Her Mother's Lover
A Novel

Her Mother's Lover
A Novel

Kelly —
Immortalize the
magic moments of
your life!
Rachelle Chaykin

Tracy Kuhn Greenlee

and

Rachelle Chaykin

KRBveritas Publishing

Her Mother's Lover

KRBveritas books may be ordered through booksellers, or by contacting:

KRBveritas Publishing
www.KRBveritas.com

Because of the dynamic nature of the Internet, any Web addresses or links contained in this book may have changed since publication and may no longer be valid.

This is a work of fiction. All of the characters, names, incidents, organizations, and dialogue in this novel are either the products of the author's imagination or are used fictitiously.

ISBN: 978-0-989-15411-6 (pbk)
ISBN 978-0-989-15410-9 (ebk)

First Edition, 2013

Printed in
United States of America

Dedicated to our Angels on Earth,

Vaughn, Zana, and Layla Greenlee,

and our Angel in the Heavens,

Michael Kriner

Chapter One

A Philadelphia Suburb, Present Day

Hi Maggie,
Thursday morning is fine to help you clean out the last 50 years
of your grandmother's lie.
Stella

Shit! She saw "lie" right after she hit send. Maybe Maggie wouldn't notice; and if she did, of course she would blame it on her absent f-key.

Life and lie. Her f-key had popped off the keyboard a few days ago, and she hadn't had time to get it fixed. If she pressed the pad extra hard, she could get her "f"; lie and life, only one letter missing.

Maggie's grandmother passed away a few days ago and the funeral had been the day before. Now the stress of settling her grandmother's estate was taking all the spare time her friend could find. She was responsible for cleaning out a lifetime of stuff in her grandmother's Mount Airy home.

The one thing Stella could offer was her time; she had a lot of it on her hands. Two years before, her daughter Sarah went off to college, leaving her feeling uncertain about her life and unfulfilled. Just as she had gotten used to her empty nest, she was faced with a temporary break from being a wife too. Her husband David worked as an engineer and although David's job didn't usually involve traveling, his company was developing a business venture with a company in China, and they expected him on site for the first six months of the project. Stella was getting used to David not being around, but she was surprised that she missed him just a little more than she expected. She decided that it all had to do with it being autumn and the beginning of the holiday season—all the festivities without the family.

* * *

When she arrived at Maggie's grandmother's house, Maggie's car was parked in the driveway and the younger woman was sitting on the porch steps with her cellphone pressed up against her ear.

Maggie watched Stella get out of the car with the take-out coffee; she flashed a relieved smile and hurried to get off the phone.

The two women had known each other for two years. Maggie had been trying to retrieve her life after her twins were born. She was struggling to find her identity and a book club seemed like a good way to get back to engaging with other adults. They met at the top of the hill in Chestnut Hill at the Borders Book Store. While waiting for the weekly book club discussion to start, they had had a heated debate over one of Oprah's book club recommendations. After the first night of polite murmuring from the other book club members, they mutually decided that the book club was too structured for them as they walked along the avenue. They had been friends ever since.

Despite a boatload of relatives, she was the only one close enough to take care of her grandmother's estate. Maggie's two brothers had returned to California and her mother was in deep mourning, so Maggie knew she had to take care of things.

"Morning!" Stella said as she handed Maggie the coffee.

"Thank God for you and Starbucks!" Maggie slurped the coffee and sighed, leading the way into the house and ending up in the kitchen. "My mom is watching the twins and they are already acting up. I think my mom may be regretting the offer to baby-sit."

"Your mom is a saint and she loves the girls. They will probably have a new collection of Barbies when you pick them up." Stella took a sip of her cappuccino, feeling anxious to get on with the day. "Where do you want me to start? It looks like you have done a lot in the kitchen." There were boxes on the kitchen table and every available counter space was filled with the contents of her grandmother's cupboards.

Maggie handed off a box of industrial-sized trash bags, "Do you want to head upstairs and start cleaning out the closets and bathrooms? We are donating and throwing out. Anything valuable has already been claimed."

* * *

After the dumpster was full of trash and the front porch was filled with donation bags, Stella went to the last bedroom to clean out the closet. She bagged up the collection of winter coats and hats and gloves on the shelf. She craved a shower after the decades of dust she had unearthed. Finally through with the last closet, she stepped back to stand on her tiptoes to make sure there was nothing left on the top shelf. That's how she saw it. Lying parallel against the bottom of the highest shelf was a wooden box. She wondered how she had missed it considering all the times she had reached up to the shelf.

She got a funny feeling in her stomach when she pulled the box from the shelf. It certainly looked old, and it had a thick layer of dust along the border of the outer edges; something had been placed on top of it for a long time. Gently, she laid it on the floor, pulled her hand over the top of it, cleaning the rim of dust from it. As if she was afraid of getting caught, she hurriedly unlatched the leather belt-like buckles that had secured it, grabbed the oiled leather handle and pulled it opened. Greeting her nose was the scent of old paint, turpentine, oil, and age; she breathed in deeply. Stella's eyes quickly scanned the contents that were stored in five or six separate compartments, each containing different art supplies—paintbrushes, dried-up oil paint tubes, and just as quickly, she closed it. She had a visceral need to own the box. Whether it was the age or the compartment tray that tantalized her, Stella could not say, but she desperately wanted to explore the contents. Securing the leather belts and picking the art box up by the worn leather handle; she went downstairs to find her friend who was cleaning out the refrigerator.

"Maggie!"

Stella's uncharacteristically sharp tone nearly put Maggie's head through the metal rack inside the refrigerator and she let out a startled yelp. She pulled her head out of the fridge and mockingly admonished her friend, "Stelllaaaa, you nearly scared me to death. What's wrong?"

"Do you think I can have this art box," Stella calmly asked, but her heart was pounding.

Maggie wiped the sweat from her forehead with her blue rubber glove, laughed and said, "You can have anything you want for helping me!" Maggie peered through her sweaty bangs at the box, shaped like an attaché case. "What's in it anyway?

"Old art supplies…I thought I might see if there was anything that Sarah could use." Stella flushed at the blatant lie she told her friend. Although her daughter was at the University of Virginia majoring in art, she was concentrating on photography. Stella had an overwhelming need for this lovely old compartmentalized box and Maggie would be less likely to ask any questions if she thought the box was going to Sarah.

"Great! Take it. It's all yours! I'm almost done too." Returning to cleaning out the refrigerator, a blob of something dark and gooey caught her attention and Maggie was soon lost in the rhythm of scrubbing the shelves to a pristine cleanliness.

Stella slipped the box into an old Wanamaker's bag and put it by the front door. She did one last circuit around the house and saw with satisfaction that it was as clean as it could get. She checked in with Maggie one last time to say goodbye. She kissed her friend's head—the only spot on Maggie that wasn't covered in smudges and grime, and then grabbed the heavy trash bag filled with winter clothes and left it with the other fifteen bags she had filled for the charity truck to pick up. Stella returned for the art box and headed for her car. As she stowed the brown paper bag in the back seat of her Volvo, she felt a nervous excitement that the art box would join the other boxes she had surreptitiously stored in her small studio.

Chapter 2

Paris, September 1928

Madalane was finally in Paris. After much debate and more than a few tears, Madalane Durand had managed to convince her parents to allow her to attend university in Paris. She lived in a converted dining room in a house for female university students just off the Rue Saint-Jacques conveniently located near the school and a few blocks from the Seine River. The housemother monitored all visitors and kept a close eye on all the girls in her charge. In many ways, Madalane was under even closer scrutiny than before she left home.

Madalane was in awe of the city and its residents. She spent most of her time walking around Paris when not attending class. Madalane could smell the dark water of the Seine River on the left bank of Paris before she could even see it. She loved watching the slow flow of the water and the way the early morning sun glistened off the surface, reflecting centuries of history.

When she had emerged from the train station upon her arrival in Paris on that early September morning, she had not been sure what was in store for her. She was disoriented from the long train journey and exhilarated to see what she had only dreamed of for most of her life. As soon as she had settled into her room, she had walked to the Pont Neuf, the oldest bridge in Paris and looked at the water of the Seine as if it would give her the courage to move forward in her new life. She felt a familiarity as she touched the ancient stone and walked along the five arches of the bridge, the castle-like bastions, the stones that lined the high wall descended into the river and protected the city from floods.

She had settled into a routine, becoming part of the machinery of Paris, exploring each section of the city with purpose and appreciation. One morning in late September, as the sun broke through the clouds, she ventured to the left bank to find the green metal quays bursting with books, paintings, and art of all sorts. Each corner of each bridge held the multi-colored magic of the city's art. Painters filled their four-foot lots with art that made Madalane want to buy each one of their paintings, all depicting the artists' image of what Paris was. Some were pastel watercolors while others were richly colored in hues of royal purple and garnet red, reflecting the iconic Eiffel Tower, the shops, and the cafe fronts filled with people. Paintings of lovers were everywhere; their lips lightly touching, immortalized forever in paint. The young woman's senses were overwhelmed by the diversity of thought, the openness of life, the revelation of freedom. She took the steps off of one of the bridges to descend to the closest level of the water; she sat and watched it flow serenely in its never-ending quest to move forward.

Madalane was surprised to find, docked right on the side of the river, houseboats where their inhabitants were starting their morning meal of tea and bread. The bows of the houseboats seemed perfectly outfitted as cafes, equipped with wicker chairs and small round tables. The umbrellas were opened and a ritual breaking of the nightly fast had begun. Herbs and houseplants cluttered the gangways as couples found their way to the decks to start their day. The young woman looked up to see the bustling city and noticed the large round metal loops mounted on the side of the Seine walls, an open hole randomly placed, appearing out of the dark, possibly for irrigation of the city. Time had slipped unnoticed as the sun shone against the stone.

She walked to the next block where she ascended to the street again, joining with the tourists, the store proprietors, the lovers strolling the quays. The blooming trees shadowed the brilliant sun and suddenly, she was part of life on the left bank. Madalane tried to store this moment inside of her memory and never let it go. She would use it to rejuvenate herself when her energy waned. She knew then the reason why so many painters lived in Paris; inspiration pulsed right there in the center of the city, invigorating all who walked her streets.

On this breezy day in early autumn, the old stone bridge supported Madalane as she stopped and stared into the brown water, swirling with eddies. She glanced at the boulevard where benches held the weight of mothers resting next to baby carriages, and the retired cast their lines into the river to catch what would soon be lunch. Madalane wondered if the sensuous flow of Paris demanded that everyone stop during their day and enjoy the bounty of Paris's circular heart. She knew in her soul that she wanted to be a person who would always stop and feel the beat of the city under her skin. She saw herself contemplatively holding her lover's hand, taking pleasure in the architecture and the people and the scents of this ancient city. Walking over the bridge, Madalane prayed that Paris would one day fill the craving in her heart.

Madalane approached a group of booths. She had walked by these artists in particular many times, but never stopped for more than a moment or two. Intimidated by the aggressive sales pitches, Madalane was nonetheless fascinated by the effortless conversation between them. She was drawn to one group of paintings in particular. These were pictures of strong women, hard-working women, old women with weathered faces and hands. The paint seemed to be layered on top of itself with a putty knife with edges of black ink creating solid lines that created a silhouette under the paint, rendering a 3-D perspective.

For several days, she had walked down the avenue peeking at the paintings, afraid that someone would push her to buy something, afraid that she would have to admit that she didn't have any money to buy their art. Finally, she mustered up the courage to stop and gaze at these paintings of old women that had so captivated her. She was lost in the vision, appreciating these portraits when movement off to her side startled Madalane.

The painter stepped into her sight line, but remained silent. Madalane guiltily glanced at the artist, dreading the sales pitch, but instead found eyes studying her the same way she was studying the paintings. Their gazes locked, and Madalane was mildly shocked to realize that the artist was a woman. At first glance, she had assumed a man, but the face, the bone structure, the softness of the artist's body clearly revealed that of a woman. Her lips pursed and her eyes narrowed as they bored into Madalane's face. Madalane had an overwhelming urge to run away, but the silent appraisal kept her rooted in one place.

Her voice was husky and low as she asked the young woman if she was interested in buying. Madalane, blushed furiously, quickly shook her head and started to leave. The painter's hand reached out and clasped the edge of the fabric of her coat. Still staring into Madalane's eyes, she said, "Stay and look today… maybe you will buy another day."

Feeling self-conscious and nervous, Madalane wanted to run away, but she also wanted to tell her that she would buy her paintings—she wanted to buy all of them, but she didn't have any money. The words stuck in her throat and she felt sick. After a few minutes of indecision, Madalane smiled and thanked her. Madalane heard her heels clicking against the pavement before she realized that she had moved away.

Over the next few days, Madalane stayed in her room when not in class. She was afraid of seeing the artist and feeling her penetrating gaze. Lying on her bed, she stared at the chandelier, her assignments completed and checked; she was going stir crazy. She had to get out of the house, but she promised herself that she would steer clear of the stalls along the river.

Aimlessly, she walked for hours trying to avoid the Seine, but all of the streets seemed to lead her back to the left bank. The sun was almost down and Madalane reasoned that everyone must have packed up for the night.

She gave in to her desire to walk along the river. The boulevard was far from empty although just a few artists were still offering their merchandise in the cool, brisk, dusky light. Young couples meandered along the river walk, whispering intimacies to one another while others kissed, oblivious to the roadblocks they created. Businessmen, dressed in identical black suits, seemed to march like a battalion of soldiers down the streets. Their walk was far too familiar for any of them to pay any attention to the gloriousness of the setting sun. A few tourists, clutching their Baedeker Guides, were still examining the paintings displayed in front of the artist's stalls.

She casually strolled by each stall, only glancing occasionally at the paintings they offered. Madalane stopped from time to time at the river wall to gaze out at the various boats silently gliding down the river; she wondered if the people on the boats stared at the people on shore like she stared at them. As Madalane got closer to the stall, where she had seen the paintings of the old woman that had captivated her, her heart started to pound. She kept her head down, but her eyes were set to the side, so she could see the paintings, but there were no rich intense paintings of women, and there was no tall, woman. Instead, a dirty young man stood behind a set of paintings in what should have been her stall. His paintings were sloppy, sultry portraits of nude women. He was smoking a cigarette, but he plucked it from his lips and called to her, "Bonjour mademoiselle! Would you like to look at my paintings? Or perhaps you would prefer a night with the painter?"

His tone was not threatening, but his provocative statement frightened Madalane. She quickly shook her head and hurried away, hearing his laugh in the wind. Suddenly Madalane was exhausted. She felt like she had been holding her breath for days, and now that she had allowed herself to breathe; she felt congested with stale, murky air. She headed back to her room, disappointed but not sure why. Back at her room, Madalane was disgusted with herself at how she had been acting. She had denied herself her daily walks just because she was afraid of seeing the woman artist again and she hadn't even been there.

Chapter 3

Immortalizing the model's soft curves, the artist's paintbrush caressed sturdy shoulders and cascaded into round touchable hips. The painting spoke of salvation, a connection between the painter and their muse. Layers of white softened the beating blush of her model's neck, the precision of crimson and ink to magnify passionate lips, which seemed to form whispered words; words compelled to speak about the secrets of love. Seductive hazel eyes gazed adoringly at her painter, their connection consuming each strand of thought; the thought of possessing the desires of a woman. The inspired portrait held more than a face and a body; the painting captured the reclined pose of the young woman as her body lay languid across time.

Stella picked up the crystal glass from her night table and swirled the Cotes de Bordeaux. She looked at the art box, the stack of letters and contemplated the painting of the woman and the sketches spread across the white Egyptian cotton duvet; she quietly studied them as they watched her. The "Flower Duet" from Delibes' opera *Lakme* floated through her bedroom, harmonizing with the delicate script of the artist's signature, E. Lavelle. She read the different dates written on each sketch and the painting, and one in particular caught her attention: *To My Morning Dove, Bonne Annee, 1930*. With the glass floating under her nose, she thought about the span of over 80 years.

Seduced by the smell of the bold fruit inviting the garnet liquid to pass her lips to tingle the surface of her tongue; she took a sip. She picked up the portrait of the woman, delicately and purposefully created, feeling the thickness of the fibers, noticing the edges frayed as if the canvas had been cut from its frame, Stella's turned it over and read the note penned in swirling ink.

Madalane,
You and Paris are my heart.
Forever, E~

Stella imagined the life of Madalane and her artist—so many years ago, the complexity of their existence. What was Madalane's life like? Who was the artist E.? She lost herself in the beauty of the model's face captured by a hand that undoubtedly loved her. She felt compelled to know more about their relationship. She put down the portrait and her wine and picked up the letters wrapped twice with a worn red ribbon. Feeling like she was invading someone's sacred treasure, she justified her need with the passage of time. One letter would be fine to read, a random letter pulled from the pack, not the first, not the last, just something from the middle. She rationalized that if she did not find the family of the owner of the art box, she would read them all, devour each one, but her own need for privacy would not allow her more than one tonight.

She pulled one letter that seemed to call to her. The aged script needed her eyes to turn the words back into life. Stella's hand shook a little as she put the rest of the letters down on the bed and slowly unfolded the one that demanded her attention, and her breath was stolen by first line.

1 January 1930

My Morning Dove,

　In my early morning quiet, the flurries are just starting to fall in the winter bitterness of our Paris; soon the windows will be white with the lace of frost locking us in our garret together. I am watching the dancing frozen miracles, remembering the soft slide of our stocking feet over the worn planked floor as we welcomed our New Year in each other's arms. I touch my mouth and feel the passion of our night; you still burn on my lips. I feel the grief of another day lost and find the scent of the night's heat contradicting the crystalline snow slowly falling. Somehow, both are married to the magic of the new day. The wind is fresh and speaking in love songs the way passion escapes from your heart, and I will say to you, I am not afraid; I am blessed.

　I am not afraid to tell you how trailing my fingers over the curves of your body bring me redemption. The whisper of your breath mortars my broken heart with the unforeseen discovery of our love. Our love cradles the fears that once lived inside of me. I pine for this love with almost a feeling of pain as I remember the faultlessness of your kiss at the strike of twelve, the way the gentleness of your mouth is alive with fire that defines the womanliness of your being. The beauty of the moment compels me to immortalize you with the eagerness of my art. I am devoted to you as my muse, my inspiration, my love.

　Your body is stretched among the tussled blanket, the pale roundness of your shoulder and a hint of your breast are my feast in this early morning. As daylight breaks, and with the dance of the single pillar's flame, I draw you yet another time with absolute knowing. Your lovely body lies over the warmth of where our bodies just lay locked in embrace. Your beauty steals the words from my mouth and saves them in the

*core of your soul. I battle my fingers with each curve I draw
to simply reach out and touch you. My hand, once embracing
the milk of your skin, now holds the black lead, and you own
the paper with the perfection of your recline. The world will
want to see your loveliness; I will be jealous (forgive me) of
each set of eyes that look upon your exquisite beauty.*

*This love we have is perfection, although perfection of
what one would define as love will battle with the perfection
of our love. We will win Dove; we will win.*
Forever,
E—

Remembering to breathe, Stella realized that she turned on
the bath water several minutes ago. She immediately imagined
water cascading across her white tiled floor. Dropping the letter
to the bed and grabbing her wine, she hurried to the bathroom.
Opening the door, Stella found herself in a storm of lavender
and musk steam, but the water had not overflowed the tub. She
closed the door behind her, and shut the silver and white ceramic
faucets off. She took a breath to collect herself.

During the past few weeks of being alone, Stella realized the
freedom was becoming more intoxicating than the wine she was
sipping. She dropped her clothes to the floor and caught her full,
steamed reflection in the mirror on the back of the door. She
watched drops of condensation slide down the mirror, creating
a shape faintly reminiscent of Picasso's cubist art. Her reflection
looked deformed; she normally saw herself the way she thought
David, her husband, saw her; the way a man would see a woman.
At this moment, she wanted to see herself more the way an artist would see her, maybe like a portrait masquerading as a love
letter. Touching the mirror, the lines of water flowed as Stella's
fingers guided them into shapely curves, a deconstruction of her
perceived reality. Stella was not as curvaceous as her mother had
hoped she would be; her tall runner's frame skirted the Monroe

look. As she stared at herself, she imagined her waist curving into wide hips, the steam adding flesh—a revelation in the width of a half-inch finger stroke.

Stella tried to remember the last time she really looked at herself in a mirror, naked and vulnerable to her internal thoughts. Maybe she looked differently than the way she felt, the way David would describe her body. She wanted E. to describe her. She was a mature woman, forty-one years old. She felt more beautiful now than she had remembered feeling in the past. Was it the words she just read? She grabbed a towel from the marble shelf and wiped the full-length mirror to have a complete look. With the mirror as her blank canvas, she felt her hipbones and then turning to the side, examined the curve of her breast and wondered if she looked like the woman in the sketches she had left lying on her bed. Stella's self-portrait began to change as she examined the silvery stretch marks left from her one pregnancy. She touched the tiny wrinkles around her face and lips and wondered if she laughed enough even to deserve them.

Embarrassed by the indulgence of her self-examination, she grabbed her wineglass and turned to face the tub with her short blond bob swaying against her face. She glanced back to the mirror and gave one last look at her tall figure from behind. What was like to be seen in a way that you did not see yourself? Through someone else's eyes? As something beautiful beyond compare, someone who was desired, a woman cherished by and filled with passion from the thoughts and intentions of another. What was it to be someone's muse?

Slipping into the white-claw tub, Stella felt her body encapsulated by the heat, the steam of the scented water and the subtle intoxication of the red wine she had been drinking. She put the crystal glass to her lips and let the ruby liquid pass into her mouth. She felt the cool of the wine and the burn of the flavors traveling inside of her. The Bordeaux echoed deep inside of her, not like the white wine she drank with David. There was a hidden truth in the richness and the attention it demanded; was red wine more like a woman? White wine was like a fast shower after playing tennis—refreshing but ultimately not as satisfying as a long soak in the tub. She rested the wineglass on her chest and the base hit the edge of her nipple, sending a flare of demand through her body. Stella's need pulled her to the bottom of the tub, under the water.

Society defined herself as a stay-at-home mother. She raised her daughter with David's help. He was a safe choice—he had adopted Sarah after all. Stella and David had created a life that was consistent, ordinary and dependable; the one she had dreamed of having. Time and reality had distorted her definition of womanhood; but she knew it was changing even now, as time slipped by and she felt her lungs begging for oxygen. As she gulped in her first breath, it occurred to her that maybe she did not want ordinary. Maybe she wanted to see life the way an artist did. Maybe she wanted to see life the way "E." did.

The air was thick and quiet, just the distant sound of the wind rustling through the trees in Stella's back yard reminded her of the world outside her home. Time, solitude, and the beauty of the letter were the only company she had tonight. She sipped from her wine glass and allowed her mind to go where she had forbidden it until recently. She thought of Victor.

Victor had been her first love, the father of her child, and the man who eventually left her. She figured he had left her behind and never looked back until his email arrived through Facebook.

Dear Stella,

I was home for a few days last month because my old man died. He had a massive heart attack in his sleep. I suppose if there is a good way to go, then that's it. I wish I had been able to stay in PA longer, but I had to get back Germany for some studio work. I've been thinking about you and Sarah a lot over the past couple of years. Maybe it's hitting forty and finally growing up, but I feel a lot of regret about how things worked out for us. I wish there had been a third option for us. Something beyond staying in PA and joining the drones or going to Europe for my career. I wish we had found a middle ground because I have always loved you the most. No one ever understood me the way you did. You were the lightness to my darkness, the sun to my moon, and the river to my rocky shore. I feel like I could have been so much more if I had had you with me.

Are you happy, my Stella-star? Do you wish things had been different between us? If I could do it all over again, I would pack you into my suitcase and drag you to Europe with our baby. I know it seemed impossible then, but I should have made it happen. Things would be so different now. I'm coming back to the states in a couple months to help my sister settle the estate and get dad's house ready to sell. I totally understand if you don't want to see me, but I want to see you. For Christ's sake, why else would I join Facebook? HAHA.

Is our baby girl happy? Did she grow up pretty like you and musical like me? Maybe there is a chance for us still. Let's get in the car and drive to the shore and talk like we used to. Remember those trips to Ocean City? Sitting on the beach late at night, playing music, knowing that love didn't get any better than in those moments. Give me one day, one hour, one minute and I know you'll remember. We can have all of that again.

Love,

Vic

Victor's handsome image floated in front of her as she realized that her glass of wine was empty and the water was quickly approaching tepid. She ran her fingers through her damp hair, pushing it from her face and felt the effects of the wine on an empty stomach. She pulled her body up from the tub and listened as the water crashed downwards, allowing her thoughts to dissipate. The thick moisture in the room awakened a part of her with need, the need to be touched, the need to belong to someone, the need to feel alive, the need to lie down with another. Her flesh blushed and the tiny hairs on her fair Scandinavian skin held captive her sweat.

Wrapped in her robe, she opened the door to her bedroom, and gazed at the sketches, the painting and the letter. They were still just as beautiful to her, but in their solemn way, they matched her solitude. She craved their story; she craved to know the mystery lying in the silent love between the painter and the model. She draped herself over David's side of the bed and hugged his pillow. She took a deep breath and smelled the familiar scent of the man she shared her life with and closed her eyes, one hand extended towards but not quite touching the mysteries of the art box. As she drifted off to sleep, her last thoughts were of the way passion was so clear in the letter.

Chapter 4

Paris, October 1928

Life became a blur of school and work. Madalane found a job in a shop and mid-term exams were approaching; when she wasn't working, she was furiously studying to ensure a solid performance. The weather was rainy and cool, and whenever she thought about walking along the river, the rain seemed to pound even harder. Madalane stared mindlessly out the window of her small bedroom as her mind wondered about the women in those paintings. Why does she paint women like them? Why not something more appealing to the tourists—like the many gardens around the city or the Eiffel Tower? Why paint these women who were defined by hard work and harsh lives?

Another week passed, and the intensity of the emotion seemed to grow numb. On Sunday morning, Madalane woke and looked out her window to see a glorious autumn day—sunny, calm, and bright. Instead of going to church, she found herself walking along the river, hoping to see the paintings of strong women and the woman artist who painted them. She walked with purpose and a sense of surety. Reaching the stalls, she quickly walked by the other artists, but as Madalane neared the woman's space, her heart started to skip. She slowed down to prepare herself for disappointment if the woman was not there. She stopped briefly and stared at the river, chastising herself about getting so worked up over a few paintings and an artist.

She felt her heartbeat calm and she moved towards the stall expecting to see the dirty young man with the terrible paintings. Instead, as she neared the stall, Madalane saw the paintings first: beautiful, heartbreaking pictures of old women. She was captivated again by their power. Madalane realized that the emotion she had been fighting so diligently was back and it slammed into her solar plexus. She could not believe how intense her reaction was. After a few minutes of gazing at the pictures, she released the breath she hadn't realized she had been holding. As she exhaled, she saw the tall young woman move towards her. She had an ironic smile on her face, and Madalane blushed knowing that she had been caught staring.

Quietly, she said, "Take one."

Madalane was startled and embarrassed being caught looking so blatantly covetous. She looked up and saw that the woman was genuinely smiling. Madalane shook her head, unsure where her voice had fled.

Stepping closer, she spoke, in a strangled whisper, "Take one, please. No one looks at them like you do."

Madalane was fascinated by her voice and the faint odor of tobacco, paint and something else, something earthy that she could not pinpoint. She shrugged her shoulders and admitted, "I have no money. I cannot buy anything."

The artist grasped Madalane's sleeve and her voice was firm, definite, and broached no argument, "Just take one. I don't want your money. It is a gift from me to you." Bitterly, she added, "No one else wants them."

Madalane's bourgeois up bringing told her that it is unacceptable to take something for nothing. But her passion for these paintings was so powerful. She could not walk away. She could not say no. She looked at the array of paintings and saw a small one, situated off to the side. It was a woman painted in three-quarter profile. She appeared hunched and her skin was pale, spotted with broken veins and dirt. She looked tired, but there was an incredible vitality in her eye. Despite the hardships in her life, she was defiant about life. Madalane wanted that one. She needed that one. Without a word, the woman intuitively picked it up and wrapped it in brown paper and string. She pressed it into Madalane's hands. The student didn't know what to say. She wanted to say thank you. She wanted to cry. She wanted her heart to stop pounding a staccato rhythm in her ears. She wanted to run home, sit in the privacy of her own room, and stare at the painting.

Madalane looked up, finding the storm-filled eyes; somewhere in her mind, she thought that the woman seemed taller than she remembered. She whispered a muffled thank you and with the painting grasped tightly against her chest, she hurriedly walked away, afraid that she would be stopped and the painting taken back.

Down the crowded avenues of Paris, Madalane hurried back to her room; she flew past the Madam of the house afraid she would ask about the wrapped package under her arm. Fumbling with her key, Madalane could barely get the door unlocked while trying to hold the painting and her bag. Once inside her room, she locked the door and, only then, did she release her grip on the package. She put it on the bed, and stepped back. She wanted to rip the paper off and stare openly at her new possession, but she was nervous. She worried that the painting would not be as good now that she could look at it to her hearts content. She relished the memory of it for a few moments, thinking of the beauty of the color and the emotion of the woman's face. Finally, the rough sensation of the wrapping paper made her fingertips tingle, and she couldn't postpone the moment any longer.

She had meant to be gentle in fear that she would damage the canvas, but as soon as she touched the string holding the brown paper in place, she knew she had to reveal its truth. She had to know, immediately, if it still affected her in the same way. As the paper fell away, she felt her breath catch and she knew that the intensity had only increased as the full face and body of the charwoman came into view. The dryness of her hands gave way to a revelation of homespun fabric, surrounding her thin wrists. The tiny brush strokes on her hands were so different than the way the woman's clothing seemed to be painted. Her brown dress looked thick and bulky, like the paint had been layered with a small palette knife, but the skin on her face was almost translucent; the blood vessels in her cheeks broken, creating faint striations across her face. In contrast, the cap, holding the woman's hair in place, seemed to be painted on with a light, ethereal stroke.

As she gazed at the painting, reveling in the freedom of ownership, she began to realize that the woman in the picture seemed to be smiling at her. Although she was shown in profile, her eyes and mouth seemed to tilt just the slightest bit. The exaggerated red lips drew the eye, demanding interpretation. Her existence was hard, and she appeared hunched and tired, but that sly grin of life in her lips and eyes betrayed her ultimate victory over hardship. Something in her world gave her the reason to live and carry on. Madalane felt odd about staring so intently at this silent woman. The longer she stared, the more she felt she was being mocked for her own middle-class expectations.

Disconcerted by the way she felt, she stood up and turned away. She looked around her small room, desperately trying to find something to focus on, but she was overwhelmed by the awareness of the painting and how this woman maintained her silent vigil from the middle of her bed. Surrendering, she looked back and saw that the woman was still frozen in time locked in her pose. She realized that this was what was intended. These women in her paintings had terribly hard lives, but they lived for something or someone. It was an acknowledgement that their lives represented hardship to her for they looked tired, work-weary, and old; however, they had something that made them happy. She thought of her own mother: pampered, but bitter. Her mother only smiled when her cruelty had hit its target—usually towards her father or herself.

The thought of her mother induced a sinking, chastised sensation. Her mother's words about her being useless echoed in her head. "You are a frivolous girl for spending so much time reading. How will you attract a husband if your nose is in a book all the time?"

Feeling off-center and confused, she sat on the floor next to the bed. She briefly thought that her skirt would wrinkle, but she pushed the ridiculousness of the concern out of her mind. She closed her eyes and thought of the painting. Was this manifestation of the old woman's secret pleasure the artist's true intention? Did she paint these women to show that they exist quite happily outside of society's definition of success? Suddenly she was exhausted. She wanted to sleep, but she couldn't bear the thought of looking at the painting again even to move it—it would raise more questions in her tired brain. Madalane leaned back against the mattress behind her back and closed her eyes.

Colors swam in front of her and images of women from the paintings seemed to parade past her closed eyes. She wanted a closer look at the rest of the paintings. She wanted to know if she was right or had she imagined all of it. She wanted to bring every one of the paintings back to her small room and examine each one with microscopic intensity. Madalane's head felt heavy and her eyes hurt. She just needed a few minutes to rest her thoughts.

Chapter 5

Maggie was pulling a tiny splinter out of Lena's finger when the phone rang. The little girl was sobbing hysterically while her twin sister held her own hands eight inches apart to demonstrate the size of the splinter. Maggie's head was pounding as the sliver of wood eased its way out of her baby girl's hand. The little girl gulped tearfully and pulled her hand back, giving her mother a searing look as she ran out of the kitchen with her sister. Maggie frantically called out, "Come back, I need to put Neosporin on your finger."

The wail that erupted from the other room stabbed Maggie's heart. This battle would be won later in the day. For now, she would see who had called during the surgery. Maggie checked the caller ID and saw that it had been Stella. Maybe she had some words of wisdom about splinters and their removal. She sighed as she dialed and waited for the call to connect.

"Hello." Stella answered the phone on the second ring. "Mrs. Richard Peters—how are you today?" Stella gave a little chuckle about her friend's name.

"Hey Stellllllllaaaaaaaaaaaaaaaaaaaa!" Maggie laughed at her own attempt at Brando's famous scream. She knew Stella hated that. "What's up? Sorry I missed your call. I was performing surgery on a four year old."

Stella loved Maggie's life even though it was hectic at times. She laughed out loud at the edge in Maggie's voice; she was always bordering on a break down with twin girls pulling at her last nerve and a clueless husband. "Who needed emergency surgery?"

"It was Lena. And you would have thought that I was sawing her arm off with a rusty knife. She can be such a drama queen, like her father."

Stella laughed at the thought of Maggie's mini drama queen. Her Sarah had been the queen of drama when she was little— she still was. "I take it the surgery was successful for Lena? No need for the emergency room?"

"Who even knows? She ran out of here like a banshee. I'll lure them both back in here with popsicles after we get off the phone, but I needed a break from being mommy. When one freaks out, the other one feels the need to aid and assist. The doctor said it's a twin thing and it's completely normal. Here's a news flash—I'm over any and all twin things." Maggie stood up and stretched her tired body.

"I couldn't imagine having two of every girl thing; you're a saint." Stella paused for moment, trying to decide how to proceed, settling on the direct approach. "I want to ask you something. Do you remember the art box I found when we were cleaning out your grand-mom's house?"

"Heart box? No, I don't remember a heart-shaped box. What are you talking about?"

"No, Mag—the ART box."

"Art box? Oh wait, you mean that old art supplies you wanted? Yeah, I remember it. Did you find anything that Sarah could use?" Maggie's attention wandered to the mostly full bottle of rubbing alcohol she used to disinfect the tweezers. She briefly wondered how it would taste in orange juice. "Hey can you drink rubbing alcohol? Do you think it would get me drunk?"

Stella chuckled, "Don't even think about it, you can't drink rubbing alcohol; have you lost your mind?" Stella's had a laughing tone, but she was on a mission so she returned to her subject. "Listen, about the art box, do you know anything about it or who might have owned it because there was some interesting things in it and I would love to find out who owned it."

"I have no idea. My grandmother never showed the least bit of interest in any kind of art. She read those dumb romance novels constantly. But you know who might know? My mom. She would know if my grandmother bought it at a yard sale or inherited from one of her aunts or uncles. You should call her."

"Okay sounds great; I will call her and see what I can find out. How is she feeling? Do you think she is up for a chat? She seemed so sad at the funeral."

"Absolutely Stella! She adores you." Maggie added ruefully, "I think you're the daughter she always wanted." Two little girls breathlessly running into the kitchen disrupted Maggie's attention.

Both girls squealed in unison, "The ice cream man! The ice cream man is coming mommy. You said we could get ice cream the next time he comes. You promised!" Angelic smiling faces punctuated their statements.

"Hold on a sec Stel, we have an ice cream emergency now." Maggie reached into the pocket of her jeans to get money and realized that her pockets were empty.

Lizzie bounced up and down while Lena pulled on Maggie's t-shirt, "Mommy we need to go now. He'll leave if he doesn't see us waiting."

"Lizzie—go get mommy's purse—Stella—I gotta go find some money and get these girls some MORE sugar. Call my mom. She would love to talk to you about the old days. Call me later."

Stella pressed the disconnect button on her phone and pulled up Maggie's mother's number.

"Hello." The old woman's voice was an older version of Maggie's.

Stella heard the cracks in Ellen's voice when she answered the phone. "Hi Ellen, its Stella Simone; how are you?"

"Hi Stella. It's so nice to hear from you. I'm okay. You know how it is. It's hard. I know mom was older, but I still miss her so much." Ellen's voice quivered. She took a deep breath. "How are you doing dear? Maggie said that David is in China on business."

"Yes, he's in China; he has been there for a few weeks now. He told me it is quite the cultural change and the food is surprisingly different—I'm sure you can imagine—it's nothing like Full Ho's around the corner." Stella was quiet hoping that Ellen would jump in. When she didn't, she gently continued, "How are you? Are you doing okay, Ellen?" Ellen had spent the past year taking care of her dying mother at her Wyndmoor home. Not having her mom to take care of left a huge void in Ellen's life.

Ellen sighed, "I always thought that losing your mother at a young age must be devastating. I always thought that if she lived a long life then it would be okay when she passed. However, it's just not true. I miss her so much; there are so many memories that creep into my mind no matter how busy I try to be. She was always there, you know. When my babies were born, when my grandbabies were born, she was always standing next to me. It just makes me so sad to know that she's not next to me anymore."

"Your mother was filled with the love from her family and the blessings of the priest." Stella thought about the services and how she spent the afternoon with the Karlz/Brown family. They were the type of family people wanted to be a part of.

"Thank you Stella. You are very kind and both Maggie and I can't thank you enough for all the help and support you gave us. Everyone has been so kind. Father Ryan has been by the house twice to check on me." Ellen's voice lowered to the point that Stella had to strain to hear the older woman. "He's worried that I haven't been to mass lately. I don't know how to explain why I am having a hard time going back to the church. The one time I did go, I left before the homily. I just kept seeing my mother's coffin at the front of the church."

"Father Ryan is a good man and if you need him to come

to you, he will." Stella paused, realizing there would not be a good opportunity to ask about the art box. Cautiously she spoke, "Ellen, how about Maggie, the girls and I come over and have lunch with you tomorrow?"

"That would be lovely. It would be nice to have something normal to look forward to. I'll make some chicken salad for us."

"Don't worry about lunch; I will bring lunch and dessert and we can be there at 12:30. Is that a good time for you?" Stella knew it may not work for Maggie, but she was going anyway.

"That's great. It'll be nice to have my grandbabies over. They are so sweet and so well behaved. Thank you Stella; you put a smile on my face."

"It's my pleasure, Ellen. I'll see you tomorrow." Stella smirked at the thought of the sweet, well-behaved twins as she dialed Maggie's number to see if they were free for lunch.

Chapter 6

Paris, October 1928

When Madalane awoke, it was dark; the evening was cool and damp. She angrily realized that she had lazily indulged herself in a nap and her body was stiff from sleeping sitting up. She felt sore over every inch of her body.

The clock told her that she had missed the Sunday meal that the Madam provided in the late afternoon. She was hungry, starving really, since she had not eaten since before she had set out for church. The walk and the painting had waylaid her appetite, but now she was ravenous. Madalane checked the small purse she kept under her mattress for her pocket money. Her job did not pay well, but she had few expenses and even fewer indulgences. She was saving to buy a painting, but now she had one and it was staring at her from the middle of her bed. If Madalane was to spend the rest of the night examining it, she needed sustenance.

On a Sunday night in Paris, there were few affordable or appropriate places to eat. The cafes were filled with couples and regulars and Madalane felt awkwardly out of place even when they were not crowded. She decided to go to a small café near the University where students could get small meals to take back to their rooms. She wanted to come back and eat while staring at her new possession. She wanted to stare at every inch, review every brush stroke, and memorize every color.

Out on the street, there was a misty rain hanging over the city. She walked quickly and tried to avoid the kissing couples hidden under umbrellas. Madalane's hair was damp and her coat was soaked when she pushed through the café doors. The madam of the café was polite and took her order quickly. She directed Madalane to a spot near the back of the café where she could get warm and not be in the way of other customers arriving in the foyer of the restaurant. Properly chastened, Madalane sat on an old church bench, feeling the delicious warmth of a full café drying her damp clothes. The small alcove afforded her no view, but she felt happily ensconced in the waiting area.

The madam peeked into the recessed room and beckoned her to come to the front. She was holding a small basket of food for the young woman. As Madalane moved through the café, she saw the flash of a recognizable face. She stopped and turned, and there sat her artist. Or rather, the woman who had created her new painting. She was sitting at a large table surrounded by a group of bohemian looking young people, including the dirty young man who had been in her space the one time. Although her face was partially obscured and it was in profile, Madalane was absolutely positive it was her. She stood, stunned and silent, staring. Something in the air must have changed because the woman's attention shifted, and she turned slowly in Madalane's direction.

Her eyes narrowed in concentration and recognition struck. She smiled and nodded at the young, bedraggled girl. Madalane was momentarily frozen, but she eventually remembered to smile back. The madam suddenly appeared at her elbow with her basket of food. She was irritated that Madalane had been standing mindlessly in the middle of her café, holding her up from other tasks. Used to dealing with wayward students, she scolded her while escorting her to the front of the restaurant. Paying for her meal, Madalane looked back and saw the woman was still watching. The student blushed and felt foolish and clumsy. Mortified, she grabbed her dinner and rushed out of the café.

The rain was pouring now and her wool coat felt heavy and hot. Madalane felt hard drops of rain pounding against her face; she was embarrassed for running out of the cafe like a child. She was angry at the madam for chastising her like a little girl—the rage burned inside of her until she tasted salty tears streaming down her face instead of rain. Madalane knew the artist would never have allowed someone to scold her like a recalcitrant child. She would have haughtily stared at the madam and slowly sauntered out of the restaurant, maintaining her dignity and control. Madalane wished she could do that. She wished that the woman had stood up from her table and come to speak to her in that quiet, hushed voice. She wished that the artist had wanted to know her like Madalane wanted to know the artist.

Madalane sighed heavily and felt her self-disgust return. Sometimes she found her own feelings impossible. She did not understand this compulsion, especially with this woman. She heard her mother's voice in her head telling her that Paris was filled with degenerates and filth. She had promised, on the family bible, to only associate with the better kind of people—university students, people from the church, good people with morals and values. Her mother's admonishment had seemed an easy rule to follow since Madalane was reluctant to talk to strangers anyway. The students at the university were nice, but like her, they were naive and frightened to have this opportunity taken away from them. The people from church and the shop were respectful, middle class, and eminently boring. The city itself was more interesting to her than the people until she had met this woman.

She shook her head—in Madalane's heart, she felt this painter belonged to her. She understood her paintings; they had that connection. She owned this incredible vision and Madalane wanted to absorb every ounce of paint, ink and canvas. Bemused by her own thoughts, she realized that her mother would be horrified to know that the most interesting person in all of Paris was an artist and she didn't even know her name.

The girl stopped suddenly in the middle of the avenue, struck by the realization that her name would be on the painting. She would have signed it. Madalane inhaled deeply; she was an idiot. Why didn't she think to look at the signature? She stared at the colors and the lines, but never once looked at the scrawled name at the bottom. She took off running through the wet streets. Her wet coat was flapping heavily and her shoes were not meant for running, but the only thing that mattered at that moment was to see her name.

Arriving at the house, she darted in to avoid her housemates who were gathered in the common room listening to an opera on the radio. The housemother liked the girls to gather on Sunday nights to chat and drink tea, but tonight Madalane didn't care about the consequences of missing the weekly ritual. She needed to be alone with her painting. She knew that she would get a stern lecture tomorrow about her absence, but it seemed inconsequential at that moment. She rushed into her room and shed her heavy wet coat, and wiped the rain and tears from her face on her blue scarf.

The painting was on the bed, waiting for her like a silent sentry, keeping watch on her small domain. Instead of focusing on the woman's eyes or her slightly up-turned lips, Madalane scanned the bottom of the painting trying to make out the signature. The first name was not written out, but rather a very thick curled "E" was emphatically placed before the slightly legible last name. The last name started with an L, but then the rest was scrawled. She focused on the last name, willing it to reveal itself to her. She traced the letters in her mind's eye, forcing loops and lines into letters. Slowly, a name seemed to lift off the canvas in front of the girl: Lavelle. E. Lavelle. Madalane's heart stopped for a minute. Suddenly, she was no longer "the artist;" instead, she had a name, a history, a world. She was E. Lavelle. The air around the girl felt warm and cool at the same time as chills crept up her spine. She felt as if she had received a religious revelation. Was God giving her the opportunity to know this woman? Would she change her destiny?

She looked down at the floor, momentarily distracted by a damp sensation on her feet. She had dripped a small puddle onto the carpet next to the bed. She was soaked to the skin, but she felt giddy, and she laughed out loud. Madalane laughed and laughed and suddenly her entire body was filled with happiness. A sharp knock at the door reminded her that she lived in a communal house. She opened the door a few inches and the housemother, sharp-eyed and vigilant, attempted to look behind her.

"Madalane, what is going on?" she asked. She was suspicious; Madalane could see it in her eyes. Realizing that if her livelihood depended upon keeping young girls on the right path, she too would be cautious.

"Nothing, Madam. I got caught in the rain and I need to change before I join you." Lying was so easy. She found that she could do it without guilt. Her mother had inadvertently taught her that lying was a skill to develop and cultivate.

"I heard you crying," the housemother persisted.

"No, Madam, I was laughing. I could not believe how wet I got." Madalane looked at her with guileless eyes. She opened the door slightly for her to see her dripping hair.

Clucking, the madam said, "Yes, you are a very stupid girl for walking in this weather. Put on dry clothes and join us." The madam checked and tightened the chignon at the back of her neck and spun on her heel to return to the sitting room.

Normally Madalane would be ashamed of being called stupid, especially by a woman who made her living babysitting adult women, but as she closed the door, she was still smiling to herself. She changed quickly and ate her cold, wet dinner from the basket. The bread was soggy and the chicken congealed, but to

Madalane it was delicious. She had seen her and she knew her name. E. Lavelle. Madalane no longer felt embarrassed over her behavior. She was just happy to have this piece of information. She came to university to learn and for the first time, she felt the world opening in front of her.

Chapter 7

At precisely 12:28, Maggie's minivan pulled onto Ellen's street. Stella had told Maggie they needed to be at her mom's by 12:00, so they were right on time—on Maggie time.

Maggie interrupted the twin's debate of whom Grammy liked best. "Girls! Please do not touch Grammy's Hummel collection. You don't want to make her cry again, do you?"

In chorus, both girls replied, "No Mommy."

Maggie turned to Stella and sighed, "My mother adores the girls and she let them play with her figurines last time. Apparently, my mother forgot that four-year olds drop things. It was not pretty."

Stella murmured in understanding, but did not comment.

"Okay girls, one more time. Make sure you kiss your Grammy. She is still sad about her mommy. Don't touch the figurines even if Grammy says it's okay, and please, don't chase the cat."

The twins nodded in unison. Maggie glanced at them through the rear-view mirror and then conspiratorially whispered to Stella, "They are up to something. I can feel it."

Maggie popped the trunk for Stella, so she could retrieve their lunch that Stella had picked up from a café in Chestnut Hill.

Ellen had been watching from the front window. As the girls tumbled from the sliding doorway of the minivan, she opened the door and waved.

"Grammy!" Both girls squealed. They ran to embrace their grandmother. Magically, the matching outfits and coordinating hair bows were still in place as Maggie watched her mother embrace her babies.

"What is it about grandparents?" Maggie wondered aloud as she helped Stella unload the trunk.

"Grandkids allow them to fix the mistakes they made with their own kids and it allows them to feel the thread of connection to the future, without worrying that they will not be good parents." Gazing at the girls explaining something to their grandmother, Stella felt wistful, "Plus, who can resist the love that flows freely from kids? Look at them; they love each other. It is beautiful to watch." Stella sighed as she thought for a moment what it would be like to hold her own grand baby and if she ever would.

Maggie hefted up one of the bags. "You are always so profound Stella. See, in my mind, it's just because my mom knows that she's not going to be blamed for turning them into the first set of serial killer twins. I'll be blamed—it's always the mother's fault."

Stella laughed and shook her head at her friend's bizarre sense of humor.

As they entered the living room of Ellen's home, the twins let out a mammoth yell. Sitting on the couch, side by side, were twin American Girl dolls. Rushing to the couch, both girls grasped their dolls with the kind of glee usually reserved for a diamond ring.

"Oh Mom... you didn't." Stella caught the roll of Maggie's eyes.

"I did Maggie. I couldn't help myself. Did you know that you can order them right off the internet? They have all kinds of stuff for twins. I can show you how to get to their website."

"Mom...that stuff is horribly expensive. They are four. They will have those dolls wrecked within a week." Maggie saw the delight in her mother's face begin to wane and she swallowed the rest of her objections. "The dolls are great, mom. Thank you."

Joining Stella to help set up the luncheon, she sighed deeply as she gazed at Stella's amused expression. "You stop smirking. You're supposed to be on my side."

The two women busied themselves with lunch preparations while the girls played with their American Girl dolls. Maggie put the food on the dining room table and then went to the kitchen to get the settings. She could see into the living room as Lizzy was showing her Grammy how perfect her dolls hair was with ribbons like hers.

Ellen called in to the friends, "Do you girls need any help out there? We are having quite the doll party out here. You might have to set extra plates for the new members of the family." Stella could feel the glare from Maggie.

"Lunch will be on the table in a minute." Maggie called to her mother and daughters through clenched teeth.

"Thank you so much girls for taking the time to bring lunch; this is really wonderful!" Ellen sounded truly happy.

Stella unwrapped the peanut butter and jelly sandwiches she had made for the girls and put them on the paper plates. She thought about setting plates for the dolls with some crackers, but that would surely put Maggie over the edge.

The twins swooned over the dolls while their enthusiastic spirit captivated Ellen during lunch. The only discordant sound was the noise of Maggie grinding her teeth as Stella tried to maintain a straight face and pleasant conversation. As they finished their sandwiches and fruit salad, the girls asked to go to the playground.

After a short, but decisive battle about taking the new dolls to the playground, Maggie prepared to leave the house with both girls, minus their dolls. Maggie accepted that she had lost the war, but at least she won this battle.

Standing in the doorway, the screen door held slightly open, Maggie reminded her mother, "Stella had some questions about Grandma's stuff."

"Right!" Ellen poured herself some more iced tea and smiled at Stella. "Tell me what you found when you cleared out my mother's house. Don't tell me that you found a lost Rockwell painting?" She smiled at her own joke.

Stella smiled stiffly and shook her head. "No, I'm afraid there is nothing that like that."

Ellen gave her a warm smile and put her hand on top of Stella's, "Thank God for my daughter and for you. I would have never been able to clear out that house."

Gently, Stella rubbed the top of Ellen's hand. Her eyes followed the blue veins lying loosely under caramel-spotted paper-thin skin. "Ellen, was this your mother's wedding set?" Stella straightened the modest wedding set on Ellen's right hand.

"Yes dear it is, or I mean it was. She wore it every day of her life. My father and mother loved each other dearly. After his death ten years ago, mother never really recovered. She took good care of him. Served him his coffee every morning, home-made dinners every night; she sat next to his hospital bed until his last breath."

"Ellen, she was a good woman." What could a woman say to another woman when there was such loss in her heart? She could only sit and listen.

As Ellen struggled to push her grief down, several moments passed before she was able to speak, "You're a good woman too, Stella. There are not many people who would take on tasks like helping Maggie with mom's house."

Feeling like this was the best chance to ask her questions, Stella began, "There was an art box in the spare bedroom closet. Maggie said that it was fine to take it, but I wanted to talk to you about it. I wanted to find out more about it." Stella took a deep anticipatory breath.

Ellen's brow crinkled. "A heart box? To be honest dear, I'm not even sure what that means."

Stella inwardly groaned. Maggie was definitely her mother's

daughter. "No Ellen, it is an ART box. A box artists use to store their paints and brushes."

"Oh...I understand but I'm still stumped dear. My mother wasn't the artistic type. I can't imagine why she would have it. Was there a name on it? Maybe it belonged to one of my uncles. Did you bring it so I can see what it looks like?"

Stella felt a surge of anxiety course through her. It was her art box now; Maggie had given it to her. Stella's insides quivered and she felt like she was twelve again when her mother had discovered her secret cache of letters from her father. Her mother had burned them in front of her, slowly, one by one, mocking her allegiance to a man who was no longer allowed in her house.

She felt sweat trickle down her back as Ellen's benign eyes gazed at her. Stella realized that she had taken the question far too seriously and she slowed her breathing, wondering exactly how much of the contents she should reveal to Ellen. She spoke with precise words, feeling the trepidation rise up again in her chest, "No, I didn't bring it with me. There were some papers and sketches in the art box; there was also letters from Paris dated from the 1930's."

"Letters from Paris? That doesn't make any sense. My family is German. I don't remember anyone speaking French. The only French person we knew was my mother's best friend—it must be Aunt Maddy's; she was French. She was such a lovely lady; she lived next door to us all my life. I don't remember her painting, but she went to museums a lot, so it's possible that it's hers."

Stella stayed silent, hoping for more. After what seemed like an eternity, Ellen continued, "She and my mom met during the war; they worked in a munitions plant down near the Navy Yard. They both had babies with husbands in the war, so I suppose it was natural for them to become friends."

"She was married to a man...?" Stella extended the "a" in man and raised her eyebrows.

Ellen appeared confused, "Well, of course dear. Who do

you think she was married to? A gorilla? The poor man died in combat. It was lucky that Aunt Maddy had a daughter. I can't imagine being a widow without a child to comfort you. After her husband was reported killed in duty, she moved into the house next to my mother's. She was our neighbor until she died in 1970." She was quiet for a few moments and then in a sad voice, she continued, "I do remember watching my mother drink an entire bottle of wine after her daughter notified her that Maddy had died in her sleep. My mother never really drank other than a beer at a picnic, so it was quite a shock to see her drink an entire bottle of wine at the kitchen table. I guess that's why it was so memorable." Ellen grew quiet again, seeming to contemplate some great mystery.

Stella's curiosity was buzzing around in her brain like a hummingbird. She had so many questions, but Ellen seemed lost in her memories. She made a mental note to ask specifically about Maddy's daughter. She might still be alive.

"Maddy and my mother were more like sisters than friends. And, they were so different! My mother was such a homebody. She loved to cook and look after us; she was always baking something. Every day after school, we would come home to find cupcakes or cookies cooling on the kitchen table. I don't know if she would have ever had had a job except it was expected during the war. Maddy was a schoolteacher; she was always working at her kitchen table. I remember it being covered in papers and books all the time. I don't think Maddy's daughter ever had a home-cooked meal unless my mother made it for her."

Stella traced the corner of the plastic place mat with her index finger while staring at a stray gray strand of hair in the otherwise dyed brown hair on Ellen's head. She watched her slip away into a childhood where cookies and cupcakes were the only things she had to think about. Now, she was the matriarch of her family.

"Ellen." Stella said softly.

Ellen's head shot up like she had been pulled from another

time, startled by the sound of Stella's voice. Gasping for breath, she replied, "What dear? What is it?"

"I'm sorry I did not mean to startle you."

"It's fine, I just find myself in a thousand different places in just a few minutes when I think about my mother. I have this urge to go and take care of her still. My days are so lonely. I try to think about the twins; it helps me to get through the hours and you know, Maggie's father has his golf friends. We go to dinner on Saturday nights. It is something to look forward to."

Stella was itching to ask about Maddy's daughter. "It was fortunate your mom had a dear friend like Maddy in such a difficult time as the war. You mentioned that Maddy had a daughter. Were you and she friends?"

"Not really. Eve was six or seven years older than me. She was better friends with my older brother. I think both my mother and Maddy would have been thrilled to see them marry, but it didn't work out that way. As we got older, we occasionally saw each other at neighborhood events and such. I always liked Eve, but we were so different." Ellen gave a hollow laugh. "In retrospect, I wanted my mother's life and Eve wanted her mother's life, but we never connected the way our moms did."

Ellen lapsed into a short silence again, lost in a world of what-ifs and could have beens. "I have some pictures from the old days. I know Maddy is in a few of them. Would you like to see them?"

Restraining her exultation, Stella smiled and nodded. "I would love to see them."

Ellen pulled herself up from the table and Stella jumped up to pull the chair for her. "You are so kind. Thank you so much for allowing me to talk about my memories of mother

"Of course, of course, let me finish up the dishes while you get the pictures. And thank you for letting me come over and pick your brain." Stella smiled at Ellen with true gratitude.

"Don't worry about those dishes. I can finish them later." Ellen moved into the living room and returned with two big photo albums. "My mother always organized her photos. Things are so different now with digital cameras. No one keeps photo albums anymore. Everything is on computers. I pulled out the old albums after mom died, so I could make the picture boards for the viewing. We all looked so young in those days."

Ellen flipped open the first photo album and Stella scooted closer to her to get a better look at the pictures. The pictures were square and black and white, each in its individual sleeve; the plastic made a sticky, cracking sound as she pulled them apart.

"These are amazing pictures. Is this when your mom worked in the city?" Stella pointed to a shot of a group of workers as she scanned the rows of pictures. In the right corner, she spotted a hauntingly familiar face. "Is this Maddy?" A chill curled around Stella's body.

Ellen pointed to a woman dressed in overalls and a scarf tied around her hair. "That's mom there." Her finger hovered over the picture for a moment before pointing to the right corner, "and that's Maddy of course. They look so glamorous, don't they? Don't you think they all looked like movie stars in those days? Nowadays everyone is so sloppy."

Ellen pulled the photo out of its plastic holder and held it out to Stella to see up close. "These black and white shots are actually quite detailed." Ellen pointed again to Maddy who was wearing a similar coverall and scarf on her head, but she seemed different from the other women. She was a little older than most of the other women; she wore a small scarf around her neck and seemed to be looking right at the camera, daring the photographer to see who she really was.

"Where did Maddy immigrate from?" Stella questioned

Ellen tapped her forehead, "Let me think for a minute. She spoke French, but many Europeans used French as their common language—German and Italian could get you lynched in those days. She taught my mother French so they could talk about things that us kids were not supposed to hear." She laughed heartily and continued, "I think she was from Paris. In fact, I'm almost sure of it."

"That is why she looks like a movie star, she was Parisian. Your mother and Maddy look like such good friends." Stella pointed to another picture of the two women with their arms wrapped around each other's waists.

"They were the best of friends Stella. No two women could have been closer." Sighing, Ellen closed the album and pulled the other one towards her. 'There are some pictures of Maddy in this one too. She and mom are much older—this is from the late 60's, right before Maddy passed away."

Ellen flipped past several pages until her eyes lit up. "Here we go. This is July 1969; I remember because it was the moon landing and the entire country was riveted. Our neighborhood had a block party. Here's mom and Maddy sitting in the front yard."

Ellen pulled the picture from the sleeve and handed it to Stella. The picture was of Maddy and Elizabeth sitting on aluminum folding yard chairs, side by side, on the grass next to the sidewalk. Maddy was wearing cat's-eye sunglasses and was leaning towards Elizabeth, with her shoulder slightly curled, like how a model would pose. Ellen's mother had a rehearsed smile on her face; her legs crossed and looked excited about the day. The slight tilt of Maddy's head led Stella to believe she had something more to say. Maddy's heart seemed to come out of her smile; she looked forlorn but experienced, modern yet classic. She owned the essence of understanding beyond explanation. She owned a peace in something that could not be seen, something that lived in her heart. She was genuinely wise as to what her future held. Stella noticed Maddy's hand resting gently on Elizabeth's arm.

"God they are beautiful, Ellen, really beautiful?" Stella wanted the picture. She wanted to study Maddy's face.

"Yes, mom was a beautiful woman. She always took such good care of herself, and us." Ellen flipped over the next page in the album. "Here's another shot of Maddy; she must not have realized that dad was taking her picture. She looks like she is watching something in the distance." Ellen removed the photo from its slot and passed it over to Stella. Ellen watched Stella's eyes grow wide and then narrow as she focused on the picture. She wondered why Stella seemed so interested in her mother's friend. Hesitantly she asked, "Would you like this picture? You could add it to the art box as a memorial to Maddy."

"Yes! Thank you so much. I will put it with the other things in the art box." Stella held the picture in the palms of her hand like a baby bird as tears sprang to her eyes in gratitude.

"Oh... where is that other picture?" Ellen pushed the photo album away and pulled the older one back to her. She started to flip through the pages rapidly. "Here's a picture of Maddy's daughter—Eve." Ellen turned the album towards Stella and pointed to a photo with two small children, standing awkwardly gazing at the person taking the photograph. The little girl had her hand on her hip and the little boy was squinting. "That's my brother who was born a few weeks after Eve."

"How precious. Eve looks like quite the strong kid, sort of feisty." Stella smiled at Ellen.

Ellen laughed. "You are so right. Maddy had a fierce temper and Eve was just like her—they were two peas in a pod. Eve was intense and Maddy indulged her interests. On a whim, they would go up to New York if Eve asked a question about a piece of art. Maddy would take her to see the painting or sculpture; the pictures in books were not enough. They were away almost every weekend. My mother never criticized Maddy, but I think she was appalled at how Eve was spoiled."

Ellen was quiet for a moment and Stella watched the memories play out on Ellen's face. "You know Stella, if this really interests you...you could talk to Eve. She still lives in the area."

Stella's heart beat a dull staccato. It was a great opportunity but with it, came great risk. "Do you think that Eve would be interested in what I found at Elizabeth's house?"

"I hate to admit this, but we haven't talked in years even though she lives a few towns over. We still send Christmas cards, and she sent me a beautiful sympathy card and flowers. It is such a kind thing to do; Maddy and my mom made sure we learned our manners. My mother would always say that good breeding stands out in the lowliest environments. You can take the girl out of the Main Line, but you can't take the Maine Line out of the girl. Anyway, Maddy's daughter traveled around after college. Then Maddy got sick and she and her husband came home to look after her. I will say this...Eve was there every minute of Maddy's last few months. After that, she stayed in the area. Would you like Eve's number?"

Stella nodded, too excited to respond. She had almost given up hope of getting any information and now she was being given Maddy's daughter's phone number without even asking.

Chapter 8

Paris October 1928

In the early morning, the artist is consumed by the life of the paint: the subtle changes in shade, the texture, and the way the colors speak to her. Each hue has a personality of its own. Each time she paints the white of stone against the white of canvas, she sees the subtle change of behavior of the white paint. It speaks to her with the clarity of truth; it knows how true it is and it knows it can be instantly changed with the minuscule fingertip of black. She hungers for the daylight to compare the intensities of the darkness of her dreams to the white of the canvas. She waits for the imperceptible sun to reveal the lucidity of its light on her humble faces. In her small bed, she waits for her inspiration; she waits for the day to invite her to the painter's circle.

In her small room, her slim graceful body slipped out from under the thin sheet and one wool blanket. One body to keep the warmth. One mouth to breathe the turpentine air. Images from the night before overwhelm her mind's eye; she thought of how beautiful the night sky was. The loveliness had made her weep. She wanted to pocket the grey night and save it for the light of day, to properly paint the tired face of the old woman scrubbing the church steps. The steps where the tourists casually walk over her cracked-wet hands; the steps that led to the building where the people worshipped the cross, the unknown, and the earth. Not the truth in their beating hearts, not the wine from the grape. This did not stop the old woman in her work. This did not stop her devotion. This did not stop her love for God. She continued to perfect the steps each day. Each day, she too, must continue with her gift from God.

She gazed at her work in progress—the old woman's portrait, the one she never posed for. She used her cigarette ash mixed with white paint to create the dry-ashy worn hands of a working woman. The small broken capillaries streaked across her cheeks matched the orange, darkening in the sky, melting into purple and red veins. It was the perfection of color; she yearned for and worshipped the perfection of color. The color of wine poured into a glass, the thick crimson of blood from a cut, the mix of Prussian blues in the sky. She wanted to submerge herself in the color.

She moved to the solitary window and waited for her sun to rise, to guide her in her work. She gazed longingly at the empty wine jug, and felt anxiety. She drinks more wine than water. She knows the water will run out of her and the wine never does. It allowed her to walk on the edge of her own existence. It filled her veins and carried her through moments where the dirt of the day had taken her heart and corroded it brown, still beating, but cracked and decayed as the dark night tortured her. She felt this pain often; it made her work harder. It made it difficult to see where her harsh life would lead her.

The essence of her life defines her paintings. She has seen the pain in people's faces and is able to render it. Her art is complex, intense, and real. Between painting and life lies madness, she knew this first hand. She sees the rough determination in women living harsh lives while she captures the soft edge of their soul with a covetous stare as their bodies are mangled in the daily wear of their work. In the darkest part of the night, she contemplates them and their path.

She took another sip of wine from her mug. As she drinks the wine, it burns her throat, flooding into her empty stomach and settling into its rhyme. She waits for her insides to calm as she waits for the sun to rise.

She knew she would have a few hours to mix her colors and plenty of time to paint; the sun seemed to have a strong start on this day. It cast the vibrancy she needed to express the small delicate lines of the everyday lives of her subjects.

She thought of the café last night. Holding her palette, she thinks of vermilion and violet, and the new face in her mind. She thinks of the girl's face. Maybe she will use this face to paint. No, she won't. She feels the consequence of arousal and the intention of need along her fingertips. Her fingertips start to burn; the images begin to lose focus in her brain. She allows the flooding to happen; she allows the paint to squeeze from the tiny tin tubes, she allows the art to come from her soul, engulfing her every stroke. Parisian colors dance in her mind. Creamy flesh bouncing to a soft beat, the round breast, the line of hair at the nape of her neck, the nakedness of a sea-shell earlobe, the soft overlay of flesh on an angular jaw and finally the thick heat of her breath.

The fresh air of the morning, the vision of the woman, the girl, her, the woman she cannot stop thinking of. A girl who stopped by her stand yesterday, a girl who carried her naked body under clothes that serve as an artificial barrier hiding who she is. It is foolish to put clothing on a leopard, covering their grace, their provenance, putting a camouflaged face on their bodies.

She has tasted the flavors of life, of women, of men. She felt the animal energy of rolling hips and a woman's scent. The essence of her skin, the powdery petals of a rose, her lips begged to touch. She made her want to paint. As the young woman hesitated at her stand, the artist studied her form. When she hurried away, her perfume lingered, mixing with the Seine air. She was seemingly becoming her balm.

With trembling fingers, she picked up a cigarette and lit it, inhaling the tobacco like oxygen. Her thoughts continued to drift like the grey smoke she exhaled. The young woman was stoic but soft. She carried herself like an unsure child, yet she seemed to have the soul of an old woman. Should she paint the woman-girl or should she put her out of her mind and suffer with the rest of her subjects? Was she a girl with a purpose? Was she a girl being taken care of by her parents?

She turned and looked out the small window, the small window that will frame the rest of her life, framing the portrait of who she is. Each tube of paint is meticulously opened and small teardrops of color are placed on her overused palette. She has limited color because she has the meager income of a street artist. She buys paint instead of food; she buys canvas instead of heat. She buys wine instead of loneliness. Her mind has driven her down a narrow road of limited choices.

She was always a bit different from the rest of her family. Her father was the only one she thought understood her nature. The father who left her at seventeen, taken by a broken heart. She wiped an invisible teardrop from her own face as she thought of her fingers touching the coldness of his absence again.

In her moment of loneliness, her thoughts move back to the memory of the girl who walked into the café where she and the other artists were drinking. She recalled an energy in the air had changed—had stolen her attention. She scanned the room and when she saw the young woman, she was paralyzed as she watched her. The new customer spoke with a disciplined courteousness to the madam of the restaurant. It was her.

She knew it was her. She felt her in her bones, and she felt it in her flesh. It wasn't but a few minutes before that moment in cafe she was thinking of her and the small painting that she had given her. She knew she would see her. She gave her one of her paintings. She would draw the girl to her. She would learn about her and the young woman's reasons for admiring her art and no one else's. She played with the rim of her wine glass. She pushed her fingers into the glass and touched the warm crimson liquid. She was craving more than her wine as she watched the girl move to the back of the café.

She pulled her attention back to the table; it was a good night to sit and laugh with the others. She liked laughing and drinking wine with Charles, especially when he offered to buy. He painted nudes. He seduced his models and then he painted them. He used the power of his sex to motivate his art. As a teenager in America, he plotted how he would get to Paris and live the life of an artist. He was a fair painter, but his art was really the life he led. He shared the stand on the Seine River with her; they also shared in the hardship and the revelry of Paris. Charles stared at his friend, noticing her intent gaze. Turning his body to look in the direction of her eyes, he saw the ordinary people talking and the normal Sunday night crowd. Shrugging, he looked back in the direction of his friend, but she had stood up.

She had to have another look at the woman she gave the painting to earlier that day. She wanted to get closer to her; she wanted to know what she thought of the painting of the old woman's face. She hoped she would feel the energy of the painting, the intention of each brush stroke, the passion of her soul. She wanted to see the girl's face, to memorize it, to have it etched in her mind, so she could see her whenever she desired.

They locked eyes. Feeling impulsive, she decided to extricate herself from the over-flowing table and follow the girl. Stunned by her face, the piercing power of her eyes and the beauty of her, she looked away to take control of her response. When her gaze returned to the spot, the young woman was out the door. Slipping out of the full banquette, she followed her. She pushed through the café door, searching the street for the young woman. Looking up and down the small street, the rain penetrated her vision, wetting her skin. Where did she go? She could not see her. She wanted to find her. She wanted it badly; she wanted to touch the

curl of the girl's hair, to feel the texture of the silky smoothness.
She was surprised by her desire for her. She knew there was more
to her, more of her that she wanted to know.

She retreated to the warmth of the restaurant, but felt the
heaviness of not knowing where the young woman went. Losing
herself in her own mind, she saw her feet led her back to the table.
The young woman's quiet eloquence and the floating movement of
her step mystified her. The disappearing act provoked thought in
her mind. Her mouth became dry, and she reached for the small
glass of red wine. She had been captured by a mystery.

Charles robbed her of her thoughts and snapped her back
into the café. "Where did you go?"

Where did she go? The artist thought how she should answer—
looking for the painting, looking for the girl, looking for herself.
She wanted to leave and find peace in her small room and wait
for the sun to come up. She did not want to lose her, yet she was
lost to the streets of Paris, taking a piece of her soul with her.

She looked down at her palette, assessing the colors in the
light. Evienne tried to remember the exact color of the girl's hair
and wondered if she could replicate it from the colors she had.

The sun blessed her today. Embracing the morning sun was
her ritual. The transparent light at her window, the fire of the
earth, the purity of the air, the cigarette she was smoking. She
wanted to take her thoughts and place them on the canvas; she
wanted the swelling of passions to stop haunting her mind; she
wanted the heart in her chest to stop pounding. Lost again, she
bent at the knees to find her balance, her mind was reeling, she
was falling; she felt tears run down her face. What was she feeling? Why the sadness? Why the feeling of need? She steadied
herself, looked out the window, and imagined the girl walking
by her little stall amongst the other shoppers. The vision cleared;
there were no people, just house tops.

There was only the gnawing anxiety of not knowing where
she was. She pulled her fingers through her hair. It was the way

she meditated; she pulled it to her face and hid her eyes. She thought of her as she breathed in the musky scent of her own hair. She wanted to touch her. She wanted to touch this young woman's hair and inhale its scent. She wanted to touch her soul.

Staring at her painting, she imagined painting her new obsession. She saw her lying across a red velvet chair. The sun beat on the smooth honeyed skin, her thick brown hair drifted across rounded shoulders; she was captivated by the sensuous splendor in her mind. She felt restless; it was dawning on her that something had been missing in her and now she ached for something she did not have. Her muse was not in the room; she was out there on the streets of Paris somewhere. She always pushed herself, but today she was disgusted with her lack of focus. She decided to head down to the river to see if she could make some money for her wine.

She grabbed her only shirt, tucked her hair into her father's wool cap, picked up her sketchbook, and headed for the street. She knew it was a uniform. The code of a manly uniform, but Paris saw art through masculine eyes. She slipped from the squat as to not be seen by the others. She attempted to be invisible while there. The other men in living there saw her as a woman creeping in on their world, like mold waiting to destroy their existence.

The day had turned into a crisp apple. She walked with a bit of freedom in her step. She was still feeling a bit worn from her emotional morning and the memory of the girl, but there was something different about life. There was a low hovering glow, reminding her of the white glisten she painted onto the edge of women's pupils. She smelled the fresh air and assured herself the distraction of the sales pitch would take her mind off her missing piece. She had a secret. For now, it was safely inside of her, buried under the distractions of the day.

After setting up the display of her paintings, she took a moment to lean against the stone wall. She closed her eyes to soak in the glorious warmth. The sapient sun pushed her salient arms into her. With eyes closed, she instantly felt the insanity of her. It started below her navel, burning and flooding over her like the river moving beside her. It made her laugh. She shrugged her one shoulder, dropped her head to the left and smiled to herself. She opened her eyes and there she was, walking towards her, the woman to whom she had given her art.

Chapter 9

Stella's hand was shaking a bit as she picked up her cell phone to dial Eve. Standing at her kitchen sink, she punched the numbers into the phone. Out the window over the sink, she watched a robin pull a long worm out of the ground and fly away. The phone rang one time, and then twice; maybe she was not home. Stella thought she would do some cleaning and take the dog for a walk. Her thoughts drifted to filling her day with chores, and then there was a voice echoing in her head. "Hello?"

Stella momentarily forgot what she was doing, as if she had walked into a room and forgotten why she was in there. She heard the woman's voice say hello again. She cleared her throat as she was stumbling in her mind for what to say.

"Hello?" The sound of Eve repeating the greeting was colored by impatience. Stella felt a surge of panic and quickly responded, "Hello. May I speak with Eve Newcastle?"

The voice had become professional and clipped. "Yes, this is Eve Newcastle. What is this in reference to please?"

"My name is Stella Simone and I'm a friend of Maggie Richards. Maggie's mom, Ellen Brown, gave me your name and number."

Eve's voice instantly softened, "Ah...I was afraid you were going to sell me aluminum siding. What can I help you with?"

"Well, I was helping Maggie clean out her grandmother's house and..."

"Oh Lord...that is a Herculean job. Elizabeth lived in that house her entire life. How is Ellen doing?"

"She is managing but sad. I sat with her yesterday. She shared some of her stories about Elizabeth." Stella momentarily thought of her own mother and if she would feel as sad as Ellen after her own mother's death. She took a deep breath, knowing the answer to that question.

"Are you close with the family? I'm afraid that Ellen and I haven't kept in touch..."

Eve's voice soothed Stella's anxiety, like a grandmother's hand patting a child's back. "I am close to Maggie and her girls."

Eve moved a pile of mail from a cluttered kitchen chair and sat down, curious why this young woman was calling her out of the blue. "I've known Maggie since she was born, but I haven't seen her in years." Eve sat back in her chair and wondered again what this call was about; suddenly, a small panic erupted inside of Eve, "Stella, is everything okay with Ellen and Maggie?"

"Oh yes" Stella quickly exclaimed. "I just wanted to talk to you about something. I talked to Ellen about your mother and she said I should talk to you, so I am calling you."

Eve's brow crinkled. This was a surprise; why would this stranger want to discuss her mother. The woman on the other side of the connection sounded too young to have even been alive in the 60's. "Did you know my mother?"

"No I didn't, but I helped Maggie clean out Elizabeth's house. There were so many things, and I found a letter that I think belongs to your mother." Stella heard a sharp intake of breath on the other side of the line.

"Why do you think it belonged to my mother?" Eve's voice was steady but skeptical.

"Can I just meet with you and show it to you?"

Eve was thoroughly perplexed, but Ellen had given this

woman her number, so she must be okay. "Why don't you come over tomorrow? I'm not doing anything until the evening. I live in Swarthmore."

Stella was not prepared for an immediate invite, but she readily agreed as she exclaimed, "Perfect".

Eve shook her head after she hung up. When she gave Stella directions to her house, Stella's whole personality changed. This woman was odd—she had seemed nervous and jittery through the entire conversation, but as soon as she started relating the directions, Stella's voice had become smooth and competent. Eve thought of the students at the college who could barely articulate their own feelings, but could expound for days on some arcane philosophical theory.

Walking into her living room, Eve's mind traveled back to that terrible day, so many decades ago, when she brought her mother's morning tea in to the bedroom to wake her up and discovered that she had slipped away in the middle of the night. Her body, just a shell of the vibrant woman she had been during Eve's childhood, was lying slack, white and cold. Eve had been taught pragmatism her whole life, but that morning, she had put the tray next to the bed and lay on the bed with her mother. She had gathered her mother's lifeless body in her arms and wept for herself, wept for her mother, wept for the life they had lived together, so many years of just the two of them.

Eve's eyes stung with tears. She hadn't felt the loss so keenly in years. So many women had complicated relationships with their mothers. She understood that on an intellectual level, but she and her mother had been very close and her mother had always been supportive and loving. Her mother had never made her feel inadequate or unwanted.

She moved out to her porch to feel the heat of the sun on her face. It was a beautiful day, so she sat on the step and let her mind wander.

Eve's reverie turned to the last big trip she and her mother had taken together before Eve's marriage. The 1964 World's Fair had been in the Queens borough of New York City, a short train ride from Philadelphia, and then the subway out to Queens. Her mother had been anxious to go, and Eve had humored her. Despite her lack of enthusiasm, Eve had enjoyed herself far more than she had expected. The silliness of Dinoland and the world's biggest cheese from Wisconsin was offset by seeing Michelangelo's Pieta at the Vatican City Pavilion. Years later, on a trip to Disneyland, she remembered that she had experienced the 'It's a Small World' ride before, at the Pepsi Pavilion during the fair as well.

Her mother had enjoyed the trip, yet she seemed bothered by the lack of European countries participating despite the massive exhibits that represented the space race and automation. Something had happened among the organizers, and many of the bigger countries had refused to take part. Her mother's beloved France had not been represented; however, her mother had uncharacteristically seemed more interested in the Spanish Pavilion anyway. They had lingered there far longer than Eve's patience had lasted. Her mother had been especially enraptured by a large sculpted piece by Vaquero Turcios called Pinta. It was a massive piece with a large arm and hand reaching out of the stone, as if trying to grasp something that was ultimately unreachable.

As Eve's mind played back the memories of she and her mother sharing a Belgian waffle that threatened to explode cream and strawberries all over both of them, she realized that it was almost fifty years since that wonderfully warm summer day in 1964. Suddenly, she felt very old. Madalane had been gone almost forty years, yet she still felt it was just like yesterday when her mother would pull out their battered old suitcases for a new adventure. With difficulty, she stood up feeling the cracks and stiffness of age. The sun was still shining down on the porch as she went back inside her house.

Chapter 10

Paris October 1928

The sky was a clear vibrant blue and the air was cool and refreshing after the previous night's down pour. As Madalane walked to classes, she looked at her surroundings with new eyes: the wounded old soldier, selling newspapers at the corner was transformed from a poverty-stricken veteran to a man worthy of respect. He was a man who maintained his dignity by holding on to his ability to earn a living. The young woman selling coffee at the cafe became a girl with a hidden life, a secret lover, an existence beyond anything Madalane had ever considered before. She was looking at the world instead of through the world.

Sitting in class, she half-listened to the professor. This class was a requirement, but it had no bearing on what interested her. She sat through another class and then another. She participated when required, but each minute that passed was a minute closer to her freedom. The freedom she craved to walk along the river and see E. Lavelle. Madalane had resolved that she would speak with her today. She felt bold and confident.

For the hundredth time, she looked at the clock. A meeting with her tutor and then she was free. Madalane adored her tutor, Madame Renard; she was a brilliant woman who functioned more as an advisor than as a tutor. She had realized that Madalane's minor inadequacies as a student were based more on bored distraction than an inability to do the work. After a few meetings, Madame Renard had spoken plainly to her, "If you want to stay at the University, you must maintain your grades."

Madame Renard was the first person Madalane had met who treated her like an adult and not a child. She was uncomfortable with being coddled and she loathed being scolded, so a dose of practical advice was extremely helpful. Madalane appreciated her honesty. She understood that she must play the game, and do the work even if it seemed pointless. After only a few weeks, her grades were outstanding and Madame Renard's role had evolved into that of a mentor.

Madalane sat across from her to discuss her classes, as she was required to do every Monday. Today, Madalane's distraction was evident. Madame Renard's shrewd eyes could see right through the young woman. As her advisor's eyebrows pinched tighter and tighter together, Madalane attempted an exhaustive review of her progress over the previous week. After allowing the young woman to flounder for several minutes, the tutor looked at her student passively, and said, "You are preoccupied by something else. Go do what you need to do, but do not let it affect your grades."

Madalane was startled and tried to defend herself. However, her tutor was not convinced, "You are clearly not in this room. I will not waste your time or mine. Just remember, some of the faculty, and you know who I am speaking of, are not enthusiastic about female students. If you are wasting time until you find a suitable husband, then you will prove them right." She turned back to her work and effectively dismissed the young woman from her presence.

Madalane would have more vigorously argued, but she knew that Madame Renard was right. She was wasting her time, but this was temporary she promised herself. She was enthralled by E. Lavelle and she just needed to see her. Before she left her tutor's office, Madalane vowed to maintain her grades, to prove the male teachers were wrong. Feeling somewhat chastened, but emphatically sure that she was choosing the right path, she set off for the stalls.

Under the brim of her cap, the woman studied the young woman as she walked towards her. Leaning against the river wall, she knew the student would come today and she would learn her name. The girl's conservative gray coat was properly buttoned and hung to her calf; her two strong calves were encased in black tights and flat schoolgirl shoes—it almost gave her the appearance of a Parisian dove. She was a dove to her. Her brown hair was wrapped in a tight knot defining a business attitude. She remembered the struggle to attend a co-educational institution— women fighting for their rights in a primarily male university. The thought made her smile. She hoped the student was more than a schoolgirl; she wanted her to crave knowledge and life.

As she got closer, the sun reflected though the red wisps of hair floating around the girl's face, like the image of an angel in a renaissance painting. As she got closer, she felt her heart knock on her sternum. She realized that she was breathing short small breaths that matched the young woman's short steps. She was surprised at how happy she was to see the beautiful young woman. A cocky smile came across her face. She settled into her most dramatic avant-garde pose and waited.

Madalane's resolve to speak with E. Lavelle was strong and resolute, but as she approached the stalls, it weakened. She grasped her canvas school bag tighter and held it close to her body; she remembered how childish she was the night before at the café and she felt her face flush. Madalane slowed as she got closer to E. Lavelle's stall. She reasoned that she would thank her for her gift and ask her name. It was polite and appropriate. Her mother would approve. With renewed determination, she quickened her pace again. The artist was there, hanging back near the stone of the river wall. Surrounded by her paintings, she was gloriously lovely. As Madalane walked past the canvases, the woman locked eyes with her and seemed to smile more than she had before.

Madalane stopped a few feet in front of her and blurted out, "Thank you for the painting." She had hoped to work up to the moment, but when their eyes met, she was unable to form any thought, except for the primary reason for her visit. So much for sophisticated conversation.

The artist saw Madalane's shamed grimace because she moved closer to the young woman and, smiled directly into her eyes. In a husky, caramel-laden voice, she whispered, "You're welcome."

The silence stretched on and the Madalane briefly wondered if E. Lavelle only spoke in whispers and hushed tones, but then she realized that the woman was still looking at her with that intent gaze. There was an awkward silence between the two women, but each felt a strange pleasure being in one another's company. The moment seemed to cover a lifetime and then the young woman broke eye contact, disconcerted by the connection they were sharing.

Agonizing over what to say, the young woman felt each second tick like a metronome in her head. Suddenly too much time had passed and now anything she said would have sounded ridiculous and trite. Futilely, she wanted to run away again, but the woman patiently stood there, quietly waiting for her to say something, anything at all. Madalane closed her eyes and took a deep breath to calm her frenzied mind, and when she opened her eyes, a quizzical look and a slightly arched eyebrow greeted her.

Madalane's eyes shifted to the paintings and words started to pour from her mouth. Everything she had thought, everything she had contemplated came out of her in a torrent of words, "Your paintings are marvelous. I don't understand why I love them so much, but I do and I am overwhelmed every time I look at them. I have done nothing of consequence since you gave me the painting yesterday, except stare at it. Why do you paint these women? What do they mean to you? What gave you the idea? What is it that you are trying to express?"

Madalane stopped when she realized that the woman was grinning, her lips quirked at the corners as if trying to define what mania had come over her. The young woman blushed and stared down at the sidewalk.

"Don't stop," the artist said in an almost normal volume. Madalane looked up and saw the truth of what she said. She didn't want her to go away and leave her in peace. She was fine with Madalane disrupting her afternoon.

"What appeals to you about the painting?" E. Lavelle asked as she fumbled for her cigarettes in her trouser pockets. Finally locating them, she lit one with fingers that betrayed her nervousness by slightly trembling. She inhaled and set the cigarette on the edge of her easel, giving her full attention to the girl.

The young woman was thunderstruck for a moment because she wasn't expecting this question. She assumed that they would discuss her art; instead, the artist had made her feel like a student.

Madalane decided to answer thoughtfully rather than just saying whatever came to mind. She allowed her mind to recall all the thoughts she had of the painting; while she considered her answer, she lowered her eyes and stared out at the Seine River. The river was moving slowly and the sun was already descending in the sky. The muted colors and the slow flow of the river seemed to pulsate with energy. Then as if in a trance, she began to answer, "Your paintings appeal to me because they go beyond the expected; they go beyond the traditional. These women seem broken, old, and tired, but there is a life in them. There is something in their eyes and face that tells me they have secrets and desires and loves that no one expects. There is so much more to them than hard work and misery, except no one sees it because they only look at their clothes and faces, and that's all anyone sees."

The woman's face had transformed from placid patience

to regarding the young woman with intent interest. Madalane stopped speaking because she was afraid that she had said something wrong, something that had offended, something stupid that she should have known better not to say. She quickly searched her mind trying to remember everything she had said and there didn't seem to be anything that was silly or ridiculous. As she stood there desperately aware that her expression had changed, she wanted to cry. She had wanted to impress her. Instead, the artist seemed frozen and distant. Madalane dropped her gaze and clenched her eyes shut.

Suddenly Madalane felt her entire body engulfed. She had been pulled into an embrace, arms wrapping around her. Stunned and momentarily frightened that she was in danger, it dawned on her that she could feel the woman trembling. Madalane brought her own arms up to hold the woman against her. The woman was so thin; she was half-afraid she would crush her. The student buried her face into the crook of the taller girl's shoulder and breathed deeply, inhaling the scent of tobacco, paint, turpentine and a woodsy clean smell. Instead of being offended at the combination of caustic odors, Madalane found them strangely comforting. They stood like that for several seconds or several minutes. Neither could tell; they were locked in an embrace of mutual acceptance and appreciation. Madalane never wanted to move again.

Some innate sense of rationality must have struck because the taller woman abruptly pulled back and turned to face the river, picked up her cigarette from the easel and took a long drag off of it. Madalane stood awkwardly, unsure of what to do. Almost as fast as the artist turned away, she returned to face the young woman, vibrantly smiling. Madalane thought E. Lavelle looked far younger than she had originally thought, almost as young as herself, maybe twenty at the most. Her face was completely unlined and fresh, but the way she carried herself was so much older. The weight of life seemed to weigh her down.

The young woman spoke to her from a place of truth. She knew because she had met liars before. Had she betrayed herself? This woman had walked inside of her with her words. The way she poignantly spoke of her art; it was as if she spoke to her lonely heart. There was a tremor in the air between them.

How does this girl understand the secrets that she has hidden, the complexities of art, the interwoven mastering of paint, the layering and lightness of time, extrapolating unseen energy into an old woman's face? She still felt the lightness in her mind, the sway of her body, the words flooding over her, the student's words and her expression so intense, so beautifully porcelain, unaffected by what society could drive her to think. Overwhelmed by the words, the brief understanding that she grabbed the girl and pulled her to her own body. The blood of embarrassment rushed to her face. She wanted her to leave, but also to stay.

She focused hard to reclaim herself. Dropping her spent cigarette and crushing it under her boot, the woman turned to face the river, and inhaled to find her composure. She moved outside of herself and noticed the blue of the sky, the china blue, the waning sun, the mix of city air. It calmed her and she then returned her gaze to the girl almost forgetting where she stood. She naively had thought the young woman would see only the surface of her art, and felt a pang of regret in realizing she was wrong and in the same breath, she was inordinately pleased. Nonetheless, it was too close for comfort. The anxiety built inside of her; she felt herself craving isolation and a full decanter of wine.

Madalane maintained her silence. She replayed what she had said, and she still wasn't sure if she had offended her or not. She watched as the vulnerability in the artist's face faded away and was replaced by a slightly mocking grin and narrowed eyes.

"Haven't I scared you away yet?" E. Lavelle snapped. Gone was the sultry whisper, and in its place was a clipped sardonic tone. Madalane stepped back unconsciously; the words felt like a branch striking her face. She immediately wanted to cry and run back to her room and shred the canvas that she had given her the day before. Madalane forced herself to stand her ground, knowing that if she moved a muscle, she would dissolve into a puddle of tears.

Resolved that this woman was not going to intimidate her, Madalane knew she had stood up to much crueler people—her own mother, for one. If she could manage to get herself to Paris to attend university, both of which her mother opposed vociferously, she was certainly not going to let some bohemian make her feel stupid or unworthy. The silence stretched on and on, and she remained staring at E. Lavelle, contemplating how much longer she should stand there. She wanted to make sure that E. Lavelle knew that she had not scared her away.

Madalane supposed it must have seemed odd to have someone staring blankly at a person after they made it perfectly clear that they wanted you gone. Nonetheless, she was feeling particularly defiant and did not want to show even the slightest weakness. The artist's face changed again, from pursed lips and clenched eyes to a more relaxed, neutral pose. Madalane wondered, was this the right time to turn on her heel and storm away, incensed at her rudeness? However, she found she could not move, but in a voice she barely recognized as her own, she asked, "Why did you say that? It was rude and mean."

In the few weeks the young woman had been in Paris, she already knew that saying something like that would be an invitation for mockery and ridicule. She wanted to smack her forehead and groan at her naivety. Instead, E. Lavelle's face transformed again and now she looked ashamed.

The whisper was back, "I apologize. You are right; it was rude."

Madalane waited for the twist where E. Lavelle would tell her to run home to mamma and cry in her lap. But no, she went quiet again. This woman was infuriating; why couldn't she have an ordinary conversation like a normal person?

Chapter 11

The following day, Stella drove west to Eve's house. A letter was sitting on the seat next to her; although she had only read two letters, she was reluctant to let any of them go. She kept glancing at it, wondering how Eve would react. If Madalane's daughter was horrified, then it would be easy. She would get the hell out of there and never tell Eve about the rest of the letters. The alternative was what troubled Stella. What if Eve wanted the art box and its contents? Was she morally obligated to turn everything over to Eve? What if Eve assumed the letter was hers and claimed it? Damn, she should have made a copy of it before she set off on this visit. A gnawing sense of anxiety played around her mind, but she tried to assure herself that she would copy everything else before she handed it over. One letter wouldn't make too much of a difference, would it?

The Blue Route always had sections that were under construction. Stella worried this would cause delays on Saturday afternoon; she hated being late. Her thoughts returned to the letters as she glanced at the passenger seat. Why was she so fascinated by Madalane? She was absorbed by a woman who lived in Paris eighty years ago.

Paris. The love letter. What if Eve was surprised by the nature of the letter? What if she was insulted by the thought her mother was with a woman. Maybe Stella was creating something that was not there. What if Eve hated her mother and it was a dead end? A dead end. Every end is a beginning. There had been many new beginnings in her life. There was room for growth. There was room for thought. Was this going to be easy?

Exit three, Swarthmore. Unconsciously, she checked the clock on her dashboard to see how long the trip had taken. Consulting the directions again, she would have to go one point two miles and make a left after merging off exit three: Media-Swarthmore to the right. Easy enough.

Should she be going to Eve's house without the art box? Yes, she should. Maybe Eve was one of those insightful, kind-hearted people. Or maybe, she would be the petty, small-minded type of person who would vilify her mother. It was the right choice to leave the box at home, Stella affirmed for the hundredth time as she steered the car towards Eve's house.

Eve heard the crunch of tires as a car came up her driveway. She had been hovering near the front window, and she was relieved to see the vehicle. She watched Stella sitting behind the steering wheel of the car. Eve was beyond curious as she opened the door and walked onto the front porch to greet her guest.

Seeing the older woman on the porch, Stella realized that it was time to see where this would lead. She checked the address and it matched the house number: 148. The older woman stood confidently, gazing at her, as if she was expecting company. Yes, it was the right place. Eve waved at Stella, partly as a greeting and partly to encourage her to get out of the car. Stella's heart was pounding, matching the barking of what appeared to be the dog of the household. Slipping the letter into her purse, she got out of her Volvo and kneeled down to give the brown Boxer a chance to sniff her hand.

Eve smiled as Stella patted Tiberius. That was a good sign; she usually liked people who liked dogs. That said a lot about a person's character. Eve watched Stella and noted that although she was casually dressed, she was perfectly turned out. From the top of her perfectly highlighted hair to the subtly expensive leather shoes, Stella looked like a woman in a Ralph Lauren advertisement. "You must be Stella. I'm Eve and that is Tiberius Julius Caesar Augustus, but he prefers Tiberius."

Eve extended her hand towards Stella. Stella reached out and grabbed it with both of her hands, cupping Eve's hand as if she was embracing her. She instantly felt like she knew this woman. Her silvery hair was pulled back in a loose knot. There were wisps framing her face. Her lips were full with a hint of pink tint to them. Stella was lost in her face for a moment, trying to see the resemblance to the woman in the sketch before remembering to introduce herself.

"I'm Stella. It is so nice to meet you and Tiberius. He is so sweet." As Stella rubbed Tiberius's head, she felt her nervousness melting away.

"Come on up to the house! Tiberius will have you rubbing his belly soon if we don't get moving." Eve moved towards the three steps that led to her wide front porch. She didn't hear Stella moving behind her, so she glanced back. Stella was staring at something along the left side of the house. Eve followed her eye line and saw what had captured Stella's attention.

"I love the sound of wind chimes—that one is right under my bedroom. Its tones are pure, helps me go to sleep. Are you a fan of wind chimes?" Eve asked.

"Where did you get that beautiful wind chime? I love the sound; it's like the sound of peace. The sound reminds me of something familiar. I am not sure. Maybe the church bells or the clock towers in Italy." The sunlight seemed to be glistening off the multi-colored glass. The sound was musical, echoing the deep resonance of a perfect tone. Stella felt a warm curl of air wrap around her neck. It sent the good kind of chills down her back. She was not sure if it was the sound of the chime or meeting this woman that made her feel this way. Everything felt perfectly aligned.

As Stella moved to the porch, Eve answered her question, "I actually made those wind chimes. I love stained glass and I love chimes, so I combined the two."

Stella was delighted to learn that Eve was artistic. Her own talents were held to an occasional craft during the holidays. Approaching the porch, Stella said, "Thank you for asking me over today."

Eve had been studying her visitor as Stella gazed at the wind chimes. Stella seemed like a nice person, but she felt a hidden recess beneath the perfectly presented exterior. "Come on up to the porch. It's a gorgeous day; I thought we could sit out here and enjoy the day. I was making up a pitcher of mojitos. Would you like one? I grow my own mint, so the taste is divine!"

"Sure, that sounds great. Your gardens are beautiful; do you do all the maintenance yourself?" Stella saw the pitcher of drinks sitting on a whitewashed wood table between two oversized rocking chairs. The mint drink did look inviting.

"I was never a big gardener, but my husband loved flowers, and I keep the gardens up to remind me of him." He taught me the basics. I find it relaxing to get dirty. Plus, the shoes are comfortable." Eve gave a hearty laugh

Stella glanced down at Eve's shoes and saw she was wearing purple crocs that were filled with Disney characters and flower buttons.

Eve led them to the two rocking chairs. Stella stared curiously at the chairs—they looked like they had been woven from small tree branches. The seat and backs were covered with what looked to be some sort of dark cotton fabric.

"I found those chairs in Guatemala. They are woven from some sort of gum tree, so the branches are very flexible when freshly cut and become almost like concrete as they die. I thought it was an interesting metaphor for our lives. The fabric is hemp that I brought back from Mexico. It can get wet and dries fast. No schlepping pillows in and out of the house every time it rains."

"You have such interesting things. Ellen had mentioned that you had done a lot of traveling."

"I have done my share I suppose. I did travel for most of my twenties—my husband and I were vagabonds. When I finished my degree, I had to settle down and get a proper job. I try to travel somewhere every year, but as I get older, my adventures are not as exotic as they used to be."

Stella had settled herself into one of the Guatemalan chairs, "I am surprised how comfortable this chair is. It is as if the chair molded to your body. It's a very comforting feeling." Stella took a deep breath of the fresh autumn air and turned to watch Eve pour the fresh mint drink into two glasses. She supposed that one drink on a warm day was therapeutic.

Stella heard the wind chimes again and felt the same calm resonate over her. "I love those wind chimes. They give me a calm feeling inside. It is weird. I never really paid much attention to wind chimes before. I think I might have been missing out on something."

"We should toast to never missing out on life." Eve stated, holding up her glass.

Stella looked into Eve's brown eyes and smiled. She liked her and was happy to be sitting on her front porch.

Eve could feel waves of nervousness falling off this woman. She sipped her drink and listened to the birds chatter aimlessly. Eve was curious. Stella had the type of look where she could be anywhere from 30 to 40. She dressed with a timeless sophistication. Eve smirked, looking at her own smudged capris, ridiculous crocs, and long-destroyed white shirt. She looked like a homeless person compared to the stylish woman sitting next to her.

Stella's mouth was dry and she took a quick sip of her drink. It was really good. She took another sip and stared out at the gardens. She had hoped Eve would get the ball rolling, but the older woman was clearly waiting for her. She wanted to know when Madalane had died, but the words came out completely wrong,

"How long has it been…since you started your gardens?" Stella mentally smacked herself, but heard herself keep talking, "I can barely keep a cactus alive and your garden is teeming with life!"

"My husband and I had only a few years together before he died. He passed away in 1975. It was a hard time for me. My mother had passed five years before that, and really, I was barely over her death when he got sick. Life doesn't always work out the way we think it will. I believe that you have to work with what life gives you." Eve pensively glanced out to the freshly blooming chrysanthemums, goldenrods, and asters she had put in a few weeks back. "You can wait for something to happen, or you can make it happen. I learned that the hard way."

Eve noticed that Stella's glass was almost empty. She quickly finished her own drink and picked up the pitcher. "Are you ready for another?"

"Yes, just one more…it is delicious." Stella thought she would have one more drink now and then switch to water so she could drive home.

"Do you have any children, Eve?"

Eve felt the tightness in her chest. She always felt this way when asked this particular question. "I suppose the easy answer is that the universe had other plans for me." Eve paused, taking a deep breath. "But the real answer is that my body wasn't able to give me what I wanted most." Eve looked away for moment. These conversations were always awkward. She knew when she looked back to Stella; there would be a look of shamed sympathy on her face. She looked down at her drink and sighed. This woman had brought up memories of her three most painful moments—her mother, her husband and the baby she could never carry to term. The Father, the Son and the Holy Ghost. Eve smiled, realizing that her mother would have been happy that some of what the nuns had taught her in school had actually stuck.

The two women sat there on the front porch and quietly studied the vibrant blooms of gold and orange. Stella knew there was vulnerability in the moment. She felt the awkward tension of Eve sharing her heart and gently broke the silence, "When I was a child, my grandmother would rock me on her porch at her place at the Jersey shore. My mother was a busy woman and never took the time to really enjoy things; I guess this is why I have a hard time sitting still, but look at me now, here I am rocking and drinking without a care in the world." Stella felt an unfamiliar sense of giddiness and wondered if she had already drunk too much.

Realizing that she was not drunk at all, just happy, she continued her tale, "Anyway, she would say this creaking noise was the gretze or gekratz, some German word that would lull a baby to sleep. Every time I hear it, I think of my grandmamma. Chairs made from green youth, now have turned to stone. It's like life and memory."

"My mother taught me that if you live in the past, you will never have a future." Even as Eve said those words, she heard her mother's practical voice reminding her of that life lesson anytime Eve complained. "She would say to me: just water from a very long river under a bridge. Her English was perfect, but she did mangle the occasional idiom."

Eve took a long drink from her glass, feeling the rum and mint and sweetness mingle on her tongue. The sun was warm, and the drink was cool. Could there be anything more perfect? Needing to dispel the torpor that had seized her, she stretched, and turned to Stella. "You said you had found something that you think belonged to my mother?"

Stella was ripped back to the reason why she was at Eve's house to begin with. She wanted to find out about her mother. "Yes, yes. Of course, the letter. I was helping Maggie clean out Elizabeth's house and found a box with a letter and other things in it, and I traced it back to you." Stella reached for her Coach bag next to the chair and gently pulled out a folded paper. She handed it to Eve.

Eve reached for the letter. The writing was a beautiful script and looked like it was written by a fountain pen—the scratches and loops on the paper reminding her of the old professors who insisted that the civilization had gone to hell in a hand basket the day the world accepted the disposable pen.

There was no envelope, but the date at the top of the letter showed it was written in the early 30's. Eve stopped for a minute, relishing the moment of discovery. Her mother had received this letter more than seventy years ago, and had kept it. It must have been important to her. Breathing deeply, she carefully unfolded the letter, noticing the creases were deep. So her mother must have unfolded this letter often. Curiosity getting the best of her, she scanned the first few lines, her eyebrows rising perceptibly higher and higher.

8 May 1934

My Dearest Madalane,
I cannot draw my eyes from you as I begin to hear the awakening of our street. I ask myself, what is this happiness living in my veins? It is you, my Dove. My heart remains encircled in your beating heart even as you sleep.

After the first few sentences, she glanced up at her visitor. "Did you read this?"

Stella looked uncomfortable at the direct question, but answered honestly, "Yes, I did."

Eve nodded and whispered, "Of course you did; I should have realized that." She continued reading the letter, trying to imagine her mother reading this letter for the first time. Trying to imagine her mother reading these words.

I draw you and find peace. Last night, the perfect fit of

your body wrapped around me and still more of my passion for you floods through my body to my pen. I cannot help myself. I cannot stop my hands from the joy of receiving the privilege of you. The perfect touch of you. The perfection of you.

I am lulled by your beauty, struck with awe. Years seem like minutes as I sit and stare at you. Watching you dream, watching you breathe, watching you, I am humbled by your beauty as the subtle sun awakens your face. You linger inside of my mind, in my blood, mixing into my black ink as you continuously inspire my paint. The passion of your love moves my brush, you paint my heart a multitude of colors, yet I am still in awe of your mere essence. My blood, my living soul, drains from me and lives in you. I give you my everything.

At this moment, listening to chattering birds outside our small window, I am in exact harmony with you and the world. I want to curl my flesh into you, melting into your peace, and cover myself with your sweet scent. Night into day, sunset into moon rise.

As I sit next to you, I will allow myself only your hand as you sleep, your smooth white skin pressed to my cheek. I feel your delicate bones and tender essence resting in between my cheek and palm and I float away in the warmth of your sea. My dearest, you bring me to my knees. And there I will honor you forever.

Forever,

Evienne

As she came to the last line and saw the signature, she chuckled. The chuckle became a laugh and then the laugh became an overwhelming howl. She couldn't stop laughing.

Stella was shocked at Eve's reaction. When she read the letter, she cried at the beauty, the heart-wrenching love, the passionate devotion in Madalane's life.

Eve took a deep breath, then another and another. How could

she possibly explain why the letter elicited such an extreme reaction? She exhaled slowly, and looked down at the curving ink outline of Evienne's name. It made her smile again.

"I'm sorry to laugh. My mother was the very epitome of the World War Two immigrant. She never wanted to discuss what her life was like before the war. I just assumed it was a life of deprivation and sacrifice." Eve's eyebrows and lips quivered with humor as she tapped the letter. "Apparently my mother had a quite different life than the hardships I had imagined for her. In fact, I don't think she was deprived of much, at least according to this letter." Eve felt the giddy humor well up inside of her again. "The fact that my mother's lover was a woman is even..." Eve searched for the right word. Her mother was the bastion of doing the right thing, the woman whose code of conduct was always so exact and correct, and the teacher who taught her students and her daughter the importance of being true to oneself.

"It's just funny. My mom was so conventional, and here is this side of her that I never knew existed. I've always loved my mother, but now after this, I love her even more."

Chapter 12

Paris, October 1928

The late afternoon sun was holding strong for a few more precious hours. Temperate autumn days in Paris always gave way to cold evenings as the breeze from the river moved down the streets and alleys of the city. Madalane stood outside the door of her school; she had stayed later than usual because she was meeting some friends at a theater on the right bank of the Seine to see The Divine Woman with Greta Garbo. She had a while before she was meeting her friends, but her brain was fuzzy from too much reading and studying and she needed some fresh air.

Truth be told, she really wanted to see E. Lavelle. Although their last meeting had been somewhat awkward, she felt like they had a growing respect on both sides and she wanted to cultivate their friendship. She felt a compulsion that she didn't really understand, but she knew not to question something that she felt this strongly about. She turned right onto Rue St. Michel, went past her flat and quickly walked towards Quai de Saint Augustins, anticipation and excitement building in her belly.

E. Lavelle was trying to work magic on this Friday afternoon. Money was sparse; supplies were needed, so sales of her paintings were necessary. Living in a squat, which encompassed her workspace, sleep area and a corner to keep the few things she owned, was the life story of any street artist. Her living conditions were unsanitary and questionable. The building was filled with too many hungry Neanderthal male artists, especially Jean, so she spent most of her time at the stand, which was her true home where she could paint and sketch without worry.

"Bonjour monsieur, the afternoon is lovely," the woman greeted each person as they walked by with a familiarity as if she knew them personally. Her charm and soft voice took the pressure off the usual sales pitch from her peers. As she scanned the strollers for potential customers, E. Lavelle felt the pang of recognition in her soul; it was the girl who she gave her art to walking towards her.

When she looked up and made eye contact, Madalane felt an electrical current charge through her. Her step quickened and she self-consciously patted her hair, hoping she looked presentable. The two women smiled at each other; it felt like they had both waited all day for this moment. Approaching, Madalane called out, "Bonjour Mademoiselle Lavelle!"

Her voice carried by the breeze replied, "Bonjour Mademoiselle." She extended her hand to the student and it occurred to her she didn't even know her name. "This is our third meeting and I have yet to learn your name."

Delighted by her interest, Madalane blushed as if she was revealing an intimate secret, "My name is Madalane...Madalane Durand."

"Madalane Durand. Madalane, hmm." The woman squeezed her hand and contemplated the sound of the girl's name coming from her lips. "Madalane, what brings you to my studio this afternoon?"

Hearing her name spoken in the artist's low thrilling tones, Madalane felt pleasure run through her body. "I'm seeing a film later with some friends from school, but I wanted to stop and say hello and see how you are doing." Mischievously, the young woman moved closer and spoke in a furtive manner, "It's only a vicious rumor that I am loitering here for purposes of a free art exhibit."

"Well then, let's fan the flame of the rumors and let me show you what I have recently finished." E. Lavelle squatted down and her long brown plait fell over her shoulder. She picked up a small painting of a much younger woman compared to the woman in the one she had given Madalane. Studying it for a moment, she then put it in Madalane's hands. "What do you think of this?" She was eager for her opinion.

The woman's face was lined but not creased, and the thick layers of paint created a creamy complexion that gave her an almost aristocratic appearance; however, the cheap gaudy clothes sent a contradictory message. Her hair was thick and glossy, highlighted by a few strands of silver. It was an interesting painting—the face of a queen, but dressed like a fishmonger's wife. Madalane was captivated by the dichotomy. "I think you like to play with people's expectations, but in a gentle way. You are not provoking any particularly strong emotion in a person, but you seem to be asking people to redefine the difference between classes." Madalane looked to see if her response was appropriate, hoping she had comported herself with some semblance of intelligence.

Madalane's words brought up one of the few good memories from the professors at art school. It thrilled the artist that she could see the interpretation she was intending. It was true; she was looking to contradict the image of wealth and its meaning. Was wealth found from the inside or from the things one acquires? "You are right Madalane. And well said." As the two gazed at the canvas, their rapt attention to the painting seemed to be enough to attract the attention of a potential buyer. A woman with a well-fashioned cloche hat and red lips insinuated herself into the conversation.

"With whom may I speak with about purchasing a painting?"

Her imperious words and penetrating gaze broke the connection between E. Lavelle and Madalane.

"Bonjour Madame. It is I you would like to speak with." Smiling, E. Lavelle slipped right into her sales pitch using the painting that they were discussing. Winking at Madalane, she retrieved the canvas from Madalane's hands and directed her attention to the older woman. "We were discussing the components of wealth; is it what we have inside or what we acquire?" She smiled at Madalane and then looked back at the women, gently placing the painting in her hands.

"You have quite a talent and I have an interest; would you be so kind as to show me some of your other work?" The artist's attention was needed and she looked back to the girl and shrugged with the nonchalance of a painter in demand.

Madalane felt an overwhelming need to stay and watch her new friend at work, yet her father's exhortations about friends distracting her when she was at work in the shop rang loudly in her head. She would prove a distraction to the artist, and that would not be helpful at all. She watched the tall lanky girl gesturing to some of the paintings lined up against the sea wall and felt an indefinable ache in her chest. She loved the way she moved so gracefully, capturing the attention of the older woman with her hands and murmuring explanations as if they were secrets for her alone. She caught her eye and motioned that she would be leaving.

She called out "Au revoir my friend."

The young woman turned and waved, "Bon soir Madalane!"

As she began to move towards the bridge to cross to the right side of the Seine, she realized that she still did not know the artist's first name. She felt silly, but she had to know it immediately. Madalane stopped, turned around and shouted, "You still have not told me your name!"

Pulling her cap from her head, she bowed low and waved towards the student, "My name is Evienne Lavelle. The famous artist!"

Chapter 13

Stella watched the older woman's head shake in disbelief, trying to wrap her mind around the mother she was learning about for the first time. Stella watched Eve read the lines of the beautifully written script as wisps of her silvery hair moved in the afternoon breeze. Eve's fingers traced the lines of the writer's name as if she was contemplating something about the mother she had not known.

"Eve, the letter is so poignant; it made my heart full and empty at the same time. The love and passion of Evienne's words is so moving." She paused before asking gently, "You didn't know anything about this part of your mother's life or who this woman Evienne was?"

Eve shrugged and took a sip of her drink, "Most children know so little of their parent's lives before they were born. My mother died when I was obsessed with my own life. It never occurred to me until I was older that she had lived an entire lifetime before I was born." Eve stood up and walked to the end of the porch; she ran her fingers along the wind chimes and the abrupt movement caused a cacophony of sound.

"The wind chimes are beautiful Eve."

Relieved to have something easy to explain, Eve spoke softly, "I made this wind chime many years ago; I was spending the summer in England and I met this lovely woman who restored stained glass for churches. She also taught classes on how to make stained glass. She was so passionate about it that I took the class and fell in love with the intricacies of the process."

Stella let the lush sound of the wind chimes fill the silence. She felt any comment she could make would be unnecessary.

Finally, Eve leaned her back against the porch railing and shook her head almost imperceptibly. "By the time I was curious about my mother's early life, she was gone. I know she was born in a small town in Southern France, I know she went to school in Paris and I know that she escaped right before the Nazis invaded the city. That's all I know about her past."

"Your mother escaped the Nazi's?"

"Yes. She left France in the spring of 1940, literally weeks before the Nazis took over. She absolutely would not discuss that time with me. She said it was horrible and the Nazis were the scum of the earth. She didn't want to waste her breath on them."

Eve walked back to where Stella was sitting and leaned against the porch railing and faced Stella. "After my husband died, I was horribly lonely. I started reading about Paris in the 1930's and early 40's, and I discovered that my mother was in the epicenter of one of the greatest literary and artistic movements in history."

"Was your mother a writer?"

"No, my mother was a teacher. Ironically, even though she was French, she taught English. She loved to read, but wrote very little; I still have most of her books. I have a few letters that she wrote me when I was away in college, but other than that, she was reluctant to put pen to paper—unless it was the red pen." Eve laughed, remembering her mother muttering in French about the atrocious grammar her students would perpetrate in their papers.

The image of her mother, bent over the kitchen table, surrounded by essays staggered Eve. It had been so long since she had discussed her mother with anyone. She suddenly felt very sad; she could feel the grief that she experienced after her mother died beginning to creep into her heart.

Eve pushed herself off the balustrade of the porch and walked back to the end where the wind chimes hung. She carefully lifted the cord and pulled the wind chime to her. She smiled as she walked back to Stella. "I want to give you this. The letter you shared with me means more than anything in the world to me."

Overcome with emotion, Stella stood up and gave Eve a quick hug. The wind chimes made small noises as they were pushed between their bodies. "Thank you so much. I will hang them on my porch as well and think of you and your mother and this time on your porch with you."

Stella could smell the hint of fallen leaves in the fresh afternoon air as she withdrew from the older woman. She felt awkward hugging someone who was a virtual stranger. "May I use your bathroom Eve; the mojitos are running through me"

"Of course. Through the door, past the dining room, but before you get to the kitchen."

Stella pulled the screen door open. It had one of those odd long springs, which pulled it shut tight when you let it go. It was another thing that reminded her of her child hood.

Eve's house was full—Stella was amazed at the piles of papers and books and wondered how one person could have so much. The surfaces were literally full—not just the tables, but also the chairs, the corners, even the television seemed buried under a pile of books. Stella found the dining room and was stopped by a gorgeous floral arrangement. The antique wood dining table held a large fish bowl type vase with branches of pink and white flowers intermittently arranged with white asters, all surrounded by stacks of books. As she continued looking for the bathroom, Stella's eye caught a small painting on the approaching wall and thought it looked familiar and it sent an uneasy feeling through her, but the mojitos were looking for escape.

Stella found the hall bathroom, clicked on the light and was shocked by the collection of pictures and shelves covering the

walls. There were literally a hundred pictures and statues representing Greek and Roman mythological characters hung from
floor to ceiling. A three-foot marble figurine of Bacchus, the
god of wine, stood next to the toilet. His wine goblet served as
a receptacle for the toilet paper. Stella forgot her nervous feeling
as she laughed at the jovial god who seemed to be quite happy
to distribute the Charmin. Eve was unusual—not really crazy—
more of a character. Poseidon was sneering at her from the seat
cover of the toilet and as she sat down, she noticed an over-sized
swan holding the soap and next to it, the hand towel bore the
imprint of tiara or crown. Stella puzzled over the connection
as she washed her hands with the little brown bar of soap and
wondered what the scent of the soap was. She dried her hand
on the embroidered towel and smelled her hands again. It was
so earthy. She would have to ask Eve.

As she checked her appearance in the mirror, she glanced at
the swan again. Then it clicked in her mind—it had to be Leda
and the Swan. Leda was the wife of the Spartan king and Zeus
came to her in the form of a swan to seduce her. She smiled
broadly, as she pushed a stray hair into place; she felt proud she
had figured out the riddle. Eve was quite charming and witty.

* * *

Eve watched Stella tentatively step into her home. She smiled
to herself, knowing intuitively that Stella's home was probably
impeccably tidy while her own was dusty, disorganized, cluttered,
and layered with dog hair. She looked down at the letter. She had
picked it up unconsciously. She ran her fingers along the textured
paper and thought of her own mother breathlessly reading this
letter. Someone felt an incredible passion for her mother. It was
an odd thing to acknowledge. In her memory, her mother had

always been middle-aged. She had been sturdy, capable, intelligent and kind. Not someone who incited this kind of passionate intensity in anyone. She studied the signature—it was familiar, but not. It struck her like lightning and she bolted into the house.

Standing there, in front of the small painting was Stella as if she had been waiting for her, staring at the painting. Eve joined Stella and both women stared wordlessly at the painting. It was a painting of an old woman. It had lines of thickly applied paint; the ink outlining the face. The old woman, the paint, the layering, but it was the ink that stayed with Stella. Her eye instinctively looked for the artist signature and she found it in the right hand corner, written on an angle.

"Oh my God—E. Lavelle." Stella whispered it. Chills crept up her spine.

"It's her, isn't it?" Eve whispered. "My mother's lover painted this."

"Yes, yes she did."

The minutes of silence between the two women filled the dining room; the essence of mystery and passion pushing them both into the past.

Eve's voice sounded almost disembodied as she spoke, "My mother was not a sentimental person, but this painting was her Achilles' heel. She made me promise that I would never sell it or give it away, but she never told me why."

"Did you ask?"

Eve looked at Stella as if she had forgotten that she was there. "Yes, of course. The only thing my mother ever said was that it was one of the few items she was able to bring with her from France. I just figured it was a connection to her childhood." Eve's eyes traced the painter's signature again, "I never would have imagined in a thousand years that her lover painted this."

"Eve, I have her art box." The words slipped out unbidden. Stella had an overwhelming realization that she was going to have to give all to Eve. Her heart sank.

Eve sighed, "I'm sorry, but I'm missing the connection. What does Evienne's art box have to do with my mother?"

"The art box has a stack of letters and drawings. I am sure the sketches are Evienne's. That is how I knew this painting was hers. She used ink in a unique way. The same as with your painting."

Stella saw the look of anger come over Eve's face. Tears filled Stella's eyes as her heart pounded and anxiety crawled through her belly.

Eve's mind reeled. More letters? How many more? Sketches? Her mother had kept all of these treasures secret and now this stranger shows up and teases her with one letter. Did Stella want money for them? Is that what this charade was about? Eve felt a wellspring of anger rising up inside, an anger she had thought she buried decades ago. Anger at her mother for dying, anger at her husband for dying, anger at herself for not being someone who could be entrusted with her mother's most prized possessions.

She stamped the anger down, and tried to sound as benign as possible, knowing her voice was hollow, "If you are looking for a payoff, you came to the wrong place. My salary wouldn't pay to even fill that car of yours."

Stella stared in horror, as Eve's tight, clipped words echoed in the room. "NO! No, I don't care about money. I just wanted to make sure you would want the letters, honor your mother's history."

Eve stared hard at Stella. This woman, standing in front of her, seemed sincere and sweet—even if she was a little deceitful. She thought about Stella's words and it occurred to her why Stella had done it this way. Heavily she spoke, "I could have been some crazed religious nut who would have burned the letter." As the words left her lips, she realized that is exactly what Stella feared. She saw Stella nod with relief.

Eve was quiet. "And my mother gave it to Elizabeth because she thought I would have judged her. And the sad thing is that I probably would have judged her if I had seen this forty years ago."

"Maybe Elizabeth was supposed to give this to you when you

got older." Stella suggested, relieved that Eve had believed that her intentions had been sincere.

"Maybe…" Eve had reached out to outline the ink on the painting with her finger; "maybe." She tore her eyes away from the painting and looked at Stella. "I wasn't callow or uncaring as a young woman; I was self-involved. I guess everyone is in their twenties. Maybe you're right and Elizabeth just forgot that the box with the letters should come to me." She sighed and returned her gaze to the painting.

Both women were lost in quiet contemplation. Finally, Eve sighed heavily which turned into a hearty chuckle, "You did a good job being the guardian to my mother's treasure. Will you come back with the art box and share the letters with me? Perhaps the universe wants me to share the secrets of my mother's life with you. Otherwise, Elizabeth would have given me the box years ago."

Stella's heart swelled with relief. Eve wanted to share the art box with her. "Yes, I would be honored to do this with you."

A mantle clock chimed the hour and broke the reverie both women had fallen under. Eve glanced over at the clock and with a start realized that the afternoon had flown by. "Is that the time? I've got to get myself cleaned up and back to the campus."

"Let me clean up outside and then we can figure out a time when we can meet to go through the art box." Stella pulled herself from the piercing stare of the painting and headed to the porch to help clean up.

As Stella gathered up the glasses and pitcher, Eve ran through her schedule in her head. Her brain felt a little fuzzy from the mojitos—she couldn't visualize her week at all. She would have to look at her calendar. As they passed through her threshold, she turned to Stella, "I need to grab my calendar; I will meet you in the kitchen."

Stella walked towards Eve's kitchen, passing the painting one more time. She read the signature quietly to herself and was immediately drawn to the intensity of the red color Evienne Lavelle used to paint the old woman's lips. It gave a youthful appearance to a haggard woman. She wondered how the complexities of this artist's talents were lost to the world. What had happened to her? She walked into Eve's kitchen and was not surprised by all the things covering her kitchen counters. Papers, knick-knacks, an array of salt and pepper shakers, even the windowsill was over-grown with plants and hanging wind chimes. This made Stella feel crazy. She wanted to organize everything and was shocked when Eve came up behind her.

Eve was carrying an iPhone. Briefly taken aback, Stella looked around again at the cluttered kitchen and then back at Eve who seemed to be expertly navigating the smart phone. Eve felt Stella's eyes on her and looked up to see the surprised expression. "Don't look so stunned. I may be old, but I love my gadgets. What did you expect? A cat calendar?" She winked at Stella and returned to her electronic organizer in her phone.

Eve advanced through the week and smiled when she saw she had already taken a vacation day for her dentist appointment. "How about Tuesday around lunch time? I have a dentist appointment in the morning, but I should be home by late morning."

Stella quickly replied, "Yes, that's perfect. Tuesday is great." She knew she had doubles that afternoon, but she would ask her friend Mindy to fill in for her at the tennis game. As Eve tapped away at her phone, Stella realized she still had not put the glasses down; she really did not know what to do with them—there was not a spot open on the counter or kitchen table.

Eve wondered how many letters there were. Should she block out a couple hours or more? Then she thought about how she felt at that moment. Even if there were only a few more letters, she wouldn't be in any shape to go out after reading them. She blocked out the rest of the day. It was hard enough having to go out tonight. She wanted to lie in bed and think about her mother. She missed her terribly even after all of these years. Sighing deeply, she looked up to see Stella standing motionless, still holding the tray with the pitchers and glasses. It made her laugh. This poor woman was appalled by her kitchen.

"Here just let me make some room on the counter." Eve pushed a toaster out of the way and then stacked some mail on top of it. She took the tray and slid it on the small space she had created.

Stella automatically handed over the responsibility of the tray to Eve, and then laughed a little while shrugging her shoulders in a bit of embarrassment. "Let me get out of your way; I know you have things to do."

Stella headed towards the front porch to get her bag and wind chimes. On the way, she gave Tiberius a pat good bye, looked back at Eve, and smiled. "Thank you again, Eve, for the wind chimes. I love them and thank you for an amazing afternoon. I can't wait until Tuesday."

The two women embraced quickly and Stella retreated to her car. Eve stood in the driveway with Tiberius heeled at her side. She waved until Stella had pulled away from the house as a million thoughts crowded her mind.

Chapter 14

Paris, October 1928

Madalane approached the booths near the quay of the Seine. She stopped when she saw that Evienne's back was to her and she was speaking to the dirty young man who had been at her booth before. She didn't want to intrude, but she didn't want to leave either. Hesitating, she felt a weariness invade her body. She had been so looking forward to seeing Evienne. They seemed to connect on the previous day and now it seemed that the Evienne had others who demanded her attention. Deciding it was futile to compete with another artist, Madalane moved to turn and leave when she caught the young man smiling at her. He said something to Evienne who laughed, the sound of her lovely voice carried in the breeze to Madalane who was rooted to the spot. The young man pointed at her and as she felt her face blush, she saw that Evienne was turning to see who had captured her companion's attention.

Evienne's body jolted when she laid her blue eyes on Madalane. The vision pulled the blood to her cheeks and nearly stopped her breath. Madalane was a few stalls down and appeared frozen in her tracks. How did Charles see her before she felt her pres-

ence? Disgust at the crass comment he had made replaced her
bemused response. Why was he even looking at her at all—she
was too young and too pure to be the object of his lust. Quickly,
Evienne shook her head at Charles in annoyance, and called to
her new friend, "Madalane!"

Dread filled Madalane as she heard her name being called.
She would have to go over to Evienne and the man. She didn't
want to talk to anyone but Evienne. Madalane felt cheated by
this turn of events. Gritting her teeth and squaring her shoulders, she walked over to where they two artists were standing.

As the sun illuminated the student walking towards the
stand, Evienne thought how lovely she was and how she wanted
to paint the girl. For the first time, she noticed the heart shape
of her face and the fullness of her lips. She was intently memorizing her features and barely heard the words coming from
Madalane's mouth.

"Bonjour Evienne." Madalane studiously avoided looking at
the young man standing next to Evienne; she hoped he would
slink away and leave them in peace. He was slouching against
the river wall, legs crossed at the ankle, with a cigarette tucked
into the corner of his mouth. She felt his eyes on her, appraising
her as if she were a steak he was considering eating.

Before Evienne could respond, Charles interjected with a
lusty tone, "Oh Ev, you have been holding out on me. Who is
this stunningly beautiful swan standing before us?" Charles felt
the young girl's attempt to ignore him. He would enjoy this new
toy that Evienne was playing with.

Clearing her mind of the anger she was feeling, Evienne
attempted to excuse her stall partner's presence, "Madalane—this
is Charles; he is the one responsible for these fine portraits of the
women." Evienne turned, stretching her arm out to indicate gar-
ish paintings of nude women in various positions on the left side
of the portraits of the old men and women that were Evienne's.

Retrieving the cigarette from his lips, Charles dropped it to the ground and crushed it with his boot. Wiping his hand on his pants, he held out his hand as if to shake Madalane's. "My God Evienne, you truly are uncouth. Allow me to properly introduce myself; I am Charles Gemello from America. And you are...?"

Madalane was taken aback at the smooth tone of the man's voice. Nervously, she held out her hand to shake his, but he grasped hers firmly and turned her hand over to kiss the back in some absurd act of chivalry. He stood, holding her hand close to his chest, waiting for her response. His chiseled jaw, dark hair and bright blue eyes combined to form a beautiful man, yet his debauched words on their previous meeting echoed in her head. He was a sleazy cad, but a practiced cad.

"I am Madalane Durand. I am a friend of Evienne's." The word friend sounded stiff in Madalane's ear, but it was true. She glanced at the subject of her connection to this moment, and Evienne had taken Charles' place, slouching against the river wall looking a bit annoyed.

"You are quite lovely Madalane. Ev has certainly improved her taste in friends. Normally I am her only friend, and I suspect you already know that I am quite unsavory." He laughed, his eyes twinkling. Madalane wondered how any woman could resist him. Briefly, she wondered if he were Evienne's boyfriend, but dismissed the idea. She could not see them together romantically. He was far too smooth for the tortured woman standing next to him. He continued to hold her hand close to his chest, and she felt discomfited by his proprietary nature. She pulled her hand away, but Charles continued to gaze into her eyes. Madalane glanced over to Evienne, silently begging for her intervention.

Feeling the sturdiness of the wall, Evienne studied her fingers and tried to scratch the paint from around her cuticle. She wanted to look better for her new friend and she was fretting about her stained hands when she heard Charles' words echo through her head, "You are quite lovely, Madalane." Evienne knew full well from their years of friendship of Charles' tactics.

He could captivate and seduce a woman like a large powerful fish could snatch bait and run with it to the depths of the sea. Neither the bait nor the fisherman would ever see him coming, but Evienne had seen it many times on her father's fishing boat, and the memory of it allowed her to confidently grab the rod. This was her moment to reel in her catch. She impulsively slipped her hand behind her friend's back and pulled her to her side, turning her away from the shark.

"Madalane, tell me, have you seen such creativity as Charles' art?" Evienne's tone was derisive as she pointed to one of the nude women garishly portrayed in electric blue on one of the canvases.

Out of the frying pan and into the fire Madalane thought as she stared at the gaudy paintings propped along the quay. "I think they are very...interesting." It wasn't the right word, but it would do. "Evienne, you know how unschooled I am about art. I can see only a slight difference between yours and Charles' work. Please tell me what I should appreciate in your friend's paintings." She turned and smiled at Charles, knowing she had trumped Evienne's play.

Charles grinned broadly, confident that he was the better artist. "Evienne, your friend has the potential to have an excellent eye for art. Madalane—I am a great devotee of Eduoard Manet. If you knew his work, I'm sure you would see that he is my artistic father. Ev prefers these gloomy women. So dreary, don't you think?"

Evienne did not want a volley of artistic repartee to trample the precious time together. "As any woman would tell you Charles, it is in the mind, not the body, that we find our greatest expression. And I am sure that you won't mind taking charge here for a time so that my friend and I may share a glass of wine."

Charles had already lost interest in the conversation as he turned to gaze at a tall woman meandering along the avenue. He nodded absently at the two women while he waited to intercept his next prey.

Evienne asked, "Would you care to join me at the Petite Cafe on Saint Michel?" Evienne slipped her hand into the crook of Madalane's arm and began guiding her away from Charles before Madalane even answered; she took a moment to casually look back at the other artist and send him a triumphant smile. Good naturedly, he tipped his invisible hat to her.

Relieved that Evienne had suggested they leave, Madalane happily waved to Charles who blew her an exaggerated kiss. She laughed and felt Evienne's hand on her arm, leading her away from the stall. "Your friend is quite the Romeo. Have you known him long?"

"Monsieur Gemello and I have been sharing this space for a few years." Evienne continued in an amused tone as they headed for the cafe. "One afternoon while I was walking the Seine, I came upon Charles and a disgruntled husband who claimed through his fist that Charles' hands had been in more places than on his brushes and paint when his wife modeled for him. I interrupted the beating that the husband was giving Charles and explained that Charles' affections were towards his male models. I guaranteed to the husband that Charles would never seduce an innocent wife, which incidentally is true. Charles likes his women willing, very willing and most wives with brutish husbands are quite willing to succumb to Charles' charms." Evienne smirked and noticed that her young friend seemed confused by the conversation, so she moved on to less prurient aspects.

"We have been friends since. It's how it works here on the quay. We have to stick together. He prefers the life of an artist more than the art itself. Luckily for him, he has a rich father who indulges him, and he in turn indulges me occasionally."

The late afternoon breeze had blown in from the Seine, forcing them to sit inside. Evienne pulled the café door open for Madalane and called for the waiter. "May I order you a glass of red wine, Dove?"

Evienne's strong jaw and piercing eyes gave Madalane no

choice; nodding to her friend, she would have agreed to arsenic if she could share it with the intriguing woman. She felt warmth suffuse her whole body when the artist had called her Dove. It was said with affection and it made Madalane feel like she was important.

"He calls me his protégé, but we both know the truth." She smiled at her friend as she pulled out the chair for Madalane to sit, and ordered them a decanter of red wine.

Madalane leaned back in her chair in the small cafe that Evienne had led them to, and looked around. It was cozy and warm, and the waiter quickly brought them a liter of wine in a glass decanter. He poured and left unobtrusively. There was a long mirror across from their table and it gave the café a roomier feel, but only a handful of the small round tables actually fit in the room. Madalane's eyes looped around the dark paneled cafe once more before settling in on her companion who was pensively holding her wine glass aloft. Madalane clinked glasses, disrupting the thoughts of her friend. "You look deep in thought. Are you re-evaluating your painting style in favor of Charles'?"

Evienne smiled gently before replying, "It is you who have been captivating my thoughts. I have a confession." She leaned in closer to her new friend and hesitated.

Rather than feeling nervous trepidation, Madalane felt pleasurable warmth suffuse her body. "Yes, Evienne. Tell me your confession."

Words slipped from her mouth as her hand slipped over Madalane's. "I attempted to follow you the other night after our eyes locked at the cafe. I was fearful I would not see you again and the rain, it was pouring. I worried about you."

Madalane felt her heart race as she heard those words. Evienne's voice, so low and intimate, the warmth of the cafe, and the closeness of their hands made her feel like this might be the most perfect moment. She felt compelled to make her own confession, "I didn't know if you would recognize me, but I knew you immediately. Then the madam scolded me and I ran away. I was embarrassed by the way she treated me."

"You have my art Madalane; I don't just give my paintings away to anyone." Evienne's voice stayed low, filled with sorrowful emotion, her face pleading for understanding. "It is just... you give me a feeling of family, like my sisters; it has been a while since I felt that way."

Aching inside, Madalane turned her hand over to grasp Evienne's tightly. "I understand my friend. I am not sure if I ever knew what it felt to be part of a family. I am an only child and my parents sent me to boarding school when I was barely a teenager. I have been on my own for many years."

"Being alone is hardening to the soul—one might compare it to the likes of a statue. The exterior surrounded by life but the inside is still stone. I suppose it is best we are not statues and that we can be protective and gentle with each other. "Evienne looked at Madalane's hand still wrapped around hers. She found herself fascinated by the smooth whiteness of her friend's skin compared to the image of her own paint-stained hand. Wanting to say so much more, but unable to formulate the words, Evienne gripped her friend's hand and sighed.

Madalane felt a surge of protective loyalty to her new friend, "You can always count on me Evienne. I promise." The young girl's solemn vow echoed in her head, and she knew she had never said truer words.

Evienne leaned into Madalane's words—it felt like crawling into a warm bed; she whispered into her ear. "You have become my church, Madalane." She paused and then spoke slowly, "Will you join me tomorrow afternoon? I have something as beautiful as you that I would like to show you."

The filled the inside of Madalane's heart. "Yes Evienne. I would love to." Madalane smiled into Evienne's eyes, feeling a fullness in her heart that she had never felt before.

Chapter 15

Paris, October 1928

Madalane Durand's earliest memory was helping her father at the counter of his store. He owned a small shop in their small village, selling the necessities for a small community. The village sat at the western edge of France near the Bordeaux region. Many of the farms in the area grew the grapes that would grace the sophisticated tables of the finest restaurants in Paris, but in most of these houses in this small village, the same wine was swallowed from earthenware tumblers.

The town was a minor stop along the way between Spain and the city of Bordeaux. Most travelers preferred to by-pass the small village in favor of pressing on directly to Bordeaux.

The shop was not isolated though. Madalane knew most of her neighbors before she started school. The warm little shop was a hub in the village for news and gossip. Madalane's father—Emile—had also been raised in the shop. His father had owned the store before he inherited it from his father. Madalane's grandparents still lived above the shop and before that, Emile's grandfather had run the store. Emile Durand's family had been part of this small community for as long as anyone could remember.

Madalane's father was the type of man who was never happier than when he was ensconced behind the counter of his shop, a crisp white coat buttoned up the front, and a line of customers who were happy to share the small bits of gossip they picked up. If a customer shared a particularly provocative piece of information, Emile would sometimes slip an extra cream cake into their shopping basket. Emile was a savvy businessman because he knew that a several small bits of gossip would often add up to one big juicy slice of gossip that would bring in the rest of the village. Everyone knew that Emile's information was the most accurate.

Madalane watched the way her father spoke with the women of the village and noticed how he preened his mustaches for some while for others, he would stand straighter and taller and smile into their eyes. Without needing an explanation, Madalane knew that her father had an uncanny ability to make some of the women feel as if their conversation was incredibly profound and important while others needed the illusion of secrecy and confidences held.

As she grew older, Madalane would emulate her father's conversational style and found that her friends would open up to her; they would often reveal more to her than they had wanted to. By watching her father, she knew when to ask questions or gaze sympathetically. Her best friend Louise would laugh and tell her that she was better than a truth serum. After sobbing and revealing the secret of her father's mistress. Louise, as well as Madalane's other friends, felt comfortable sharing their lives with her.

From the time she was little, Madalane had spent every waking minute in the shop with her father. Even when she had to go to school, she would rush from the schoolyard to take her place behind the counter. There were two pegs behind the counter for the white coats they both wore. These pegs had been there since before Emile could remember. One was for the senior shop clerk and the other was for the junior shop clerk. The day she came to the shop and found a much smaller version of the white coat on the junior peg made especially for her was one of the happiest days of her life. She imagined spending the rest of her life working behind the counter, listening to the stories of the villagers, and one day when her child would become her junior, she would buy him or her a miniature clerk coat.

This idyllic existence in the shop was a sharp counter point to what occurred in the Durand home. Madalane's mother, Marie Durand, was very unhappy with her lot in life. She imagined herself the wife of a wealthy businessman, and not a man who owned a small shop in a parochial village. At night, as Emile and Madalane walked home from the shop, Madalane could feel her father's light-hearted demeanor change to a somber expression of melancholy. They would enter the house, carefully scrapping the mud from their shoes, and both would take their place at the table. Marie's brittle, clipped speech would immediately put both Emile and Madalane on edge. Even before she realized what was going on, Madalane knew that the tension around the table was thick.

Emile's attitude of careful and practiced charm would dissipate under Marie's intense scrutiny. As Emile ate, Marie would pull out a small red ledger, and she would demand to know the sales for the day. If the sales were low, Marie's displeasure would be palpable as she interrogated him about who came into the shop and who bought what. She believed that he spent too much time chatting with the customers and not enough time pushing them out the door. After dinner was cleared, Marie would demand the invoices from vendors and she would scribble those figures in her red ledger—all the while commenting that the suppliers were over-charging her husband or shorting him on the actual weight. Every night, as Marie pored over the figures in the red ledger, she would list all of the areas that Emile needed to improve. She knew, without a doubt, that if he paid more attention to business and less attention to the customers, they would be rich.

Madalane would escape to her bedroom as soon as dinner was over to complete her homework and write poetry, but she heard her mother's caustic words echoing through the hall and into her room. Her father would age a decade each night.

One day, while her father was in the back of the shop speaking with a vendor about one of his wife's cost saving ideas, Madame Seicy came in. She was the queen of the village information pipeline. She was in the unique position of being the housekeeper of the parish priest as well as wife to the town's doctor. Madalane had watched with dismay the night before as her mother had mercilessly shredded her father during dinner. Madalane did not understand why her father would have married such a woman. Although she loved her mother because she was her mother and it would be a sin not to love your parent, she saw her mother as the weed in their happy life.

Madame Seicy was browsing amongst the jams and currants near the counter. No one else was in the shop; Madalane knew that Madame Seicy knew as much as her father about the village, so she took a chance that her question would be answered. She waited until Madame made her choice and was approaching the counter with her small shopping basket. Madalane's tongue suddenly felt thick and dry in her mouth, and with a trembling hand, she started to write up the receipt. Her voice, sounding incredibly foreign to her, was low and raspy, "Madame, may I ask you a private question?"

Madame Seicy was momentarily taken aback, but quickly found her voice, "Of course."

"Why did my father marry my mother?" Madalane could scarcely believe the words had left her mouth even as she heard them with her own ears.

Madame Seicy was quiet. She looked at Madalane intently. "Isn't that a question for your father?"

Madalane let out the breath she was holding; she had half expected that Madame would not answer. She wasn't sure if she was relieved or disappointed, but she felt a certain hopelessness overcome her and tears started to form at the creases of her eyelids. She closed her eyes and tried to get control of her emotions.

Madame Seicy saw the turmoil in Madalane's face and took pity on her. She looked around the shop and saw that there were no other customers. She reached for Madalane's hand and grasped it tightly. Madalane, surprised by the touch, looked up. Madame Seicy's eyes had narrowed, and she quickly said, "It is your parents who should answer this question, but I will tell you this. Your mother thought she could change your father into who she wanted to marry. She didn't know that your father was already happy. And now, as you know, neither is happy."

As the last words rang in Madalane's ears, she heard her father laughing with the vendor as they came into the store. Quickly, Madalane finished writing up Madame Seicy's order. As she finished wrapping up the package, Madalane mouthed a silent thank you to the Madame. Madame's eyes traveled from Madalane to Emile, and then she smiled and turned to leave.

After the encounter with Madame Seicy, Madalane resolved to speak with her father. Although divorce would never be an option because they were Roman Catholic, he should stand up for himself. He was a respected member of the community; many of the women who came to the store would gladly have traded places with Marie Durand. He was a kind man who everyone liked. His shop always had a steady stream of customers and although they would never be rich, their family was very comfortable. Madalane knew her mother was not someone with whom she could discuss anything.

It was the end of another day as Madalane and her father walked home together. The weather had cooled as the sun began to set in the western sky. The long days of summer were waning as autumn neared. Emile had been pensive for most of the day, which was very unlike him. Madalane had watched as he had allowed her to assist most of the customers who had come in that afternoon. It had been a week since her conversation with Madame Seicy, and she had found a different reason each day to avoid the question that was sitting on the tip of her tongue. When she had noticed her father's quiet mood, she had decided to postpone the question again.

As they walked in the quiet watching the sun make its descent along the horizon, her father reached down and grasped Madalane's hand. She was momentarily bewildered because he had not done that since she was a small girl. There must have been a surprised look on her face because her father stopped and smiled at her. She felt the depths of his eyes penetrate hers as he smiled.

"Madalane, I am very proud of you," her father started. Her confusion continued to grow and his smile stayed fixed on his face. She realized that this was the smile he used when a customer had grown wearisome. "And you are a marvelous junior clerk. You know how much I love having you work in the shop with me." Madalane felt her stomach tighten; she knew something terrible would be said. All at once, she wanted her father just to blurt it out, but at the same time, she wanted to run before he could open his mouth again. "Your mother and I believe that it is time for you to consider your future. There is a very good boarding school close to Bordeaux that will give you the opportunities that you cannot get here."

"But Papa, I want to work in the shop with you. I want to stay here. I don't want to go to Bordeaux." Madalane's voice attempted to calm her voice but it sounded shrill and she felt a hysterical sensation well up inside of her.

Her father's tone was sharp and abrupt, "You are not a child any longer—you will be thirteen this year and it's high time that we plan for your future. It is already decided Madalane; the plans have been made. Your cousin Michel is coming live with us to help with the store." Her father let go of her hand and started to walk away.

"Papa....please....papa...listen to me. I want to stay here."

Madalane felt sick and dizzy, an overwhelming feeling of bitter cold creeping into her. Her father's back was to her; he stood ramrod straight as she continued to beg. The tears that she had tried to hold back suddenly let loose in a torrent. How could he send her away like this? She had always worked hard. Her cousin was a dolt, lazy and stupid. What had she done wrong? She wracked her brain trying to remember the last few days and then she realized that this type of plan would have taken months, not days or even a few weeks.

With a shiver of realization, she understood that they had been planning this for a while. In a plaintive wail, she screamed, "Papa!" It was her last ditch effort to grab onto to some semblance of her life as it disappeared like the sound of her voice dying in the wind.

Her father turned, and she saw the tears coursing down his face. Through clenched teeth, he said, "It...is...decided."

That night, as Madalane and her father returned home, Marie uncharacteristically stood in the doorway. Madalane pushed past her, ran to her room and slammed the door shut as her father heaved himself through the doorway. Madalane lay upon her bed and cried at the thought of leaving her father, her friends, and her home. She heard footsteps outside her door a few times, but no one came in. When her eyes were swollen and sore from crying, she stared at the ceiling, trying to imagine what it would be like to sleep in a different bed, attend classes in a different school, live without her father's reassuring warmth. She felt the tears begin again as they squeezed out of her eyes and fell backwards along her cheeks and down the length of her ears. She knew in her heart that it was not her father's idea. Her mother was behind this.

The next few weeks were a quiet hell. Emile's actions had spread throughout the village, and many of the women had come to him to whisper a private word. Madalane belonged in the village; she belonged at the shop. He staunchly, steadfastly stood by the decision he and his wife made. Only when the store was quiet, and Emile's attention drifted did he allow himself a few moments of terror that he was pushing his little girl away. His wife was right though. If Madalane stayed in the village, what would she become? She would marry and run the store. A tiny voice in Emile's voice asked him what was so wrong with that, but he knew that he needed to get Madalane away from Marie. He could not escape her, but he would do anything to give his daughter a chance of finding a life that did not include Marie.

He thought back to when he met Marie. She was so pretty—he was dazzled by her dark eyes and luscious figure. His own mother had warned him that it is better to marry a woman who can be your partner than a woman who will only warm your bed. He had been betrothed to one of the local girls—a girl he had known his entire life—she was more like a sister in some ways. This made Marie even more enticing; they had met when Marie's father stopped in the village to sell pots and pans. Her father was an itinerant salesman, and when Marie's mother died, she joined her father on the road. It was a hard life for her, but she had a goal. She wanted, no—needed to marry a man who could give her a good life. She knew she was beautiful and even though, she slept in the back of a caravan most nights, she made sure she was always dressed well and her hair and appearance were perfect. When she met Emile, he became another mark in the small red book she carried with her. He was definitely a potential husband—his family owned a thriving shop on the way to Bordeaux.

On the return trip, when her father stopped in the small village, Emile threw caution to the wind and begged Marie to marry him. The way she swayed when she walked, the curve of her smile as her eyes met his convinced him that no one else could ever rule his heart.

The breaking of his engagement caused a small furor in Emile's village, and many of the older women clicked disapprovingly each time they entered the store. Nevertheless, Emile was madly in love and when he and Marie married, he felt that this woman would prove to be an outstanding helpmate. The first few months were filled with joy tempered with occasional bursts of displeasure. Emile was an easy-going young man, but Marie would often fly into fits of rage because he seemed to her too lackadaisical. Marie refused to step foot into the shop; she hated the idea of waiting on her neighbors. Even though Emile could have used the assistance, he came to enjoy the time away from Marie. A tiny nagging thought that his mother had been right played at the edges of his mind, but he would quickly dismiss even the thought of it.

A year into the marriage, Marie announced she was pregnant. She seemed to change overnight—she nested, made baby clothes, and set up a nursery in their small cottage. She was convinced it would be a boy, and she would name him Mathias, after her father. As she became plumper and happier, Emile remembered why he had married Marie. She was affectionate towards him and invited his mother in to help with the preparations. When the day came and her water broke, she was deliriously happy. She even managed the labor with good humor; Emile was completely enamored with his wife again.

At the final push, when the squirmy pinkish-white bundle of flesh was finally revealed to the world, the mid-wife declared the baby to be a healthy girl. Marie's face registered disbelief and then she lay back in the bed and wept. Only after much coaxing by the mid-wife and Emile's mother would she even hold the baby. Marie refused to name the baby; she fell into a deep depression and Emile's mother moved in with them for the first year to help with Madalane, since Emile had finally decided the baby needed a name. He named her after his own mother's mother. Madalane's first year of life was filled with the love of a grandmother, while her own mother lay in bed staring listlessly at the wall. The mid-wife called a doctor because this type of behavior was completely outside of what she understood.

The doctor came and examined Marie. Physically she was fine, but she had truly believed that her child would be a boy, and this had caused her to disconnect from being a mother. To Emile's mother, this seemed like a bunch of malarkey. Women have babies every day, and Marie just needed to get out of bed and start caring for her child. However, Emile was hoping that his beloved Marie would rediscover her happiness, so he gave in to her wishes to be left alone in their bed.

When Madalane was one, Emile's father suffered a stroke, and Emile's mother needed to devote her energies to her husband. She went into Marie's bedroom one morning right after Emile had left for the shop, and sitting on the edge of the bed, she quietly explained that it was either time for her to get out of bed and raise her child, or get out of bed and leave forever, so Emile could find another wife. Marie's face did not seem to register what she had said at first, and then with an exasperated huff, Marie finally rolled herself out of the bed.

Emile's mother asked, "Are you leaving?"

"No, I will feed and bathe the child."

"You must also show her love and affection for her to grow."

Marie's dark penetrating eyes flashed, "No Madame, God did not grant me my prayers, and it is not in me to love her."

Emile's mother was horrified, but she knew she had no choice. Her husband could not even feed himself, so she had to allow Marie the chance to be a mother. Deep in her heart, she hoped that Marie would find some love for the little girl. She desperately hoped that her granddaughter would be loved.

Chapter 16

Stella looked at the seat next to her and realized that this would be the last moments alone she had with the art box. She put her hand on the smooth hard wood and thought of the journey the box had taken, wondering if Eve's house was going to be its final resting place. The sketches of the women were so beautiful and sensual. Love and admiration flooded through the ink; the love between the two women was apparent. It made a smile slip across her face. She was eager to read the rest of the letters and learn more about the two women who had infiltrated her world.

* * *

Eve had made her best attempt to tidy up the living room and the coffee table. She had moved most of the papers that tended to pile up. The night before, she had tried to imagine what reading these letters would be like. It had made her impatient and nervous. To calm down, Eve had sat on the couch and excavated the various piles on her coffee table. Most of it ended up in the recycling bin, but she had found a few papers and cards that she wanted to keep. It had helped keep her mind off the letters, but only a little.

After the dentist, she had stopped to buy something for lunch. She decided that wine was absolutely necessary—if not for Stella, then for her. If she were going to plumb the depths of her mother's affair with her female lover, then she would need fortification.

* * *

Stella finally arrived at Eve's road and turned into her driveway. The popping sound of the gravel brought Eve's Boxer running towards Stella's car. She glanced back at Granger who had left nose prints all over the back seat window where she had strapped him in with the doggy seatbelt David had bought her for Christmas. She hoped that Tiberius and Granger would get along, or else it would be a long day of keeping them apart. She checked her watch and found herself right on time. It was twelve thirty.

Eve heard the car coming up the drive; she took a deep breath and headed out to the porch. She watched Stella get out of the car, and put a lead on the dog in the backseat. Tiberius loped over to check out the new dog. After much sniffing, they decided that the other was not a threat. Stella leaned over to pet Tiberius.

Eve waited until Stella looked in her direction before she said anything. Stella was perfectly pulled together in jeans and a tailored white shirt. How did someone look so good without effort? "Hi. How was the drive? Did you hit any traffic?" Eve felt like she was watching a scene in a play, as if she was reading from a script.

"It's a beautiful day; the ride was nice." Stella called. She had a big smile across her face and her heart was fluttering in excitement.

Eve saw that Stella pulled a bottle of wine and an old wooden box from the front passenger side of the car. She realized that it must be the art box. She hadn't been sure what to expect. It looked like a natural wood—pine maybe—and it was definitely weathered with age. She closed her eyes as a memory trying to push itself forward—was this the box her mother kept next to her bed? Being old was a hassle. She pictured, in her mind's eye, her mother's small bedroom. It was always neat as a pin. Under her bedside table, she had kept a pile of books, but underneath those books was a box. It looked similar, but it was so many years ago. Was it wishful thinking on her part or could it be the same box? Eve came down the steps to help Stella who handed off the bottle of wine as she gripped the leash and art box in each hand.

Stella's exuberance was palpable as she exclaimed, "It is so nice to see you. I am so excited to be here." Unable to contain herself, she pulled the older woman into an embrace.

Eve was a little surprised at the crushing hug that Stella gave her, but it felt good to have the excited energy flowing between them. The art box, between them, was like an umbilical cord, connecting them to a shared life, a shared story. She smiled at Stella, "Are you ready to do some reading?"

Stella pushed the box into Eve's arms as they separated. Stella was so excited to see her face, but instead she saw pain ripple over her Eve's face. Stella wrapped her hand under her friend's arm; the two women, their dogs and the art box moved into the sitting room of Eve's cottage.

Eve's mind was churning. Her mother, the most important influence in her life, was really a cipher to her. She had examined what she knew about her mother over the past couple of days, and everything boiled down to the fact that she knew nothing about who her mother was other than her role as her mother.

Realizing that she defined her mother solely as a maternal figure was a revelation. Even as she had gotten older, it had never really occurred to her that her mother was someone with a life or purpose outside of raising her child. Now, she was about to read the love letters her mother had kept next to her bed for her entire life. These letters were so important to her mother that she could not destroy them, even when she knew she was dying.

Giving them away gave them a mythic status. She wondered if Elizabeth really had forgotten to give them to her or if her mother just couldn't bring herself to destroy them and she had asked Elizabeth to do it.

Eve squeezed her eyes shut, trying to stop the tears from forming. She focused on the sound of her own breathing, slowing it down. She felt Stella's hand rubbing her back, comforting her like a mother would a child. It almost made Eve start bawling for real, but she steadied herself.

"Let me get you some tissues Eve." Stella stood up from Eve's overstuffed sofa and looked at this woman cradling her face. Stella's heart felt her pain. She was a woman, an older woman, crying openly in front of a stranger but they weren't really strangers, were they? Stella felt odd for a moment; she wanted to wrap her arms around her to take the pain of loss from her. She obviously loved her mother deeply. Stella didn't have that kind of connection with her own mother. Feeling like she stood there staring a second too long, she turned quietly towards the bathroom in search of tissues. She had to pass the painting. It really was intricate and impressive. Evienne Lavelle was becoming her obsession, an artist she wanted to understand.

She clicked the light on in the bathroom and was surprised again by the huge amount of mythological knick-knacks. Stella thought of Eve in an affectionate way. She was an interesting woman. Even her house was starting to grow on her. The clutter seemed to define Eve in some way. She grabbed the tissues from the back of the toilet and headed to the living room.

Eve felt the power of her grief overwhelming her. When Stella had stood up, Tiberius had taken her place. His big square Boxer head was resting on her thigh and she reflexively reached down to rub her fingers through his fur. She looked at his big brown eyes. She loved how the expression on a dog's face looked like they truly cared. She needed to get a grip on her emotions or she would never make it through the afternoon.

Taking a deep breath, she exhaled slowly, willing herself to find her equilibrium. She closed her eyes, visualizing her mother's face. She felt peace seep into her heart. When she opened her eyes again, she saw Stella standing in front of her, holding a box of tissues. Eve wondered briefly if Stella regretted pursuing this. Had she expected a hysterical reaction? She was mortified that she couldn't contain herself, but Stella's steady gaze reassured her that she wasn't being ridiculous.

As she handed the tissues to her, Stella softly asked, "I love the smell of the soap in your bathroom, what scent is it?"

Eve gratefully took the box of Kleenex and tried her most lady-like nose blow. Stella, if truth were told, intimidated her a bit. She was elegant. Eve had given up feeling inadequate years ago, but this stranger was seeing her at her most vulnerable, and it made her itchy.

At Stella's question, Eve felt the flood of tears threaten to return. She smiled at Stella, thinking it must be some karmic message from the Gods that this woman was the messenger that was sent to her. "It's sandalwood. My mother adored the scent— she always wore perfume, but the smell of the soap is the scent I always associate with my mom. When she kissed me goodnight as a child, that scent was always there. She never switched soaps even when we were so poor, we could barely afford our bills. She wouldn't buy new shoes when she needed them, but she always bought this expensive sandalwood soap. Some people smell chocolate chip cookies and become nostalgic. For me, it's always been sandalwood soap."

Eve felt an awkward silence permeate the room. Stella had an expression of sincere sympathy on her face, and Eve hated knowing that her pain was evident. She briskly stood up and walked towards the kitchen. "What do you think? Is it too early for a glass of wine?" Without waiting for an answer, she pulled a bottle of red wine to her and efficiently sliced into the cork cover.

Briefly disconcerted by Eve's desire to drink, Stella's mind rebelled. Her conscience was reprimanding her again; I'm drinking by one again. Stella silently retorted, I would drink too if I just was handed a box of stuff that my mother saved from her lover. Stella sat down on the sofa next to where Eve had been sitting and looked at the art box sitting on the cluttered coffee table; Granger came over and settled next to her on the floor. She straightened her jeans with her palm. She was sweating a little. She looked down and adjusted her wedding set to the center of her finger. Stella resisted the urge to organize the table in front of her. She put her hand to her face, smelled the soap again, and thought how nothing good reminded her of her own mother. Then the thought occurred to her, what if her mother had a past she didn't know about. Just as quickly as that idea flitted into her mind, she knew she wouldn't want to know anyway. The distance between them was just fine. Her mother had always put herself first anyway.

Stella thoughts were interrupted by Eve calling from the kitchen, "I hope you like a French red."

Stella replied, "I love red. I really love red." She picked up the art box, put it in her lap and waited expectantly for Eve's return with a smile on her face.

Eve walked back into the living room carrying a tray with two glasses of water, a bottle of Cahors and two wine glasses. Seeing Stella there, sitting so serenely, cradling the art box, gave her an overwhelming sense of calm. If nothing else, this woman who randomly wandered into her world would be an anchor for this afternoon. Eve set the glasses and wine down on the table and poured two glasses of wine. Sitting down next to Stella, she handed her visitor one glass and then took the other for herself. She clinked her glass against Stella's and muttered without irony, "To mom and her lover." Both women drank deeply from their wine glasses. Eve would have drank the entire glass down in one long swallow, but didn't want to appear to be a total lush in front of her new friend.

Eve put her glass down carefully. Clearly, Stella would never spill anything—so she would be extra careful today. Turning to Stella, she noticed that Tiberius had joined Granger on the floor and they were leaning against each other.

"Tiberius and Granger are getting along just fine, aren't you babies." Stella rubbed the top of each dog's head and looked back to Eve. "I didn't know how much I loved red wine until my husband went to China."

"Your husband moved to China?"

Stella continued, "He is on an extended business assignment in China and won't be back until May. It's been interesting getting used to being alone. This wine reminded me of the other night; I was standing in the liquor store feeling lost and realized I always picked what made him happy. I really don't mind, but I put myself aside to take care of him and Sarah. I think most woman do this. Don't you think?"

Eve remained quiet.

Stella pondered the silence for a moment. "It's funny how you forget who you are when you share your life with someone day in and day out." Stella swirled the wine in her glass and watched the legs glisten down the inside of the globe. She returned her look to Eve. "This art box," Stella gently rubbed the top, "has changed something inside of me. I feel like I am learning about who I am. Who I really am. It sounds crazy, I know. You're probably thinking how could I not know who I am. And then I think there is something hidden inside myself that I need to know about. There is something deep inside me that I have forgotten about. A treasure and somehow I feel like this art box and you are a part of this process."

Eve gazed in wonder at the composed woman in front of her. She was well studied in maintaining a facade, but Eve could see the vein throbbing in Stella's throat and the tears welling up in her eyes. She would normally have pulled a friend into a hug and let them have a good long cry, but she still felt distant from this woman. Instead, she picked up the box of tissues that Stella had given her a few minutes before and offered them.

Stella met Eve's eyes and they both realized the absurdity of this moment and broke into laughter. Their combined laughter brought Tiberius and Granger to their feet, looking back and forth between the two women. Simultaneously, they both picked up their wine glasses and finished off their first glass. Eve picked up the bottle and poured them another round. "It's a good thing I buy this stuff by the case! We might go through several bottles before this day is out."

Stella gathered herself and focused on the art box in her lap. Eve stared at the box, trying to remember her mother's bedroom. "I think my mother kept that box under her bedside table when I was young." Her voice had taken on a disembodied tone, lost in the memory of a distant childhood. "You know what it's like as a child; you are barely aware of your own world, much less someone else's. I have an image in my head of my mom's room— it was always so immaculate and organized. Under her bedside table, she kept a stack of books—she was always reading—and underneath those books was a box—this box, I think. I just can't be sure though. Memories are tricky as you get older; sometimes you want something so badly, your brain gives you the white-washed memory instead of the boring reality."

Shaking her head to clear the cobwebs, Eve grinned at Stella. "Let's get this started! What's that old proverb? A journey of thousand miles begins with a single step. Let's take the first step! I can't wait any longer—open her up!"

Chapter 17

Paris, October 1928

Evienne's tall figure appeared in the distance. Madalane waved at the artist, but Evienne's head was down, seemingly to buffet herself from the winds of the day, despite there being no wind.

Madalane started to walk towards her and when she came within a few yards of her, Evienne finally looked up and gave her the kind of smile that let her know with a certainty that she was glad to see the young woman. Evienne tightened her coat to help keep the warmth inside her. Seeing Madalane made her feel apprehensive yet at home at the same time. She wanted to run, fading into the coming night. But mostly she wanted to stay.

Stepping in close to Madalane, Evienne lowered her head to kiss both her friend's cheeks. She pulled back and smiled into eyes that were bright and happy. This moment, when they greeted each other was the only time they both let their guards down long enough to reveal their mutual joy at spending time together. They grinned at each other, both feeling a little foolish.

Evienne feared she had let her own mask fall too long; Madalane was always so full of warmth and sincerity. She made Evienne want to fold her in her arms and embrace her genuine kindness. She worried she might have revealed how glad she was to see the young woman, so she quickly turned the attention towards the point of their meeting.

Evienne has been showing Madalane the city. They always started near the stalls, and the young woman would take Madalane down a new narrow street each time. Her knowledge of the city was remarkable and she explained things with an artist's eye. Today, Evienne was taking the student north across the Petit Pont to the Notre Dame Cathedral where beautiful stained-glass windows and incredible sculptures were housed.

At first, as they walked down Quai Saint Michel, they were both quiet and awkward with each other, but as Evienne told stories of some of the unfamiliar places, they both forgot to be nervous. She pointed to the shop where a gypsy woman worked her spells—the rumor being that this gypsy had cast an enchantment over the owner and he had given her the shop—lock, stock and barrel—before he vanished completely. She then pointed in the direction to a particularly unsavory looking alley where the best restaurant in the city was located. Evienne was animated and Madalane was spellbound by the hidden stories of the city.

Madalane could smell the warm breath of her companion on her cheek as she leaned over to share a sordid tale of the Russian woman who lived at the top of a beautiful apartment building and how she afforded to live there. Blushing at the tawdriness of the woman's story, Madalane felt strange warmth suffuse her body and lips. It was an odd sensation that she quickly stamped down.

"Evienne, you tell me so much about this city, but you never tell me anything about you."

Evienne seemed to ignore this statement as she led her over the Petit Pont.

"Where do you come from?" Madalane was annoyed at herself as soon as the words left her mouth. Why was she compelled to ruin a perfectly good day to probe into her new friend's life? Surely, Evienne would have told her if she wanted to.

Sighing, Evienne responded, "I am a self-made woman. I came from the sea. I learned life from the streets and put what I know on my canvas. It is simple enough."

Madalane had heard similar words before. Evienne always seemed to speak in riddles. She was a flesh and blood woman, so why couldn't she just tell her where she was from. She sighed and closed her eyes, turning away.

Sensing her friend's discomfort, Evienne tried to ease her tension. "It is all right that you ask that." She pulled her closer at their locked elbows. "I wonder the same about you. Where are you from?" Evienne paused, thinking about the words, "It is a funny way to ask such a thing about a person's life, don't you think? As if where you were born defines who you are?"

They had reached the church and were standing at the front of the cathedral. It truly was the majestic moment that Evienne had promised although Madalane's heart was heavy with frustration. She could not admire something of such great beauty in this state. She glanced up at Evienne and tried to determine if she was mocking her. Madalane had shared some things about her life, but felt awkward about revealing much since her new friend was so reluctant to tell her anything.

Evienne felt the aggravation of her walking partner and guided her to a bench near the church. The two sat down and Evienne took her friend's hand in hers. "Close your eyes Madalane."

In her calmest voice, she spoke to Madalane, "Does the site where the stone was quarried define the history of this church?"

Madalane's body deflated and she felt the frustration rise again. Slowly, she shook her head. She had lost her temper and now she felt the rage circling her spine.

Evienne's voice, calm and filled with intention, whispered in her ear. Madalane listened to the story of the fight between the pope and the bishop of Paris, and how the money was raised for churches by taxing the sins of the rich.

Madalane didn't care; she was furious at Evienne and she was even more furious at herself because she never got an answer, but was still compelled to keep asking. Eventually Evienne's voice began to soothe the boiling heat in her chest.

Autumnal breezes blew through her hair as realization dawned on her. She understood what the artist was saying, and she felt like a spoiled child. The church had existed for hundreds of years and will continue to exist. Evienne had existed for decades before they met, and she will continue to exist for years to come, with or without their friendship. Mortified, Madalane stared down at her lap. Tears of immaturity slipped from her eyes and splashed against her gloved hands.

Evienne watched the tears stain the dove-gray gloves. She kept her voice soft and steady, "How was this church made? How was it designed? Imagine the hours it took for the craftsman to lay out, cut and wrap lead around each piece of this stained glass window." Evienne gazed from the peak to the grand doors. It is time that creates a piece of art. It is time that creates the things in life worth working for. Beauty has a miraculous way of creating emotion, that emotion living inside our souls. Eventually the truth will be revealed. Our emotions will not allow us to hide from the truth."

Her voice was low and lulling. Madalane felt a level of peace overcome her and she wanted to grasp Evienne to her and lose herself in the warmth of the tall woman's arms. Madalane remained perfectly still and listened to the words flow gently like a river. This is how Evienne would tell her about her life— through the words that described buildings and paintings and windows. Madalane felt so childish around Evienne; she could be so profound and insightful. Madalane felt the urge to curl in her lap like a cat and just listen for as long as her friend was willing to sit. She felt like she could be the brilliant person she dreamt of being if she could only spend every waking moment with Evienne.

"Sitting in front of this grand stone church," Evienne continued, "do you feel the energy of time and history? Can you measure the sharpness of one of her many steeples? Can you run your fingers along the curve of the archway? Touch the circular metal of the leonine doorknocker? Open your eyes Madalane and notice the changes of the color of the gray stone as the sun starts to set; the sun turns the stone to cream." Evienne sensed the calmness blanketing Madalane as she spoke to her. Evienne wanted to tell her everything she knew; she wanted to fill her heart with happiness.

Evienne's voice described the depth of color, the geometry of corners and Madalane finally looked up at her friend and stared at her beautiful face. The angles of her cheeks and the color of her eyes seemed to reflect the austere beauty of this church. Madalane watched her lips and how they formed the words; it struck her, as if like lightening, that she was not French. Although she spoke French like a native, her words were too perfectly enunciated. She spoke French like someone who learned it after she had matured.

Mind churning with possibilities, Madalane wondered how she could find out where she was from originally. Evienne was smiling at her and Madalane smiled back. Despite her warring emotions, Madalane wanted to see the stained glass even as her energy was completely focused on the words—trying to figure out what accent lay beneath those carefully spoken French phrases. Her dialect was almost perfect, but there was a slight hitch that Madalane had taken for thoughtfulness, but really, she realized, it must be a moment when the right word eluded the non-native speaker. Madalane was flushed and her heart hammered against her chest with the joy of discovery.

Unsure of her friend's thoughts, Evienne took Madalane's arm and led her into the church. A rush of cool air greeted them as they descended into the dimness of spiritual house. The two women seemed insignificant compared to the size of the church. Quietly, the two walked towards a pew in front of a statue of Jesus and Mary—La Pieta. Behind it was a mosaic of stained glass that formed a halo over the head of Mary. They stared at the stained glass window as the colors slowly began to change into something ethereal, matching every emotion the two women felt.

The stained glass windows were exquisite. Madalane was awestruck as the sun gleamed through the iridescent colors and the red and blue glass shimmered catching her eye. The pew that Evienne had navigated them towards was in front of the sculpture of Jesus and his mother after his descent from the cross. He lay motionless against her thin body. Mary's body enveloped her son and it was her tears and her agony that infused their hearts with a wretched sadness.

The colors of the stained glass sliced into Evienne's heart as the marble Christ was embraced by his mother. She felt the darkness of pain, of loss, of death, of hate, and of abandonment. She wanted to pull her heart out and throw it far away from that moment, so she would never feel loss again. Every inch of her body trembled; the beauty and the pain overwhelming her. It was all she could do to not close her eyes and cry until tomorrow.

The pain on the faces of Jesus and Mary made Madalane ache and she looked over to Evienne, seeing tears running down her friend's face. Evienne's pain was palpable and she could feel her agony though the rigid posture. Madalane reached out and grasped her friend's hand. It was cold and trembling. At this moment, in the solitude of the church, she knew that she loved her. She felt it with a certainty.

A huge desire to comfort her friend overwhelmed Madalane. Sitting side by side with Evienne, unsure how to act, hearing her own heartbeat in her head, ticking off the minutes as the two women were consumed by the cavernous silence. Resolved to act, she disentangled her hand from Evienne's grip. Reaching around to her own neck, she slipped the clasp of the chain she wore around her neck. Grasping the small silver box in the palm of her hand, she reached over to Evienne's hand again and slipped the gift into her friend's palm.

Shocked from her mind's million-mile journey, Evienne looked to her own hand to find Madalane's hands encapsulating hers. Evienne opened her hand and looked into Madalane's eyes with an unspoken question.

"It's for you Evienne. It is something my father gave to me when I was sent away to boarding school to remind me of my family." Madalane paused for a moment, allowing the memories of her father's tearful farewell at the train station wash over her. "I want you to have it because you have given me a new family. Paris is my new family and you have given me that gift."

Tears continued to fall from Evienne's eyes. She was incapable of words. She could only hope that when she looked back to the palm of her hand, it would not fill with her tears. Madalane moved her hand and allowed Evienne to see the treasure she had given her. A small rectangular box rested perfectly in the palm of Evienne's hand. The silver was polished and soft, almost a liquid in her hand. Feeling the moment of a priceless gift, she flipped the box in her hand and was struck by the masculine engraving of the letter E.

"Madalane, I could not take this from you. I could never take something as precious as this."

"But you must Evienne. Don't you see? I was destined to meet you. Look at the monogram! My grandfather was Emile. My father was Emile. How in the vast world we live in could I have ever found you? God sent you to me Evienne. You are my gift. God would not look kindly on me ignoring such a significant message." Madalane's tone dropped to a hushed whisper. "I don't know if you can understand how I feel, but you feel like my family now. You give me such comfort. Please accept the vesta case—it will hold your matches, and maybe you will think of me when you light your cigarettes. I want more than anything in the world for you to have it."

Evienne continued to stare at the small silver box as she whispered in a husky, urgent voice, "Family has lived far from my heart, Madalane. I almost don't remember what being part of a family feels like. Thank you for this." Evienne moved her eyes from the box and stared deeply into Madalane's eyes. "I will cherish your gift and I want you to know that every time I look at it or feel the heat of the silver lying next to my heart, I will know it is a piece of yours."

Madalane gazed intensely into her friend's eyes, but she didn't say a word. There were no words needed. She placed her hand against the larger hand and sat quietly, enjoying the stillness. The small silver matchbox sat between their palms, the heat from their hands mingled in the alloy of the metal. Madalane felt content. Life was a challenge, but suddenly she knew she wasn't alone anymore.

Evienne slowly said in a tremulous voice, "I will cherish your heart, forever. Forever, Madalane."

The sun slowly set in the body of the church, dusk blanketing the two women who sat in her pew.

Chapter 18

Stella turned the art box like a book in her lap and began the process of opening it. Stella continued explaining, "I did some research and found out it was purchased somewhere in London—the shop emblem is faint but I could make out that it was from L. Cornelissen & Sons; by the way, they are still in business today. It made me wonder if our artist was English."

Eve grunted, acknowledging the information, but not caring. She was anxious to see what was inside.

Stella unlatched the fastened hooks and opened the box. The aroma flooded both of their noses; Stella inhaled deeply, smelling the now familiar scent.

Eve attempted to calm her anxiety. How would her mother feel about her daughter looking at her private papers? Would she feel exposed or would she be relieved that her secret was finally out in the open. When Stella looked into her eyes, Eve gave a barely perceptible head nod, indicating that she should continue.

"This box is curious because of its many compartments. Either Evienne came from money or whoever gave this to Evienne must have known she had true talent because at the time, this box cost a bit of money. Can you smell the paint and turpentine?" Stella picked the art box from her lap as she would a baby and encouraged Eve to smell the air hovering over the paints and brushes.

Eve tentatively sniffed the air; she wasn't sure what she should smell. She liked art, but much like cooking, she didn't want to be too involved in the actual craftsmanship.

Stella gently placed the box on the coffee table in front of them and unlatched the easel compartment to release the prize of pictures and letters. "I am sure this is what you have been waiting for." Stella collected the tied letters, pictures and drawings and handed them to Eve.

Eve reached for the bundle. She was surprised at how many letters there were. How long was her mother with this artist? The letters were tied tightly with a faded red ribbon. Without thinking, Eve pulled the packet to her face and breathed in deeply. She did not know much about painting, but she knew this scent in an instant. It was sandalwood. It was hidden deep in the pores of the paper. Heaviness hit her heart—her mother's scent was so powerful on these pages, even if it was only in her mind. She pulled the pack of letters from her face and brought them to her heart to try to hold the moment inside of her. Eve's hand shook as she placed the letters in her lap separating the tied pack of letters from the collection of sketches. The sketches were folded in half, keeping the mystery private to a casual observer. She unfolded the first sketch.

Stella could tell watching Eve's hands shake how intensely moving this must be for her. It was a private moment she was witnessing and she thought it better to say nothing.

Eve unfolded the paper. Her eyes filled with tears as they both stared at the languid women wrapped in each other's arms. The sketch in front of Eve might be the most erotically lovely picture she had ever seen. It was impossible to see where one woman's body stopped and the other woman's body began, the limbs intertwined, organically growing like two branches of a tree fused together.

Eve closed her eyes; she needed to get control of her emotions. She looked at the sketch again—a conversation she had with her husband years ago played around the edge of her consciousness. As the memory became clearer, Eve laughed and shook her head to dispel the image, surprising Stella.

"Are you okay?"

"I'm sorry—I just keep remembering all of these incredibly naive things I thought about my mother. I told my husband that I thought my mother was a virgin when she got married. I guess this sketch throws that theory out the window." Eve let out a short sigh that turned into a tight laugh, "I think my family tree just got a hell of a lot more interesting."

Stella begrudging realized how difficult it was accepting her own daughter's sexuality let alone how hard it was for Eve to see her mother's. The sun was shimmering gold through the small square windows framing the door that led to Eve's porch. Stella took a sip of her wine, and busied herself by making space to lay the sketches out.

"Can I spread the sketches out for us to look at?"

Nodding vaguely, Eve swirled the red wine, half looking at the picture. "I'm not sure how I will feel by the end of the day, but I want to thank you for bringing me these letters and pictures. I can't think of a better person to share this experience."

"Of course. I feel honored to be here with you. I am oddly motivated by this whole thing—compelled to learn more about your mother and Evienne.

Both women were lost in thought when Granger got up and started circling the room, Tiberius soon joined him. Stella laughed, "I think the boys need some time in the great outdoors."

Stella jumped up, straightened out her shirt, and headed for the porch with both dogs trailing, thankful for the chance to get some fresh air.

After Stella left the room with Granger and Tiberius, Eve sat back for a moment and considered her day so far. The sketch of the two women lying on the cleared space of the coffee table stared back at her. Her mother reclined, naked and curled around her female lover. This was not the mother she knew—the woman in the sketch was a woman that Eve was getting to know forty years after she died.

The rest of the sketches were still folded in a pile. Eve opened each one and laid them out creating a line of sketches on the coffee table. Eve recognized the sketch of the old lady—it was the same woman from the painting in the dining room. The other sketches were done in the same style—the pencil strokes that illustrated the majesty of a beautiful woman's body.

She opened the last sketch and laid it on the coffee table with a sharp intake of breath. The last sketch was a close up of her mother's face. Her mother's face—unlined and guileless—stared back at her as if daring her to judge her. Eve felt the tears erupt and stream down her face. Eve had assumed this to be a sexual affair, not necessarily a love affair. It was easier to think of her mother walking away from sex than from love. The artist who had made these sketches had loved her mother intensely. Staring at the picture, she saw the slight hint of a smile in her mother's face—this was her secret love—this was the secret that lived in her heart all those years.

Trailing the dogs, Stella returned to the room and stared down at the drawing in front of Eve. "I knew it was your mother in these drawings after I met you. I saw your eyes in her face. The resemblance is unmistakable."

Stella was silent for a few minutes and then gave in to temptation, asking in a heightened tone, "Eve, do you think your mother named you after Evienne? Is your full name Evienne?"

"I wondered that the other night." Eve slumped against the back of the couch and sighed. "It's mind-boggling how much I have already learned about my mother and frankly, myself too, with just a few drawings and one letter."

Stella crossed the room and sat down next to Eve, gently resting her hand on the older woman's.

"I'm a little disconcerted by this whole thing. When I was

a kid, I asked my mom why she named me Eve. She told me that eve meant the start of something very special and I was the start of something very special in her world. Now, I think she was creating a fairy tale for me, a myth like Santa Claus. She named me after her lover, which I suppose is a nice sentiment. I just don't understand what happened between them. She barely knew my father when she married him. It was one of those wartime things—young GI going overseas, looking to marry to have someone to come home to because he was facing certain death. Why was he more important than the lover she spent the rest of her life thinking about? Why name your child after your ex-lover?"

At a loss for how to respond, Stella said, "Untie the ribbon and start with the one on top. I think that the letters are the way your mom last read them."

Eve looked up at Stella and nodded. It struck her again that the letters were so carefully tied together—exactly how her mother kept her important papers—everything tidy and organized. Her fingertips traced the top of the ribbon once more, as she tried to picture her practical immigrant mother carefully tying up this ribbon after furtively reading them late at night in her tiny bedroom.

Placing the packet of letters in her lap, Eve gently pulled the ends of the ribbon. The ribbon was a faded red and had old-fashioned tiny lace loops around the border of the fabric. Eve felt a momentary impulse to toss the ribbon aside and dive into the letters, but she felt an energy emanating from the cloth and carefully set the ribbon off to the side on a small table next to the couch.

Tracing the indentation the ribbon left on the letters, part of her wanted to use the soft, cotton gloves that the librarians used when going through archives of valuable papers. Ruefully, she realized that no one else valued these letters like she did. She put the stack of letters on the coffee table in front of her and reached for the first one. There was no envelope, just a folded piece of what felt like sketch paper—the same kind of paper that the drawings were made on. She unfolded the letter and noticed the date—October 1928. Her mother had been in her late teens—so young, it was almost unimaginable to think of her mother ever being that young.

As she read the salutation—*My Dearest Madalane*—, her eyes filled with tears and her hand began to tremble. Christ, what was wrong with her? Eve looked up at Stella who was gazing at her pensively. "Will you read it out loud for me? This is more difficult than I thought it would be."

Stella extended her hand and the letter seemed to float between the two women. "Of course." Stella wanted to race through the letters so she could know everything about the lovers, but she felt the sorrow and anxiety coming from Eve. She intuitively knew she had to tread gently.

Leaning forward, Eve bowed her head as if in prayer, hands clasped together, supporting her forehead. Stella's voice shook as she read the first line, but as she warmed to the flow and rhythm of the words, her voice exuded a growing confidence.

16 October 1928

My Dearest Madalane,

    I live humbly by the gracious fingertips of Paris. She has shown me the flavors of her heart, infusing the flowers of her breath into my lungs, filling my mouth with her red wine. Paris lives in the dark seductive shadows of the Eiffel Tower and in the depth of the Seine River; I will follow her wherever she takes me as I followed your lips enjoying a glass of her wine. The reddened hues pour from the bottle like the setting sun shimmering in your hair.

    I have learned to trust in the nature of my city; she has been my family. I welcome you to her arms.

Thank you for the pleasure of allowing me to show you
her radiance.
Forever,
Evienne

As Stella's voice whispered the last line, Eve raised her eyes to Stella. "Thank you."

Stella held the letter in her hand, staring at the fine, purposeful penmanship. She wondered what life was like for Evienne and Madalane in Paris. Why she would say she lived by the gracious fingertips of Paris? How poor was she? Did she live on the streets before she met Madalane? Where was her family?

Abruptly, Eve stood up. "I need to use the bathroom. Give me a minute."

Both dogs stood at attention, but sat back down as they watched the older woman move through the dining room. Stella watched Eve glance at the painting of the old woman as she walked past, shaking her head.

Perhaps this was something Eve needed to do alone. Stella wondered if she should she even be involved in this mystery of Eve's mother's love story? She really liked Eve and didn't mean to upset her. Stella resolved to give her the option when she returned. Stella stood when she heard the bathroom door open and she gently put the open letter on top of the art box.

Eve walked back into the room and saw that Stella was standing. She felt a pang of disappointment as she said, "Are you leaving?"

"I just want you to know I will leave if you want me to."

"No, please don't leave. I'm sorry. I am a little unsettled by what I'm learning about my mother and I'm a little off-balance. I want you to stay. Please."

"Of course, I will stay as long as you want." Stella smiled, hoping her gentle tone calmed Eve's frazzled nerves.

Eve let out the breath she had been holding. "Thank you."

She nodded feeling a little ashamed at her display of emotion. She blotted her face with the tissue and proceeded to shred it as she held it between her fingers. "In Buddhism, there is a saying that a man who loves fifty people has fifty woes, and a man who loves no one has no woes. I would always prefer a life filled with love than a life absent of it, no matter how much pain it causes. You have brought me knowledge that is causing me more pain than I thought I could bear, but your presence is also lessening the pain; you are easing the agony I feel. I want you to know that I appreciate you so much."

Stella's face was soft and sympathetic, and Eve felt an overwhelming sense of kinship with this virtual stranger.

Stella crossed the room to where Eve stood and wrapped her arms around the woman in a ferocious hug. Stella rubbed Eve's back like she used to rub Sarah's.

Eve chuckled after a few minutes and picked up her empty wine glass. "I think I need more wine!" A little embarrassed, Eve pulled away and went into the kitchen. Both dogs watched the exchange between the women and then looked at each other. Granger sat down next to his mother and Tiberius followed Eve.

Chapter 19

"Would you like me to read the next one?"

Eve nodded and Stella reached for the next folded letter on top of the pile and started to read in her clear contralto voice:

30 October 1928

My Dearest Madalane,

You are the face I see in the words I write; each stroke of my brush—the image of you. As I sat with you today at the church, melting into the colors of the stained glass, I wondered where you came from. My tears seem to be the only part of myself I can share with you because death and disappointment has put a coffin around my heart. My older brother died in 1922. His death broke my mother's heart and my mother died not long after him. And finally, my father couldn't take the loneliness and passed in 1924—the same year I decided to move to the city. I was leaving my small fishing village, the only home I knew, and my two younger sisters went to Boston in America to live with our aunt.

Death has made me a vagabond, fueling my body to search endlessly for life. Death has made love and tenderness untouchable, a thing of the past until you. Your kindness

*infiltrated me as we sat in the church. Your kindness, like the
sun illuminating the face of the Virgin, her gentle heart peer-
ing into the shadowed window of my soul, showing me you.*

*As a woman, I would sit alone staring at Mary, praying
I was that child resting in his mother's arms, safe and loved.
I was the dead waiting to be revived. I swallowed the wrath
of time. Yesterday, I was numb, but today your spirit made
sharing the magnificence of the stained glass a treasure. You
immortalized time in my heart's memory when you slipped
your father's vesta case into my hand. I was no one until I sat
next to you, and in this moment, I feel I am born.*

Forever,

Evienne

As chills ran down her arms, Stella got a flash of the small
metal box hidden in one of the covered compartments in the art
box. Stella had assumed it was Evienne's since it had the engraved
E. She looked at Eve who was lost in thought. Stella pulled the
art box towards her, resting it in her lap, and unlatched the small
compartment. Inside was a tarnished silver matchbox.

"Eve." Stella said to her friend and then repeated her name.
Her voice interrupted Eve's thoughts and she looked at her. "Give
me your hand." and Eve did exactly as she asked and Stella placed
the box onto her palm.

Eve's reverie was disrupted by the feel of something cool being
slipped into her hand. She knew Stella had been speaking to her,
but the spirit of the letter had captured her mind. This was the
first time she felt she knew the woman Evienne was writing to.
Her mother would have changed another's life. She had influenced
hundreds of students over her teaching career and these words
in the letter were prescient of the woman Madalane had become.

Opening her palm, Eve looked down at the tarnished piece
of metal. She rubbed the flat of the metal and saw the glint of the
monogram. "I don't know what a vesta case is. Is this it?" Eve's

voice sounded bewildered and almost girlish in her confusion.

Trying to contain her excitement, Stella jumped closer to Eve on the sofa, so she could explain the vesta case to Eve. "I believe it is. This is the case that your mother gave to Evienne, and now it's being given to you.

Stella continued, "A vesta box is the name for a match box. See…" Stella pointed to the top of the box,"…let me see it for a minute and I'll show you—you open the lid here" Stella pulled open the hinged lid and showed Eve the inside, "and then this is where the matches go and look here on the bottom, this is where you strike the match. This matchbox was your grandfather's." Stella put the open box back into Eve's hand for her to examine.

Overwhelmed by the feeling of holding something that once belonged to her grandfather and mother, Eve looked at Stella, "How did you know what this is? Do you collect antiques?"

"I collect boxes….all kinds. I have seen vesta cases online but I never bought one."

Eve nodded. "I need a minute—I think my blood pressure is spiking." She leaned her head back, feeling dizzy as she closed her eyes and breathed deeply.

Stella felt the energy in the room begin to calm. Her eyes glanced back to the stack of letters and noticed that Eve had put the tarnished vesta case on top of them. She looked down at her own hands, feeling the emptiness when there was so much to hold and examine. She straightened her wedding ring. Eve's breathing was deep and steady; Stella wondered if the older woman had fallen asleep. She couldn't resist picking up the vesta case, polishing the blackened metal with a napkin as she gazed at Eve sitting next to her. With her face in repose, Eve looked older than when she was alert. Stella tried to imagine what Eve had looked like at forty. She then tried to imagine what she herself would like in her late sixties. Her mother's many plastic surgeries made it impossible to predict. She envied Eve's sense of identity. Her thoughts traveled to her own family's life and lies.

Stella felt that nothing was worse than not having a connection to a past, not knowing where your parents were from. Nothing was worse than a mother who had changed her past to look good to her country club friends and potential husbands. Stella knew what was true about her own life, but her mother created a story to fit the friends that she kept. Stella had a hard time knowing what fact was and what was fiction about her mother. She didn't have the real history that Eve did. Stella continued to polish the little box, thinking about the hands it had passed through.

Eve desperately tried to empty her mind, trying some deep breathing exercises. Her brain was crowded with images of her mother, everyday images of Madalane sitting in her reading chair, book in her lap or strolling through a museum with her arm tucked into Eve's as they discussed the difference in the use of light between artists. Too many memories and too many years to try and bridge; she sighed again as she opened her eyes, glancing at Stella. Slowly she stated, "I know this is going to sound repetitious, but this is much harder than I expected."

Stella nodded but didn't say anything.

"I never had any family growing up except for my mother, and all of a sudden, I am dealing with a family heirloom. It's just an odd thing, Stella. I appreciate your patience though. The vesta case is startling to say the least, but to be honest the thing that threw me for a loop was the reference to the stained glass window in the church."

Stella nodded; she had not made the connection before. "You love stained glass."

Eve took a sip of wine before speaking, "Yes, I thought it is a by-product of being raised Catholic." She stopped and laughed. "Boy, that's a hoot considering mom's love life. Anyway, we used to go to this old church near Lansdowne—Our Lady of the Virginal Aspiration or something like that. After mass, she used to walk us around the stained glass windows so we could study them. She told me that art was how pre-literate societies were taught, through the stories represented in the picture."

Feeling confident in the connection, Stella insisted, "Your mom must have loved stained glass because it reminded her of Evienne. They connected in the pew of that Paris church. She wanted to give a piece of herself to Evienne."

Chapter 20

23 November 1928

My Dearest Madalane,

At dawn, I panicked for my vesta case; it assures me that you are real. I trace the etched silver and search my mind of our evening's pleasure; my dream-like state transports me home to my fishing village where many times my family enjoyed bread and wine. You have given me this comfort, a tradition pulled from my past. As I lay in my bed, noises of the street and looming scents seep into my lungs and I realize— I am awake in Paris.

I block them and allow my thoughts to wander to the warm kitchen of my mother's fire. We knew love through laughter and the ache of a full of stomachs when my father was fortunate to catch a prize and would honor my brother by allowing him to present the fish to our mother. I, being the eldest sister, provided guidance and devout protection while my middle sister would debate and educate, and our youngest, the baby, was the greatest love.

My mother said with our combined passions, we represent a well-rounded woman and we had much to learn from each other. We each held the strength of our convictions, and truth be told, my mother had the final judgment. Our family eve-

nings reminded me of our stroll through the Jardins du Lux-
enmbourg last night. As we discussed your studies, touching
on the Judgment of Paris, I fear I will end up as the golden
apple for you. I have felt the chaotic energy of decisions spin-
ning around my mind and you seem immune. You effortlessly
stroll next to me, inviting my guidance in art. I am in awe
of your grace, and your steadfast commitment to letting your
passion shine. My mother would have been honored to have
known you as I am.

    Thank you for our lovely Parisian feast last night although
my mind hungers for our stroll through the gardens.
Forever,
Evienne

Stella's clear voice faded as the letter came to an end. Eve's
eyes remained closed as if she were listening to a silent postscript.

    Eve finally opened her eyes, "Evienne is quite the writer,
isn't she?" She glanced over at Stella who was still staring at the
letter she held in her hands. When Stella did not respond, she
continued. "I mean, Evienne is a painter, but she wrote equally
compelling letters."

    "I think that she defines herself to Madalane through the
images she mentions. Think about it, the reference to the Judgment of Paris and the golden apple. She uses art and history to
explain who she is." Stella studied the letter with conviction to
support her theory.

    Eve grinned. "You know that reference!" She was delighted by
Stella's grasp of the esoteric allusion. "I am beginning to believe
that Evienne is far more impressive than some grungy street artist."

    Seeing Stella frown, she tried to explain what she meant. "I
mean that Evienne clearly interested in the themes of art and
literature. The Paris of Judgment and the golden apple are much
more obscure than something from the Bible. I think it's very
interesting that she used Discord's golden apple that started the

contest to explain her own concerns. That allusion would have made perfect sense to my mother—she was a huge fan of mythology and its use in literature. Because Paris is forced into judging who is the most beautiful of the three goddesses, he will undoubtedly cause chaos by whomever he chooses. It is an untenable position to be in and Evienne must have felt an incredible pressure to make my mother happy but also to make the right decision. I am beginning to see why my mother liked Evienne so much."

Stella quietly remarked, "She loved Evienne."

Good-naturedly, the older woman smiled and nodded her head. "Point taken, but at some point, she liked Evienne before she fell in love with her." For a brief moment, she felt an odd sensation saying those words—it was the first time she had felt the love between the two women. "My mother was not a person who trusted so easily. She played her cards close to her chest. However, there must have been something about Evienne that my mother valued and I'm seeing that Evienne was a much smarter woman that I thought she was."

"I think she was struggling with feeling vulnerable. She wanted to strip herself naked and find the freedom to love someone wholeheartedly. To love the way she had only dreamed she could love—to feel the emotions of love and rage, and of possibly losing love. I think so many things had been taken away from her, except her art. That was the one constant." Stella looked to Eve to see if the older woman agreed.

"I want to know why my mom never said a word to me about Evienne."

"Maybe it was too painful. Sometimes thinking about an old love is incredibly excruciating and raw."

"You sound like you speak from experience," Eve murmured.

Stella gave a small smile and nodded. "It was a long time ago and to this day, I usually don't allow myself to think about Victor."

"Victor?"

"Yes, my daughter's father. It's actually ironic that I am talking about him now. I have literally not talked to anyone about him since he left us, but he sent me an email several weeks ago. He wants to see me."

"Do you want to see him?"

"I'm not sure. I loved him more than anyone else, next to my daughter of course, and it wasn't enough to keep him. I am still mad at him, but I'm afraid that I will melt into a puddle when I see him and do whatever he asks."

"You're not a kid anymore. You grew up." Eve was quiet for a moment before speaking again, "Have you told your husband?"

"Not exactly—I didn't tell him about Victor. I've been unhappy.... that is not the right word...I have been unsatisfied since Sarah left for college a few years ago. I feel like the life I have been living is a lie. I told David that I thought we should separate for a while. It's why he took the assignment in China."

"So he is okay with a separation?"

"No...not at all. He's a good man, so he gave me what I asked for, but he is mad at me." Stella's thoughts went to the email she received a few days ago.

```
Stella—

I have tried my best to give you the time and
space you need to figure out what you want. I
know I promised to let it "sit" until I'm back
in the US, but I don't understand any of this
quite frankly. I am angry, confused and I feel
helpless being so far away from you. I have
questioned myself, my actions, my feelings...
everything since you asked for the separation.
And NO--it didn't make it any easier to do this
in China. I am halfway around the world, and the
one person who I counted on in my life is not
sure she wants to be stay married to me. Over
```

the last month, I have asked myself a hundred times what I have done wrong. I love you with all my heart. I love Sarah with all my heart. I know I'm not the most handsome guy or the most charming, but I have tried and I know I can do better if you tell me what I should do.

If you have found someone else, you owe it to me to tell me. While I am chewing my leg off to get out of this trap, I can only imagine you in the arms of someone else, planning your life with him. I know you said that this is about you, not someone else, but how the hell am I supposed to know that? I held up my part of the bargain. I loved you, supported you and never once even thought of cheating on you. Have I disregarded your feelings? Not listened to you? I am always willing to listen, but Stella--you are not always willing to talk. You sit in silence, like a statue, and I'm supposed to read your mind? It's not fair. How can I wait until May when I am so tied up in knots. If you want a divorce, tell me. I can't stand feeling like I am standing on a surfboard that is going to slip out from under me because of an undertow.

I am not trying to make this harder on you. I am in agony over this and I know you. You cannot be totally unaffected despite your poker face. If you choose to stay married to me, please be honest with me. Tell me what is bothering you. I want to help you. I want to be your partner, not just your husband. If you want me to move out, then so be it. I will. I love you too much

to fight you on something so important. You
know me and you know I wouldn't have written
this email unless I was in hell. I need to put
my feelings in perspective. I am hurt that you
may not want me in your life, but I will survive if you don't. I will leave and give you
the freedom you want to live life on your terms,
as you phrased it.

Despite the pain I feel right now, I love you.
I will always love you. You are the woman I
want to spend my life with. I understand if you
don't feel the same, but it will never change
the way I feel about you.

David

"Not many men would be so accommodating." Eve murmured.

"I know. I am just confused and I don't want to cheat David or myself out of happiness if we can have it with someone else."

"Do you think you could be happy with Victor?"

"That's the million dollar question. I don't know."

"Are you going to see Victor?"

Stella looked at Eve and shook her head, "I don't know that either. Like I said, I have no idea about anything anymore. All I know is that your mother's letters have brought me a sense of purpose more than anything else in a long time."

Eve glared at the still relatively large stack of letters. "There are so many of them. Did you check the dates to see when they end?"

"No, I only read enough to find you." Stella caught Eve's eye and smiled. Glancing at her empty water glass, she needed more water; her mouth was dry.

Stella stood and pointed towards the kitchen, "I'm going to get a refill. Would you like one?"

Eve shook her head, pointing to her barely touched glass of water. "No, I'm a firm believer that it's healthier to drink wine than water. There is a Brita pitcher in the fridge and the glasses are above the toaster oven which may or may not be covered with the mail."

Chapter 21

My Dearest Madalane,

I repeat your name over and over in my mind as I paint this morning, and I thank you for coming to me. I feel like every face I sketch is your face, every woman resembling you might be you. In truth, I catch my heart as it leaps in hopes it will be your face smiling back at me.

Last evening, as we walked down the rue Bonaparte, I pulled you close to my side. Completeness came over me, softly as the night dropping around us, and I looked at you and found Paris in your eyes, as if the other half of my soul was standing next to me. I pray this is not foolish and you feel the truth of my heart for you.

Sitting in Café de Flore, I looked around at the other patrons and gave thanks. Thank you for sharing bread and cheese and wine. You are the dearest dining companion an artist could ask for.

What am I to do when you leave for home? No fire will warm me as your company, the bread will taste plain, the

wine like water, and laughter only a murmur until you are
back in our Paris.

    I long for your return and you have not yet even left our
beautiful streets.
Forever,
Evienne

Madalane left the college as soon as classes were over and walked quickly back to her room at the boarding house on Rue Saint Jacques. It was bitterly cold, and the chill would get even worse once the sun started to set. In a few weeks, she would be returning to her village for a few weeks to celebrate Christmas with her family. She dreaded seeing her mother and undergoing the interrogation she had almost grown accustomed to when she returned on her rare visits home from school. Nonetheless, she was eager to see her father and her friends around town. She winced as she realized that she would also have to see her cousin, Michel, who had taken her place at her father's shop. Michel could neither make accurate change, nor inventory a shelf, nor charm a customer. Being a shopkeeper required being nimble in at least two areas, but poor Michel could not even spell nimble. Deep down Madalane felt a malicious satisfaction knowing that her mother and father had not been able to replace her so easily.

As she turned the corner of her boarding house, she saw a familiar tall figure standing near the wall, buffeting herself from the harsh winds that tore down the street. Madalane's heart gave a little leap and she walked faster. Evienne's head was down and she was trying to smoke a cigarette, cupping it in her hand. She must have seen movement out of the corner of her eye because she turned and saw Madalane hurrying towards her. As they came together, Evienne leaned down, gave Madalane a kiss on each cheek, and then bent for third kiss on the left cheek again. As she drew her lips away, she whispered huskily, "You look like a country girl out for a walk on the moors." Then Evienne slipped her arm under Madalane's.

Madalane blushed. Evienne knew she was reading Wuthering Heights and this little allusion to the story made Madalane feel a warmth that Evienne paid attention. They went up the stairs to the boarding house, Madalane let them in to the house and they quickly moved into Madalane's room. The student's door was the first one on the right when you came in the house. Although it was on the ground floor, and in the fall, the street sounds lasted well into the night, Madalane preferred this room. It was right inside the entrance and the Madame of the house rarely saw Madalane except for the dreaded house dinners on Sundays.

Madalane lit the small fireplace in her room and slowly added wood until the fire caught and the room started to heat up. She turned to look at Evienne who was vigorously rubbing her arms.

"Why don't you wear a heavier coat?" Madalane asked. Evienne's jacket was not much heavier than a man's dinner jacket.

"Why do you not live in a castle and have a private tutor?" Evienne cheekily replied. "I am warm with this fine jacket. It was given to me in a trade from a lovely seamstress; her customer did not come back to pick up his jacket so I traded her with a small painting for her sister in India."

Madalane got the point—Evienne was incredibly poor. They both knew it, but rarely discussed it. This was one of those moments that Madalane's bourgeois lifestyle intersected with the desperation that Evienne's life often faced. Impulsively, Madalane removed from her own neck the heavy wool scarf she had knitted a few years before and wrapped it around Evienne's neck. The scarf was a dark royal blue. The wool had come from a traveling Spanish woman who had needed food for her children and had no money. Madalane had traded the woman food for the wool and paid for the food out of her own small allowance. She had knitted the scarf in secret, so her mother would not see the vivid color. Her mother would find it shocking to see such a color wrapped around her plain daughter. "This will keep the wind from your neck Evienne. My grandmother always said to me if you keep your neck warm you will never catch chill and you will never get sick."

Evienne rearranged the scarf around her neck. At first, she had wanted to push it back at Madalane, but she recognized that Madalane was doing this out of love and concern. Evienne had to remind herself that Madalane only wanted to give her something to keep her warm. So she kept it and allowed the scarf to embrace her.

Madalane put a kettle on the hook in the fireplace, and removed the books and papers she let pile up in the extra chair in front of the fireplace. The last remnants of the sun were filtering through the lace curtains of the window and the room took on a cozy glow with the orange flames of the fire contrasting with the sepia tones of the sun setting.

"How are things with Jean?"

Evienne scowled. Jean was an artist who lived at the squat. He was rude, drunk and worst of all, a bad painter. He had also decided that Evienne should be his woman. Not his wife or girl-friend, but merely his woman. He had stumbled into her room repeatedly over the past few weeks. Evienne could scarcely get any work done because he was always intruding. Luckily, she assured Madalane that his stink preceded him, so she always knew when he was near.

"He attempted to share my blanket again last night."

Madalane's eyebrows rose, but she stayed quiet.

"I had to show him his presence was not appreciated or wanted."

That's when Madalane looked down and saw Evienne's right hand; her knuckles were bruised and swollen.

"Did you hit him?"

"His face smashed into my hand. It was an accident, of course." Evienne's lips had curved into a sardonic smile. She leaned towards the heat of the fireplace with her left hand planted firmly on the mantel and her right displayed at her hip.

"Oh Evienne, what shall we do with you." Madalane laughed as she said this, but felt a tiny flicker of fear for her friend erupt inside of her gut. "You need a safer place to live Evienne. You must know that."

Shrugging, she replied, "Sure and I must buy a heavy coat, be a famous artist and drink better red wine. Madalane, you know I invest my money in art supplies, which leaves very little, and I must live where I can afford. I have been managing for years here in Paris. She is my lover and will always take care of me. She always does." Evienne looked down at the fire; she watched curls of steam come from the spout of the teapot. "I think the water is boiling." She looked up to find Madalane looking directly at her.

Madalane was quiet. The thought she was about to express had been floating around in her consciousness for weeks, but she had been unsure whether to suggest it. Now, with Evienne's bruised, sore hand staring at her, she knew this was her one chance. "Come live with me." There was a long still silence. Madalane was not sure what to do; it was as if Evienne did not hear her. "Come live with me Evienne. There is plenty of room." Madalane scanned her small dorm room trying to ease the awkwardness.

Evienne thought maybe the heat was burning her cheeks; she searched her pants pocket momentarily for a cigarette. She slipped both her hands down the sides of her chest looking for them before finally finding them in the outside pocket of her jacket; she was relieved to give her hands and mind something to do. Evienne's long fingers pulled one from the pack, slipped the Gauloise pack back in the black jacket pocket and reached for a match from the mantel tin. She struck it on the stone front of the fire place, the match balanced between middle and index finger, she brought the cigarette to her lips, curled her tongue around the end paper of the cigarette, wetting it so it will not stick to her lips, cupped the flame to the end, drew in the first hit of fresh tobacco and as the heat reached her lungs, her eyes closed.

Smoke curled up, winding around her face and as Evienne exhaled and opened her eyes from her ritual, Madalane was still standing in front of her staring. Evienne turned away, quickly taking another drag, balancing the cigarette on the mantel and retrieved the steaming kettle from the fire. "I will make the tea tonight—having tea with you is a privilege, but I am not used to having hot tea every day, I am really more of a red wine woman."

Chapter 22

My Dearest Madalane,

Yesterday, Paris was my truest companion—the scented breeze wrapped her arms around my soul, the wine of her river filled my belly and the colors of her city inspired my paint. This dawn, I sit in my cold room and realize you triggered emotions forlorn in my paint-stained world. Ominous clouds pillow the sky, below the horizon births peach slivers of light, a morning reminding me of you. I would not want to be a burden to your future. I would not want to drag you into my darkness.

I have been separated from life, needing resourcefulness to hide my maddening solitude. I, like you, should have love living in the veins of my heart, not lies. The truth of this day holds your true heart in God's hands. Your kindness, an untouched angel, makes me question my purpose. Am I even worthy to share the air you breathe, to be blessed with the thoughts that you think? Your essence drives me to paint the poetry in my mind. The mere thought of you quickens my own heart. It is you I feel when I sleep; it is you I think of when I wake.

> *Out of many, there is one.*

Forever,
Evienne

Eve watched the emotions wash over Stella's face as she had read the letter. Eve knew she listened with a critical ear, wondering how this woman's absence could break her mother's heart so completely.

"Evienne seems like she had a hard life." Eve's words even sounded hollow to her own ears. She was trying hard to be sympathetic, but she felt anger more than anything else. Her mother had spent a lifetime alone. What did this woman have that no one else could give her mother? She glanced at the letters, knowing that somewhere in those pages were the answers to the questions that ran through her mind.

"Evienne was hurt by years of loss. She desperately wanted to run into Madalane's arms, but was scared by the fear of being abandoned again." The words poured from Stella's lips, "She said it all here...*I would not want to be a burden to your future. I would not want to drag you into my darkness...Your kindness, an untouched angel, makes me question my purpose. Am I even worthy to share the air you breathe, to be blessed with the thoughts that you think?*" Stella stared at the letter and whispered in a strangled tone, "I think she feels unworthy."

"Everyone has a hard life Stella. You had a mother who was less than maternal and I grew up without a father. It doesn't negate a person's responsibility to the people in their lives." Eve's frustration was palpable in her words and she knew her tone was overly harsh.

Stella pleaded, "It's your mother's love story. Everybody should have at least one and this is your mother's."

Eve sighed. "I know, but a love story always ends badly right?"

"Honestly Eve, no, they don't always end badly." Stella was feeling a bit foolish for being so emotional. Desperately trying to regain some dignity, she looked back at the letter and read the lines, "*it is you I feel when I sleep, it is you I think of when I wake'.*"

Eve felt a stab of anger and countered without thinking, "I think your husband would disagree."

Stella stared hard at Eve, unable to speak. She felt her world crashing in on her. She wanted to run out of the room, screaming. Instead she gazed downward at her wedding set, centering the diamond of the engagement ring with the diamonds in the wedding band. Unbidden, tears began to flow as Stella struggled to get a hold of herself.

"I'm sorry Stella. I shouldn't have said that."

Choking on tears, Stella shook her head. "You're right though. I was David's love story. He rode up on a white stallion and saved me."

Eve had no idea what to say. She felt terrible for imposing her frustration on the younger woman. "Life is not a fairy tale. Girls don't need a prince to save them anymore."

"I needed David. I don't know how Sarah and I would have survived if I hadn't met him when I did."

"You were surviving."

"Barely."

"As you get older, you become your own woman. You don't have to be indebted to someone forever."

"It's not about being indebted to David. I do love him. But I'm not sure I love him enough."

"How does anyone measure love? How can you tell when it is enough?"

"I don't love David the way I loved Victor. Victor made me insane with love. David is more of a comfortable robe you put on in the winter. Victor made me feel crazy. David makes me feel warm. What if I am cheating David?"

"What makes one better than the other?"

"That's part of my problem. I don't know what is better for me. I feel like getting that email from Victor was serendipity. I had asked for the separation a full month before I got the email. Maybe this was all meant to be. Maybe it's God or the universe telling me to go for it."

"Then why haven't you agreed to see Victor?"

"I don't know."

Eve sighed, unsure again what to say. Finally, she said, "Time will tell you what to do. Sometimes you just have to wait for the right moment."

Chapter 23

Eve offered to show Stella some pictures of Madalane, and while Eve retrieved the photo album, Stella brought the dogs in and they settled in the living room, each keeping an eye on their mom. From the recesses of a cabinet in the dining room, Eve had returned with a thick photo album coated in dust. Cracking open the photo album, Eve remarked, "I can't remember the last time I looked at this old thing."

She quickly flipped through a few pages before stopping; Eve laid the album on the coffee table and gently pulled the plastic off the page. Gingerly, she pried the picture from the page and took a closer look before passing it off to Stella. "That's mom and Elizabeth, probably around 1953—we had just gotten a new car and I can see it in the background. The car was a lemon, so we only had it for a year or two before mom traded it in for another car."

Stella peered into the frame of the black and white photo: self-consciously the two women stood together in the driveway of a house, arms looped around each other's waists. Madalane looked directly at the camera while Elizabeth's gaze was turned towards something in the distance. Madalane had a sleek bobbed haircut and wore a small scarf around her neck with a white shirt and tight peg pants and her waist cinched by a wide belt. Elizabeth had the tight pin curls so evident of the times and she appeared to be pregnant, wearing a shapeless housedress.

"The two look like they were really good friends. Do you always remember Elizabeth being in your mother's life?"

"Oh yes—I knew Elizabeth my entire life. I think I was around ten when I discovered we weren't actually related. I knew my mom was an only child, but I think that I had somehow got it into my head that Elizabeth was my dad's sister." Eve reached for the picture to return it to its place and pulled out another picture. "This is all of us kids and mom and Elizabeth at one of our picnics. They would pack sandwiches in the summer, we'd all troop over to the park, they would sun themselves, and the kids would run around like a pack of wild wolves. We're all sitting very tamely in this picture, but by the end of the afternoon, someone would always be bleeding." Eve laughed at the memory. "Elizabeth was my second mom for a long time, and now she's gone too. When I heard she died, I couldn't get myself to the funeral. It was just too hard. It felt like my mother had died all over again."

Stella was quiet for a moment, feeling the pain that Eve's voice held. Finally, she remarked, "You have lovely memories of your mother. My clearest memories of my mom are of her moving from one man to the next. I had too many dads and uncles to remember, but never any aunts. My mother never had any close women friends; she saw women as competitors, not friends. You had two wonderful women who made you feel special."

Eve's sorrow gave way to anger. "Your mother seems very foolish. A woman needs woman friends. It helps her cope with the vagaries of life, of children and God knows, of men! I think my mom and Elizabeth were each other's sanity. There were days that my mom would take me and Elizabeth's four kids to the drive-in theater just to get them out of her hair. Of course, mom sat in the front seat chain smoking and reading a book while the rest of us sat in the backseat, waiting breathlessly for the chance to go to the snack bar."

Eve accepted the photo that Stella held out and replaced it, scanning the rest of the photos on the page to see if Madalane were in any. She flipped a few pages and came to a photograph that made her chest ache. It was her mother, sitting in a chaise lounge at the pool, wearing a one-piece bathing suit, smoking a cigarette with a tall glass sitting next to her. She was laughing at something Elizabeth, who was next to her, had said. She looked so much like the woman she remembered. She wordlessly passed it over to Stella who gazed at the photo, as if memorizing each element.

Curious, Eve asked, "Did your mother's lack of friends impact your ability to make and sustain friendships?"

"I never really had a close friend, not like your mom did. I had Sarah. I convinced myself she was everything. When Sarah got older and wanted some independence, I took up tennis—I was varsity in high school, but had not played in years. The women I play against are friendly, but not my friends. Maggie is probably the first real friend I have made in years."

Stella was quiet as she allowed her feelings to wash over her, "It took courage for me to even come here and talk with you. I convinced myself it was because of the art box, but I am realizing it is a whole lot more. I need to reach out and see what I am missing in my life. I see what you grew up with and what I did not, and what you are sharing with me now. You had amazing mother in your life." Stella was quiet for a moment and then asked, "Did you ever have a close relationship with a woman like your mother had?"

Eve impulsively laughed, "Do you mean—did I test drive the Sapphic route?"

Eyes wide in mortification, Stella shook her head, "No, I mean it's fine if you did, but I meant a best friend. Someone you could turn to in times of trouble."

Eve was still grinning at the younger woman's embarrassment, "I always had a strong support system...wonderful friends, incredible mentors and of course, my husband and now Hank.

I have a few best friends—women who have held my hand during the worst parts of my life. I thank God for them. I'm not as exclusive as my mother was. She seemed more of a one-friend woman. She had other friends, but none of them were as close to her as Elizabeth." Eve sat for a moment staring blindly at the photos on the page before she continued.

"I think that if I had children, I might not have been so open to all these wonderful people who came into my life. I would have been myopic and focused on my children, as you focused on Sarah. You know the old saying: God takes away with one hand and gives with his other. I had a lot of friends instead of a baby. It's still not an even trade in my book, but I'm an old lady now and quite frankly, I am not sure if I would have been a very good mother. I'm a very selfish person. I like things my way, often to the detriment of others. Trust me, Hank would totally agree!"

Eve flipped through the photo album, scanning shots of her teen years, feeling completely detached from the young woman smiling in most of them. She finally came to the shot she remembered with distinct clarity: her graduation picture, standing in a black cap and gown, looking extremely happy and relieved. Her mother stood next to her. Madalane wore an expression that Eve had not really paid any attention to before. She was smiling, but her eyes were troubled.

"This is the day I graduated from high school. Class of 1960. Let me guess, you weren't even born yet." Eve chuckled and handed the photo to Stella. "My mother has such a stoic expression on her face. She knew I was leaving soon, leaving for good. I never thought of my mother having abandonment issues, but it's written all over her face in this photo."

"I don't think Madalane thought you were abandoning her. She wanted the best for you, but she felt the pain of being alone again. You talk of leaving as if you are guilty of something extraordinary, and never came home again, but you did. Why do you feel like that? I look at your mom and I can feel the same pain I have felt in her eyes. I can understand where your mom is coming from, it can make a mother heartsick to let her child go, but you have to honor the fact that you did the job and it is time."

"Tell me about Sarah's father. Why did you and he break up?"

Having delved so deeply into Eve's life, Stella felt obligated to answer the question, despite the anxiety she felt exposing her life. "Victor was a musician. He left when Sarah was a toddler. I encouraged him to go and live his dream. He was my boyfriend; we never married. He was a wild passionate man who felt life through his music and his guitar. He would sing to me, write me love songs and promise me that he would come back and we would live around the world while he played concerts and recorded. We would have our happily ever after. I waited and waited. We waited, Sarah and me. Ultimately, I was stupid to wait." Stella eyes started to fill. She did not realize how thoroughly he had abandoned her. She suddenly felt sick.

"I am so sorry. I know how much it hurts to lose someone you love. I think losing someone who you love because they are selfish must be even worse." Eve considered her words before she continued speaking. She feared she had insulted Stella with the statement that her ex had been selfish. "I know you told him to go, but every man knows that women are the ones who sacrifice, so it was his responsibility to stick around and ignore what you said. If Hank deserted me every time I told him to hit the road, we would never have gotten past the first year."

Stella laughed a little as she slipped her finger under her eye to catch the tears that escaped. Her thoughts quickly turned to her mother; men were disposable to her—they still were. When she found a richer one, a more generous one, she kicked the current one out and moved on. She could never do that to David. The small voice in her head asked if she was sure about that.

"Did you really try to kick Hank out? I mean really he sounds like a good deal."

Eve ruefully nodded. "We have discussed moving in together.

I am going to retire in a couple of years and he is already retired, and one house would certainly be cheaper than two. I guess we will have to cross that bridge when it comes time. I suppose it is inevitable, but for now, we both like our own space. Plus, can you imagine if he was underfoot while we were doing this? He is a dreadful pest, always wanting to be part of whatever is going on. I had to ban him from the house or he would have showed up to mow the lawn or fix a shelf that has been falling down for five years." Eve chuckled as Hank's crestfallen face passed through her mind.

Stella handed the young picture of Eve back to her and realized that Eve might be a bit lonely like herself. It was a relief somewhere deep in her soul to have a confidant like Eve. She usually stored her emotions, neatly tucked into boxes of her mind, but with Eve, she felt the need to share, as if she were her mother—the way Sarah would blurt out something to her in spite of her quest for independence.

"I married David because I felt safe and cared for. I am going to be honest with you—he was not the love of my life; Victor was. David was the safe choice who turned into a good husband— sometimes a great husband. We like the same things and we get along really well. Sarah likes to beat me up about choosing the country club over poverty—she has her father's romantic soul." Stella picked up her water and finished it giving her enough time to contemplate the truth. "I did it for my daughter. That is honest, and luckily, it worked out."

Eve shook her head. "David wasn't the safe choice. He could have ended up being a total shit to you. He turned out to be a good man. You can't discount the value of that. Safe is being alone for the rest of your life. "Safe is—" Eve indicated the corners of her room— "is filling your life with so much clutter that you force yourself to be alone." Eve's expression was stoic, but her voice held a tremor. "Safe is never allowing the hole in your heart to heal, like my mother did. You are brave. You took a chance with your husband and you won. Many people would envy you. And remember, your daughter is a still an adult-in-training. She has no idea how hard and harsh the real world can be. Romanticism is a tale told by poets and Disney. Real life and real relationships take work. Your daughter will learn that soon enough."

Stella's eyes widened; she had assumed Eve was happy with her choices, but maybe she wasn't. Did the fear of losing someone again stop her from committing totally to Hank? It seemed the holes were not as filled in as much as she had thought. She felt the taut strain in the air between them and tried to diffuse it. "Shall we read the next letter? Maybe Evienne and Madalane know the answers to the secrets we seek."

Eve nodded, sipping her wine. She felt tired, and wondered if a cup of coffee would perk her up as she gazed at the pile of letters that had barely diminished.

As Stella reached for another letter, the sound of wind chimes seemed to emanate from her purse. Putting the letter gently back on the pile she reached for her bag knowing it was her phone. She wondered who would be calling her in the early afternoon. It was the middle of the night in China and Sarah usually called at dinner time. Finding her phone, she looked at the caller id and saw that it was Maggie. Quickly, she answered the call, "Hi, Mag."

"Oh thank God I reached you! I am desperate. The girls are supposed to be picked up from their preschool in 45 minutes and I'm still at the doctor's with mom. I don't think I will make it back to Chestnut Hill in time. My back-up carpool mom is not answering her damn phone. Who doesn't answer their damn phone these days?" Maggie's voice was frenzied and her rising tone echoed through the speaker and into the room.

"Of course I can get the twins." Stella's voice was soft and reassuring. "Honey, is everything okay with your mom?"

"Oh yeah...mom is fine. She has her annual visit to the cardiologist and it's taking forever. You know how it is, you make a one p.m. appointment, and we're still waiting at three p.m. It's infuriating but there was some sort of emergency...I think one of the patients had a heart attack during their office visit...all kinds of chaos around here and an ambulance came and went a little while ago. Things have settled down now and we are next according to the receptionist. Are you sure this is okay? Am I messing up your afternoon?"

"No, it's fine. I'm at Eve's house in Swarthmore so I will have just enough time to get there."

Stella hit the end button and looked to Eve. "I'm sorry—it looks like our day is coming to an abrupt end. I have to pick up the twins from preschool for Mag. She is stuck at the doctor's with her mom. Everything is fine, but the office is in some upheaval. Would you like me to come back later this week or next?"

Secretly relieved that the day was ending sooner than planned, Eve stood up to get her planner. "I have to check my calendar. I can't remember anything without it anymore. My brain has turned into a rusty sieve."

Eve went into the kitchen and Stella heard a variety of curses and thumps as Eve searched for her Blackberry. Time was getting tight and Stella felt the urgency of Maggie's anxiety strike her.

Eve returned scrolling through the tiny screen, "The rest of the week is a wash for me. I am teaching and covering for a colleague plus a few committee meetings thrown in just to torture me even more. How about next Tuesday? I teach in the morning but then the rest of the day is free."

"Perfect, I'll be here. You're a teacher Eve? I can totally see you teaching."

Eve laughed. "Yes, I am definitely my mother's daughter, except I teach history instead of English and college level instead of high school. Young adults at least pretend to be mature."

Stella laughed and checked her watch. "I gotta run and get the girls." She patted her leg and Granger who had been lying next to Tiberius, immediately stood up. "Come on boy, we have to go."

Eve walked the younger woman and her dog to the door and stood on the porch as Stella raced out to her car. "I'll text you with the time for next week, okay?"

"That sounds great." Stella turned around and waved, "Sorry to leave so quickly. I look forward to seeing you again and thank you." Stella impulsively blew her a kiss as she unlocked her car and ushered Granger into the back seat.

Chuckling as she closed the door, Eve felt a wave of relief wash over her. Her mother had been a private person, yet Eve had never felt any distance between them. She felt betrayed that her mother had not shared this piece of her life, yet there were many things that she had never shared either. Weren't boundaries necessary and healthy between mothers and daughters? Eve shook her head, trying to clear the sound of Stella's voice reading the letters. She would read the letters again at some point when she didn't feel quite so emotionally exhausted. She would read them as a historian and not as a daughter.

Chapter 24

Paris, December 1928

In the early morning light, Evienne is consumed by the life of a painter. Upon waking, she usually thought of her painting, but on this morning, she woke thinking of Madalane. She thought of the subtle changes in her expression, the texture of her hair, and the way the color of her eyes speak to her. She laid in the small hard bed and waits for light to transform her into an artist.

In her small damp room, she pulled her black wool pants up her long legs. She wrapped twice around and buckled her leather belt remembering how beautiful the evening sky was. The memory made her chest tighten for the colors of the night. She wanted to pocket the blue and save it for the light of the day.

Shirtless, she looked at the canvas she had been working on—the tired face of the old man who begs for alms at the foot of the church steps. Evienne envisioned his life of pleading and hoping for a few centimes. Even as evening comes, and the old women gather to gossip on a nearby bench, the old beggar continues his rosary of solicitation. The haggard man blesses every soul; it is his service to God. Does God notice the tourists who casually walk beyond the old man's beseeching hand to visit the antiquity of the Saint Pierre Church between Place du Tertre and the Sacré-Coeur? The tourists worship the ceilings of God, the unknown retrieval of stones to build houses, the young man who inhabits multi-colored shards of glass, but not the earth that the old man inhabits.

Evienne sat on her stool in her small room at the squat and studied the painting of the man's face by the first flush of sunlight—the dingy collar of a cheap black suit, the tobacco stains of mustard yellow blended along the ends of his mustache, blue eyes beclouded with pain and whiskey regret; the old man was a host of perfect imperfections. The glow of morning light intensified the mix of color, highlighting and enhancing the perfection of his image.

The dried drops of paint that coated Evienne's easel inspired her—sometimes she studied them, they taught her the detail of color. The colors displayed the changes in depth and intensity as wine poured from bottle to glass; showing her how the thick crimson of blood from a cut dried into a dark brown; showing her the evolution of Prussian blue to red in the sky. Evienne thought of submerging herself into color as her morning wine dyes her lips. She thought of what color she is—today, she is red. She moved to the solitary window and waited for the sun to rise, to guide her in her work.

Evienne felt the pain in people's faces and she painted their furrowed thoughts. Her art is complex and real and somewhere in the madness, she allowed her paintbrush to guide her life. She painted the rough determination in men and women while capturing the soft edge of their souls, fading into the harshness of their lives. It is apparent in their stare, mangled from the daily wear of their work. That is how Evienne survived. She blended into other's lives and was grateful to have art to keep her.

Evienne waited. She folded her arm over her bare breasts and waited. Evienne hid in the dawn, hid behind the empty spaces of her art, slouched in silence in front of a canvas, smoking her winged Gauloise.

Soon she will begin the ritual of painting. Her paintings are small and tight, a canvas pulled taut over a square wood frame. Parisian colors danced in her mind. Standing half-nude in her locked room, a black plait of hair falling from the nape of her neck to lie between her round breasts, the complexities of her mind ignoring the gray cigarette smoke puddling thickly along the ceiling. The fresh air of the morning, the vision of the young woman, the woman Madalane was becoming; she could not stop thinking of her. As she hesitated at her easel, she studied her own mind and realized that Madalane has become her balm.

Evienne turned and looked out her small-framed window. Her mind drives her down a narrow road. She feels her as she sees a new face emerge from the canvas. Evienne touched her energy with her paintbrush; she feels her energy in her bones. The desire of her soul seeks the divine.

Finally, the sun blessed her window fully. The dancing light at her window, the heavens, the heat of the earth, the purity of the air, her fingers stamped out the butt of the glowing end of her cigarette. Lost again, she embraced her muse, her mind is swelling, she is falling; she feels tears running down her face. She steadied her body and looks out the window as if the girl is looking in. She knew there were no people just rooftops. She pulled her fingers through her tied hair. Soothing herself with her hair, she pulls the long plait over her eyes, and meditates. She thinks of Madalane as she breathes in the musky scent of her own being. She wants to touch her. She wants to touch Madalane's soul. She wants their souls wrapped around each other.

Evienne shakes herself back to what grounds her, her painting. She tries to push out the coursing energy that occupies her mind. Again, she thinks of painting her obsession. Back and forth. She imagines her as she always imagines her: lying across a chair, worn but well built. Her smooth skin heated by the sun, hair drifting across rounded shoulders; it is how she lives in her mind. Evienne felt restless and unfocused.

Frustrated by her thoughts, Evienne pulled on her shirt and sweater, donned her cap and headed out to sell some paintings.

Distraction often leads to inspiration. She walked down Rue Dauphine, making a left heading towards the Seine.

After collecting her paintings from the storage shed, she set up her side of the stall; it is Saturday and she knows Charles will be here to sell later. He will charm the tourists and be invited to dinner at some cafe to talk of his life a painter in Paris. He has talent Evienne thought, but he sacrificed his art to satisfy the expectations of the tourists. As she leaned her paintings against the sea wall, she thought how he painted cupids instead of gargoyles on the tops of Paris architecture. Lovers overcome their resistance, pull the money from their pockets, and put it in his.

Evienne took a moment to lean against the barrier wall of the Seine. She closed her eyes to soak in some of the glorious warmth and thought of the painting he did of Cupid and Psyche. She instantly felt the insanity of her again. She remembered how Charles told her of the beauty of Psyche, and Evienne thinks of the student. The feeling starts below her navel, burning and flooding over her like the river moving beside her. She thinks of Cupid and his arrow. In her mind, she sees how the sapient sun splashed a perfect light on her alabaster skin. Evienne prayed for Madalane to be standing in front of her, but when she opened her eyes, it is a tourist.

"How much?" She says pointing to a delicate painting of the five-arch Pont Neuf. Evienne picked up the painting and started her pitch, "Here stands a bronze equestrian statue of Henry IV of France. He protects our oldest bridge in Paris from the clochards." The tourist seems intrigued as Evienne continued. "And inside the statue the sculptor Lemot," Evienne points toward the actual bronze, "put four boxes inside, one containing the life of Henry IV, and another box containing 17th century parchment documents." Evienne whispered in her best patriotic tone, "A Parisian secret you can tell your friends. May I wrap it for you?"

The tourist seemed unsure.

Evienne put her hand to her customers elbow and said "And

you should walk and enjoy the new bridge and visit my friend's café for a hot chocolate. Later, when you gaze at this painting, you will remember the perfection of this day in Paris." The tourist's reluctance gave way and she happily agreed. She received more than a painting; she had a painting filled with history and a painter named Evienne Lavelle. She happily gave the woman her asking price, tucked her wrapped painting under her arm and headed towards Pont Neuf.

Evienne felt the coins in her pocket and knew that they were hers. A day holding the sun and the moon, one always chasing the other. She thought how funny it was, how one event led right into the other, how change created fear and fear created strength. She knew that tomorrow, Madalane would get on a train, leaving for her month-long trip to her parent's home. Evienne turned back to watch the Seine and wondered why she had not noticed the tiny flowers growing out of the stonewall where she almost daily stood; so delicate, they reminded her of life with Madalane. She knew life would change at the next sunset. She felt the fog of loneliness curl around her.

She felt the trepidation of missing Madalane and tried to hide it from herself by convincing herself that home was where her boots were planted. She could survive as the delicate vine of flowers did in the winter. The sun began its fall behind the Gare d'Orsay; Evienne knew it was almost time to stack and store her paintings and finally find her way to the Sorbonne to meet Madalane. Evienne had written her friend a bon voyage letter and decided that she would buy her some sweets for her trip. Evienne cut across Boulevard Saint -Michel to her favorite shop, Bonbons. She asked the Madame to wrap exactly twenty-eight cherry candies in a box with Christmas paper. Evienne wanted to give something to her friend at the train station. She wanted it to be her heart, but the candies would have to do in their small box.

Madalane quietly shut the door behind her as she left Madam Renard's office. She had taken her last exam, she had turned in her last paper, and she had completed her last meeting with her tutor. She was officially finished until the new year. All she had to do was finish packing for her trip home tomorrow morning. Ever since she had been sent away to boarding school, she had felt ambivalent about her breaks at home. A few times in secondary school she had stayed with friends rather than go home to feel like an interloper. Nonetheless, she was expected home and at least her father would be happy to see her. The halls were already mostly empty and she heard the click of her shoes as she walked towards the exit. The hollow sound echoed in her ears as she tried to step lighter to muffle the sound.

The sun had begun its crawl down the horizon as the cool air hit her cheeks; normally she loved dusk, but tonight it felt like the city was closing itself to her. She pulled her coat tighter around her neck before descending the steps to the street. As she stepped towards the left to go down Rue Saint Jacques, she felt a presence behind her. She looked back and saw her friend standing there with red, wind-burned cheeks and hair askew from the breeze. Evienne winked and smiled at her, and Madalane threw herself towards her friend seeking the comfort of Paris.

Evienne met her friend's embrace with a deep purposeful inhalation and open arms. She captured the scent of her wool coat and the intimate perfume of her hair. Evienne leaned down to kiss both of her cheeks and embraced her for a second time as she spoke. "Bonjour, you must be pleased your studies are finished until the new year?" Evienne felt the feeling of completeness and the feeling of loss at once looming and wearing at her like a blistered heel after a wonderful walk.

"I am happier that you have come to see me." Madalane was truly ecstatic over her friend's unexpected arrival. She had dreaded the cold walk back to her room. She had dreaded the long lonely night that stretched in front of her. Most of all, she had dreaded only seeing her friend for a few minutes before she left for home the next morning.

Clasping Evienne's arm in hers, they started to walk along the Rue Saint Jacques. Suddenly the setting sun was not so dreary. It almost seemed to be winking at her in good humor. "Will you come back to my room and help me pack?"

"I have moved so many times Madalane; I am the best packer ever. But on the way home, we have to stop for some wine and bread. I am ravenous!" Evienne pulled Madalane closer to her side, "We can eat while we decide what books you should bring for your train ride." Evienne smiled at her friend as the two closely interlocked strolled into the evening.

The two women made it back to Madalane's room in record time, carrying their dinner and wine. The room was cool from being empty and as Madalane unpacked their purchases, Evienne laid a fire to warm the small space. When she turned around, she saw their gourmet feast laid out on the small desk. Madalane had poured their wine into small glasses and she was holding one out to her friend.

"Joyeux Noel Evienne. Thank you for spending the evening with me." The women clinked glasses and Madalane sat on the bed as Evienne sat on a chair.

Evienne stretched and crossed her long legs, put her left arm to the back of her head and allowed a sip of red wine to warm the chill of the day from her bones. "Will you write me while you are playing shopkeeper with your cousin?" Evienne smiled and winked at her friend, accidentally her forearm pushed her cap off her head and it toppled in front of her face to her lap.

She laughed as Madalane's hand automatically reached out to save the cap from falling to the floor. Realizing the foolishness of rescuing a cloth cap, she laughed. She was about to hand the cap back to Evienne when the subtle aromas of her friend struck her from the lining of the cap. Suddenly it was too seductive to return this treasure. She offered the cap, but as Evienne reached for it, Madalane pulled it back and placed it on her head. It was too large and drooped over her forehead, so she resettled it towards the back of her head.

"I don't think I carry it off quite as well as you. Do you think it looks fetching on me?" Madalane mock posed to give Evienne a full view. Evienne nodded and laughed, delighted by her young friend's exuberance.

Adoring the way Evienne looked when she was happy, Madalane pulled the hat off her head and offered it back to Evienne. Evienne shook her head, indicating that Madalane should put it back on. Madalane settled it back on her head. She could smell the sandalwood and the tobacco and the paint—the wonderful mélange she associated with her friend.

"Why do you wear this cap Evienne and not a beret? Hasn't Mr. Picasso made berets de rigueur for all the artists in Paris?"

"When our painter friend, Mr. Picasso wants to paint me as he has painted a portrait of Ms. Gertrude Stein, he will be happy to paint me with my cap on and know I am my own artist." Evienne assumed a regal pose on the hardback chair.

"Mr. Picasso is this an acceptable pose?" Evienne stated her request as she answered.

"Yes Ms. Lavelle," Evienne's voice lowered to mimic Picasso's voice. "You wear the cap of a fisherman. Is this your talisman, your trademark, your fortune?"

Evienne shifted her body to answer her invisible interviewer's question, "Why yes Mr. Picasso. My story starts with a mermaid who traveled from the far seas and searched me out. A budding painter walking on the beach of a small fishing village on the coast of England." Evienne leaned into Madalane as if to tell her a secret. "The beautiful mermaid stretched her body on the sandy shore, her long hair mingled with seaweed and shells. She said to me, Evienne, your world will be guided by the sun and your soul inspired and warmed by a wool cap."

Evienne's face took on a look of bewilderment and she

searched her own head in amazement, but there was no hat there. "The mermaid continued, the day you stop believing in yourself is the day your hat will fall to shreds. And just as suddenly as she appeared, she dove back into the sea, never to be seen again." Evienne sighed very dramatically and continued, "I being a young lass did not understand the need for a cap until I found a paint brush and needed to block the sun from my eyes. And this is why, Mr. Picasso, I wear a cap. I wear this cap because the mermaid told me to."

Evienne reached to the table, ripped a chunk of bread, and emphatically pushed it in her mouth content with her explanation of her father's cap.

Madalane grasped a piece of the bread that Evienne was still holding and popped it in her mouth. "You, my friend, should have been a writer of tall tales. I am never quite sure what is real or unreal when I am with you."

Evienne merely laughed, but offered no reply. The evening had taken on an anxious pause as the sight of Madalane in her father's cap gave her a feeling of uneasiness. Like colors blending, Madalane had suddenly become part of her history, of her family, of her life. It made her feel off-balance to see the woven tapestry of her life grasping at new threads and weaving them into her life. Feeling a weakness infuse her, she reached for her cigarettes and quickly lit one as Madalane stood up.

Madalane was highly entertained by her friend's unguarded revelations. The allusion to an English fishing village was caught and filed for later analysis. She did not want to ruin their last evening together with questions that made Evienne uncomfortable.

"Tell me your plans for Christmas while I get my clothes together." Madalane crossed to the wardrobe where all of her earthly belongings hung. A feeling of sadness overcame her as she gathered up the few dresses she owned. There was so little of hers back at her parent's house; it had been so long since she lived there for any amount of time that she no longer had even a spare coat in that house. Shaking off her emotional apathy, she turned to her friend and smiled brightly.

"Come on Evienne. Tell me what Paris is like at Christmas. Does Father Christmas visit all the children, even the over-grown ones who have paint splattered all over their boots and ink under their nails? Even the ones who have been naughty and have not kept the wine glasses filled?"

Evienne stood and filled the glasses and offered her friend more bread with cheese. The night was quickly passing and she knew she would have to head home soon. Evienne drank more wine. "What will I be doing when you are sitting around the cozy fire with your family chatting and admiring your glistening holiday tree? I suppose I will sell many paintings as the most divine presents for my bourgeois clients to give."

Evienne knew the holidays well. They represented just another day, a solemn day, a day for memories to flood her lonely mind. Putting her glass down, she picked up Madalane's gray sweater and carefully folded it and tucked it in her friend's case.

Envisioning Evienne's cold damp room, Madalane ate another piece of bread and cheese, watching Evienne add items to her suitcase. She wished that she could bring Evienne home with her, but she would not subject her worst enemy to her mother's bitterness. However, if anyone could deflect her mother's criticism, it would be Evienne. She could confound the most acid tongue. Still curious about Evienne's plans, she asked, "Do you go to church on Christmas Eve? Christmas morning? We go the night before because my father opens the shop for a few hours on Christmas morning. Someone always forgets something for their feast. It is his Christmas gift to the village."

"You must not worry about my faith Madalane. I will go to church for candlelight mass on Christmas Eve, and pray for you and your feast. It's getting late, you must hurry to bed; your train will be departing quite early in the morning." Evienne knew she would pray for 1929 to begin to make the holiday season go quicker.

Already feeling drowsy from the wine and the heat from the fire, Madalane was reluctant to let her friend leave. "Evienne you should sleep here tonight. If you are walking me to the train station in the morning, it seems an awful waste of time to walk all the way home and all the way back in the morning. It is already so late and it is freezing out. I need you to get a good night's sleep so you can carry my very heavy suitcase for me. If you are cold and tired, I will have to find someone else to carry it and that would be such a bother on such short notice. So really, you would be doing me a favor by staying here." Madalane tried to sound light and teasing, but she was desperate for her friend to stay.

In the quiet recesses of Evienne's heart, the questions arrived. Should she stay, or should she go walk the streets; conflicting thoughts ran up and down her spine. Evienne watched Madalane finish packing, close, lock, and put her suitcase at the foot of the bed. She was more than capable of handling her belonging, maybe she did want her to stay for companionship, not the heavy lifting.

"It is bitter outside at this hour, stay here with me, we need an early start. I won't be able to sleep if I am worried about you out in the freezing cold." Madalane was persistent as she busied herself with which book she wanted to bring with her on her trip. Finally, she placed The Great Gatsby on top of the suitcase.

"You are right Madalane; I will stay and not miss the opportunity to carry your case to the train." Evienne smiled at her friend as she sat to pull her boots off.

"It is the best choice Evienne, thank you."

They both easily prepared for bed. Evienne stripped down to her underclothes as Madalane unbuttoned her dress with her back to Evienne. Evienne tried not to stare overtly but the temptation was enticing. The flames of the fire showered gold across Madalane's back. Evienne's reverie was interrupted when Madalane said something about eating the sweets for breakfast and how Evienne should take the leftover cheese so it would not go to waste. Evienne was frozen in her feet by the natural beauty illuminated in front of her. Her own clothes puddled in her arms.

"Will you take the cheese Evienne? Hang your clothes on the hooks and hurry. I feel the morning coming too soon." Madalane turned and looked at her companion as she quickly jumped in the single bed pulling the covers over her head.

Evienne moved swiftly; she pulled the letter she wrote earlier that day from her jacket pocket and slipped it into the book Madalane had put on top of her case. Joining her friend in the narrow bed, Evienne moved against the warmth of her friend's body and curled against the heat, wishing the night would never end.

Chapter 25

As she channel surfed, Stella picked a baguette crumb from her shirt and then put it in her mouth. David's purple button-down shirt was the perfect pajama top. It was the last shirt he wore the day before he left for China and Stella could still smell him on the fabric. Smells are interesting she thought—they were transporting and reassuring and can make you feel fear or happiness all through a scent.

She ate the remaining piece of cheese and noticed the little flowers in her china were the same color as David's shirt. She was staring at the dish then the shirt, comparing the colors intently and caught herself in the act and laughed. She shared her insight with Granger who was lying on the couch with his head resting on her thigh. He was a good listener she thought. His scruffy white head didn't move from her leg as she scratched him between his ears. Granger was content. He was not usually allowed on the sofa, but tonight Stella was happy to have woman's best friend next to her.

She had received an email from David that morning. He seemed resigned to their separation, and his email was filled with details of working in China. It was as if he could express nothing in his heart, so he focused on the world in which he was living. She had also finally responded to Victor's email with a short note telling him that she would think about his request. She ended the email with an update of Sarah's school life. She kept it brief because she didn't want to share too much of Sarah with him. It would be up to Victor to ask about Sarah—she would not impose her daughter onto Victor.

Stella's reverie was interrupted by the sound of the door opening. Granger's ears perked up, but he didn't move. Stella felt a lazy lassitude and briefly wondered if a serial killer would come through the front door or use the back. She knew if Granger wasn't barking, it was someone he knew. In the recesses of her mind, she thought briefly that David had flown home to confront her. She whispered to the dog, "Is it David? Has he come home to us?"

Instead, her daughter Sarah walked into the living room, holding a large laundry basket filled to the brim. "Hey mom! I came home to see how you're doing!" The words died on her lips when she saw Stella on the couch, dressed in David's shirt and nothing else.

"You what? " Stella could barely get the words out of her mouth as she struggled to sit up, trying to move a very uncooperative dog.

Sarah looked uncomprehendingly at her mother. The dog was on the couch. The dog was never on the couch. Her mother's bare legs had rested on the coffee table and there was a half-empty bottle of wine sitting next to her toes. "Uhm...mom, what's going on? Why don't you have any clothes on?"

"I am wearing clothes—I have on a shirt and well..." Stella looked down at herself as the dog looked up at her.

Over her initial shock, Sarah realized that she needed to change the subject or she would never get what she came for. She tried a different tactic. Sitting down next to her mother, she winced as she saw her mother's naked thighs and instead focused on the wine bottle on the coffee table. "Aw mom...do you really miss him so much that you have to get drunk? You should have called me...I would have kept you company." As soon as the words left her mouth, she knew they sounded much nastier than she intended.

Stella finally collected herself, pushed a very unhappy Granger to the floor, and pulled her feet from the coffee table, crossing her legs at the knee. "What are you doing home Sarah?" Stella said in a firm voice.

Feeling discombobulated by her mother's odd behavior, Sarah stared at her mother with a concerned expression that bordered on confusion. What was going on? Her mother was having some sort of weird breakdown. Sarah had showed up at dinnertime to ensure a well-cooked meal, but instead her mother was sitting half-naked on the couch with the dog, with a half-empty bottle of wine, and glancing at the book lying face down on the couch—oh God—a book of stories by Anais Nin. Sarah colored a deep pink. She didn't want to know what her mother was up to. She felt a little light-headed as she flopped back against the back of the couch. She decided to act like everything was normal and just get the business done.

"I'm starved, what's for dinner mom?"

"Baby, dinner has been served on the Food Network. Why didn't you call and let me know you were coming home? I would have pulled something out of the freezer." Stella tucked David's shirt between her legs, trying to preserve some modesty.

Not to be deterred, Sarah cocked her head and smiled. "I bet there are grilled cheese fixings and maybe some soup, right?" She put on her best puppy-dog face and tried to look as hungry as possible. Why was her mother being so weird?

"Honey, your dad has been gone for a month and I am fine. You have not called me in weeks and now you show up. What is going on and why are you home? Is everything okay with you and your girlfriend?" Stella hated using her name. "Did you two have a fight? Is school okay? You didn't drive six hours to have a grilled cheese." She knew when Sarah was looking for something and getting her mother off the couch to make her a sandwich was not it.

"I just figured that you would be lonely without David and I haven't seen you in a while, so I just got in the car and came up." Sarah warily watched her mother's reaction. When Autumn had suggested borrowing the money for the ski trip, it seemed so easy. Of course it sounded easy when Autumn laid out the plan, she barely knew Stella. Sarah realized that she would have to step up her game if she was going to get money.

Sarah waited for a response, but one didn't come. She stared at her mother, trying to read her expression. She decided to try a variation of the truth. "I just needed a break for a couple days. And I really did miss you." She smiled broadly hoping that she looked sincere.

Stella looked intently at her daughter's face, trying to discern what she was up to. "Come on, I'll make you that grilled cheese."

Chapter 26

Paris, December 1928

Madalane's eyes opened; a thin line of orange separated the night from the morning. It was time to get up and head to the train station. She rolled over to face her friend who had kept her back warm through the night hours.

Evienne's warm breath pushed into Madalane's neck. Evienne was barely awake, but she intuitively wrapped her arm around Madalane's frame and pulled her into her body. She could smell the mix of soap and Madalane's intimate scent from the slope of her shoulders. Evienne breathed in deeply as she pushed her lips to her friend's neck. Evienne's hips slowly matched her breathing as she pulled her even closer to her body. A soft sound filled her ears. "Evienne."

Hearing her own name coming from Madalane's lips shocked her out of her hypnotic haze. Groaning, she replied, "I know, Mad, we have to get moving but I'm so warm right now." Evienne reluctantly pulled herself from her friend's body, sat on the edge of the bed, and stretched. With her back to Madalane, she questioned herself while Madalane felt the rush of cold air assault her exposed body.

Disconcerted by Evienne's movements, Madalane turned and stared at her friend's back for a few minutes. She felt a strange sensation in her chest. The year before, at boarding school, she had met a boy at a mixer and he had taken her for a walk behind the dance pavilion. He had held her against a tree and given her a kiss, her first kiss, and as he held her against the tree, he had grinded against her. She had panicked and fled back to the dance. But this was different. When Evienne had, in her sleep-fogged brain, pulled her close and moved against her, she had felt a burn working its way through her body. Her own voice sounded foreign to her as she breathed out her friend's name. She hadn't wanted her to stop, but the sound of her name woke her friend from the languor of the moment. Begrudgingly, Madalane swung her own legs over the side of the bed and began to get ready.

The room was cold and both women dressed quickly. Evienne laid out the leftovers from the night before as Madalane brewed their tea. They were quiet and reserved, knowing that in an hour they would be separated for a month.

Evienne was deep inside her own head as she wrapped her leather belt twice around her thin waist and tucked in her shirt. Finishing, she sat down at the small table where Madalane was confidently attending to the tea.

The young woman moved ritually with the teapot, holding the handle with a towel and then slowly poured the amber liquid into Evienne's cup. The steam lifted and blocked Madalane's vision for a moment. She glanced at Evienne and felt a chasm of loss open inside of her. How many people had she poured tea for that she would never see again? She was adrift and alone in the world except for these comforting domestic practices. Setting the strainer on her own cup, she poured again watching the steam rise between them. Would this be the last time they would share tea? Evienne's life was not filled with structure; she could easily leave Paris for another city anytime she wanted. Setting the pot on the cork pad, she smiled at her companion as they began their meal. Realistically, she knew life would continue on much as it had before, but pain engulfed her heart as loneliness spread through her body. Looking again, she noticed that she held Evienne's attention. Smiling brightly, she resolved that if this were the last cup of tea she would share with her, then it would be a happy memory.

Sharing tea in the early morning was a lovely intimate act that spoke of Madalane's gentle kindness. Evienne was captivated by the quiet contentment between them. She wrapped her fingers around the warm cup, leaning into the steam, hoping the heat would take the chill from her thoughts. She contemplated what her friend must have been thinking; her smile seemed forced although still beautiful; even the sweet cakes did not seem to hold their normal appeal. Evienne wanted to say something to her friend, but she could only reach across and offer her friend the plate of cakes.

After their brief repast, the two women tidied up and did one last check of the room. Madalane's eyes flitted across the room, looking for anything she might have left behind. This had been her home for the past three months and except for a few books left on the desk and the painting she received from Evienne, it bore no evidence of her stay. As Evienne left with her suitcase and Madalane locked her door, it occurred to her that when she was dead and buried, her books and painting would be the only things left to let the world know that she had been alive. Instead of terror, it somehow filled Madalane's heart with peace. She didn't know why, but she felt tranquil for the first time in a long time.

Clasping her purse and book to her chest, Madalane asked her friend. "Ready?"

They left the house and headed north towards the train station.

Walking along a small cobblestone walkway, Madalane turned to Evienne and asked her the same question that she had been asking since she had met her. "When you paint, what does it feel like?"

Evienne was surprised by the question, but saw the sincere interest in Madalane's question. "When I was young I would see the sparkle on the ocean water when I was out fishing with my father. I would concentrate deeply to memorize each color, each blue and silver until it became the only thing that I saw. It gave my mind peace, so when I paint, it gives me peace."

"Sometimes it almost seems like it makes you angry." Madalane ventured.

As they approached the river, Evienne stopped walking and looked pensively at the water. It appeared that she was speaking to the dark waters of the Seine. "People who do not understand the process make me angry. I find peace in painting the beauty of a haggard face. I find peace in the mixing of colors. I find peace from looking into your eyes. I find peace knowing that you are interested in who I am, not what I am."

Madalane was momentarily startled at the Evienne's words. She looked away and a small furrow appeared on her brow as she wondered what that meant. Evienne was so open this morning, which was rare. Perhaps, it reflected the resignation that they wouldn't see each other for a month. She usually did not answer questions so directly, normally evading them with elliptical conversations that brought the topic back to Madalane. The student glanced warily at Evienne as they resumed walking easily carrying her heavy suitcase, shortening her stride to match the shorter girl's pace.

Madalane impulsively decided to press further, desperate to maintain this openness. "When you paint, how do you see faces? Do you see only a tiny part of the canvas at a time or do you see the whole thing at once and you have to focus on the perspective?"

"Why does it matter how I paint? I put paint on a canvas and it becomes something. It is not complicated." Her tone was gentle, but it was clear that she had tired of her friend's questions.

Madalane felt the familiar sense of frustration entering her body. Evienne hated discussing herself, but Madalane loved talking about art, especially her friend's art. If only she could get her friend to understand that she wanted to know what it was like to see the world filtered through color and lines. "You say it is not complicated, but I can barely draw a stick figure. I am fascinated at the way you can translate the mundane into something that has depth and meaning and substance."

Evienne sighed, "You have asked me this question many times in the past few months. You should know by now that I cannot answer your question. Not because I don't want to, it's just that I don't know how. It is something lives inside of me."

Madalane nodded, finally realizing that her friend was telling her the truth. "I understand Evienne. I apologize if I antagonized you, but you are so interesting to me. It's been a long time since I met someone who is truly unique. I want to know how you see the world around you. I want to know how you filter images through your eyes."

Evienne was beginning to believe that Madalane wanted to know her. At first, she had considered her friend's curiosity as intrusive, assuming she wanted to know a bohemian who she could brag about to her housemates. Reconsidering for a moment, she looked into Madalane's eyes, seeing only sincerity. She shook her head at the earnestness of her friend's expression. Smiling indulgently, she replied, "It is not my talent that allows me to paint the truth of an image. It is following the slightest change in light that allows me to see the emotion of it. I go so far as to show you how it looks, how I see it. It is in the shadows of color that I know where to put my brush. It is in the darkness that I am revealed a person's soul. In the light, I paint for you what I love, and in that, the dark and light of color and life becomes my art. I devote my life to my portraits, so difficult and yet so beautiful at the same time, and hope that my vision gratifies. And after each painting, drawing—where I thought I knew love—I know love more seriously and intensely than before."

Evienne's words were unexpected. Madalane had not anticipated such a complete assessment of the artist's methods. She knew that she often pried too deeply with Evienne, which made her uncomfortable; however, it was exactly this kind of answer that gave her insight into this mysterious woman. Madalane realized that they were still standing in the middle of the sidewalk, people grumbling as they walked around the two women. Evienne was staring at her with an amused expression. Madalane blushed; embarrassed that she had been rendered speechless.

Resuming their walk, Madalane felt an overwhelming sense of gratitude towards the artist. "Thank you Evienne. I hope I am not being too intrusive, but I have never known anyone like you. I find you and your abilities a source of endless fascination."

"Talking about art is interesting. Talking to me about me is boring. We should talk of more interesting things…like you, Madalane." Evienne smiled but her jaw was clenched tightly.

Madalane knew from Evienne's tone that this topic was now over. Evienne had grown weary of her intense scrutiny. As the two women crossed a small street, Evienne slipped her free hand along Madalane's back, guiding her to the other side. She felt the connection of their bodies and she sighed at the warmth. With the train station looming, Madalane turned her face to look at the river one last time. It was beautiful, as usual. Madalane allowed her mind to wander as they neared their destination. She felt warmth on her hand and looked down. Evienne's hand had drifted from her back gently to clasp her own. Madalane was overwhelmed by a sense of comfort and happiness. She curled her fingers tightly around her friend's larger hand. The two women stopped and stood motionless as they arrived at the train station.

Evienne looked down at the beautiful delicate hand resting under the harshness of her rough skin. She thought she might weep knowing her hand was touching Madalane's alabaster skin. Studying their clasped hands, she memorized each line and each vein. She would immortalize this moment.

A man cursed the two women as he tried to get around them,

breaking the spell of solemnity that had descended upon the two young women. Evienne laughed aloud and saluted the man with her chin. Madalane chuckled at Evienne's good-natured response. Facing the doorway to the train station, the two women entered the cavernous space, hands still clasped.

Standing in front of the departure board, the cascade of clicking sounds reminded travelers that life was ever changing. Madalane's train was on time and it was boarding; they headed towards the tracks.

Evienne pulled her hand from Madalane's and reached inside her coat for the box of hard candies. The little box was wrapped in Christmas paper with a gold seal from the store. She hoped she would think of her over her break every time she unwrapped one of the red candies.

Evienne's chest started to tighten; she did not like to say goodbye, she did not want her to go. "I bought you candy—the cherry ones you like. Don't eat them all at once or your stomach will hurt." Smiling, Evienne held the box out to her and then wrapped her other arm around her. She held her friend desperately, like it might be the last time.

Madalane's heart felt like it was going to burst. Every bone, tendon and muscle in her body told her not to get on the train, to stay in Paris with Evienne. Enveloped against her friend's body, she felt an awful ache spread through her whole body. Struggling to maintain some semblance of sanity, she burrowed tighter against her friend. She would be back in a month and things would pick up just where they left off. She repeated this in her mind over and over, hoping to believe it soon, hoping it to be true.

The conductor swept past the women, loudly announcing the final boarding call. "Final boarding call for Bordeaux and all points south."

The conductor's voice echoed in Evienne's head, the message spiraling down her spine, "Madalane, have a Merry Christmas; I will be here waiting for you when the train brings you back to our Paris." Evienne whispered into her ear.

The whistle blew its final warning, letting the passengers know that time was not stopping. Evienne pulled back, kissed both of Madalane's cheeks, and then looked towards the cab door, yet Madalane did not move. "Come on my Dove, you have to go." Evienne picked up Madalane's case.

Grudgingly Madalane hopped up onto the train step as the train started to move. Her suitcase was heavy and the book and purse made it even more cumbersome, yet she wouldn't move away because she was watching Evienne, memorizing her face, her smile, her presence. Finally, the conductor asked her to move and she slipped into the train car, but stood at the window, waving until the train had cleared the platform and her friend was no longer visible.

Chapter 27

With as much dignity as she could muster, Stella stood, straightened her purple shirt as if it was a formal gown and collected her wine glass. Heading for the kitchen, Stella sighed; She had a gut feeling Autumn had something to do with this visit. Hanging with a bad girl made Sarah want to be bad.

In a flat tone, Stella asked, "Do you still like the yellow mustard on the one side and not the other?"

Sarah frowned as she followed her mother into the kitchen. Her mom was different tonight; she was calm, yet confrontational. She was used to her mother retreating to her 'studio' whenever Sarah challenged her. "What's up with the outfit mom? You never wear dad's clothes."

Stella felt the soft cotton fabric and the thought crossed her mind to go put her pajamas on. Why did Sarah make her question herself? Why did she feel like she was making her mother a grilled cheese sandwich and not her daughter?

"It's an old comfortable shirt and I can wear what I want to wear. Why are you interrogating me Sarah?" her stomach tightened from the confrontation. "You didn't answer me dear, do you want yellow mustard on one side or not?" she said in a firm tone.

Sarah winced at her mother's words, and then growled, "Yes. You know what I like." The only sign that her mother had heard her was the mustard that appeared on the counter. Sarah felt a surge of anger welling up inside of her. Why was her mother being so combative?

Stella's jaw tightened and she briefly disappeared behind the fridge door as she got the butter. "Did you come home to fight with me about your dad's clothing or is there something else you want to fight with me about?" Stella's steady blue eyes penetrated Sarah's hazel eyes.

Sarah spat out the words, "David is not my father." Her eyes blazed with indignation.

Stella looked at her daughter with disgust. She was enraged by those words; she felt the frustration creeping into her by her daughter's old accusations about the choices she had made years ago. She smelled the grilled cheese burning behind her on the stove, and only then broke eye contact to retrieve her daughter's sandwich.

Despite the roiling anger inside of her, Stella was surprised how calmly she was handling the situation with Sarah. Normally she would have fled to her room and David would have dealt with Sarah; she hated confrontation, especially with Sarah. Tonight though, Stella felt strong and clear with her words. She knew the direction Sarah was heading and felt a new confidence, like a veil was lifted and her power was activated to get directly to the heart of the matter.

Stella placed the grilled cheese down in front of her daughter, and stated, "David became your father the day I married him."

Sarah was seething now. "Don't blame me because you married him. You didn't marry him so I could have a father, you are the one who wanted the big house, the tennis club membership, the easy life. You're just afraid to admit it." Sarah punctuated her statement by biting into the grilled cheese. "Don't we have any goddamn chips?"

"Those chips are in the pantry and if you want them, you can go and get them yourself." Stella's fury was nearing its boiling point. All the effort and sacrifices she had made for her daughter seemed futile. Sighing deeply, Stella felt exhaustion taking over her body. "Why are you here Sarah? Just tell me. Let's get past this. I don't want to fight."

Sarah stared at her mother, but said nothing.

Annoyed at her daughter's sulky behavior, she spoke with steel-hardened words, "You are a woman Sarah, start acting like one. Take responsibility for the viciousness of your own words. Your words hurt David, yet he always forgives you. You want to blame me for giving birth to you and providing you the best life I could. If it is unacceptable, then forgive me and go make one for yourself."

Sarah felt her own anger surge, "Do you think I want to rely on you when you've seen me as a mistake since I was born?" She stood up, her face beet red and her body trembling with anger. "I ruined your life mom. I know it. If there were any other way to pay my living expenses, I would do it. That damn credit card you gave me is maxed out and David hasn't paid it off. What am I supposed to do for food? Gas? Go hustle some business on the corners? You may have given me a life, but I won't be a whore for some man like you are."

Stella's anger disappeared as she realized that Sarah just wanted money. She felt like laughing out loud, but she knew that would only exacerbate the tension in the room. "Okay Sarah. I understand. This is not about who your father is or who I married. You need to learn how to manage a budget. David and I are not giving you any money until next semester—we already told you that. You need to learn when to use that credit card—it is for living expenses, not a lifestyle. People raise their kids on less money than you blow at restaurants and shopping." Stella took a deep breath, feeling emboldened by the righteousness of her argument, "I am nobody's whore or fool. Go make something out of your anger and come back when you know the difference between insolence and respect."

Eyes narrowed and body tense, Sarah's voice was full of fury, "You know what mom? It always comes down to the fact that you're still mad that I'm a lesbian. The only reason you hate Autumn is because she is a woman."

Stella's palms were sweating as she straightened her wedding band. Bitterly, she thought Sarah should go into politics—she could switch around an argument and spin it to her benefit every time. Since Autumn had arrived on the scene, Sarah had been spending vast sums and still wanted more money. Nothing was below her to get her way.

"I don't care that you are a lesbian Sarah, but I see you are having a hard time accepting being an adult. Look at the way you blame me for your choice by slinging your lifestyle at me. It is your life, not mine and your behavior sends a red flag—maybe you just a rebellious brat trying to guilt your father and me into giving you money?"

Sarah glared at her mother. This was not the plan. Autumn would go on the ski trip without her and meet some snow bunny. There was no way that Stella would back down now. She would have to let her mother calm down before she tried again. Sarah moved to the foyer, allowing a few tears to form as she whispered, "You know what mom? I came today because I missed you. I was worried about you. Instead, you acted like I had no right to care about you. I will leave you in peace."

With the words still hanging in the air, she stormed out of the house and got back in her car. As she pulled out of the driveway, she wished David had been there. At least, he would have slipped her some cash and quieted them both down. Fuck it. She was done. She needed to clear her head.

"SARAH REIN!" Stella shouted as she dropped into the kitchen chair like a stone. Under her breath, she muttered, "You forgot your laundry."

Chapter 28

Paris, December 1928

Madalane's face framed the doorway of the train as Evienne's arm extended over her head waving as the train slowly accelerated, creating a distance far more painful than Evienne expected. The screeching sounds of metal-to-metal reminded her of the weeping mourners at funerals; the departing train carried her heart like a processional. Evienne wanted to run after the train and jump on it, but her feet would not move, frozen, cemented to the platform. She memorized her friend's face until the white of the smoke enveloped her. The steam turning from white to gray to almost transparent and tiny curls of white lingering and mixing into the air and then it was gone like Madalane. She could not see her any more. Not the color of her eyes, not the shape of her face, not the waving of her fingers; she had disappeared with the steam.

Evienne reached into her breast pocket looking for her cigarettes. She tapped the open pack on the palm of her hand and let one white cigarette fall into her palm. Feeling her hip pocket of her jacket for the vesta case, she recognized the package of bread and cheese Madalane must have put in there for her. The gesture made her smile and choke on the growing sadness creeping inside her. A tear fell as she tried to light her cigarette.

Standing on the train platform, Evienne silently wondered where she should go. Smoke curled in front of her face and she prayed for time to flood past her, to hurry the time dividing her from the girl on the train. She turned to find herself alone among strangers finding their way out of the station. Evienne pulled her cap lower on her forehead and thought of the alabaster of Madalane's hand and the strong bones that the creaminess covered. Evienne left the station to find comfort in Paris.

* * *

Making her way down the narrow hallway, Madalane found a compartment with two older women and a child. She slipped in and stored her case under the seat, nodding to the women and smiling at the child. The women were speaking quietly and the child appeared to be occupied by the passing landscape beyond the window. Madalane sat on the gray felt bench seat, opened her book, and started to read about Jay Gatsby.

An hour went by and Madalane's eyes were tired. She closed the book with her finger holding her place, and leaned her head back along the headrest, allowing her eyes to rest. The little girl who shared her compartment sat next to Madalane and was now playing with a doll. Across from Madalane, the mother and the other woman were quietly talking. The cabin was hot, but no one seemed to mind. She let her mind wander to the story she was reading. She had felt like Gatsby all of her life, gazing at the green light, knowing there was something out there that would change her life for the better. She had worked hard at boarding school, ensuring good grades, ensuring letters of recommendation, ensuring that she would make it to Paris, ensuring she would make it to the Sorbonne.

Until she had met Evienne, she had worried that she had made a terrible mistake. Paris had not been the city of lights, but another cold, impersonal experience for her to endure. And then Evienne had entered her life. Evienne had become her green light—the promise of something better. She craved more from Evienne, but she wasn't sure what she wanted.

The train screeched around a corner, bucking the compartment with a jolt. The book flew out of Madalane's fingers and onto the carpeted floor of the train. Groaning at the disruption of her thoughts, she leaned over to retrieve it. Sitting back up, the little girl next to her said, "Miss, your paper fell out of the book."

Without thinking, Madalane leaned over again and saw that there was a folded piece of paper lying at her feet. Picking it up, she opened the paper to see what it was. The carefully written words jumped out at her as she recognized Evienne's distinctive handwriting.

All at once, she felt the oddest combination of loneliness and joy. Her friend had slipped the letter into the book, so she would find it after the train had left. This was exactly the reason she adored Evienne. No one had ever made her feel so completely appreciated. Her hands smoothed the paper and her heart filled as she read the words her friend had written to her.

19 December 1928

My Dearest Madalane,

I think of you before a single line of color is drawn to the morning horizon, and I see you in the silver belly of every moon. The chilled air curls inside me while the warm sun dances on my face; it is hard for me to decide which I should resist and which I should love—to feel the cold or to feel the warmth in the shadow I cast. Today I wanted to run into the shadows.

Growing from a crack in the barrier walls of the Seine are weeping tiny flowers—How can life last in the beginning of a cold winter? Is it the well of the Seine that replenishes the delicate rosy cups? Is it the mysteries that Paris desires to spread in the ropey vines with an unquenchable thirst for our pleasure?

My choices have been questionable to some—I was too radical for the Female Art School in London and encountered a debacle of fighting at the Slade School of Art. The subordinate position of existing in a co-educated university infuriated me; my free spirit claimed its path when I decided to move to Paris. The air of Paris seduced me, filled me with a home, and allowed me the temporary position at the Académie Julian.

Seasons came and left and my education became her cobblestone streets and wooden benches, haggard faces, and bartered wine; Paris continues to nourish my soul. Each change in my solitary life created more vulnerabilities—am I worthy of bringing my vulgarities to your world? Where your world contains caring family and friends, mine only holds distant memories of a mother and father, sisters and a brother.

In the quiet of my mind, I thought of my friend Charles' painting of Cupid and Psyche. Where Cupid withered for the love of Psyche, I fought in art school and was scarcely able to continue my love of painting. I worry for your mortal beauty, your kindness, your delicate nature. I pray I will not lead you to the harsh reality of my life, my barren contributions to a folly of fallen attempts.

Now, I am consumed by my life as a painter and when I look to you, I am mesmerized by the subtle changes of your life, Madalane. The texture of your hair, the way the hazel of your eyes blends from gold to green. Madalane—each hue houses a secret of its own. Madalane—thoughts of you consume me. Please embrace your family, breathe in the safety

of knowing you are loved, be filled by the overflowing well
of comfort and the hearts around you.
   I will miss your smile and during our separation, we
should look for the sun and have faith that its warmth is
from one another's arms.
Forever,
Evienne

Another screech from the train going around the bend punctuated the last few words of the letter. Madalane's heart was full
and happy. She slipped the letter into the middle of the book
and pulled the book to her chest. She would read the letter again
and again; she would read it every day, but for now, she wanted
to revel in the sweetness of Evienne's intention. The little girl
sitting next to her had whispered something to her mother and
they both got up to leave the cabin. As they left, the mother
looked back to Madalane and quickly spoke, "Please feel free to
take the window seat if you would like. My daughter is going to
nap when we return."

Feeling like this was a gift from the universe, Madalane slid
over to stare out of the window. A few grubby fingerprints left by
the child did not mar the austere beauty of the countryside that
flew by. She reached into her purse and pulled out the small box
of candy that Evienne had given her. She offered the box to the
remaining woman who shook her head politely refusing. Relieved,
Madalane pulled one cherry candy out of the box and returned
the box to her purse. Slowly she unwrapped the cellophane, relishing the sound of crinkling as she freed the candy. Popping it
into her mouth, she immediately felt the explosion of cherry on
her tongue. She watched the fields roll by and turned the candy
around in her mouth. It was slowly dissolving; the sweetness
coated her tongue and she surreptitiously licked her lips to feel
the stickiness hold onto her mouth. She pushed the candy under
her tongue, holding it in place and feeling the sweetness drip

down her throat. It was an exquisite taste and it reminded her of Evienne's disarming appeal.

The train flew past more pastures, harvested before the winter's wind had come, crows pecking at the bare ground, hoping for sustenance. She opened her book and stared at the crisp white sketch paper that Evienne used as stationary. She didn't need to re-read the letter now; there would be time enough for that later. The candy was getting smaller as she rolled it around in her mouth, pensively considering her friend's actions. Until this day, Madalane had felt like she had foisted herself on Evienne. Now, the sweetness of the candy reminded her that Evienne had done this for her. Evienne had written this letter for her and hidden it in her book for her. As the last sliver of candy melted in the heat of her mouth, she smiled at the barren landscape.

Chapter 29

Sarah peeled out of the driveway and floored the gas pedal through the quiet suburban streets of her mother's Chestnut Hill neighborhood. It could not have gone worse if she had tried. Why was her mother so unreasonable? David was the only one who could get her to compromise. Remembering she had left her laundry basket in the middle of the living room, Sarah slammed on the breaks as she approached a stop sign.

Sarah was stuck. She knew she had to apologize to her mother, but she wasn't ready to yet. She didn't want to talk to anyone. She didn't want to see anyone. She didn't want to think about anything.

Slowly she took her foot off the brake and headed through the stop sign, driving at a much more legal pace. She decided to head to the bookstore. She could stay there until they closed at 11pm and read some trashy novel without spending any money. She hoped that her mother would be asleep before she came back to house.

* * *

Stella stretched her hand to the empty side of the bed realizing again that David was not there. She got the god-awful feeling in her stomach as the high-speed train of memories emerged from a dark tunnel. She rolled over and listened for the birds, hoping this would calm her mind. It was so quiet in her house. Stella called Granger's name ready to give him his morning scratch, but she didn't hear his shuffle towards her; she looked over and he was not in his bed. She had a curious feeling and then she smelled inviting scent of coffee. David always made the coffee in the morning; she was still getting used to brewing her own since he left. Realization hit-Sarah was making the coffee this morning.

She lay back in the bed and thought about the fight with Sarah. It was a game of Jeopardy having a twenty year old. It was hard enough to know the correct answers, and even more difficult to figure out the right questions. She hoped Sarah's night gave her time to think about her words and actions.

Stella pulled herself out of bed, remembering a dream she had had last night. She was walking the streets of a small town and looking into doors and windows of people's homes. Life seemed to be normal to the people living in the row homes although despite many attempts, no one acknowledged her presence. She was invisible. As she walked around the town, she came to an outside café where many customers were enjoying their meals, engaged in their conversations; still no one spoke to her and there sitting at one of the tables was her own mother. She was properly dressed, posture straight and legs crossed; her purse precisely placed in her lap. Stella stood next to a giant green fan palm that framed the sidewalk restaurant and tried to initiate contact with her mother, while she wondered why she had not been invited to the gathering. Eventually Stella walked to her mother's table and went so far as to touch her shoulder and her own mother turned and asked in an ambivalent tone, "What is your question dear?" It was as if she was a stranger asking for directions.

She opened the bathroom door and dropped her hand over David's robe that was hanging on a hook. The robe smelled like his cologne. She buried her face into the terry cloth of the robe and cried. She thought it would be easy to be alone and now she felt the vacancy of her husband. How he would talk her through these fights with Sarah.

She wondered if she was treating Sarah the same way her mother had treated her. Stella's opinions and choices put a gray cloud over the appearance of the perfect party her mother threw. Stella was a disgrace to her mother until she married David. He took the responsibility of her daughter's life and mistakes, making her mother's conversations effortlessly picturesque at her bridge game. In her mother's eyes, David was the shining prince who saved her daughter from a life of bad choices and single-parent poverty.

Stella resolved that she was not going to ignore her daughter's choices as her own mother ignored and dismissed her choices. If her daughter needed money, she would find out what it was for and then decide if she should give it to her.

The day she found out she was pregnant with Sarah was the day she made the conscious decision to change herself. She was going to be a better mother than her own and not repeat the same mistakes.

Chapter 30

Madalane's Parents' House, January 1929

Madalane sat at a small table in her parent's sitting room. It was more than a week after Christmas and the only letter she had received from Evienne lay open in front of her. Her eyes dropped to it again, reading and rereading the lines that held no affection or emotion. The writing was scrawled and barely legible as if Evienne had hurriedly dashed off the letter to fulfill an obligation. She had waited so patiently for a letter to arrive and now that it had, it felt even worse than the waiting. What had happened to her Evienne?

1 January 1929

Dearest Madalane,
  Bonne Annee!
  Glistening raindrops garland the bare avenue, Parisians bustle by exhausted by the festivities of the holiday, and sadly, my Paris slumbers in your absence. I've taken up rooms with Charles; the company is suitable.

My muse has turned into a frozen statue perched on a marble pedestal, I pray for your return.
Forever,
Evienne

She read the lines again, feeling the tears blur the hastily formed words. Evienne had moved in with Charles. Obviously, this was a rejection of her invitation. She had hoped that if Evienne refused her, that it would be a gentle, regret-filled no. Instead, the no was casually added in a vague mention in a letter squeezed between Bonne Annee and see you in a few weeks. Madalane felt ill—she was heartsick, tired, and alone.

Charles was such a cad and Evienne often railed against his treatment of his models. He seduced all of them and then tossed them away when he finished his canvas. Madalane was bewildered by the idea of Evienne falling for Charles' charms. Evienne had once alluded to being immune to Charles' seductive powers, but she had not made it clear why. Perhaps they had been in a relationship that had ended, but now had resurfaced. Madalane covered her face with her hand, trying to block out the images of Charles possessing Evienne.

The harder she tried to make her mind blank, picture after picture assailed Madalane's mind. Sadness and hurt transformed into anger and she stood up, grasping the letter in her fist. Storming into the backroom her parents had given her during her infrequent visits home, she stored it under the pillow of the cot pushed up against the pantry shelf. Her old bedroom had been given to her imbecile cousin. Years ago, on her first visit home, she had found her meager possessions packed up in a few boxes and her cousin's belongings scattered throughout her former bedroom. Her mother had haughtily pointed to the pantry behind the kitchen, indicating her new status in the household. She was a visitor; she no longer lived there. Her mother had brooked no argument, clearly stating that her cousin earned his keep and should be given a room of his own.

Wrapping an old gray scarf around her neck and shrugging on a heavy coat, Madalane fled from the stifling environment of her parent's house. She walked through the town with her head down, avoiding eye contact with the neighbors who had known her since she was a child. At the end of the street, she briefly hesitated, considering if she should go back to her house. No one was waiting for her there. Her father and cousin were at the shop and her mother was at the church, arranging the spring calendar with the priest and the other women of the town.

She decided to keep walking. It was bitterly cold, and her coat was an inadequate barrier to the chill winds, but walking felt good. She mirthlessly wondered if she could walk until she made it to Paris. This visit home had been worse than usual. Instead of her mother's general indifference, her mother seemed hostile and annoyed with her. The first few nights, as they sat around the dinner table, she had mentioned the wonderful art that the street artists created. She had planned to mention her budding friendship with one of the painters, but her mother's horrified look stopped her in mid-sentence.

Her mother's voice crystallized in her head, "Have you been associating with bohemians?" The way her mother said the word, she might as well have been saying prostitutes.

Stammering, she backtracked, "No, I meant that the art you seen on the street is almost as good as the art you see in the museums."

Her mother gave a non-committal grunt as she frowned. "I certainly hope you are not wasting your time and my money gallivanting around Paris when you should be studying."

"No, of course not." Madalane felt the weight of her mother's disapproval settle over the dining table as she returned to interrogating Emile about the day's receipts. Her mother's hair had grayed slightly and her skin was less firm, but her pinched stare and tight voice were exactly the same as it had been six years earlier when she had been sent away.

She had spent a few days at the shop with her father. Ostensibly, she was graciously giving her cousin a break from the day-to-day grind of being a shopkeeper, but really, the thought of being with her mother all day felt unbearably stifling. Her cousin had been thrilled with the break and he had gone home for a few days before Christmas to visit with his mother and father. Madalane had angrily wondered if his bedroom had been given away in his absence.

Working with her father again at the shop had been bittersweet. The neighbors and her friends from grammar school had stopped in to say hello and find out about life in Paris. Some of the older women were fascinated that Madalane was so brave to live alone in Paris while others thought it was shockingly inappropriate that Madalane's parents had been so cavalier in letting her live in the city without a proper chaperone. Cheerfully she deflected their criticism while deftly appreciating the compliments about her independence. Unfortunately, her cousin had returned the day after Christmas and had once again reclaimed his spot behind the counter.

A few of her old friends had invited her to dinner, which she had gratefully accepted. Most of their lives had changed little. They were engaged or waiting to be engaged and they were only marginally interested in her life as a student in Paris. They preferred to discuss their impending weddings and their plans for their own homes. Listening to the minutiae of their plans was infinitely better than feeling the omnipresent pressure of her mother's disapproval and resentment.

As her walk took her further and further from the town center, she felt the gloom of her parent's house drop away. The town had given way to a clearing that led to a cluster of woods. As a child, she had been frightened of the tight darkness that the forest had represented, but now it felt like freedom. Walking another kilometer, she came to small stream. Sitting on a downed tree, she watched as a few twigs and leaves meandered along the icy water. The quiet was jarring for Madalane; having lived in the city for a few months, she was used to the raucousness of a city street. Even living in town, she was used to noise infiltrating her consciousness at all times. Here, though, it was completely still. She knew if she screamed out her frustration, no one would hear her. As tempted as she was to let her emotions cacophonously erupt, she felt it would be just be futile to listen to her own dissatisfaction echo from tree limb to tree limb.

She pulled her coat closer around her body. She was freezing cold, but this moment was the first moment she had felt sane since she had gotten off the train. Closing her eyes, she imagined Evienne sitting in a warm café with Charles by her side. Maybe his arm was slung around her shoulder or perhaps they were just sitting close to one another. It was not in Evienne's nature to express physical affection and Madalane could not imagine Charles being too keen to identify himself as her lover. Madalane doubted whether Charles would ever be someone's exclusive lover. Evienne's face, serene and somber, swam in front of Madalane's eyes. How could such a perfectly lovely woman allow herself to be part of Charles' harem of women?

Tears pricked at her eyes; the coldness turning them from hot to icy in seconds. Madalane wanted to go back to Paris. For what reason, she wasn't sure. If nothing else, she could see Charles and Evienne together as a couple. That would cure her of her infatuation with Evienne. At the same moment, she never wanted to go back to Paris again. She never wanted to see Evienne or her dorm or the school ever again. She would beg her parents to allow her to stay. She would marry the first boy who asked her and she would forget this foolishness. She would disappear from Paris, from Evienne's mind, from the world she had grown to love over the past four months.

She wiped her face with her hand. She was chilled to the bone. A sly voice in her head whispered that she could sit out here for the rest of the day and night and there would be no more problems. She could marry the coldness seeping into her body and not wake up. Would God understand her reasons? Would she be committed to an eternity of damnation to pay for one sin? Miserably she pushed her head back and stared at the darkening sky. Praying to God for an answer to a question she didn't understand, she waited, watching the steam of her breath come out in short bursts. A shadow crossed over the treetops and she saw a falcon catching the breeze with calm patience and seemed to float indulgently before diving down a few yards from the stream. Snatching up a field mouse in its talons, the falcon paid Madalane no mind as she looped back into the sky and disappeared.

Disconcerted at the closeness of the predator, Madalane shook out her skirts and headed back the way she had come. Had Charles swooped down on Evienne while she was vulnerable and missing Madalane? Is that what God was trying to tell her. Confused yet determined, Madalane was beginning to see that hope was not lost. Surely, when she returned to Paris, she could convince Evienne of the rapacious nature of Charles' love. He would use her and then discard her as he did all the others.

As much as Madalane wanted to ignore the ambivalence of Evienne's letter, there was something nagging at her; she would write her back as soon as she got back to the house. She would write her a letter filled with love and longing. She would make sure that Evienne knew what it felt like to be loved by someone with a pure heart.

The walk back to town was long. Madalane was surprised at how deep she had gone into the woods. Her fear of the mysterious woods had vanished in the face of her misery. Looking back at the area where the falcon had snatched its prey, she memorized the spot. She would remember this moment where she had created her own destiny and not merely acquiesced to the demands around her. She would neither be the falcon, nor the mouse. She would find another way—a way that was gentle and kind.

An hour later, Madalane was back at her desk re-reading the letter that Evienne had written her. The sun was almost gone for the day and the chill that had enveloped her during her walk was slowly dissipating. Her father and cousin would be home soon. Her mother was already home when she returned from the woods. She scarcely glanced at her daughter as Madalane moved through the kitchen to hang up her coat and retrieve the letter from her temporary quarters.

Resolution was easy; the hard part was putting pen to paper to express to Evienne how she felt. She thought of the first day she had seen Evienne, selling her paintings amongst the others. It seemed like years had passed except it had only been a few months. Evienne had changed her life. She had given her a life that she didn't know she could have. Now she needed to exercise her will.

4 January 1929

My Dearest Evienne—
   I wish you great joy and felicitations for the New Year. I can feel in my heart that 1929 will be a year of great happiness for us both.

Madalane stared at the words. They seemed so horribly inadequate and impersonal, but she resolved to keep writing and perhaps out of the miasma of feelings, something of quality would emerge and speak to Evienne's soul.

   I received your letter with the utmost happiness and appreciation. I have missed you more than….

Madalane stopped and stared out the small window in front of her. How could she express how much she missed her when it felt like she had lost a limb? How could she tell her that each minute away from her was excruciating? How could she write that each morning, she mentally crossed off another day on the calendar knowing that each cross would bring her closer to returning to Paris and Evienne? Evienne was skittish and Madalane worried that if she expressed herself too plainly, it would frighten her. On the other hand, she didn't want to be too mild. Evienne had to understand, no feel, the sheer desperation that Madalane felt without her.

I received your letter with the utmost happiness and appreciation. I have missed you more than the moon misses the beauty of the night. Being with my parents has made me realize that my home is in Paris now. Paris has become my mother and you, my dear friend, are my sister. You once told me that Paris keeps you warm even in the coldest weather and I truly understand that now. I don't belong in this town as much as you wouldn't be happy anywhere but in Paris.

Madalane paused again, reading the words she had laboriously pulled from her heart. Evienne's letters were so magical and the words flowed across the page as the Seine followed its path through the city. Her own words seemed stilted and forced, but still she continued writing.

I watched a falcon fly through the empty sky this afternoon. She was fierce and free and she reminded me so much of you. I watched her until she was no longer visible on the horizon and I prayed that she would invigorate my soul to endure another few weeks with my family. I think God sent the falcon to remind me that your spirit lives inside of me, even when we are apart.

Hearing noise from the kitchen, Madalane realized that her father and cousin must have arrived home. She would have to finish the letter later after dinner. Hurrying to avoid being asked why she was idle, she gathered up Evienne's letter and her own half-written letter and hid them in the book she carried with her at all times. Each and every one of Evienne's letters resided within the pages of this book. She almost left the small cache of letters in her dorm, but she knew Madame would snoop in her absence and she couldn't risk any of her precious letters being callously examined.

After dinner, elbow deep in hot soapy water, Madalane considered her unfinished letter. What was the point of the letter? It had seemed so clear a few hours before and now she was lost again in the swamp of words that crowded her mind. She just needed to finish it and send it off in the post the next morning. If Evienne was lost to her, then so be it.

Retrieving her book and the letters, she perched on the side of the cot. She read the words that she had emphatically placed on the paper; they already felt foreign to her mind. She needed to be frank and if she scared Evienne then that was the consequence she would have to live with. Gripping the pen tightly, she continued writing:

I miss you Evienne. Each day I am away from you feels like an eternity. Surrounded by friends and family, I have never felt so alone. I only want to be back in Paris with you, walking along the Seine and exploring my new life. Each year I have lived away from my family, I have detached myself from their lives and vice versa. I am barely recognizable to them as they are to me. When I close my eyes at night, I see only your face. I see your profile in every shadow and your warm smile in every sunbeam. An hour doesn't go by when my thoughts don't turn to you and how you would find something amusing or appalling in equal measure.

I hope your New Year's celebration was memorable. I wait to hear every detail of the debauchery and decadence

of our wonderful city. I am counting the days until I return.
Madalane

Emotionally exhausted, Madalane stretched out upon the cot and fell into a deep slumber. It was done. She had cast her net on the sea and now it was up to the fates to decide if Evienne would be waiting for her when she returned to Paris.

Chapter 31

Sarah heard her mother's footsteps on the stairs. She was ready to make nice. She didn't want to go back to Virginia with the terrible feeling that she left with last night. She looked up as her mother walked in the door of the kitchen, "Hi mom."

"Coffee smells good. Hand me the cup you bought me for Mother's Day last year; I love that one."

Sarah winced as she poured her mother's coffee in her special mother's day mug. She had bought it at the drug store on her way home from college. She had felt badly about the lameness of the gift, but clearly her mother had liked it. Looking at her mother with familiar eyes, Sarah noticed that Stella was wearing the pajamas with the sheep on them under a light robe. They had been a gift from David; he was more whimsical than her mother was. There were many occasions where she would have to convince David that his latest flight of fancy was just not the right thing for her mother. She had been asked by Stella to keep an eye on the various gifts he would buy after the notorious singing-fish birthday gift.

"I'm really sorry mom....about yesterday. I didn't mean what I said." The words came out hesitantly at first, but then in a rush. She felt a wave of regret as she remembered their fight.

"Sarah, baby."

"I know mom...I was so wrong yesterday. I feel a little over-whelmed right now because I want to tell you something." Sarah watched her mother's face go pale and hurried to reassure her.

"No, it's good news. It's great news actually. I have been offered a paid internship." Sarah hesitated. She knew her mother would be thrilled, but how could she explain her own ambivalence. "It would be in Europe for the summer—Italy, France, Holland and England. I would work in different museums; I would be doing stuff for their photography exhibits."

Smiling proudly, Stella exclaimed, "Honey this is great news. Why didn't you tell me about it before?" Sarah was silent and she winced as Stella looked into her daughter's eyes. "What is it?"

"It's just that I'm not sure if I really want to go away for three months. I mean I know it's a great opportunity, but still...that's a long time to be away."

"Why are you worried about being away for three months?" Stella knew that she was setting herself up for the Autumn saga, but she wanted Sarah to know she was supportive of her feelings. She looked down to stir sugar into her coffee.

Sarah knew she had painted herself into a corner, but she needed to talk about it. Her friends were sick of her constantly discussing Autumn. They had tuned out and only offered the most benign advice these days. She had, she realized too late, burned a few bridges for her relationship.

"It's um...Autumn. She doesn't want me to go. She said she would not be willing to put her life on hold while I go off gal-livanting around Europe." Autumn's words had echoed through her mind often enough that she knew them verbatim.

"Oh honey, I will say from experience that if a person truly loves you, they would not set limits or restrictions on you and your choices in life. They should want you to grow, and you going to Europe to work in museums is not gallivanting."

Stella saw the pain in Sarah's eyes. Sarah appeared really to love this girl and separation was a challenge for her. "Baby, the thing about choice is you only have yourself at this time to consider, take the question to your heart and know the choice is yours. Would you regret not going because of another person's demands on you? When September comes and you stayed home, would you regret not accepting the internship? How will you feel if you never get an opportunity like this again?"

In her heart, Sarah knew her mother was right, but still the nagging fear remained fixed in her heart. "I know what you are saying, but what if I'm wrong. What if Autumn is my destiny? If I walk away from her, will I ever get the chance to feel this much love ever again? She is going on a ski trip at Christmas and I am terrified I will lose her." Sarah's voice strangled over the few last words. She knew Autumn wasn't perfect, but she couldn't imagine her world without Autumn being there. It made her ache even to consider the possibility her girlfriend being with someone else.

Stella measured her words carefully, knowing she was treading on sensitive ground, "Being in love with a person is not to live in fear of them leaving us. We share in that person's life and walk a similar path with them. If you are meant to be together, an ocean won't matter...or a ski trip."

Sarah listened to her mother's words. When her mother gave advice, it always sounded so reasonable, so practical, and so eminently logical. How could she explain the feeling of dread that overwhelmed her when they fought and Autumn disappeared for the day? Sarah felt so weak around Autumn; she needed her, craved her at times. If she went to Europe and Autumn moved on to another girl or even back to her old girlfriend, Sarah knew she would die of a broken heart. Her mother would never understand something like that.

She looked at her mother who was sipping her coffee and watching her. Sarah looked down at her own coffee mug and quietly asked, "Would you be disappointed in me if I chose to stay in Virginia for the summer?"

"It is not me who would be disappointed; it would be you who would have to live with your choice. Stella hoped she would be able reach Sarah's sensible side.

Sarah started to feel edgy and knew that if they continued the conversation, it would get ugly again. She sighed and realized that ultimately her mother made a good point. Some tiny rational part of her mind was thumping her on the forehead, asking her if she had lost her mind. Three months in Europe versus fighting with Autumn over money in Virginia.

"I don't know mom. I know I have to think about it some more before I make any decisions." Sarah poured herself more coffee and reached for her mother's cup. "Are you ready for more?"

Stella understood the implication of Sarah's words. They were both ready for a break.

Chapter 32

Paris, December 1928

It was all Evienne could do to keep her mind on task. It was a week since Madalane had left and she would not be back to the university until well after the New Year. Looming over her shoulder was the feeling of something missing; she kept trying to convince herself it was the lack of family during the holiday season, but this was not her first Christmas alone. She did hear from her sisters, they were kind enough to send paints and brushes. Usually this would make Evienne ecstatic, but the paints still sat in their untouched box. Evienne looked at the paint and thought of attempting a portrait, but the inspiration was not there.

The lull after Christmas was bitter for sales. Most people were away visiting or were staying warm and cozy inside because of the cold weather. Spending so much time in the damp squat was nerve racking for Evienne. Jean, the artist in the squat who desired her, had an ego the size of the Eiffel Tower and she had had just about enough of him and his unwanted attention. She needed the companionship of a woman, the conversation of a woman. She was pleading inside for something, asking for change, but she wasn't sure what that change should be.

Evienne had thought if she talked to her friend Charles, he could get Jean off her back, but it seemed they were on the same team—Charles had told Evienne that Jean was harmless and to let him have his fun. Evienne was exhausted and charred from the winter, especially from the constant harassment by Jean wanting to share her bed. He was always touching her long brown plait, dropping crude remarks about wrapping his hands in it.

All Evienne could think of was Madalane. She was the last thing she thought of before she went to sleep and the first thought she had when she woke. There were times when she thought she would feel Madalane coming towards her and turn to find only the wind. The mere sensation would take her breath. She would wake in the morning thinking she was lying next to her, yet the small cot was holding only her. The thought of Madalane gave her life happiness. The thought of her not being in Paris was chest crushing. Evienne's thoughts started to suffocate her, she wanted to walk the streets, feel the icy air, and remember why she lived in Paris.

Evienne put on her father's old cream cable sweater and overcoat; she adjusted the blue scarf on her neck that Madalane had given to her. Smiling, she realized she only took the knitted scarf off to bathe. She loved it; it reminded her of a place she could call home. She unlocked the chain on her door and looked in the direction of the noise of Jean and his friends—they were distracted with a card game. She wanted to go unnoticed, slip away into the day, and enjoy the tiny bits of sun. She passed unnoticed through the squat to flaneur the streets. Maybe she could find a face to sketch or a conversation.

The cold air chilled her cheeks as she strolled towards the river. She would cut down the side streets to shield her slim frame from the wind. The bare trees seemed to salute the chill of the bank and the glorious sun that had not been out for days, shone with a brilliance that she had almost forgotten. Evienne was happy to walk with her faint shadow. She leaned on the stonewall of the

Seine and contemplated the water's cold sadness. Evienne looked at her hands and saw the red chap of winter. She pushed them in her overcoat pockets and found the remnants of the baguette that Madalane had put there before she left on the train. Evienne took it from her pocket and ate it now. She thought about the morning Madalane left and the hot tea as the crunch of the stale bread echoed in her thoughts.

Evienne yawned because sleep was sparse at the squat. Her long walk tricked her mind into thinking she would be seeing Madalane; every afternoon held the same longing. Evienne watched the sun start to sink and the gray begin to loom over her head. She thought maybe she should try to sell although people were scarce on the streets. It was the tiny bit of sun that tricked her into spring. The winter was still firmly planted. She should paint she thought as she yawned, heading back to Rue du Gril; she would sleep the afternoon away and be one day closer to Madalane's return to Paris.

Evienne was vaguely aware of sounds as she slept on her narrow cot. She heard voices— jeering and loud and she tried to ignore them as her body floated back into sleep. A loud crash slammed against her consciousness and her eyes flew open. Jean was staring down at her from the foot of the bed, leering at her and smelling of cheap whiskey. Her brain fogged with sleep couldn't understand why he was there and she glanced around and realized that he had four equally drunk friends with him. The smell coming off the men made her want to vomit. Her door broken, hanging on one hinge made her panic.

In a loud, triumphant voice, Jean sneered, "Bitch, I'm going to teach you how to be a real woman today." The other men laughed.

Evienne's body reacted before her mind registered what was happening. She leapt off the cot and moved to bolt from the room. As she pushed one of the men out of the way, she felt an excruciating tug on her braid. Jean had grabbed her plait and pulled her back to him. The other men closed in around her, grabbing her arms and pinioning them behind her back; the smell of stale cigarettes, vomit and whiskey permeated her throat. She gagged as Jean pressed his mouth onto hers. Feeling his tongue worming into her mouth, she bit down, hard. Against her chest, she felt him flinch and he jerked away, slapping her viciously across the face. She felt the tingling of blood rush to her cheek as her heart throbbed in wild panic against her ribs.

Jean stepped back and lit a cigarette, staring hard at Evienne's flushed face while addressing his friends. "The putain likes to fight like a man. I think it's because she thinks she is a man, yes?" The men laughed and Evienne felt her arms held tighter. Jean continued, this time addressing her. "You are not so pretty. In fact, in this light, you are quite ugly. But the red in your cheek from my hand is quite lovely. Maybe you need some more. Perhaps some violet too?" He chuckled as he drew smoke into his lungs and without warning, backhanded her other cheek.

The pain was shocking and Evienne felt it through her whole body. She was tempted to say something belligerent but she held her tongue, hoping the beating would end soon. Leaving the cigarette dangling between his lips, Jean motioned for the men to continue holding the young woman. He smashed his fist into the upper part of her nose, between her eyes. Evienne staggered, seeing stars. She heard laughter and Jean explaining, in clinical detail, how a boxer had taught him that move to disable an opponent. He resumed slapping the young woman, right cheek, left cheek, and right, left. Evienne allowed her face to move with the pressure of his hand, knowing that resistance would make the bruises deeper, and they would take longer to go away. Somewhere in the clouds of her mind, she hoped that her face would be healed by the time Madalane returned.

Blood flowed freely from her nose and mouth. Her eyes were so swollen, she could barely see out of them. She had lost count how many times Jean had slapped her. She wasn't even sure if she was conscious anymore until she heard Jean coughing and spitting uncontrollably. From the small slit of her swollen eyelids, she saw that the cigarette had burned down to embers between his lips. Thankful for a small reprieve from the relentless pain, she warily watched him. Jean spit a few times on her cot and wiped his mouth. "Now, that is a beautiful woman, don't you think gentlemen?"

The four men laughed nervously. The young woman was barely standing on her own and somewhere inside them seeped the knowledge that this wasn't right.

"Put her on the bed and keep holding her. You will each have your turn when I'm done my lessons."

The men pulled the young woman to the cot. Evienne realized the enormity of what was going to happen and she began to struggle. The men pushed her onto the cot face down and looked expectantly at their leader.

Jean tried to pull her pants down, but her belt held secure and he snarled at his collaborators, "Turn the bitch over. I want to bite her tits."

The four men looked to each other for guidance. Unsure, but committed, one man grabbed her head and pressed his thumbs into the raw flesh of her cheeks. The other three men picked her up and turned her over. The pain from the man's fingers pushed against her face almost made her pass out. She couldn't breathe through her nose; it was broken and filled with blood. Barely able to open her eyes, she could see Jean standing over her smoking another cigarette, maliciously smiling at her.

Making sure that each limb was held down by a friend, he leaned over and ripped open her shirt, revealing her breasts. He took the cigarette from his mouth and extinguished it on the skin above her left breast. He muttered viciously as the pain seared through her body, "I will leave a mark on your heart that you will never forget."

He tossed the cigarette onto the floor and bit down hard on the top of her right breast. The pain was horrific and Evienne felt an overwhelming desire to sleep, to give up, to abandon hope. She felt more bites as Jean navigated around her chest, moving up to her neck. Tears sprang unbidden from her bruised eyes. Through blurry eyes, she stared at the ceiling. The paint was peeling; her brain noted the irony of that. A painter living in a room with peeling paint—the whole experience had taken on a surreal experience as she felt herself leave the wretchedness of her body. Detached from the experience, Evienne wondered if this is how it would end; such a ridiculous way for her life to close. Where was the nobility in this act? Was this the truth of her life? As that thought entered her mind, Evienne imagined Madalane's return to Paris. Madalane would not understand giving up. Madalane would fight until her last breath.

Deep in the tortured well of her soul, she felt a small spark of energy. Jean had backed away from her neck and was fumbling at her belt buckle. He released the catch and tried to pull the leather from around her waist. Wrapped twice around her body, it only tightened the more he tugged on it. He swore in frustration. His distraction turned into her opportunity. One of the men holding her legs had moved to help him remove her belt and with her free leg, she kicked towards him as hard as she could. She caught Jean squarely in the crotch and his face seemed to drain of blood immediately. The other men were motionless, shocked at the intensity of her action. She kicked again, this time against Jean's chest and she heard the whoosh of air leaving his lungs as he fell back, off the cot, and against the floor. She couldn't see him but she heard the gasping. Her arms, which had been held securely against the cot, were pulled back towards the floor by the two men. She felt the pull and then pop of tendons pushed beyond their normal limits. The other two men struggled to gain control of her loose leg as she wildly kicked about, randomly hitting the men as she continued to struggle.

The men were screaming at each other. Evienne heard the string of obscenities hurled towards her, but she kept fighting back. Her wrists were on fire; her face was burning with pain, yet it felt like she had some control back. After what seemed like minutes, the man who had lost control of her leg threw himself on top of her lower body, effectively staunching her kicks. The four men held her down, but didn't move.

Jean was still collapsed on the floor. Evienne's chest heaving and the pain in her body exploding, she desperately tried to think of a way to escape.

"Hello boys. Am I interrupting your party?"

A sound filtered into the room. Was that Charles' voice? Or some random fantasy her mind had created to deal with the inevitability of her situation?

In a nonchalant voice, as if walking into a gang rape was an everyday occurrence for him, he continued talking, "Ev—I hate to ruin your little party here, but you promised to come have dinner with us."

Oh God, Evienne felt like weeping, it was Charles. Through the smears of blood blanketing her eyes, she saw Charles standing in the doorway, casually smoking a cigarette with a few horrified faces behind him.

The four men released Evienne immediately without a word. Charles entered the small room, stepping over Jean and offered his hand to his friend. Evienne's whole body was wracked with most intense pain; she knew she had to force herself to get up and get out. She lifted her hand to grasp Charles' hand and the pain shot through her like a lightning bolt. Nonetheless, she held on, as if for dear life, standing up on unsteady feet.

Moving automatically through the room, she heard the men move to Jean's prone body. Whispering to Charles, she gasped, "My bag, my art box." He nodded and reached for both and handed them off to a woman standing in the arch of the doorway.

As they walked, Charles grabbed her coat and gently maneuvered her towards the steps beyond the doorway of the set of small rooms. Once beyond earshot of the room, Evienne stopped, breathing heavily with exertion. She turned to Charles and said, "Thank you."

He looked at her. Her face was disfigured with swelling, purple and bloody. Her shirt still opened revealed bite marks and the burn; her hand, still held in his, was misshapen and cold. His bravado in the room left him as he gathered her to him. His kindness, his momentary retreat from indifference, was too much for Evienne. She leaned against his taller body and she just let go. She passed out, terribly aware of the agony she had just endured.

* * *

Evienne was pulling a huge fish in onto her little dingy. Her burly fisherman father was standing behind her whispering, "You will overcome this burden, my girl; you will overcome the weight of this. You must be strong and believe in yourself."

Something from far away was slamming into her mind. She jolted in fear, trying to open her swollen eyes. Her arms flew up to protect her face. Searing pain in her wrists, pain demanding her breath, her chest had pain, her stomach had pain, pain that left her exposed to yet another hell she had once visited. The swelling burned in her eyes. She could barely breath, her heart was pounding and sweat began to form in cold beads at her forehead. She was the fish with a glassy stare, slowly dying on the drying wood of the dock.

Evienne forced her eyes to open. The room was dimly lit by a candle in the far corner. The window offered a faint shadow of morning. She recognized the sketches in Charles's studio. Her breath shortened making her chest heave. Her eyes burned with the salt of tears. Whimpers of sound escaped with each uncontrolled breath; she cried until she could not remember who she was and she fell back into unconsciousness.

Evienne tried to shake herself out of her dream world. Her lips were peeling, parched, and dry. She tried to sit up, forcing her hands to the sides of her prone and stiff body. Pain from her flexed wrists seared up her arm, crashing in the middle of her chest. She screamed out, the unfamiliar sound of pain waking her. She felt a light cloth cover her eyes. Her mind asked if it was a shroud. Sometimes, a cold breeze would drag her into a hazy reality. Kicking and screaming, "Bastards. You can't hurt me." Fighting off her own body as it attacked her; her pain matched the blood surging through her temporal veins. Her head would slowly roll back and forth until she was lost in the waves of yet another dream.

Slime coated her hands as she tried to unhook the seething eel from her one-inch hook. It had been a good fishing day as she looked out over the vast harbor. The eel slapped against her sandy feet. The water shimmered silver in the morning light, it made her want to dive into the cooling clean ripples. Evienne knew it would not be easy to unlatch the prehistoric creature. She watched its clicking jaw gasp for water. As she tried to grasp its head, the eel's tail wrapped his wild body around her arm, its tail growing and wrapping around her neck leaving a coating of slime, covering her body. She fought to get away, to maneuver her frame from the body of the eel. The serpent was strong, consuming her. She was fighting for breath. She was screaming for help. Her younger sister watched in the distance as Evienne called out to her for help, but she did not answer. Evienne stared at her sister until her face transformed into the old woman she had painted cleaning the church steps. The elderly woman's face spoke to her. "You have to wake up my child. You have to finish cleaning the church steps." The old woman walked towards Evienne, her blue eyes burning into her as she slipped the eel and the slime from her and settled her into a warm bath.

"Evienne you have to wake up," the familiar scent of smoke filled Evienne's nostrils. Her tongue was stuck to the roof of her mouth; the voice was familiar as she heard it again. "Ev... You have to wake up." Charles said.

Charles sat near the window, smoking a cigarette, watching the young woman. It was early morning, the sun was strong and its light fell on the young woman's face. He was tempted to retrieve his sketchpad from the table, but his concern for his friend over rode his artistic impulses.

Evienne had slept non-stop for two days. His favorite model, Patrice, had volunteered to keep an eye on the young woman. She had been the one who stood in the doorway behind Charles, horrified at the devastation that had been wrought upon the young woman. Charles had taken over the model's vigil this morning, sending her home with some extra money and a promise to paint her soon.

He heard a low moan from his friend. She seemed to be surfacing from her dream. He urged her to wake, "Ev...you have to wake up." His voice sounded desperate and he tried a lower tone, trying to regain his casual tone. "Ev...don't be a pain in the ass... get up and paint with me."

Evienne moaned louder this time; he knew she was waking up and feeling the pain that coursed through her. He had given her opium for two days, hoping that the narcotic would ease the pain, but now it was time to feel alive again.

Evienne shook her thoughts into place as Charles' voice registered in her mind. "Water." The whispered word from Evienne's mouth were raspy and hoarse, but the voices in her head screamed loudly at her—Get up, get out, you have to get your stuff, you have to go and get Madalane at the train station. Get up, Evienne get up! You will be late!

Charles moved quickly to her side. He picked up the mug of water that Patrice had left there last night. In a stern voice, he commanded, "Evienne, you must lie still or the water will spill."

The girl looked at him in wide-eyed panic. He immediately softened his tone. "Let me help you sit up so you can drink." He sat on the chaise and cradled her shoulders with one hand and he held the cup to her swollen lips with his other. The girl gulped at the water. It spilled along her neck and landed on her pillow, but she did not seem to care. She was aching with thirst. As the cup emptied, Charles withdrew it, promising to fill it again so she could have more. He stepped towards the small table near the window where the water jug sat. He looked out the window, shaking off the horror of the beating his friend had endured.

Turning around, he saw that Evienne was attempting to stand. Her face was locked in a rictus of pain, but he felt an overwhelming urge to laugh at her stubbornness. No one else but Evienne would try to rise in this condition.

"Where do you think you are going?"

"I have to get back to the squat and get my art box. My sisters just sent me paint for Christmas—I have to get it, Charles. I have to get my kit. The pain in her body pushed the tears from Evienne's eyes. She looked down at the source of her most excruciating pain and saw her wrists, disfigured with swelling and shades of blue and green. "Oh God, my hands."

His heart went out to her. As a painter, your eyes and your hands were your truth. "They will heal. But you must keep them wrapped and not put pressure on them. Patrice's sister is a nurse. She came and wrapped your wrists and gave us a balm for your face and the burn on your..." He felt he should not mention the angry bullet hole that the cigarette burn had left on her breast.

He turned to the table again, and pulled out her art box. "We brought the box that night. You wouldn't leave without it. I went back later and got the rest of your belongings." He watched Evienne's body slump back against the chaise. He saw the tension leave her body as he gently laid the art box in her lap. Her hand, purple and green from the bruising, caressed the wooden box and her eyes closed.

Fearing she would go back to sleep, he spoke loudly. "You can't go back there. It is not safe for you in that sty. It is only for pigs and others who wallow in shit."

Evienne's heart throbbed in her chest as her fingers rubbed the wood grain of her box. It was the one consistent thing in her life. It was her heart. Her eyes closed with relief as she agreed with Charles to stay. "Merci, Charles, merci." A line of tear drops rolled down her face.

Charles watched the young woman drift off to sleep again. The anxiety that had been gnawing at him all morning was somewhat abated. He lit another cigarette and watched her sleep. The city was awake and he itched to join the world. Shaking his head, he laughed. He was no hero, nor was he inclined to accept the mantle of heroism although the admiration of the models had certainly benefited his reputation.

He snuffed out the cigarette and tossed it out the window. Evienne would be fine. She would sleep the day away and have no idea that he had left. Maybe he could get one of the girls at the cafe to stop in and check on her. He refilled her mug and placed it next to the chaise. Fleetingly he thought that he should kiss her forehead and whisper in her ear that he was leaving, but what was the use? She knew him. She knew who he was. He would leave her alone; he was good at that.

Chapter 33

Later that afternoon, Stella and Sarah returned home after spending the morning and early afternoon shopping. They had had an easy day. Forgiveness is easy with your child.

As they sat in the kitchen, Sarah remembered who she had seen the night before at the bookstore. "You will never guess who I saw last night."

"Who did you see; wait let me guess, umm..."

"Come on mom." Sarah whined.

"Was it...the man with the white dog? Sarah laughed because all she could think about was the old man shuffling up and down her street with his little dog on a short leash.

"Jesus, is he still alive?"

"Yes, I think so. Come on—tell me who you saw." Stella chuckled reaching for Granger's head.

Sarah leaned forward a bit and whispered conspiratorially "Courtney Kelly."

The wheels in Stella's mind churned as she tried to place the name. "Oh...your babysitter. How is she these days? Did she finish college? What's she doing back here? Visiting?"

"I don't think she finished college. She has a two year old and her boyfriend bailed on her. She had to move home. She seemed fine. We only talked for a couple of minutes. Her two year old was a terror. I think she wiped her nose on my car door and licked my window."

Stella laughed out loud at her daughter's disgusted face.

"I'll tell you this. When I saw Courtney walking down the street with her daughter, it made me realize how hard it must have been for you. I don't think I could have done what you did."

"You do what feels right inside your heart, honey and you were right inside my heart. I loved your father, Sarah; God knows I loved that man." Stella felt the pang of absence settle in the worn spot of her heart. She had always tried to keep the love she had for Victor hidden, but David's absence gave her the freedom to reflect.

Feeling the hair on the back of her neck rise, Sarah listened intently to her mother's story about her real father. Stella barely ever spoke about him. The few conversations they had had about him happened many years prior. She had been eight when Stella had married David and found stability. But Sarah remembered the crappy little apartment they lived in, the bill collectors calling and being left alone in the apartment when Stella couldn't find anyone to watch her while she worked.

"When Victor left, why didn't you move in with grand-mom?"

"My mother told me that she had raised her child. She wanted to live her own life. When I needed her to be a mother or a grandmother, she was busy playing bridge with her friends."

Stella remembered how she would sometimes beg her mom for help. She would not answer her phone or simply not show up when she said she would help. Motherhood was a chore.

"She resented me for letting Victor go. She wanted your father to get a nine-to-five job to take care of us. That might have worked for some, but it would have killed your father. That life would have stolen his dream."

Stella reached for the pen on the counter island and spun the pen as if it were the wheel of destiny, hoping it would validate her choices. She watched the pen slow and come to a stop, pointing at her daughter. "I loved your dad and I was not going to stop him from living his dream any more than I could stop loving you. I loved him enough to let him go. I wanted him to do what he needed to do. Your grandmother used men to take care of her own needs. She chased my own father away when she had the chance to trade up."

Stella had never spoken so honestly about Victor or her own father. Tears were flooding her eyes as she looked at her daughter. Stella could still see Victor's eyes in Sarah. She could still feel the passion of his heart in her daughter's spirit. Sarah was the best of Victor.

Her grandmother's words echoed in Sarah's ears. "Your father was no better than a bum. I always said good riddance to that man." She knew her father had been a musician that her mother had had a relationship with, but she had never heard her mother say that she missed him. Sarah didn't even remember him; he was gone years before she started to develop memories. Her first memory was celebrating her fourth birthday with her mother and the lady who lived next door in their dingy little apartment.

"Did you ever speak to Victor after he left?" It made the young woman nervous to ask that. Even though she liked to pick on David, he was the man who raised her, offered stability and ultimately gave her a father. She hated the idea of her mother betraying David's loyalty and kindness.

"Love is a funny thing. Not always what we think it should be. It would take me weeks to get over something as simple as a post card from him. I felt abandoned. He wrote a few letters to us, but soon he was lost to the other side of the ocean. I felt helpless and lost, and after a few years of sporadic communication, I asked him never to contact us again. It was the hardest thing I ever had to do."

Stella sank into herself. The crack in her heart felt as fresh as it was when she was in her twenties. She wanted to lay her head down and cry, but she knew she had to maintain herself for Sarah's sake. She always did.

"How did you know that you had to let him go?"

Sarah's voice sounded to Stella's ears like she was six years old again and asking why God let her goldfish die.

"I had to choose whether I wanted to live in his shadow or not."

"Do you ever wonder how things would have gone if you could have convinced him to become a music teacher or something? Don't you ever wonder if he loved you enough to sacrifice his dream for yours?"

The realization that Stella made the right choice hit her hard. "Victor's lifestyle would have made me chase him and then I would have resented him. I made the right choice for you and me. You have to know your limitations Sarah; you have to know what you can tolerate in a relationship, what will help you grow or what will eventually suffocate you."

Her mother's words were simple, but made so much sense. "Mom, do you still have that photo album of you and Victor from back in the day? It's been a million years since I saw it."

"Do you think we should take a stroll down Sarah Rein's memory lane?" Stella forced a smile.

The tension that had been building through their conversation suddenly lifted. "Yes—I want to check out those happening 80's outfits again. Maybe I will get some tips on feathering my hair and popping my collar." Sarah gave her mother her best bratty smirk.

Sarah was anxious to see her mother and Victor through the eyes of an adult. The last time she had seen those pictures, she had been in elementary school. "Do you know where the album is? Want me to get it for you? Is it in my box or do you have a separate Victor box?" Sarah's teasing tone tugged at the anxiety Stella normally felt when anyone saw her closet of boxes.

"No, you get us something to snack on. I'll run upstairs and get the album." Stella headed for the staircase and thought about the boxes of memories she had in her studio. Her studio was a small bedroom that David had turned into a sitting room for her as a birthday gift when she turned thirty. She kept her life in that room. She collected her memories in that room.

She clicked on the Peter Rabbit lamp she had rescued from Sarah's pre-college Goodwill pile and opened the closet door feeling a sense of home as the familiar colored boxes, suitcases, photo boxes, and tins stacked chronologically from the beginning of Stella's life filled her field of vision: various family letters and cards were in a Gimbels' hat box retrieved from her mother's obsession with fashionable chapeaus, and on top of that box, she had a popcorn Christmas tin filled with pictures from her high school photography class. She scanned the Bass shoe box with the letters from old friends and the perfume box of postcards from her father and a few greeting cards from her mother. In that moment, Stella realized that there were far fewer boxes since she had been with David.

Catching Stella's eye was her decoupaged wooden wine box. She looked to the studio door, thought of Sarah downstairs, and decided to take the extra minute to pull the box containing her 80's memories. Reaching up and grabbing the box, she remembered cutting and pasting her favorite keepsakes on the box. Decoupaged to the front was the orange jacket of David Bowic's single, Let's Dance, with the two black stick figures dancing. She had listened to and sang that song and The Rise and The Fall of Ziggy Stardust and The Spiders from Mars a million times. Her fingers traced the arch of a rainbow and the heart that proclaimed "I Heart Rock and Roll."

She put the box down and opened it. How many years, she thought, had flown by? Lying silently on the top was a letter from Victor; she instantly recognized his poor scratch that passed for writing. Should she read it? Noticing that it was postmarked early in the 1990's from London, she shook her head and grudgingly accepted that she had to read it.

Hey Stella-star!

*How's my favorite girl? I hope you and baby-girl are
doing good. We are on our way to Germany for a gig near
Berlin. A few of us want to perform at the Berlin Wall but
rumor has it that we'll get arrested and cause an international incident. Sounds good to me! Watch the news and you
may see me getting carted off by the police.*

*Things are fine with us. Jimmy is pissing everyone off with
his bitching about missing his wife—we may need to find
a new drummer. I think he's gonna flake and go home. The
guy has no backbone.*

*We met Bowie last weekend. I know how much you love
him. He was with the black chick he's dating. She was super
sexy but she kept rattling on about starvation in Africa. Looks
like Bowie is a little whipped, if you know what I mean.*

*The boys are getting hungry, so I gotta go. I will write
next month and let you know how the Berlin show went.
We are playing a little shithole, but it's supposedly where the
music execs hang out. This could be our big break baby and
then I'll be driving up in a Porsche when I come home to you.*
Love,
Vic

Tears clouded Stella's vision as she reread the last line—a
Porsche! He had left her with a one year old who he didn't even
refer to by name. Realization and anger poured into Stella's heart
as she admitted this was not love. He didn't even know what
love was, and sadly, she realized, neither had she at the time.
She vaguely remembered being thrilled that he had remembered
that she loved David Bowie. Now it seemed pathetic; Vic was
selfish. Pursuing his own happiness and his own life came first,
while she had hoped that she was important enough to warrant
an occasional letter. She had raised their daughter while he took
care of himself, never once thinking of Sarah or her, not even

offering an apology.

Stella threw the letter back into the box without even putting it into the envelope and closed the box, putting it back on the shelf. Evienne and Madalane flooded her consciousness drowning Victor's trite words.

Her gaze moved up to the top shelf of the closet; a yellow suitcase lay on its side. It was the old kind of Samsonite suitcase, which she had picked up at a thrift store when Sarah was a baby. Stella grabbed the handle and pulled it from the shelf, smiling at the creamy yellow pleather. Their lives and memories were mixed together inside the suitcase. Sarah's first knit hat from the hospital, a worn onesie, a scrapbook, and a photo album of her time with Victor. Was she strong enough to go through this with Sarah? It had been a long time since she visited that part of her life.

Chapter 34

Paris, December 31, 1928

Patrice, Charles' model and sometimes lover, poured the jug of warm water over Evienne's long hair. The water was finally running clean. It had taken several buckets of water to wash all the dried blood out of Evienne's hair and it hurt Patrice's heart to think of the violence this young woman had experienced. She gently wrapped the long hair in a sheet and helped her back to the chaise.

It had been ten days since the attack and Evienne was getting stronger, but the model enjoyed tending to her. Evienne was fragile in her bruised and beaten state, but her body was recovering. Her wrists were taking the longest time to heal. Evienne had learned the hard way about doing certain tasks for herself. The pain from the popped tendons was relentless, so she allowed the model to wash her hair and help her change into a new shirt. No matter how many washings with lye, the charwoman was unable to get the bloodstains out of Evienne's old shirt. Patrice unwrapped the new white shirt that Charles had unwittingly given her money to buy—he thought he had given Patrice money to buy a new outfit for their New Year's dinner, but he underestimated the power of a good sale and a motivated caregiver.

Slipping the shirt onto Evienne's almost gaunt frame, the model averted her eyes from the still-present purple bite marks and the scabbed red flesh of the cigarette burn. Buttoning the shirt, she smoothed the crisp cotton over the young woman's shoulders and belly. "Bien—it fits perfectly."

It took mental patience for Evienne to accept charity help, even if it was from Charles and his friend. Evienne looked down at her new white shirt. It had been years since she had a new shirt. How was she ever going to repay Charles and Patrice? Their generosity was palpable and uncharacteristic. She sat on her chaise and let Patrice work the knots, one after the other from her matted hair with the wood comb she had brought with her. "Am I hurting you Evienne?" She asked as she sectioned off the hair, finding knot after knot.

"No Patrice, it is fine, my scalp is tough." Evienne closed her eyes and thought what it would be like to have Madalane's fingers touching her hair.

Patrice watched a blush rise through the Evienne's face. She had been so stoic through her convalescence; this slight reddening of her cheeks was the only sign that the model's closeness affected her. She had heard that Evienne was indifferent to men, and clearly, she had been punished for that. As she braided the girl's long hair, the model pushed her body closer to Evienne giving her a chance to feel the softness of her skin. She found the impossibility of Evienne's position erotic. Men lunged and grabbed, but Evienne seemed to shrink away from her touch when she came too close. Patrice liked Evienne's reluctance. Despite the fact that she enjoyed male company a little too much, she found Evienne's shyness alluring.

Disappointed she had finished her tasks for the day, she stood up, grazing her bosom against Evienne's arm. "Is there anything else I can help you with today?"

Evienne reached for her, dragging her almost useless fingers over Patrice's arm. Patrice gazed at her. Evienne struggled to form the right words, "Patrice I would have died without you. How can I ever show you my gratitude?" Patrice kneeled and leaned into her, grateful for the praise of her nursing, but careful to avoid pressing against the bruises that peppered Evienne's upper body.

Evienne accepted the touch and simply kissed her cheek. Patrice pulled back and gave her a portrait smile, the kind painters clamored to paint.

Evienne saw the perfect smile and she briefly wondered if she would ever paint again.

"And now I must make myself beautiful for Charles. He won't tell me where he's taking me, but he promised me a New Year's supper to remember. I suppose I should make sure he has a New Year's night to remember." With a wicked smile, Patrice wrapped her heavy cape around her shoulders. She looked at the young woman who had moved to look out the window. Feeling an unfamiliar longing in her heart, the model turned away confused by her own reaction and walked towards the door. As she left the studio, she called back, "Charles, the silly boy, left some wine sitting unattended in his room this afternoon. I put it in your water jug—you need a little New Year's cheer. I will be back tomorrow to see you."

Evienne turned and waved as the model sailed elegantly out of the room. She leaned over and sniffed the jug. The wine filled her heart with memories of Madalane and the last meal they shared before her friend left to visit her family.

* * *

Evienne was startled awake by Charles and Patrice coming in the apartment door. It was blindingly dark in the room and Evienne's heart pounded erratically as memories flashed to what had happened to her just days ago. She pulled her bandaged hands to her chest and tried to settle her frayed heart. Lying on the small chaise with her eyes wide open, she saw nothing, yet she wanted to feel something. She prayed for her life and thought of the only one who could put a smile on her face. She wanted to write a letter to her friend; she started writing it in her mind.

My Dearest Madalane,

    I wake in the middle of the night and I think of wrapping my arms around your waist. I think of pulling your warmth into my heart. I know your touch would heal me and yet I can only think of what I do not have in my hands. I have been crying frozen tears. I want to pull myself from this wretched lounge to wrap my arms around you, but I can only write you a letter in my mind.

    The thought of writing steals your loveliness from my mind because it initiates excruciating pain in my wrists. My hands are not the fluid brushes I once knew. I dream of what they were to me. I dream of how my fingers covered your creamy hand the morning you left, how I have not immortalized the image of you in paint. I turn my mind from them and I think of you. I dream of you next to me, healing me, saving me from the evils of my memories. I pray for the light of day. Lighting a match seems as difficult as holding a pencil to write to you. I pray for the morning as I sit in the dark and think about you. Madalane, I love you and miss you terribly. I see your face in every thought, in every breath, and I want you to come back to me.

Desperate to write Madalane a letter, Evienne wrapped her leg around the foot of the lounge to raise herself to a standing position using the strength of her stomach muscles to ease the burden on her wrists. She quietly moved through the dark room to the window and sat on the stool to maintain a vigil for the sunrise. She thought of Madalane and what it would be like to see her face, it has been so long; it has been so quiet in her heart.

She meditated on the roof top shadows of early morning until her eyes slowly fell shut.

The sun with the hues of purple and orange shone on Evienne's face, waking her from her sleep on the bony chair. Almost falling, the jolt sent the memory of pain riddling through her. The sun that she had been waiting for was now here. Evienne stretched her back and stared at the pencil. She reached for it and slowly rolled the pencil back and forth contemplating its use. She thought it might be more than she could handle, holding the pencil inside the pinch of her fingers. She didn't care. She needed to write, she wanted to tell Madalane everything that has happened. She wanted to unburden her heart. She promised her she would write.

Evienne's hand gingerly held the soft wood between her index finger and thumb and she hoped her choice of lead would make the gift of writing easier. The cumbersome bandage made holding the pencil awkward. The sun dripped delicate oranges and reds on the wood table where she sat. Evienne was stirred by the colors, stirred by returning life.

She looked at her hands and thought about how she could casually wrap one of her paintings in brown paper, and how she could write her signature on her art. How some clients liked a hand written note, written in her beautiful flowing penmanship. She thought of the blue wool of her scarf and how Madalane's fingers knitted it. How she could rip a piece of baguette and eat it. How she could maneuver a paintbrush and create delicate veins in the faces of her paintings. She thought of taking the lids off the tiny tubes of paint and squeezing vibrant colors from them. Would she ever be able to paint again? She felt defeated.

Evienne stared out the small studio window as the sun rose over the roofs, enticing her to memorize pictures of Paris. She picked up the pencil again and readied her sketching paper. *My Dearest*—she winced with pain as the wood shook in her hand. Her fingers gripped the pencil with white intensity. She stared at the purple bruises in contrast to the white of the bandages. Her mind traveled to the gnarled hands of the old people she painted and the uselessness of their fingers. *My Dearest Madalane*—her name was complete. A fine sheen of sweat covered Evienne's forehead. Each letter seemed to take a lifetime to construct. How was she ever going to write all her thoughts to Madalane? How was she ever going to tell her everything she thought? She struggled through *Bonne Annee*.

Her mind screamed over and over again, as she struggled to write. This is not the letter I wanted to write, believe me, but it is the best I can do. Do the best you can Evienne, do your best for Madalane. Tears filled her eyes as the ache in her wrists became constant.

Evienne controlled her breath and thought how she did not make it to Christmas mass. Madalane will be disappointed in her, Christmas was a week ago, and she didn't care. She needed to get through this letter. She would take a walk to the river after dropping the letter at the corner shop. It would be good to take a walk. It would be good to have fresh air. She needed to think about what she was going to do; she could not stay at Charles's place much longer.

Glistening raindrops garland the bare avenue—

Evienne's tears made her think of the cold rain. There is nothing to look forward to until your return. She looked at the completed letter, which was more like a note and realized it would have to do. Evienne was shocked from her reverie by a knock on the door.

"Good morning Ev...Happy New Year! Patrice made some tea, do you want some?" Charles asked.

"Yes, come in." Evienne was relieved for the interruption.

Charles entered the small studio, carrying a tray with tea and a chunk of baguette. He looked slightly worse for wear after his

New Year's night, but he was smiling which usually meant that it had been a very good night. He placed the tray on the small table next to the stool and moved to the window to look out at the daylight. "Uh....does it have to be so bright in here?"

"Charles, have some tea it will help with the morning." Evienne stared at the serving and waited for her friend to pour.

"Patrice went out to buy more wine. I am not done celebrating yet. No tea, but I will have a cigarette." He lit two Gauloise and handed her one. She took it gingerly and put it between her lips. He poured the tea for Evienne and leaned against the wall and looked out the window again.

"Charles—"

He turned to face the young woman.

Evienne looked into Charles' bloodshot eyes; her voice cracked as she spoke, "Thank you Charles. Honestly, thank you."

"I spoke to Patrice's sister—she said that she might know of some nurses looking for a roommate."

Evienne was stung by Charles words. "I am going back to the squat." She knew she would live on the street first, but she was angry that Charles disregarded her attempt at thanking him.

Charles looked at her as if she had lost her mind. "Do you have a death wish? You made Jean your bitch when you beat him up and look what happened. Do you think you can go back there like nothing happened? He would have killed you if I hadn't shown up. You can't treat a man like that without consequences."

"To hell with him. He is a slug and I could care less." Evienne stood and tapped her ash, swallowing the pain from the tenderness in her wrist, into the small ashtray near Charles.

Charles laughed mirthlessly, "He will send you to hell if you tangle with him again. I'm serious Evienne. He will kill you if you go back there. You humiliated him."

"My friend asked me to move in with her." the words fell out of Evienne's mouth.

"The student? The one who moons over you at the stand?"

"She is my friend Charles." Evienne felt anger welling up inside of her.

"She is your sycophant, but she is pretty and is clearly sincere. So, the problem is solved. You move in with your friend and she will be your slave. Every artist needs slavish devotion."

Charles words infuriated her. "You are a pig." Evienne picked up the cup, wincing at the pressure in her wrist, and took a sip to stop herself from saying more.

He grinned. "Yes, I am a pig, but I am also a pussycat who loves to curl up in his lady's lap and purr."

Evienne rolled her eyes at Charles' words. He was incorrigible. Pensively, she tendered an idea, "I am going to raise some money and move to America to live with my sisters. I am not sure Madalane really wants me to move in with her anyway."

Why would you leave Paris? Do you want to become a cowboy? No Evienne—you don't want to go to America. You would hate it—too many cars and cowboys. Plus, no women look like you in America. You would have to trade in your pants for a skirt."

"I would be spared this wretched life and I could start over. Those stuffy Americans would get used to me." Evienne hated conformity.

Charles shook his head, stubbed out his cigarette butt and lit another. "Darling, the Americans are still puritans. They would tie you to a stake in the center of their town square and stone you to death for wearing pants. Janet told me that a woman can get arrested for wearing pants these days. How much art will you get done in jail? Stop being ridiculous. Stay in Paris. Move in with your little friend—what is her name—Margareta? She loves you. You will have a nice life. She will finish school, get a good job, and support you. You will have everything that an artist needs—a patron, a warm room, plenty of wine, a paintbrush and a soft body to fuck at night. It's perfect." He considered his words for a moment, and then continued, "If you don't move in with her, maybe she would consider me?" He laughed but quieted when he saw Evienne's expression.

"Her name is Madalane." Fuck her? He was so crass sometimes; the words coming out of Charles' mouth made her seethe. "I might move in with her; I'm not sure. She might be more work than I need." Evienne's blue eyes became black as she stared at Charles, furious at his profane words.

"It is only work if you allow it to be work. If she gets out of line, move on to the next girl. There are many girls in Paris who like girls. Your friend is just one of many who would open her legs for you."

"I'm not fucking Madalane, Charles. Stop talking about her like she is one of your whores." Nonchalantly, Evienne took another drag off her smoke and stood. She fiddled with her blue scarf and thought how Madalane would be horrified to know they were discussing her like this.

Charles looked honestly puzzled. "You aren't fucking her? Why not?"

Evienne flipped him a look. "She happens to be my friend. Not that you would know anything about that." Evienne regretted the words as soon as they came from her mouth.

Charles tilted his head and examined his friend. His eyes narrowed and a deep, hearty laugh echoed from his chest. "Ah, my dear friend—you are smitten with the girl. Don't try to deny it. I can see it on your face. This makes it even more perfect. She loves you; you love her. All you need is a few dogs and you can be like Ms. Stein and her friend."

"Charles, I love Paris and no other. I need some of her fresh air. Do you want to walk down to the river with me and we can discuss in further detail exactly what kind of dog you think Madalane and I can afford." Evienne was itchy. She wanted to walk until her feet ached. She wanted to shut her friend up. She wanted to love Madalane without the feeling that it was wrong. "What do you think, you want to walk?" Evienne put out her cigarette and grabbed her letter, looking towards her infuriating friend.

"No, I'm going to stay here and wait for Patrice. I'm quite fond of her whatever you might think of my relationships." Charles took another drag of his cigarette and looked at his friend thoughtfully, "You really should move in with Madalane. She would be good for you. She would never let you starve and there is something to be said for devotion." One last pull off his cigarette and he tossed it out the window. "Think about it Evienne—you don't want to leave Paris. Even if things don't work out with the girl, you have somewhere to go for now that is safe. Worry about things not working out when the time comes."

"Perhaps. I'll think about it on my walk."

Evienne was finally able to breathe again as she headed down the steps from Charles' apartment. She turned left out of the doorway and walked to the corner shop to drop the letter she had written to Madalane. The cold air hitting her lungs was fresh. She needed the clarity of the air to clear her mind. She walked into the shop and a small hanging bell rang as the door closed behind her. She chatted briefly with the shop owner and collected a stack of letters from Madalane. She impulsively purchased a bar of chocolate with some change she had in her pocket. The candy made her think of Madalane. As she strolled, she thought of how Madalane would surprise her with sweets hidden in her pockets. She was the most thoughtful person she knew. The chocolate was rich and dark and melted on her tongue. It was the first real pleasure she had felt in weeks.

She leaned over the river wall and contemplated what she should do. The shimmer of water beckoned her attention. She found the water to be her guide, a sanctuary of her mind; she prayed and asked the spirit of her father what to do.

She needed a sign. Anything. Evienne heard the faint laughter of a child. The high pitch brought her out of her reverie to the moment at the river. She looked up and saw a father gingerly helping his young daughter reel in a fish. They were floating down the river on a small boat. It was the middle of the winter, the air was so cold. This would not be something one would see this time of year. It reminded her of her own childhood in England. Her father would take her out fishing early on Saturday mornings, sometimes allowing her to miss chores. It was the time they were able to talk and share the daily happenings and their dreams. The little girl on the boat was no more than seven or eight. Her father's large frame steadied them as she squealed with the excitement of catching the fish. It was not a big fish and she really did not need the help; it was the surreal act of love that two people shared.

This image playing in front of Evienne's face brought happiness to her heart. She remembered her father's loving words and kind touch and realized this was her sign. It had to be; God knows it was the middle of the winter. Her father would say to her, "Do what will make you happy, Evie. Follow your heart; it will always guide you to your truth." The feeling of relief and calm came over her, if Madalane was serious about her moving in, she would do it, but she would wait for her to bring it up again. She felt the spiritual happiness of having made a good decision moving up the back of her neck, knowing she would say yes. As if God was applauding her decision, the bells of Sainte-Chapelle started to peal.

Evienne looked again for the father and daughter but they had vanished. She wondered if she made the whole event up as she scanned the river towards Pont de Sully. They were gone. They were like angels, maybe they were.

Evienne felt Madalane alive inside her again. She wanted to talk with her, share with her. She instinctually headed down Rue Dante towards 33 Rue Galande. She knew she was not there although memories of their time together offered her comfort. Her energy was running low; she needed to head back to Charles although it was not where her heart was meant to lie.

Hours later, Evienne opened the door to Charles' small studio and paused to look at the room. She had been in the room for

almost two week and had become numb to the sketches tacked
on the wood walls. Poses of naked women, necks and the curves
of breasts. She had not noticed the scent of paint and turpentine.
She looked at her small pile of belongings in the corner, including her art box. The box her father gave her. Her stained shirt,
perfectly folded by Patrice, lying on top of her small bag. She
hung her coat and curled up on her chaise, studying the sketches
of women hanging on the studio walls. Without thought, her
eyes closed, dropping her into dream-filled sleep.

Madalane's face emerged from the dark water. Her hand
reached for Evienne; Evienne took her delicate fingers in hers
and she easily gathered Madalane's naked body from the river.
The two women embraced; they missed each other. A sweet
jasmine scent fell from Madalane's skin and Evienne breathed
the essence into her soul, filling her with a transcendent energy.
Evienne heard her name called and turned from the apparition.
A large portrait of Madalane was in front of her. Her dark wavy
hair cascading over her shoulders, chestnut wisps framing her
face. The mystical portrait spoke wordlessly to Evienne. "Come be
with me, come let me love you." Her hand extended through the
canvas and gently touched the painter's face. She lifted her spirit,
guiding her soul into the painting with a gossamer softness. The
two bodies mixed and floated in the clouds of the leathery canvas.

Chapter 35

Opening the fridge, Sarah noticed that the usually stocked shelves were mostly empty. She mused that David's absence must have made her mom stop her regular meal cooking. She grabbed a block of cheese, the mustard, and some pickles. She looked for the white wine, but there wasn't any. Closing the fridge, she scanned the kitchen perplexed. There were a couple bottles of red sitting on the counter. She briefly wondered why her mother had suddenly developed a taste for red. Shrugging, she grabbed the bottle and the opener and laid it on the table next to the cheese. Opening the pantry, she found a box of Triscuits and a jar of olives. Not quite a feast for the ages, but enough to satiate their hunger.

She peeled off the wine cork cover and she heard her mother's light step coming down the stairs. She was apprehensive and excited. She felt a connection with her mother for the first time in a really long time.

Swinging the case as she came down the stairs Stella made a promise to herself to make this about Sarah, not about herself. "Found it. Oh great you found us some food too. I'm starved."

Startled by the sight of her old suitcase, Sarah forgot she was in the midst of uncorking the wine. "Oh my God. Where did you find that relic? I thought we had given it back to Goodwill years ago."

"You remember it? Of course, you must. I thought it was a cool place to store our memories." Stella put the overnight-sized suitcase on the kitchen bar and clicked open the locks.

Sarah laughed. "I'm surprised those locks still work. I played with them day and night. Remember, I used to keep my Barbie's and stuffed animals in there"

Sarah reached out and ran her fingers along the top of the case. This was the one constant in her childhood. No matter how many times they moved, no matter how many crappy apartments they briefly lived in, this suitcase had been hers. She felt an overwhelming urge to cry, but turned away lest her mother should see tears over this ridiculous pleather suitcase.

Sarah grabbed the wine and finished removing the cork. Her mother opened the top and as she did, the light reflected the dent in the top. Memories came rushing back into Sarah's head. "Hey...check it out...this is the indentation on the top from where I used to sit on it as I watched TV." Sarah's hand laid flat against the indentation when Stella lowered the lid to see it. A lifetime ago, she had sat on the suitcase, alone in an apartment, waiting for her mother to come home from work. For some reason she couldn't remember, the suitcase had been her safety spot. She had felt like it would protect her from anyone who walked past the flimsy door separating her from the yelling and noises emanating from the hallway.

"Mom—if you ever want to junk it, give it to me. Please?" Sarah's tone had become almost child-like.

"Of course I will give it to you." Stella smiled warmly at her daughter as she opened up the treasure of memories. Perfectly folded on top was an infant-sized outfit. "Look, it's your little dress you came home in from the hospital." Stella picked it up gently and embraced it as if her daughter were still in it.

Sarah rolled her eyes at her mother's dewy embrace of her baby outfit. "This is a motley collection of stuff. What on earth compelled you to save my baby clothes?" Sarah picked out a stuffed bear that was disintegrating and had lost both of its eyes. "Is this Rupert? I threw him away when I was 14. How did you find him?"

"Bad habit baby, you know I can't throw anything out. Here is the photo album you wanted to see. Stella pushed the suitcase aside to make room for the album; the cover had blue and green psychedelic flowers and a huge gold spiral binding, a relic of the 1980s. Stella put it down on the counter and opened it to find that the first picture was of her and Victor at an outdoor concert. Stella was surprised at how young she looked and how happy her expression was.

Sarah looked at the picture and saw a girl who looked a lot like herself, but with feathered bangs. The young man standing next to her had a similar hairstyle, but that's where the similarities ended. Victor appeared scruffy in an old concert t-shirt while Stella wore a perfectly pressed polo shirt. His arm was wrapped securely around her body and Stella looked incredibly happy.

"You have your Vic's eyes, Sarah. You have lovely eyes." Stella tenderly put her fingers under her daughters chin and tried to see Victor in her. It had been so long since she allowed herself to think so intently about him.

Sarah felt sad that her father was unable to be the man her mother needed. She felt sad that her mother had to settle for someone who she knew would take care of her instead of the man who made her smile.

"Do you wish that things had turned out differently?"

"I can't answer that question Sarah. It would be like you wondering what your life would have been like if you never met and loved Autumn."

Stella was flipping through the album now, laughing and remembering her youth. She stopped for a minute and pointed at a shot of Victor holding a guitar while she sat off to the side, but she couldn't find the words to explain why it was important. She remembered that picture like it was yesterday. She had just discovered she was pregnant, but hadn't told anyone yet. She quickly flipped past it and soon there were shots of Victor with his hand covering her belly.

"How long did Victor hang around after I was born?"

"Your father left for good when you were almost three."

Sarah felt her mother's heartache and consciously decided not to pursue her questions. This walk down memory lane was getting uncomfortable. She was ready to move around. "Let's take Granger for a walk and get some fresh air before the sun sets."

Stella nodded and stood up and Granger instinctively knew it was his turn for some attention just by the glance in his direction. Sarah took the leash off the hook near the door. The dog did his "I'm going out" dance as Sarah tried to click the leash into place.

With the leash firmly clicked into place, the two women headed out the door. "I'll say this mom. You are a much nicer person than I am. I don't think I could ever sacrifice myself so willingly for someone else. No matter how much I loved them."

Stella smiled lightly, but knew in her heart that her daughter was more like her than either of them had ever realized.

Chapter 36

Outside Paris January 1929

Madalane's head was throbbing. She was exhausted from the train ride, from the weeks spent with her parents, from the fearful knowledge that Evienne might have moved on in her absence. Initially she had sent Evienne letters every other day. When she received little or no response, she stopped writing. She had received a couple from Evienne, but despite her friend's continuing communication, she was anxious. The first letter had been a heartbreak, and by the time the second letter came, Madalane had hardened her heart against Evienne's ambivalence. The second letter proved to be just as infuriating as the first.

8 January, 1929

My Dearest Madalane,

I reside in the tangled webs of Charles's antics; it is entertaining but less than productive. You must cherish the solidness of home, I am sure I would—wild engagements fog the necessities of my art.

Your memory breathes inside of me, each day the sun

rotates closer to my heart and you will soon be here to pro-
vide the warmth.

When will spring come? I anticipate your return with
great joy; I will meet you at the station in eight days from
today.
Forever,
Evienne

Was Evienne with Charles? The young woman supposed that
Evienne seeing her and living with Charles were not mutually
exclusive. She needed to see Evienne. That would be the only
thing that would make her feel better. She would get used to Evienne's romance with Charles. She had learned to endure anything.

She looked out the window as the train approached Paris. It
was rainy, gloomy and cold. Madalane felt the chill run through
her body and into her bones. She hoped the weather was not a
sign of things to come. She opened the last of the cherry candies
Evienne had given her when she left Paris. She had realized that
there were twenty-eight pieces of candy, one for each day she
was away—she suspected that Evienne had planned it that way.
She had coveted the last piece through the entire ride north. She
hoped it would be a good omen to end her trip the way it began.

Madalane stood as the train slowed. Her back hurt, her
head hurt, she felt nauseated from hours of swaying motion of
the train. The city looked dark and gray, just like her mood. She
had written to Evienne with her arrival information, but with
each passing day and then with each passing mile, she knew it
was less and less likely she would be met by her friend. It was not
the kind of day anyone should leave the warmth of their home,
especially a cozy love nest.

She gathered her suitcase, now much heavier because her
father had given her a huge tin of chocolates, cookies, and biscuits.
She would be glad of it later when she felt a craving, but every extra

ounce seemed to add more bitterness to Madalane's foul mood.

* * *

Evienne stood in Charles' small studio gazing at her image in the mirror normally used by his models to perfect their look before posing. She gently touched the soft skin under her eye, hoping the yellowish-green shade wouldn't be noticed by her friend. The day was wet and cold and the train station was a bit of a walk, but Evienne headed out early for the station so as not to miss the return of her friend. She thought about bringing her sketchpad, but rejected the idea. Her wrists were finally feeling stronger although they were still tender. A poorly rendered sketch would be worse than no sketch at all.

Walking through the dismally cold city, Evienne worried that it was a bit excessive to wait a few hours, but Madalane was all she could think of. She would be happy to wait—it gave purpose to her day. Once she arrived at the train station, she checked the arrival board. It was so early; Madalane's train wasn't even on the list yet. Evienne settled herself near the board to keep a vigilant eye out for the train from Bordeaux.

After hours of watching people walk back and forth from the platforms, the Bordeaux train was at the top of the arrival board. She had made her way to the platform, and Evienne felt the ground tremble from the approach of the train; it matched the excitement in her body. Her heart was pounding as she watched the train approaching from the distance. Impatiently, she paced while the train pulled alongside the platform. She wanted to run up and down the length of the cabs to check each window for her friend.

The train came to a creaking halt, steam blasting out from the under carriage of the cars. There were at least twenty cars as the train was filled to capacity due to the travelers coming home from holiday visits. Evienne searched to find Madalane amongst the crowds of people now beginning to exit from the train. The travelers were happy finally to put their feet to the ground after an eight-hour train ride from Bordeaux. Searching each face, Evienne started to feel the panic of not being able to find her friend, her heart rate accelerated. She searched through throngs of people, trying to stand on her toes to peek over the top of hats and umbrellas.

Finally, with an overwhelming sense of relief, she saw Madalane, feeling instant recognition in her blood. Madalane stood with her back to Evienne, looking towards the entrance of the station. Evienne felt a surge of instant happiness after not seeing Madalane for four weeks. She quickly walked up behind Madalane, taking her bag from her and surprising her at the same time.

Madalane face was filled with pure shock and relief when she snapped her head in the direction of the person grabbing her bag. Shock turned to delight as Madalane realized Evienne had taken the burden of her bag from her. Transported by sheer bliss, Madalane threw her arms around Evienne and grasped her tightly. She breathed in the comforting smell of sandalwood and paint that defined her friend. She had never been so happy in her life to see someone. The gloominess she had felt was gone, completely and utterly gone.

"You came!" The only words that kept running through Madalane's mind abruptly poured out of her mouth. Their hug turned into a major obstacle to those trying to get around them on the busy train platform. Evienne's eyes opened and she saw the scowls of harried travelers. She smiled at the absurdity of the moment, but continued to hold her friend tight and close.

Madalane's name was the only thing Evienne could think of; she wanted to burst into tears, but she held her friend tightly and felt the heat from her body. Her healing body still felt the echoes of pain, but it was the sweetest pain Evienne had ever felt. Evienne looked into her friend's eyes and she was joyously aware that Madalane's happiness was as crystal clear as her own. As the travelers moved around the two women, Evienne pulled Madalane to her and kissed both cheeks twice. The kisses were warm and she let her lips linger on the warmth of her friend's cheek.

"I could not wait to see you; I missed you." Evienne whispered the words directly from her heart into Madalane's ear. As the platform thinned of passengers exiting, Evienne smiled, "Shall we?" Madalane's joy was palpable as she nodded. Evienne grasped the heavy suitcase, her wrists numb to the pressure of the past; the pain was secondary to her joy. Madalane tucked her arm around her friend's free arm and they moved off the platform and into the cold, rainy streets of Paris.

The walk was long, but it felt like mere minutes to Madalane. Evienne's tall, lean body striding next to her with her suitcase in hand was comforting. The day was getting darker and the cool breeze that blew off the Seine made the approaching evening colder. Neither felt the cold though as they walked through the lanes to Madalane's room. To fill the silence, Madalane related a funny story about her incompetent cousin at the shop, involving his inability to measure anything accurately.

Evienne laughed with unmitigated joy as Madalane recreated her father's outrage at her cousin's stupidity, and before they knew it, they had reached Madalane's rooms. They quietly let themselves in the front door. The house was dark; most of the other girls would be arriving in another day or two, and the housemother stayed upstairs in the evening.

Evienne took the keys out of Madalane's hands and opened the private door to her small room. Madalane stopped before entering her room and turned towards the staircase. "I must let Madame know I am here, or she will come down in her most frightening nightgown and face cream."

Evienne laughed as she carried the suitcase into the room. "I will light a fire while you appease the beast." Madalane felt an overwhelming sense of relief that Evienne had not planned to leave right away. A sick feeling surged in her as she ascended the steps that Charles might be waiting for her friend. Shaking the image from her mind, she tried to calm her nerves. She knocked on the housemother's door. After several interminable minutes of interrogation, the housemother was satisfied that Madalane had had a lovely holiday and was looking forward to the new semester.

Madalane forced herself to descend the steps slowly. She quietly opened the door to her room, praying that Evienne was still in there and had not bolted without saying goodbye.

Evienne was surprised how relieved she was to be with Madalane. She didn't want to question her feelings; she just wanted to be there with her friend and feel the warmth of their companionship. Small flames popped and licked the small pieces of wood. She feared the Madame would come downstairs to Madalane's room with the student. As she heard footsteps outside the door, she held her breath until Madalane's face was the only face she saw.

Evienne was facing the door in front of the fireplace when Madalane walked through the door and directly to the fireplace. "Mmm...the fire feels so good." Madalane started to unwind her scarf from around her neck. Evienne approached her, took the ends out of her friend's hands, and unwound the wool in a leisurely manner; it gave her a chance to study and memorize the planes and curves of her friend's face.

Standing so close together, Madalane felt herself falling into Evienne's body. She leaned against the chest of her friend and wrapped her arms around the slim body. She felt her body relax; the warmth from the fire and the warmth from her friend's body seemed to surround her. She was content for the first time in weeks.

Now that she was warm and had her dearest friend with her, she realized that she was starving. She abruptly pulled back and shamelessly smiled at Evienne. "I have chocolate...and lots of it!"

Evienne's sweet tooth was unknown to most, but Madalane had discovered that Evienne's weekly treat was a chocolate bar. It was one of the reasons that Madalane had so readily accepted the tin of sweets her father had presented her. Evienne's eyes lit up like a child presented with a new toy. Madalane reached into her suitcase and out came a box of chocolates, carefully wrapped in brown paper and string from her father's store.

With mock seriousness, Evienne beseeched her friend, "Will you share your chocolates with me? I did carry your bag through the damp cobble stone streets, made you a cozy fire, and I will take off your shoes and rub your tired feet if you bestow upon me one mere piece of chocolate."

Madalane burst out with an uproarious laugh. Evienne did a little dance of excitement and jumped on to the bed to wait patiently for her treat, like an over-sized poodle anticipating its reward for doing a good trick.

Madalane was stunned. She had never seen this side of her friend before. Evienne was positively giddy with excitement. Overcome by the pleasure of seeing her friend so happy, Madalane thrust the box at Evienne and said, "They are yours...all of them."

Evienne looked at her like she was giving her a pot of gold. "No, they are yours..."

Madalane smiled at her friend, and replied warmly, "No, they are ours...untie the string and let's have some chocolate."

Having this kind of treat was an unexpected delight for Evienne. "You are an angel, Madalane." This statement was not far from the truth for Evienne. She quickly pulled the string, releasing the brown paper and exposing the box. She pulled off the lid and found to her surprise a box stuffed with chocolates. She wanted to fill her mouth with the delectable chocolate, but instead held the box out for Madalane to have the first. She gazed up at her and smiled, "You first."

Madalane reached for a nougat and then stopped; she considered her options and stalled examining all the different kinds her father had included until she heard a sigh of exasperation from Evienne. Madalane looked up into Evienne's eyes and winked at her as she went back to her first choice. She loved teasing her friend just a little. She normally didn't feel this level of confidence, but with a huge box of chocolate, she felt safe that Evienne would not pull away.

Evienne reached into the box and pulled out a caramel. Madalane knew that this would be her choice. She watched Evienne's face contort with extraordinary pleasure as the chocolate melted on her tongue and the caramel oozed into her mouth. Madalane felt a carnal sensation watching Evienne enjoy the chocolate. Seeing her friend's face relax and then the small smile that played around her lips as the chocolate blended with the caramel made her stomach clench and her heart skip.

Evienne felt the cream of the chocolate move down her throat. This was the ultimate pleasure for her. She smiled and closed her eyes. The day was ending on a sweet note combined with comforting pleasure of her friend's presence.

Madalane stared at the soft lines of Evienne's face. She was not sure if she had ever seen her look so rapturous, but there was a shadow under her eyes. She looked closer and realized that there were several shadows along her jaw line and cheeks.

With seriousness, Madalane asked, "Are those bruises on your face? Were you in a fight?" Inside, her chest clenched with fear.

Evienne immediately stopped chewing, reciting her rehearsed answer, "We had a little too much cheer on Christmas. It was just a bar brawl. I thought the purple looked quite fetching with my skin tones." Evienne laughed, trying to lighten the heaviness of the moment as she wiped the chocolate from the corner of her mouth.

"Whatever shall I do with you? You are such a hooligan sometimes." Madalane chuckled. She felt that Evienne was not telling her the whole truth, but she didn't want to ruin the perfection of her homecoming. Her headache lessened with each minute they spent together.

They continued to eat chocolate. Madalane's sweet tooth had been sated much sooner than Evienne's, but Madalane continued to take pieces because she knew Evienne waited for her to take a piece before she would reach for another. The room was so warm, and the chocolate had been filling and sweet. Evienne was telling her a story about a tourist who had purchased a painting on the day after she had left. Evienne's voice was low and lulling and Madalane felt her eyelids drooping.

There was an indefinable air of contentment in the room. Madalane could barely keep her mind afloat after her day's journey. She lay back on her pillow and closed her eyes from fatigue. Evienne watched her friend quickly fall asleep in front of her. Evienne slipped of the bed, placed the box of half-eaten chocolates on the bedside table, removed her friend's shoes, and took the folded quilt from the end of the bed and covered Madalane's sleeping body.

Sitting on the edge of the bed with the sleeping Madalane, Evienne gazed at her friend's secret world of sleep and dreams. She watched and memorized the miraculous vision of her friend dreaming, peacefully moving from place to place in her esoteric dreamland. The vision made her think of her own dream from the other afternoon when Madalane's dream presence offered her salvation and redemption. It made Evienne's heart ache to see Madalane so vulnerable and beautiful. The chestnut curls that framed her friend's face gave her an ethereal appearance, as if she were still a dream. She reached out and gently moved a lock of hair just to make sure this moment was real.

Evienne heard wind and rain lashing against the windows. She looked at Madalane's sleeping form. She had a small bit of chocolate on the side of her mouth. Evienne felt an overwhelming urge to lean over and lick it from her lips, but instead she stood to put her coat on.

Madalane's eyes opened and she crinkled her brow. "Where are you going?"

Evienne knew in an instant that she would not be leaving tonight. She put her coat back down and slipped her shoes off. She got into the small bed and whispered, "Nowhere Dove, nowhere." Madalane's back was to her front and she felt Madalane relax against her. She smiled and snuggled closer to Madalane. Madalane's hand reached around and pulled Evienne's arm around her. There was no space between them.

Evienne nuzzled her nose into the back of Madalane's neck and she took one last deep breath. She was filled with happiness, the warmth of the hearth, the smell of her friend's hair, and the feeling of security. Evienne felt a heat inside of her. She felt a passion, long thought dead, begin to stoke into a flame. However, Madalane's angelic sleeping form combined with the heat in the room and the fullness of her belly allowed her to fall into a deep, dreamless slumber.

Evienne woke to the sound of birds greeting the morning, the normal commotion in the outside world. She didn't think she moved a muscle all night, as she realized her arms were still securely wrapped around Madalane, both women still fully dressed. Evienne had not slept this soundly since she lived at home, sleeping with her sisters. She pressed against Madalane's body and felt the natural way they fit into each other. Their bodies were molded into each other, from the graceful lock of their ankles to the heat of their thighs pressed onto each other, blending into the curve off Madalane's back pushed against her breasts. She wanted to memorize everything about this moment as she would a face before sketching. She listened to the small breaths of Madalane's sleeping rhythm. Slowly Evienne slipped from the bed.

Madalane felt the cool air on her back and it momentarily confused her. She lay for a minute trying to get her bearings. She opened her eyes and the events of the previous night came rushing back to her. Evienne had slept in her bed, with her, wrapped around her. No wonder she had slept so well—the usual crushing worry of Evienne's safety was not a concern last night.

She heard Evienne quietly stirring the fire. She wanted to

ask about Charles, but wasn't sure how. In an almost whispered tone, Madalane asked the dreaded question, "Are you worried Charles will wonder where you slept last night?"

Evienne turned and stared at Madalane. "I don't think he cares where I am. He was probably quite happy to have his studio vacant to fondle one of his models." Evienne raised an eyebrow and grinned.

"You are living in his studio Evienne? Why are you living in his studio?" The silent stare from Evienne manifested every worry Madalane could have had for her friend. "Did you fight with Jean? Did you need a place to go?" The picture became clear to Madalane from the look on Evienne's face. In the morning light, Madalane could easily see the bruises that clearly marked Evienne's face.

Evienne felt tears flooding her eyes. She did not want to tell Madalane about her attack; she did not want Madalane to feel sorry for her. She did not want her to think anything other than she wanted to live with her. "Madalane, you are worrying too much. It was fine. It was just time to leave. Charles's place was just a convenient option."

"Please live with me," the plea spilled from the Madalane's lips.

Evienne staggered as she heard the words: "Live with me." The day at the Seine came flooding back to her. Madalane was reading her mind and it was the deal she had made with herself. It was the message she had hoped for. Madalane had said it; she had heard it with her own ears. She had promised herself that if she were to ask again, she would do it—she would move in with her. Evienne took a breath, walked to her friend, and looked deeply into Madalane's eyes. She had a radiant beauty and the quietness of sleep and worry draped over her. Evienne became lost in the image before her for a moment.

Evienne perched on the bedside and gracefully moved her hands to her friend's face. She slipped a palm to her cheek and said, "Good morning, Dove. We should start this day again."

Madalane looked at her. "Evienne, please I am worried about you."

Evienne kissed both of Madalane's cheeks and then whispered into the warmth of her neck, "You have cared for my heart and allowed gentle kindness to fill my life. Yes, I think it would be a wonderful thing to share tea with you every morning."

Smiling, Madalane relaxed her head on her pillow, pulling Evienne to her and hugged her, never wanting to let her go again. She had finally received the Christmas gift she had prayed so fervently for.

My Dearest Madalane,

Paris has been a mother to me. She is ever changing and nurturing, and I try to flow like her river. I only want what is best for you and taking a chance on someone of my likes is comparable to buying art from a street artist. Although you think I have talent, I am but a rebel painter, living by the graciousness of her muse. Some think I should change my approach, but I can only be who I am.

Please Madalane—know I will leave your room if the situation compromises your education. I want nothing more than for you to succeed, and having someone like me sneaking from the street through your unlocked window may look a bit more suspicious than friendly. I would not question your choice. I would not hold you responsible. I would know in my heart it is what is best for you. Don't think twice, my Dove, about taking care of yourself first. I have little to offer other than my fine ability to lay a fire and of course make a cup of tea…
Forever,
Evienne

Chapter 37

Carrying a bottle of wine, Eve circumnavigated the room avoiding the piles of paper she had organized on the other furniture. She promised herself daily to start going through the piles, but that particular task always seemed to drop to the bottom of her to-do list. She poured for herself and Stella, and sat down next to the younger woman who wore an odd expression.

Stella took a sip of the wine and adjusted her wedding set. Sarah's surprise visit home had been a blessing despite the wretched way it had started. She realized how totally abandoned she had been by Victor. She had sent him an email after Sarah left. It was short and simple—she appreciated his interest, but she was a different woman now. She could not go back to the way things were. She knew she would hear from him again, but after hitting send, the lightness in her heart reinforced her decision. He had the power to make her crazy, but frankly, who wanted craziness these days? She was happy in her life, even if she was still unsure about David. The nagging feeling that she was using him wore at her. Feeling uncomfortable, she focused on Eve and her mother.

She tried to imagine Madalane raising Eve by herself. So much like her own life, but much more difficult—an immigrant with no identity other than as a refugee with a baby. It gave her hope for Sarah since Eve turned out okay. She wondered if Sarah would become so grounded and content.

Eve picked up her wine glass and sipped the Cabernet while surreptitiously studying Stella, "Is something wrong? You look like you have something on your mind."

"I have been thinking how hard it must have been for Madalane to raise you alone. What was your Mom like when you were a child?"

Eve drank from her own wine glass to fortify herself. It hurt to think of her mother because her absence had lain so heavily on her heart over the course of the last week. As the seconds ticked by, Eve felt conflicted, but decided to open up to Stella.

"My mother was, as you can imagine, intensely private. She rarely spoke about herself or where she had come from, other than an occasional rant about French politics. Like I told you before, Mom moved to the United States right before France was invaded by Hitler. She lived with some friends of her family in Boston for a while; they sponsored her immigration." Eve sipped her wine again before resuming, "She met my dad and she moved to Philadelphia and started working in the Frankford Arsenal in the Northeast when he was shipped off to the European front. The munitions factory is where she met Elizabeth. They both had small children with husbands in the war, and they bonded despite my Mom being a foreigner, which meant she was ostracized by most of the girls at the factory. After the war, they both moved to Chestnut Hill and they were the best of friends until Mom died."

"Was she a good mom to you Eve? Do you think of her words when you look for guidance? Would you have gone to her in need?" Stella desperately leaned towards her friend. "I want to know what kind of mother she was. I need to know that there are good mothers out there. I feel broken as a mother at times. I just need to know if it's possible to be a good mother through instinct alone or am I just kidding myself?"

Eve realized that Stella's curiosity was based more on her own problems with motherhood. How could she begin to explain Madalane's influence on every aspect of her world and how even to this day, forty years after her death, that she was still there in her mind, offering advice and solace.

"Stella, being a mother now is much different than it was fifty years ago. Parents didn't put so much pressure on themselves to be super heroes. My mom's style of parenting would not work for most people. She treated me like an adult when I was five years old. She gave me autonomy to make my own choices, but she made sure I understood the consequences of the choices I made."

Eve took another sip of wine, not sure if any of her words answered Stella's question. The younger woman looked miserable, head downcast, body slumped forward, her fingers on her right hand playing with the wedding ring on her left. Eve felt an overwhelming urge to try to help her, "My mom was an odd duck in certain ways, but she was always there for me. I suppose that is the main thing. I never doubted that she would be there to bail me out of trouble or support me in some cockamamie plan I concocted.

"When do you know you have reached the point where you have done your job? Did I even know how to be a mother, not being mothered myself? My daughter is a good person—I just hope I didn't tarnish the opportunities she could have by not teaching her the skills she needs. How do you even know if they listen at all?" Checking her anxiety, she looked to Eve, hoping for the answers she needed to believe in herself.

The tone in Stella's voice made Eve wince. How could she, not even a mother herself, offer advice to someone who has raised a child to young adulthood? Anger and resentment flooded Eve's belly, but she remained silent. What could she say? Images of her own mother flickered like old home movies through her mind. Madalane had not been a conventional mother—she had been more of a partner in crime. Memories of breaking into a writer's long-shuttered house crept through her mind—her mother leaping over a stone fence to find a way in, leaving a stunned Eve in her dust. Suddenly the sorrow that had been threatening to engulf her evaporated, leaving only the feelings of love she had for Madalane.

"My mother would know exactly what to say. She always did. I am not so lucky—I feel that my advice is usually banal. Mom was always at the kitchen table, grading papers when I came home from school. She'd have a glass of red wine at her left side and a crystal ashtray at her right side. If I had a problem or needed advice, I would sit down across from her with my own glass of wine and explain my issue. She was a great listener. She didn't interrupt ever—she would listen and then ask about anything she didn't understand after I had laid the problem in front of her. I can see her now—smoke curling around her face, her eyebrows pulled together in concentration, and her amazing eyes. She had the most beautiful soft hazel eyes. She would gaze at me like she could see into my soul. Then with startling clarity, she could get right to heart of a matter and help me see the best solution. But just remember, I never gave her any credit. I was a total brat, just like every other kid."

The two women were silent for a few minutes as Eve fell back into thoughts about her youth. When Eve came out of her reverie, she realized that Stella looked even more miserable. "Listen Stella, my mother had a horrible mother herself. My grandmother was the reason my mother left home when she was a barely a teenager. She resented my mother for reasons that my mom never understood. My grandmother probably hated her daughter because she was competition. From the little that mom told me about her, she seemed very male identified. She only valued men, so she would have to compete with a daughter for her husband's attention. My mother did love her father, my grandfather, but she never saw him after she left for college. She would get a letter from him every once in a while, but he died before we had the money to return to France. You don't have to have a wonderful mother to be a great mother yourself. My mom was evidence of that." Eve's words trailed off and she hoped that Stella would find some comfort in them.

Stella looked up took to her friend. She stared at Eve, realizing that she did give her the answer she was looking for. She would listen to Sarah and then give advice—it was Sarah's decision to take it or not. She didn't need to overreact and try to force Sarah to be someone she did not want to be. She would simply listen and try to understand.

"My mom was always so busy telling me everything I was doing wrong and what I should be doing to look better for her that she never took the time simply to listen to me. I think I am guilty of this with Sarah. She has a chance at a photography internship in Europe this summer and I really want her to take the opportunity. She is struggling about leaving her girlfriend for the summer. I want Sarah to leave her behind—but really, it's not my choice, is it?"

"It's not your choice, but you certainly have a say in the matter. Sarah is your flesh and blood and her destiny is not to be left to post-adolescent whimsy. She needs guidance and support. My mother and I did not always agree, but her words resonated inside of me with every decision I made. I think those early adult years are the toughest. We have to be grown-ups, but we are still working with teenage impulses. I desperately wanted to take a year off of college to backpack around Europe, but mom convinced me to finish college and do my European tour before I started grad school. I fought her tooth and nail, but you know what, in the end, I stayed and finished my bachelor's degree. It was a good decision because when I did go to Europe, I didn't come back for a long time. When I did come back, I was not starting from scratch. If you taught Sarah how to make a good decision, which I think you did, then she'll make the right one.

If she chooses to stay home with her girlfriend, then that was the right decision. We only know if our choices are correct if we examine them in retrospect. Don't beat yourself up Stella if she disagrees with you. You have to give up any illusion that you can control her behavior, but you gave her the best of yourself for the past twenty years, so I'm sure she will make good choices, even if it's not the choice you would make."

"You make it all seem so logical and simple. I think that I have been over thinking all of this. My only option with Sarah is to let time unravel the mess and then move on." Stella stared as if the answers were held inside the globe of wine sitting in front of her. "The crux of the matter is that I have to have faith my daughter will use the tools I gave her and let the pieces fall where they fall."

Chapter 38

Paris, February 1929

The wind and rain of January in Paris pounded against the windows, but the room was warm and brightly lit. The two girls had been living together for a few weeks and between their respective schedules, they had not had a chance to relax and enjoy each other's company until this night.

Madalane's room had been a dining room before Madame converted the house to a hostel for students. It was a lovely room with a large window facing the street; really, it was almost too perfect for their situation. Evienne could come and go without too much notice merely by using the window. Before Evienne had joined her, Madalane had often been woken up late at night by voices passing by the window. When she first moved in, she had been frightened that someone would try to burglar the house through her room, but Evienne's solid presence helped her sleep easier. She knew that Evienne would never let anyone hurt her.

Madalane laid on the bed, half reading a book and half watching her friend. Evienne was relaxing in the club chair next to the fire as she sketched a woman's form from memory. Madalane felt an indescribable sense of contentment. She was back in Paris, her friend had moved in and although school had just resumed, it seemed to be going smoothly. The further she was away from the Christmas break she had endured with her family, the less she thought about her parents. Each occasion she had to spend time with her parents, it felt like she was being force fed a bitter pill of familial poison. However, she was in Paris—far away from her family—and mostly importantly living the life she craved with Evienne. She rolled over on the bed and laid her face against the soft quilt. She was relaxed, not tired. She heard a page being turned on the sketchpad and briefly wondered if Evienne would sketch her. It was a challenge to know that Evienne's sketchpad was an extension of her hand. If it wasn't within her grasp, it was a few feet away. Madalane let her mind wander as she heard the furious sounds of a pencil moving against the thick paper.

Madalane focused on the textures of the quilt, the warmth in the room, the emotions inside of herself and promised to memorize this moment so she could touch it when she was unhappy. Although at this moment, she couldn't imagine ever being unhappy again. Evienne's move had been surprisingly smooth. She didn't own much, so the clandestine transfer of a bag, a few canvases and the art box through the street window was accomplished relatively quickly. Evienne left with Madalane in the mornings and she would walk her to her first class and then head off to the quay to sell her paintings or return to the apartment to paint. They had quickly settled into a routine of seeing each other as often as possible during the day—Madalane found she couldn't resist visiting her friend during her breaks from class and Evienne consistently resisted invitations to stay out drinking at the cafe with her fellow artists at night.

Madalane rolled over again and squinted towards her friend. Evienne was completely focused on what she was drawing, but she must have felt Madalane's intense gaze because Evienne looked up and smiled at her. Madalane picked her book up and tried to read. Her mind had its own agenda though. She stared at the words but they were not capturing her attention. She was so incredibly content, yet there was this nagging feeling inside of her that this was not enough. But she couldn't understand what more she could want. She had gotten what she wanted. Evienne lived with her now. It wasn't the best of circumstances with Evienne having to use the window for entering and exiting at times, but it was wonderful to have her friend next to her at night. Over the past few weeks, Evienne had even begun to open up to Madalane a little about her family life and where she grew up.

She was the oldest child of a fishing family from the northwest of Britain. She had three younger siblings—two sisters and a brother. Her father's income afforded them a comfortable life. Eve, the name she was born with, went to the village school until she was twelve and then she stayed home to help care for her two younger sisters. Evienne loved to draw, and each day after lunch, she would go down to the beach and draw huge designs in the sand, sometimes fifteen feet wide. The pictures in her head pulsated with life and as she drew them out in the sand, she wished she could color them in.

Occasionally, a stranger would be sitting on a beach with a set of watercolors and a canvas. City people would drive along the coast and stop to paint the beach where Evienne created her natural canvases. At first, she had kept her distance from these strangers, but eventually Evienne's curiosity got the best of her and she moved closer to their easels. Most of the amateur artists were very nice and did not mind the young woman watching them work. Evienne was fascinated by the initial harsh whiteness of the blank canvas and the way the colors would bleed into each other as the watercolors were mixed together. Evienne was a beautiful young woman and she knew that the men were friendly to her because they appreciated her long hair and youth. She learned that if she flattered their prowess with a paintbrush or leaned against them while they painted and asked simple, easy questions, they would offer to show her how to paint. These lessons were uneven since some of the men were actually quite dreadful, but when she held a paintbrush in her hand, she felt completeness.

As time went by, her ability to simper and seem unschooled became harder and harder. She wanted to work with her own canvas and not small sections of someone else's canvas. She was curious about oil paints and charcoal and the other methods that some of the men had explained to her. Her ability to translate the beach scene into a watercolor drenched with cool blues and hot yellows far surpassed any of the amateur efforts of the men who sat at the easels. In her mind, the colors mixed, blended and evolved into translucent echoes of the scenes in front of her.

She went to the sundry shop in the village. There were no art supplies there, but Mrs. Mulcahy, the proprietor, would know where to get them and how much they were. Evienne had no money, but her birthday was coming up and she knew that her parents would indulge her if the price were not too high.

A few weeks later, Evienne sat on the beach with a gleaming white canvas and fresh set of watercolors. She stared mindlessly at the crashing waves, the line of the horizon, and the small boats in the distance. She wanted to paint all of it, in one go, but she had painted this scene a million times in her head. She turned her chair around, and faced the village. The small houses with their chimneys and fenced yards seemed too ordinary to paint on her first canvas. She was momentarily at a loss as to what to paint. In her frustration, she closed her eyes and the image of her father walking from his boat towards her formed in front of her. She quickly opened her eyes and began to paint the clothes her father wore every day: his fisherman's cap pulled low, the bulky cable knit sweater, his wool pants held up with his thick leather belt. The watercolor did not allow her to add the detail she saw in her mind's eye, but she could feel the paintbrush moving as if her mind was willing it instead of her hand.

Her brother, who came after her in birth order, died when he was barely in his teens. He had started going out with his father in the morning to help pull the nets. He was not a natural fisherman, but he was a hard worker and would one day inherit the boat as the only boy in the family. One morning, he woke up feeling poorly—he looked pale and he felt too weak to get out of bed. Within a month's time, he had died. The doctor said there was something wrong with his blood.

Evienne's mother died shortly after her brother. She had been heartbroken at the death of her only son. She seemed to just waste away in front of people's eyes. Evienne, her father and her two younger sisters watched in stunned silence as the two family members died in quick succession. Evienne's father would stay out on his boat from sunrise to sunset, unable to face their home now that his wife and son were gone. Evienne's life became one of being a mother to her younger sisters and a cook and housekeeper for her father.

Evienne still had two blank canvases and plenty of watercolor paint left, but she had no time, nor did she have the desire to pick up the paintbrush and try to make something beautiful. She couldn't even face walking down to the beach. She was heartsick over her mother and brother, she was heartsick that her father hid on the boat and she was heartsick that her two little sisters would grow up without the mother or father she had known.

Every evening, Evienne's father would trudge through the door and sit heavily at the table. Evienne would put food in front of him, which he ate quickly. Then he would sit in front of the fire, smoke his pipe and stare at the flames. He looked older than he was. She knew he had a hard life out on the boat, but he loved it. Occasionally he would bring in a huge fish, one that would set the buyers at the market angling for a look. There would be a gleam in his eye as he recounted the buyers arguing over who would have the great fortune to buy such a fish. She loved that gleam and the way his craggy face would split as he smiled like a schoolboy when he finally finished the story by declaring the final price (which was always higher than he expected and lower than they needed to make ends meet).

She wanted so much for that gleam or the smile to return, but her father seemed covered in a blanket of sorrow. She felt the same sorrow and she buried herself in grief and work. She took in sewing from the widowers and bachelors of the village to earn extra money. There was nothing she wanted to buy, but she wanted to keep busy and their small family always needed something. Her hands needed something to do.

As each day ended, Evienne prayed that her father would be the man he had been before her mother and brother died. But each day, he seemed to sink deeper into an abyss of quiet and sadness. One day, as she listened to the constant squabbling of her sisters, she felt a cool breeze blow against her. She turned to see if someone had opened the door, but nothing was different. Her sisters were only a few years younger than she—they were twelve and nine to her sixteen years, but they seemed untouched by the sorrow that hung over their father. It had been two years since their mother had died, and nine year old, Mary, barely remembered what life had been like. The twelve year old, Ruth, remembered, but she refused to fall into the trap of endless mourning. In many ways, Evienne envied Ruth because she was defiant in her quest for happiness.

Late at night, as she desperately tried to summon the image of her family before their tragedy, she would see the faces of her mother and brother grow hazy. As the years went on, it was harder to remember the days when her family would sit around the table in the evening and enjoy the warmth of the kitchen. Her father's stories were the centerpiece and her mother's love would feed the family with a poignancy that made her weep. Now, her father would sink into his memories in silence. Her sisters were a counterpoint to his melancholy. They were loud and rambunctious and they got on her nerves. In more rational moments, she would realize that they were the normal ones and the somber attitude that she and her father had adopted was wrong.

To ease the stagnation of their environment, she started taking the girls on picnics to the beach, and she brought along one of her blank canvases one day. It was a warm day and the girls were ecstatic that Evienne was making an effort to have fun. They swam in the cool water and then flopped down on the rocky shore to warm themselves. Evienne painted their young, smooth bodies and felt the tears begin to stream down her face. But she continued to paint, watching the colors blend into one another as the girls came into focus on her canvas. She cried as the sun burned into her fair skin and she cried as the water crept closer to her spot on the beach. She cried for her sisters and her own inadequacy as a mother substitute. She cried for her father and his inability to recover from the sadness that permeated their home.

When the canvas was done, her tears stopped. She told the girls it was time to go home. The girls came over to see the painting. The picture was exquisite and even in their youth, they understood what it contained. It was so much more than a portrait of two girls on the beach; it was the portrait of love and family, sadness, and hopefulness. They both hugged Evienne. The three girls stood on the beach feeling the intensity of being a family for the first time in a long time.

Later at home, Evienne had shyly displayed the painting to her father. Overcome by the moment, he had said little, but a few weeks later, he had given her the art box. It had been expensive—far more than his meager earnings could afford, but she knew that it was his way of thanking and supporting her. From the minute he had gruffly thrust it at her, it had been her most prized possession.

Weeks turned into months, and the Evienne felt more alive each day. She began to meet her father at the dock each afternoon to walk home with him, as she had done for years before her mother died. At first, their walks were silent, but as the weeks went on, he opened up—first talking of the weather and the fishing, and then slowly he started talking about her mother.

He was dying of a broken heart. One afternoon, as the sun was setting in the horizon, they walked along the sea wall that protected the village from the sea's occasional violence. He stopped and stared at the purples and oranges in the sky.

"I don't think I will see the next full moon," he said quietly.

Her first instinct was to scoff and tell him to snap out of his maudlin thoughts. Then she understood that he was serious. She was suddenly terrified of being alone. How would she raise her sisters? With a trembling voice, she asked "Why?"

Squinting at the sunset, he continued to look away from her, "I can feel it. I know it the same way I know when there is a net full of fish below me." He attempted a smile, the exhaustion clear on his face, "Like how you know that there is a mermaid swimming next to the boat Evie."

He started to walk again, and Evienne slowly followed. She was worn down. She finally felt alive again, and now her father was giving up.

Before reaching the house, he stopped again. Looking at her, he pulled her to him and whispered, "Do what you want when I am gone. This is your life. You need to find what will make you happy. Always hold onto your mother's pearl—she will protect you—she is our angel."

True to his word, he died within the fortnight. She woke one morning to make his breakfast and he had died in his chair in front of the fire sometime during the night. She placed a hand on his face and felt the coldness of absence enter her again.

Her father's sister showed up a few days later. Evienne's aunt was a kind woman who lived near London. Her father had asked her to look after Mary and Ruth. She was to sell his fishing boat and divide the money between the three girls. Her aunt sat her down after the funeral and asked her what she wanted to do. Her aunt and uncle were planning on immigrating to America; many members of her uncle's family had already settled near Boston and she could certainly find a new life there. Her two sisters would be coming with her aunt.

Evienne sat there looking at her father's older sister; suddenly she had options. When she had found her father's body, she thought she was going to have to find a husband to marry, so she could care for her two sisters. The money would not be a lot, but it would be enough to live on for a few years. Her aunt was quiet and let her think as she mulled over this information.

"I want to go to art school," Evienne declared.

Her aunt's eyebrows rose incredibly high on her forehead. This was not what she was expecting. "I'm not sure that is what your father would have wanted you to do."

"It is. I know it. He would have approved. I want to become an artist."

Her aunt shook her head and gave a frustrated sigh. "What are you to do as an artist? Teach? What is the point of art? I am worried for your future Evie."

It was an apt question that she had never considered before. What was the point to art? Evienne sat quietly looking at her hands trying to put into words the feelings that art made her feel. Finally, she said, "Art is alive. It is the only thing that will live on years after I am gone. My mother is gone. My father is gone. My brother is gone. I have nothing left but my memories. I need to use my art as a way of immortalizing their lives. I can make them live again through my art."

As she talked, Evienne pulled the canvases she had painted out from behind the chair where she was keeping them. She showed her aunt the painting of her father. Evienne's father, with his craggy face, disheveled hair and handsome smile, seemed to jump off the canvas and fill the empty spaces in the room. Her aunt started to weep. Nodding her head, and resting her hand on her niece's shoulder, she gave Evienne her blessing. To seal the agreement, Evienne thrust the painting into her aunt's hands, knowing the die was cast.

Mary was angry when they heard the news, but Ruth understood the desire to be happy. She and Mary would live with their aunt in America and they would discover their own world. Ruth tried to reason with Mary, but for the past few years, Evienne had been Mary's mother, and she felt deserted. She ached inside knowing the pain she caused her sister, but she was young, and her aunt and Ruth would provide stability and a sense of family that they all longed for.

Evienne's aunt stayed for another month with the three girls while their father's estate was settled. She created a trust for Evienne out of the proceeds from the sale of the boat. It wasn't much, but it seemed like the pot of gold at the end of the rainbow to the young woman. Her aunt had also made inquiries as to where a young woman should study art. She discovered that London had the Female School of Art. The only problem was that Evienne had had no formal art training and therefore, no one to recommend her for the school. Her aunt had broken the news to her niece with gentle care, secretly hoping the young woman would abandon her ambition. Instead, it filled Evienne with resolve.

Evienne's first step was to create a portfolio of paintings that showed versatility and then travel to London to meet with the Dean of the Female School of Art to prove her worthiness. She knew, in her heart, that this was her destiny. When Evienne explained the plan to her aunt, the older woman shook her head in exasperation, but supported her niece nonetheless.

The young woman needed time to work on her portfolio and she needed to buy ample art supplies. Her aunt wearily agreed to help her and she spoke to a woman in the village who would give Evienne a room to live in while she worked on her paintings.

Her aunt finally arranged passage for herself and Evienne's sisters to America. For all the young woman's bravado, she was momentarily and desperately afraid. She had never been alone in her life, and now she would be living in a small bedroom in a neighbor's house with some arcane plan to get accepted to a school that might not care about her or her passion for art.

The night before her family left, they sat down for a large feast. Mary was still not speaking to Evienne, but Ruth was chattering and trying to maintain an atmosphere of happiness and expectation. Evienne's aunt was subdued, but she was truly glad to be going home to her family. Evienne felt sick and wanted to throw herself at her aunt and beg her to take her to America with her sisters.

That night, Evienne tossed and turned for a few hours, and eventually gave up trying to sleep. She would not be going far in the morning. The neighbor she would be staying with was only a few hundred meters away and her meager belongings would be transported in just a few trips. The young woman wrapped herself in a blanket and moved out to the kitchen. She had been born in this house and had known no other. After tomorrow, another family would be living there. Their children sitting at the kitchen table and another mother stoking the fire in the morning as another father shaved in icy water next to the sink.

She stared at every inch of the room, attempting to memorize every splinter of wood, every crack in the bricks that outlined the fireplace, and every divot in the floor where her brother's knife had gouged the wood. She felt the tears building up in her eyes, knowing that she would never cry in this kitchen again. Evienne's feelings of loneliness were exploding inside of her when she heard a door open from her sister's bedroom. It was Ruth and she too had wrapped herself in a blanket.

Ruth walked towards her older sister and sat on the bench next to her. She was trembling slightly and Evienne opened her blanket to let her sit close and feel the heat from her body. Her sister, who was always so cheerful and happy, looked forlorn. She wanted to ask her why, but Evienne already knew in her heart. Instead, the two sisters sat, side by side, feeling the cool air blow through the cracks between the doors and windows. Evienne felt her sister's heartbeat slow and match hers; the universe reminding her that her sister shared the same blood and the same life.

Tonight, that life would end and the two girls would both move on to different lives. Evienne prayed that both of her sister's lives would be filled with warmth and love; she prayed that Mary would forgive her one day; she prayed that she would not appear to be foolish in her quest to be an artist. Ruth's hand found hers beneath their shared blankets and Evienne knew that she prayed with her. For the rest of the night, the sisters sat together in quietude as they prayed for their futures.

As the morning turned from black to gray, the two girls stood and went into their room to dress. Evienne looked out the small window of the room, saw a pink glow on the horizon, and felt it was a good omen for her and her family. Today was a new start for all of them, and soon the excitement of activity would overtake all of them, but for now, she stared out the window and watched the pink turn to gold. Everything was packed except for the canvas that Evienne had painted of her sisters. She carried it to where Ruth and Mary were sitting.

Mary turned her face away but Ruth gazed at the watercolor. "'Twas a grand day," she stated wistfully.

Evienne looked back at the painting and felt a surge of sadness strike her heart. "I want you and Mary to have this—to remember me by."

Ruth's face crumpled into tears and she nodded. Mary's head had fallen and she too was sobbing. Evienne laid the canvas against the wall and gripped both of her sisters in an embrace that would last for the rest of their lives.

* * *

Madalane felt a deep satisfaction knowing that her friend was beginning to trust her and yet she wanted more. She wondered if she had a crush on her friend. Crushes at the boarding school were commonplace and the nuns rigorously attempted to suppress these relationships. Nonetheless, when an institution puts two hundred lonely adolescents together, the search for intimacy was unquenchable. Madalane's dearest friend at fifteen had been a girl of similar age, ambition, and demeanor. Bookish and studious, the two girls had spent every waking moment together. They shared their pasts and their hopes for the future until the nuns had separated them onto different dormitory floors. No longer in the same group, and the ever-vigilant pressure by the nuns proved to be too much. They drifted apart and Madalane witnessed her friend forge a new intimacy with another girl. She had learned two important lessons from this experience. The first was to hide your feelings from the world. Maintaining a sense of neutrality became imperative in all of her friendships; she desperately feared being abandoned again. Rejection was bad enough but being forced to walk away from someone was soul destroying. Her second lesson was that no one would love you forever. She realized that no matter how intense a friendship was, it would end eventually. Madalane knew she had to enjoy it while it lasted before circumstances separated a friendship.

Maybe that's what the anxiety she felt was about. Perhaps she was already predicting the demise of her friendship with Evienne. Evienne would one day walk away and not look back. A new friend or a new situation would separate them and then it would be over and it would be time to move on. Madalane felt a brief panic overwhelm her and she wanted to rush to Evienne and throw her head in her friend's lap and beg her never to leave. Instead, she closed her eyes and calmed her breathing until the panic subsided. She opened her eyes and saw that her friend was staring at her quizzically.

Evienne could not help herself from questioning the uneven breathing in her friend, "Are you okay Madalane?"

Madalane stretched and put her book aside, relieved that her friend wanted to talk, even if it was only briefly. She did not like the way her thoughts were going and a distraction would be helpful.

"I was thinking about the boarding school I went to in Bordeaux and how glad I am that I'm not there anymore."

Evienne looked down at the sketch of Madalane's face and asked, "What happened there?"

Madalane laughed and shook her head. "You know how it is...nuns telling you what to do every minute of the day. No warmth or comfort. Just the drudgery of school every day." Madalane stopped speaking, hoping Evienne would move on to another subject, but the artist was quietly contemplating her friend. Madalane's discomfort grew and she continued talking to fill the awkward silence. "It was a lonely experience for me." She didn't know what else to say. How do you explain loneliness to a person who seemed to thrive on it?

"Why were you so lonely?" Evienne looked at her friend.

"Loneliness, I suppose, is knowing that no one will remember you after you are gone." Madalane knew her words were dire, but that's how she had felt at the boarding school. She had friends, she always did, but no one who really made her feel loved or cared about. Friendships had always been a crutch to ease the rejection of her parents, but they were surface and carefully controlled by the nuns and, to be honest, by herself.

"I will never forget you Madalane." Evienne's tone was even and sure.

Tears surged to the surface of Madalane's expression. Evienne always said the right thing to her. No wonder she felt this ache when she was with Evienne. Trying to stop her voice from trembling, Madalane echoed the sentiment, "Evienne, I will never forget you. I promise that you will forever be in heart and on my mind."

Chapter 39

Paris, February 1929, the same night

Reaching into the cabinet next to the bed, Madalane pulled out the biscuits her father had sent. Evienne climbed on to the bed, sitting crossed legged in front of her friend. "These are the best tasting biscuits. They remind me of being a kid."

Madalane's ears perked up, hoping for a childhood reminiscence from her friend. Evienne continued to crunch the biscuit with a melancholy energy, so she decided to prod her friend a bit. "So, what do they remind you of?"

Evienne gave a small smile as she began her story, "They remind me of long salty trips out in the ocean with my father. My mother would pack lunch for my father and me when we would be out fishing all day. Sometimes I would get seasick. I would throw up over the starboard side of the boat so my dad would not see me and then I would eat some of those biscuits and they would make me feel better. I never wanted to be separated from papa's world, so I never let him know. Do you think he knew I got sick?"

Madalane felt her heart tighten at her friend's memory. Half of her wanted to laugh at the absurdity of this tall, strong woman furtively vomiting over the side of the boat. The other half wanted to gather her friend in her arms and comfort her. "I don't think it mattered if he knew or not. I think he loved having you on the boat with him. That's what's important."

Evienne continued to crunch on the biscuits when it occurred to Madalane that she might not realize how important she was to her father. "Evienne—did your sisters go on the boat with your father or were you the only one of his daughters who went?"

"I was the only fisherwoman; I was my father's daughter much more than my mother's." Evienne grew quiet, remembering how being relegated to the kitchen chores was the worse punishment she could endure. Getting up to get a cigarette, Evienne returned to relax on the bed, blowing smoke rings at the ceiling. "Who you miss the most, Mad?"

Madalane felt a tremor of anxiety. Clearly, Evienne had reached her limit with talking about her father. She thought again about whom she missed. Except for her grandparents, she had not had to deal with death up close. Abandonment was the only thing close to death that she could understand. Faces and names of childhood friends passed through her mind as she rejected each as being not interesting or important enough to mention. Finally, there was one name she had avoided—Sabine—her roommate when she was fifteen. She had rigidly prevented herself from dwelling on their friendship, but Sabine was the only one who she missed desperately.

"I had a roommate in secondary school. She and I became very close friends despite the fact that we were very different. She was not like the other girls—Sabine was interested in science and she loved being outside with the plants and being at the lake near the school. I miss her. She was unique and I found her fascinating."

"What was it that made her fascinating?" Evienne wistfully wondered if she could be Madalane's fascination.

Madalane reached for another biscuit. She felt her stomach lurch and briefly wondered if seasickness was contagious. "Sabine just didn't care what people thought of her. She wanted to be Marie Curie and work with chemicals and other stuff that girls are usually not interested in. She showed me that just because I was a girl, it didn't mean that I had to focus only on boys and having babies. She made me realize that I could escape my provincial little town and get to Paris. She's really the reason I'm here today. She gave me the belief that I could be more than what others expected of me."

Evienne smiled and replied, "I love Sabine's spirit. It is one of the reasons I love Paris so much; the city is filled with people who think the same way. Women are strong, women have opinions, women can learn, and women are smart. Your friend gave you excellent advice and she bought you a ticket to Paris and Paris gave you to me."

"Yes, she did give me the chance to meet you. I should find her and let her know that I made it to Paris and I have another wonderful roommate!" Madalane smiled at her friend and moved to stuff the remainder of her biscuit into Evienne's mouth. Evienne accepted the cookie and leaned back on the bed. Madalane settled down next to her and they laid in a companionable silence for a few minutes, both lost in thought.

Evienne thought of how she had felt the top of Madalane's finger inside her mouth, touching the tip of her tongue. She wanted to suck on her finger, but instead she allowed the dry white crumbs to dissolve in her mouth. Evienne need to take the focus off of her thoughts. "What ever happened to Sabine?"

Feeling a sharp stab of memory, Madalane rolled onto her side, facing the wall with her back to her friend. She whispered, "The school discouraged especially close friendships between us girls. As long as you kept your friendships superficial and casual, the nuns were happy. Sabine and I became very close, and the more time I spent with her, the less time I spent with the girls who talked endlessly of getting married. The mother superior wrote to both of our parents and told them that we were being separated because we demonstrated an unhealthy attachment to one another."

Madalane closed her eyes, feeling the piercing humiliation that she had felt when she discovered that her parents had been informed. "We were moved to separate dorms. We were warned to stay away from each other. I was very good at following rules. She attempted to communicate—through notes, but I was afraid." The words echoed in Madalane's ears. She wasn't sure what she had been afraid of, but she had felt fear every day until finally Sabine walked by her without even a glance in her direction. "After a while, I just forgot we had been friends. Her parents moved to England and she left the school."

Evienne knew the feeling of having to leave people. It was not easy on the heart. "Madalane," Evienne put her hand on her friend's shoulder, "I am sorry you had to lose your friend because of stupid rules. It's not fair." Evienne curled her body around her friends to alleviate both of their pain. She knew Madalane was crying and she wanted to take her away her pain, but all she could do was to pull her closer to her heart. She could smell her scent, she could feel her breath; she wanted to open her own body and pull her inside to keep her safe. She whispered the only words that came to her mind, "There are no rules here; we are artists and students of life."

The feelings of loss that had infiltrated Madalane's heart were filled by the warmth of Evienne's words and the solid presence of her friend behind her. The two women lay in silence. Madalane felt her body relax into the artist and she felt a measure of peace. As she felt her body begin to drift off into sleep, she was struck by a hammer of anxiety. What if she lost Evienne? She had really liked Sabine but she would die if lost Evienne. Trembling, she burrowed back into her friend's warmth, trying to ease the cold anxiousness that had covered her. Madalane's usually clear voice was thin and raspy, "Promise me, Evienne, please promise me that you won't go away."

The words thundered through Evienne's head. She had not considered Madalane's feelings about her. She automatically thought Madalane would leave her for a better quality of life, to have someone who would care for her needs. It never occurred to her that she was needed by Madalane. The feelings made her nervous. Evienne smoothed the flyaway hairs resting on her friend's shoulder and arm, and felt the definition of her bone structure with each gentle stroke. A thousand images came to her mind as the words repeated themselves in her mind, promise me you won't go away, please. Promise me. Surprised by the ease, the words echoed from her own mouth "I promise you I won't go away my dearest friend. I promise." Evienne whispered the words to her friend, her lips brushing the curves of her ear. "I promise."

Hurt surged from a place forgotten in Evienne. She prayed to God to help fulfill her promise. She held Madalane even closer as memories passed like photographs in her mind: her father's hand, the comfort of her mother's lap, braiding her sisters' hair, the sea, painting Paris, love and fights and surviving. Their friendship was transforming her ambivalence into kindness. She wanted to tell her everything, saving her from the despair of nothingness, the chasm of loneliness she had learned to live within.

The young woman's body relaxed against the artist. Evienne felt Madalane's body fall into a restful sleep. Evienne's mind crept to the days she spent on Charles's sofa; she continued to whisper into Madalane's ear as if confessing her sins, "I thought you would never come home. I thought I was going to have to forge through alone again. I was no better than a picture frame being put into a pen of pigs. I cried as I stared at the cracked ceiling of Charles's studio and prayed to know more of myself—to understand my heart, to forgive my need to isolate. My wrists bruised, my eyes swollen, my body aching for what lesson? I fought with anger and fear as Jean and his thugs tried to rape me, but I realized I fought because I finally had something real again in my life. I fought because I had you. Maybe I am stubborn, maybe I am too proud, maybe God took my hands so I would see clearly what was right in front of me."

Madalane did not respond. Evienne was relieved not to have to discuss her admission, but she also felt compelled to keep talking to her friend who was lost in her own dreams.

Evienne's tears blended in with the flow of her words as she laid them out over the quiet in the room. "I know now where I belong, I know now I will never leave you. I know now that I am a better person and artist because of you."

The confession turned into a homily of Evienne's self-worth. The words settled into their new resting place, allowing fresh air to enter Evienne's lungs as she matched the slow breathing of her friend's. Her final prayer, learned and often recited aloud at the wheel of her father's fishing boat, blessed the sleeping room, "God, at whose command the winds blow, and lift up the waves of the sea, and who stillest the rage thereof. We thy creatures, but miserable sinners, do in this our great distress cry unto thee for help: Save, Lord, or else we perish. We confess, when we have been safe, and seen all things quiet about us, we have forgot thee our God, and refused to hearken to the still voice of thy word, and to obey thy commandments: But now we see, how terrible thou art in all thy works of wonder; the great God to be feared above all: And therefore we adore thy Divinity. Amen." The words fell over the two women like a blanket. It was the prayer Evienne's father had said daily as he left port. Evienne repeated her promise as she felt sleep overtake her, "My dearest friend, I will never leave you."

The artist's mind, body and soul were spent. She snuggled closer to her friend and fell into a deep sleep. Madalane's eyes opened in the dark as the tears slipped from her eyes. Evienne's words were so painful; she had yearned to turn and embrace her friend; however, she knew that Evienne would never accept sympathy. She grasped the artist's hand and held it to her chest. An overwhelming need to protect infused her; she would never let anything bad happen to her friend ever again.

My Dearest Madalane,

Tonight the velvet of your skin softened the fear covering my flesh. It is so quiet, the caring between us, I almost did not notice its presence becoming part of me. Trust is the darkness that breathes under our sheets as we lie together in our warm little world.

I know my abandonment as a girl birthed a survivor, and I believe we are two survivors that have found each other. Sadness held hands with trust, and at times, I had mistaken them for the same thing. In darkness, during our nights Madalane, I found a home that is warm and safe and lets me sleep to wake refreshed and safe, ready for a new day. You are a better place than any I have ever known, and any place is better now that I am with you.

I smile thinking of you as I am a daydream looking down at the Seine. The sun is shining on me and I laugh because we come from different sides of the river, yet we spring from the same water. How did God know to send you to me when I could barely feel his presence? Now the world is alive. We are a family now for I have learned to trust you and love you in a way that I have missed for so many years. I have missed the closeness, the knowing that someone is there, that I am here for another. You have given my head a shoulder to rest upon.

You smell like a walk through Paris; will you walk with me and be my family tonight in the moonlight.
Forever,
Evienne

Chapter 40

Paris, March 1929

Evienne watched the tourists strolling along the boulevard. It was almost springtime and the sun was shining brightly even though there was still a bite in the air. She and Charles were taking advantage of the beautiful day to sell some paintings. The tourists and locals were out in droves, invigorated to see finally the start of better weather. Leaning against the sea wall, both artists appeared nonchalant, but they kept a keen eye on the people walking by, ready to pounce if anyone showed any interest.

Charles lit another cigarette and sardonically asked, "How is your little friend Ev?"

As a smile played around her lips, Evienne leaned into the sun and smugly replied to Charles. "Madalane is fine, thank you for asking."

Charles glanced over at his friend, curious about her expression; he decided to tease her a bit. "Have you seduced her yet? Or are you still worshipping her purity?"

This question annoyed Evienne, "Good God Charles, you are crass! Give me a cigarette."

He laughed, handing her a cigarette and his matchbox. "Do

you want me to smoke it for you too?" Evienne rolled her eyes at him and he laughed again. "You are certainly happier than I have ever seen you." Pensively he gazed at her, and touched his nose as he continued, "But I don't think you have fucked the girl yet. I don't know what you are waiting for Ev. She is going to get snapped up by one of the young bucks who will be sniffing around soon. You know what French men are like in the spring!"

When Evienne didn't reply, he continued, "She needs to be told that she is desirable. Trust me on this. I know women. She is young but she wants to be a woman. She is holding out for your attention, but if you don't show her that you crave her, she will look elsewhere. Mark my words my friend." Charles dramatically inhaled his cigarette to punctuate his statement.

The conversation made her burn inside. Evienne prayed that she would get a sale so she would not have to respond to Charles. She tipped her head at him. "I am taking care of her, don't you worry, chum. I understand the needs of a woman better than any man." She took a drag of her cigarette and winked at her stall-partner.

Charles knew his friend would offer no prurient details. He would have to make something up later for Patrice. She became incredibly aroused when he whispered a fictional telling of Evienne's passion for her little friend. He would definitely benefit from a little tweaking of the facts. Truth, as he often said, was a flexible concept.

"How is it painting in her little room? Can you get anything done? Is there enough light?"

"Not like the digs you have Charles, but better than the squat. Madalane is very accommodating if you know what I mean. Sometimes I draw her. She is a pleasure to sketch." Evienne thought she should play the game for her friend, but she felt disdain towards herself, knowing she was painting a fake picture of Madalane.

Charles pitched his cigarette into the Seine and turned to his friend. "I am feeling overly generous today for some reason—perhaps Patrice has more talents than looking pretty." He smirked at the memory of the bite she left on his belly that morning. "You should use my studio in the mornings. I don't paint until late in the day and really, Patrice is no good to me until the sun has been up for hours. You should use the space. You could get your little friend to pose for you. I won't even charge you for any stains you leave on the chaise."

Charles was leering at a pretty girl walking by as Evienne turned her head to see if he was serious. Oblivious, he kept speaking, "Of course, Patrice is quite fond of you. You brought out the nurturing side of her during your convalescence. I think she would be happy to pose for you, but I may need to observe your technique." He leered at her in case she missed his meaning.

Rolling her eyes at him, Evienne was tempted by Charles's offer. This could be the break she needed, and he offered Patrice to her. Memories of her old three-way love affair surfaced; it made her cautious to consider the young model. She would have to think about working with Patrice. Her life was different now. She had Madalane; she didn't need to share a lover with anyone, ignoring the faint voice in her head that reminded her that Madalane was not her lover. "Your generosity makes me think you are fond of me Charles." Evienne took a leisurely drag off her cigarette as if in deep contemplation. "I will take you up on the studio time. Maybe your success will rub off on me."

He grunted, imagining Patrice's long limbs intertwined with his friend's. Patrice would put on a show for him, but Evienne would never allow it. On the other hand, he knew that Patrice could be very convincing. He would, at the very least, hear all the details if she was able to seduce Evienne.

"Use it any morning. Patrice will get up early if you want her." Charles' words held a certain meaning that Evienne ignored.

The two artists stood watching the crowds. An American couple approached their booth. The man made a move to look closer at Evienne's painting of an old man.

Charles whispered under his breath, "Looks like you have one on the line; reel it in Ev!"

Unexpectedly she sold four of her paintings to an American couple who seemed quite taken with her technique. Because she spoke English fluently, she was able to communicate much better with the American tourists than most of the artists along the quay. Americans in particular seemed to get flustered quickly by accents and uncommon words.

This American husband and wife had asked her numerous questions about how the ink outlines impacted the layering of paint. They were older and didn't seem frivolous. She was reasonably sure that they would buy one of her paintings, but when the husband picked up two and then the wife picked up two, she was completely taken aback. They paid her the asking price without haggling. The husband asked her to sign her name legibly on the back of the painting of an old flower vendor. Smiling, she happily complied with the request.

They walked off with their wrapped purchases, and Evienne felt the weight of the coins the husband had given in her pocket. This was more money than she usually made in a week. She was already in a good mood, but now, she was ecstatic. Madalane's birthday was approaching and she could finally buy her friend something perfect. She had secretly been working on a sketch of her friend's face, and she knew that Madalane would blush, but be secretly pleased with the portrait. She also knew that she had wanted to repay Madalane's kindness with something more special, but business had been slow and she was scraping by just to replenish her paints and buy bread.

Charles' paintings were also in demand on this cold morning. An older woman, with a fox fur embellishing her shoulders, had engaged his attention. She was clearly enamored with him. She knew his pitch all too well. While Evienne considered what to buy for Madalane, she watched him lean in close, whisper a price into the older woman's ear and inhale her scent at the same time. He was smooth and she knew he would personally deliver the painting to her apartment. The woman pulled out a card from her small purse and handed it to him. Evienne watched him run his thumb along the thick paper, gazing longingly into his customer's eyes. The woman turned and headed back the way she came. He gave a short wave and returned to Evienne's side, slouching against the sea wall.

Charles lit another cigarette and quickly removed it to spit a piece of tobacco onto the sidewalk. With a casual confidence, he filled her in, "I am going to stop by Amelie's apartment with the painting. She wants to learn about my art."

Evienne laughed out loud and clapped him on the shoulder. "I'm sure that she wants to be your patron. You just need to make sure she pays the price."

He scowled again and scratched the scruff on his chin. "Hmm…perhaps I should be a gigolo and forget art completely. The lifestyle would suit me quite well."

Evienne was gathering her sketchbook and art box as he said this. Still laughing at his attitude, she whispered in his ear, "Perhaps you should invest in a bar of soap and a razor first."

Charles laughed and nodded, understanding her point. Evienne kissed him lightly on both cheeks and headed off to run her errand.

Not far from the artists' stalls, on Rue de l'Odeon, there were two bookstores that she frequented. She rarely ever bought anything, but both stores stocked photography books and when Evienne needed inspiration or an idea for a painting, she enjoyed the warmth of the stores and the conversation that the patrons had with the owners.

She went into Le Maison des Amis des Livres. The woman who ran the shop didn't seem to expect anyone even to purchase books. She allowed customers to borrow them first before they decided to buy them. Evienne was not sure how this made her

money, but the bookstore had been around since before the Great
War. The brightness of the day brought out shoppers, and the
little store was quite busy. As she entered, the bookseller, Adrienne Monnier called out, "Bonjour."

"Bonjour, Adrienne."

"We have some new photo books from America." The key
to Adrienne's success, Evienne thought, was remembering what
her customers liked.

"No, nothing for me today. I would like to buy a gift for a
dear friend."

When Evienne declared an intention to buy, Adrienne raised
her eyebrow in surprise and came around the counter to help
Evienne. "What does your friend like to read?"

"Um...she is a student, so she reads everything."

"Come now, is she a realist, a fantasist, a romantic?"

"She is a realistic romantic." She felt pleased that she could
clearly remember the conversation they had about Madalane'
loathing of the story of Jane Eyre because Mr. Rochester kept
his first wife locked in the attic.

"Does your friend like poetry?"

Evienne felt pressured; she wanted to look around, not to
be interrogated; however, Adrienne had been very kind to her
for many years, so she forced herself to keep her frustration in
check. "Yes, I know she does."

"Bien, I have just the section." She led Evienne to a small section of poetry books. "This is the biggest selection of women poets
in the city, and sadly it doesn't fill an entire shelf." Her voice held
an ironic tone and Evienne nodded, understanding the meaning.

"Is your friend a close friend?"

Evienne replied without censoring her statement, "She is
the dearest friend a person could have. She is kind, selfless and
incredibly loving."

Adrienne's flexible eyebrow rose higher than Evienne had
ever seen them go before. "That is high praise."

Evienne's excellent spirits were not diminished by the slightly unusual tone in Adrienne's voice. "She is the best person I know and she has made me a better person."

The bookshop proprietor's wandering eyebrows finally settled into place as she put her hand on Evienne's wrist. "Browse as long as you wish, but I think your friend would enjoy this author in particular." The shopkeeper pulled out a slim volume of poetry by Edna St. Vincent Millay and handed it to Evienne.

Evienne sat down and started to leaf through pages. Adrienne was right. These poems were beautiful and lovely, like Madalane. She took the book up to the counter to pay. "Thank you Adrienne; this book is perfect."

"I think you will find it most entertaining."

Evienne watched as Madalane's gift was wrapped in a brown sheet of paper. Adrienne held on to the book as she searched a drawer in the desk made counter. "I have the perfect addition for your friend's birthday present. Ah, here it is!" She pulled 2 feet of red ribbon into the air. "Shall we tie it into a bow?"

The artist nodded happily. The feeling was still disconcerting, but she was getting used to it. She had forgotten what it was to be happy, but Madalane had reminded her. "She will love it! Thank you so much."

Adrienne smiled thoughtfully at the young woman, "Evienne…I have not known you so well in the past, but I feel we have a similar way of thinking."

The artist was immensely pleased but uncertain of what drew the comparison. "Adrienne, I am honored to be compared to you."

The older woman gave a hearty laugh. "No, that is not what I meant at all. Listen, Evienne, my friend Sylvia and I host a salon in the spring after hours in our apartment. We invite writers and artists—and I think you should come and bring your friend. I think you will find it most entertaining."

Although Evienne was startled by the impromptu invitation, she was equally thrilled. "Yes, a salon? That would be divine."

"Excellent. The first one will be in May—the second Friday. We close the shop at 8 p.m. and generally, people start showing up at nine. It is the doorway next to the shop door—just ring the bell."

Evienne smiled warmly, "Thank you Adrienne. I would be delighted to attend."

"And bring your friend. I would like to meet the woman who has captured you so thoroughly. What is her name?"

Evienne blushed at how Adrienne had so keenly understood her feelings for Madalane. "Thank you. My friend—her name is Madalane—will be very happy to hear that we are invited to your salon."

Evienne slipped out the door with the securely wrapped book under her arm. What a strange conversation that had been, but she was deliriously happy and headed back to their room on Rue Galande.

Chapter 41

Paris, March 1929

Madalane sat nervously staring at anything but her friend. She was nude except for a sheet—Evienne called this a modesty drape. How could it refer to modesty when she was sitting naked on a chaise in Charles' studio? How did this happen she asked herself for the umpteenth time. She had misunderstood Evienne's announcement of Charles' invitation. Charles had uncharacteristically made a generous offer to Evienne that his studio was always available to her. Madalane initially thought that Charles wanted Evienne to move back in with him, but that had not been the case. She hadn't realized this as she stood on the street in disbelief that her friend was already moving out after just a couple of months living together.

Madalane's heart had turned to lead and before Evienne had had a chance to explain; Madalane had volunteered to do anything if she would stay. Evienne had looked at her with a fierce intensity and nodded without saying a word. Madalane inwardly groaned at the memory. She remembered feeling like she had outplayed Charles. Later, after they had eaten dinner and both women were sitting by the fire enjoying the warmth, Evienne had clarified the invitation. Madalane felt her stomach rise up to her chest as Evienne quietly and graciously accepted Madalane's offer, requesting that she pose for a painting. Madalane smiled and nodded, hoping that Evienne would eventually forget and she would not be scrutinized with Evienne's usual intensity when she drew or painted.

A day went by and then another. Madalane assumed that the artist had forgotten the promise. She was mostly relieved, but a small part of her was angry. Why was she not good enough to sit for a painting? Was she too ordinary? Too plain? Then, after classes had ended on a Thursday, while the two girls ate their evening meal, Evienne informed Madalane that she would have Charles' studio all day on Sunday. Charles was taking Patrice to the racetrack as a treat—it would be an all-day event. Evienne had wryly noted that it was definitely more of a treat for Charles, but Patrice would enjoy showing off to the crowds at the race-track. The artist had decided that it would be the perfect day to use Madalane as her model.

So here they were—Madalane draped in the modesty cloth while Evienne organized her ink and paints. On this Sunday morning, a perfect light illuminated the room with such intensity that the young woman felt the heat suffuse her entire body. With Evienne's back to the window, the light would also shine on her canvas. The chaise was opposite the window, so the morning sun shined brightly upon Madalane's face and body. She had disrobed behind a small screen and had wrapped the sheet around her like a mummy. Her heart was pounding as she stepped away from the screen and walked nervously to the chaise.

Although they shared a room, their small private bathroom allowed them to maintain their modesty. Evienne had no qualms about taking off her clothes in front of her friend, but she had quickly learned that Madalane would turn pink and face the wall each time Evienne started to disrobe. Evienne, understanding the young woman's discomfort, had adapted and changed while

Madalane used their small lavatory.

Perched on the chaise, Madalane waited for instructions on how to pose. Evienne turned to look at Madalane sitting straight backed on the chaise, and was stunned by the loveliness of the woman in front of her. She stared at her as she had never seen her before. Madalane had let her hair down and it was lying effortlessly over her shoulders. The cascade of brown curls held golden hues and reds of a sunrise. Her eyes held the stark white of the sheet wrapped tightly around her.

Madalane fidgeted under her friend's intense stare. She felt like Evienne could see right through the sheet and was appraising her nude body. She waited for instructions, but none came. Sitting, perched on the side of the chaise, she felt awkward and unnatural. She could smell the age of the chaise and she wondered how many women had posed confidently before her. Her words trembled as she spoke, "Should I sit back? Or maybe lean against the side?" Madalane hoped that her questions would distract Evienne's focused gaze.

Evienne was pulled abruptly from the ocean of her imagination. The chaise, the window, the pictures all reminded her how desperately she had wanted Madalane here over the weeks of her recovery. The pain of her absence was frantic, yet there she was sitting in front of her. No words fell from her lips; no sound was forced from her strangled windpipe. She held her eyes as she shook inside, reliving the hell of those lonely weeks.

The artist pressed her hand against the white shirt over her heart. She moved her hand over the cotton to the buttons and began slowly unbuttoning her shirt. She never painted in her button down or in her cable sweater; she preferred naked from the waist up but today she stayed in her thin undershirt. Clothing was too cumbersome to deal with and not practical considering her sparse wardrobe.

As she pushed each button through the slit in the fabric, she thought how stunningly alluring Madalane was before her. She would rarely have the opportunity to look at the creaminess of her skin or the contrast of her brown hair lying in waves over her shoulders. One brown wave slipped delicately into the crevice between her breasts. The vision barely allowed her to breathe. Some days, as they sat at the cafe while Madalane studied, Evienne would study her and imagine what shape her collarbone would take as it sank into the depth of her neck and lost itself in the round of her shoulder. Today she mused how the small dip where her neck turned into her chest could hold a pool of water and that water would follow the same path as the brown hair presently slipping over her white skin. Evienne studied her pale skin, wondering if it was ever touched by the sun and formulated how she will use the transparency of the white canvas to capture the blue of her skin. Half way down her own buttons, Evienne had the urge to smell her friend's hair and bury her face in the luxurious silk. To feel the warmth it held from her body's heat, to know the texture one more time. Madalane's eyes captivated her. The colors of earth swirled inside each iris, the trees, the rising sun, and sweet fall leaves sheltering the earth. Evienne found Madalane's eyes portraits of her existence; a complex exhibition to capture.

Evienne's shirt lay open, exposing her body to the room. Evienne did not care what Madalane saw; she only dreamed she would make her proud with the art she was going to create. Evienne pulled her shirt off and fixed her leather belt as she walked to the door to hang the shirt on the hook. She felt Madalane's eyes track her and she stopped and turned to her friend. "Are you ready?"

* * *

Madalane watched her friend stand like marble; she was so intense when she worked. At first, it was a curiosity for Madalane, but it was becoming commonplace as the weeks passed and she watched Evienne enter her creative haze. Having her eyes bore straight into her soul was discomfiting, so Madalane looked up and focused in on the sketches pinned up around the room. Most of them appeared to be Patrice—each one representing a different angle of the young woman's body. Madalane's face colored as she stared at one that showed the model's face and upper body. Her bosom was defiantly placed across the bottom half of the paper. Embarrassed at her own reaction, she forced her eyes down to the floor. She stared at the parallel boards, noticing the pattern of alternating wood grain. Madalane thought about the provocative sketches scattered around the room. Evienne had lived in this room for weeks; she had stared at these drawings for hours. Madalane knew in her heart that Evienne would have memorized the lines and curves of each picture.

A beautiful woman, nude and seductive, stared back at Madalane as she glanced up to the wall again. Madalane felt awkward and prudish as she looked down at the white sheet wrapped tightly around her. At that moment, her modesty felt like a heavy burden. She released the fabric that she had gripped tightly in her hand. The crinkled sheet loosened but did not fall away. Relieved for a moment, she then realized that she would have to stand to remove the sheet. That would be too humiliating. She sat, sitting slightly forward on the chaise for a while longer. Abandoning the idea of graceful revelation, Madalane contemplated how she could pose, chagrined that Evienne was offering no preference. She leaned back a bit and as she did, she saw the sheet drop to the top of cleavage. She automatically stopped, slightly shocked by the cool air hitting her flesh.

Her heart pounded relentlessly. If she leaned back a little further, the sheet would slip over the curve of her breast and she would be nude from the waist up, like Patrice. Evienne's face was an impassive mask of concentration. Blankly staring at her, she seemed only to see Madalane as lines and shades. Madalane wondered if she let the sheet slip, would Evienne even twitch?

Would she care? Would she raise an eyebrow? Would she mock her? No, Evienne would be kind and supportive. Nervously, she glanced down at the sheet tenuously wrapped around her breasts. Would Evienne look at her as a model, like Patrice? Or as a friend simply helping another friend out? She stared up at a sketch. It was Patrice lying on the chaise, left arm thrown over her head and the right arm extended across her body, cradling her nude breasts. She tried to envision herself in that pose. She shook her head at the absurdity of the scene. Sighing heavily, the sheet slipped another inch and her body froze.

Evienne noticed her anxiety, "Sitting as a model is tedious, are you sure you want to do this? It might be easier if you just recline on the chaise and close your eyes and forget where you are."

Madalane nodded tensely.

"Do you need anything? Do you want wine? Are you cold?" Evienne wanted the experience to be easy for the young woman.

Combined with the sketches and thoughts about her friend undressing, she barely heard the artist. Madalane's nervousness had been thrust into high gear as she had watched the artist remove her shirt. Although she had seen Evienne in an undershirt many times as was her habit when she worked, watching the casually competent undressing was unnerving for her. She had recently allowed herself to imagine what it would be like to watch Evienne undress for her with a sensual intention. She had initially been horrified to think of her friend in those terms, but as the fantasy played out in her mind, it evolved into an intimate and passionate image. In class, while professors droned on, she would access this imagined event over and over again. It gave her comfort as well as ensuring a warmth that would blanket her body and make her smile.

Finally, she realized that a response was required. "Yes, I would love some wine."

Evienne poured the deep ruby-red wine from the ceramic jug, walked over to the young woman and handed it to her. As

Madalane reached for the goblet, the sheet slipped and dropped below the curve of her breast. Madalane froze again, staring up at Evienne.

The artist's face was blank. She turned and walked back to the stool behind the canvas. "You need to find a comfortable position because you must hold it for a while; don't fight the urge to take a nap."

Madalane glanced at the sheet puddled around her waist. She was still slightly sitting up, bent over, and her breasts between her arms. She felt uncomfortable and since the sheet was already down, she leaned back against the side of the chaise, tucking her legs into a curled position. She looked up at the sketches of Patrice as she took a huge swig of wine, feeling the burn down her throat, hoping for liquid courage. She saw a similar pose to the one she was attempting. Patrice's left arm dropped behind her body and her right arm cradled her head. Madalane mimicked the pose, realizing that Patrice had used that pose to ensure her bosom would be more prominent. Instead, she curled her left arm around her stomach, which was more comfortable, and she could reach her wine more easily without losing the pose.

Settled into her spot, she looked at Evienne. She realized the advantages of being a model. She could stare at her friend all day without shame or self-consciousness.

Evienne considered her model; you could learn about a woman's life by the curve of her neck, just as you could understand her purpose by her hands. A woman could hide her truth behind make up and lipstick but a woman's neck and hands always exposed her secrets. Some necks did not take the brunt of life and remained supple, while others were robbed of moisture. Madalane's neck smoothly curved like water running over marble, and her hands unaware of her future. Madalane did not hold the knowledge of her own potential, what her naked image could inspire. She did not understand the passion that moved through the arteries in her neck causing the flush in her cheeks moving to her chest matching the red wine on her mouth. She thought of Madalane's heart as she formed her face and neck and contemplated the pose on the canvas.

The transition between studying Madalane and sketching was hypnotic for Evienne. She needed neither words nor comfort. She wanted to master the perfection of Madalane's image. The process was fluid, automatically capturing the body in repose in front of her. Slowly, Madalane appeared on her canvas.

Evienne stopped for a minute and stared at Madalane's exposed body. She was fixated on her face and had momentarily lost sight of the whole picture. Madalane had her eyes closed and was lost in thought. Her neck, breasts, and stomach flowed with the gentleness of velvet nearly matching the color of the sheet. Her body, in contrast to the deep burgundy of the chaise, was compelling, almost too distracting. Evienne held the urge of her own body, directing it through the fire of her art. Evienne wanted to cover Madalane's mouth with hers; delicately dancing her fingers over the pink of her nipple but she was disciplined to her purpose. She saw her model's eyes open and she hurriedly looked to her canvas. Evienne could never love her as she deserved. She would not let herself fall in love and she knew she couldn't just seduce and leave.

Although the canvas was not large, there was a significant amount of work needed to paint her subject. Evienne sat back to stretch her back and reached for her cigarettes. It gave her a moment to contemplate her model; Evienne took the top off of the burnt sienna tube and mixed a small drop onto her pallet. She was in the process of replicating Madalane's hair. She looked to Madalane who finally seemed comfortable. She was opening another part of herself that Evienne was quietly seduced by. She no longer had the burden of her physical form; she was at peace. She seemed lost in the ether of her mind.

Evienne took another drag of her Galois and balanced it on the bottom of her easel. Was she turning Madalane into the person she wanted or was Madalane changing her? Was Evienne breaking down Madalane's walls of innocence and opening her to the world of erotic pleasure or was this the emergence of love? Madalane lounged like a contented cat, not like anything Evienne had ever seen. Or maybe she had, but only in her mind's eye. A smooth ribbon of words came from Evienne's mouth. "Tell me Madalane, what is love?" She said Madalane's name as a whisper of pleasure.

Madalane felt a band of heat streak across her chest from Evienne's question. She felt hypnotized by the sun warming her body from the window behind Evienne; she paused to admire the sturdy confidence of her friend's stance. She took a sip of wine while she considered the question and felt the calming taste of the alcohol. She never drank wine in the morning but when Evienne had offered her some, she gladly accepted. It had a somnolent effect on her and now she felt a mellow comfort swimming in her veins. Evienne's question floated in the air in front of her. Normally she would panic at a question like that; instead, she just answered without thinking about how she would code her words.

"I don't know what love is Evienne." Madalane took another sip of the red wine, feeling the burn down her throat. "I know that my parents cannot possibly represent true love. My mother is a bitter woman who has made my father equally bitter and very unhappy. He cannot divorce her because of the church, but I know he could love and be happy with someone else."

Madalane was quiet for a minute. She tried to remember what she had been thinking before her parents' relationship popped into her mind. She had been thinking of Evienne. Evienne was her definition of love, yet she knew if she said that, Evienne would change the subject and Madalane would feel the cold crawl of humiliation.

"I only know love through books and movies, and they don't seem very accurate from what I have seen of real life. I am unprepared to define love, but I think..." Madalane grasped helplessly for words thinking of the interminable weeks she spent at home missing Evienne, "love is about yearning to see that person, wanting to talk with them, wanting to curl up in their arms and feel safe." Madalane took another sip of the wine. "Maybe I am naive because no one has ever loved me, but I think love is about trusting someone and knowing that they feel about you the same way you feel about them." She felt hopelessly awkward, but she defiantly maintained her pose and her expression.

Like a breeze, Madalane volleyed the same question, "Have you ever been in love, Evienne?"

The words caught and spun around Evienne's chest. Yes, she had been in love; yes, she loved a woman. She loved and loved until it hurt. She loved a woman who loved a man. It was complicated. She had been so young, yet it was not so long ago. She wanted to forget and now it was a looming truth suspended in the air between them. Madalane trusted her. Madalane would define her by her answer. Madalane should know the fear that pressed into her when she thought of love.

"Love is one of those complicated mazes we try and figure out on the journey, Madalane. I experienced a love between my family, between my mother and father, but I was young and my world crumbled as death slowly took the souls of my family. As I buried each one, a part of my soul was buried with them. I felt dead inside. I felt alone, art was the only thing left to console me; I learned how to escape into my paintings."

Madalane stared at her friend's praying head hanging at the altar of her canvas. She was afraid to move, knowing it would deflate the energy in the room. She was frozen in the intensity of the moment.

Evienne continued as she painted and smoked. She dragged the back of her hand across her face, pushing her fingers into her hair. "I was alone in London. I won't lie—there were many times I was scared. Life scared the fear right out of me at times and then I would just laugh. When I came to Paris, I met some helpful people in the art community. And that is when it happened."

Madalane wanted to know every detail; she wanted to crawl into Evienne's lap and know everything about her. "What happened?" Madalane asked trying not to sound too anxious, trying not to break her pose.

"There was this couple who took me under their wing. The man was an artist and his woman was his model. She wanted him to fall in love with her. She wanted the lifestyle of a muse." Evienne murmured, staring at her canvas, avoiding Madalane's eyes.

"What happened?" Madalane cautiously asked.

Evienne looked up from her painting, "I fell in love with the model, Madalane. I did not even know it was happening. They took me places, kept me warm, and fed. She treated me as her lover and I craved it. The two of us, her man and I fulfilled all of her needs. I was really nothing in their world; I served as a lure like chum in the ocean. And then..." Evienne stopped.

"Yes Evienne, what happened?"

"They left me and they moved to Sweden. They just left. It was for the best. A few kisses on the cheek, only two train tickets, and goodbye."

Madalane was thunderstruck. Her friend had been involved not only with a woman, but a woman who loved a man as well. She stared at the artist, trying to find the words to respond. The way Evienne phrased the affair sounded like she had been part of harem, but instead of the man being the sultan, it had been the woman.

Evienne continued applying paint to the canvas occasionally taking a drag from her cigarette. She was so nonchalant, yet Madalane's entire foundation had been shaken. It was times like these that she truly felt out of her depth. She had read about these types of relationships furtively in the library, standing between the stacks lest someone should see what she was reading. Now face to face with a woman who had lived this life and she was speechless. Madalane realized that she had been quiet for so long that Evienne no longer expected a response, yet she felt she should offer something. "I think they were both fools for letting you go."

Evienne grunted but seemed completely focused on the painting. Madalane took another sip of the wine, which the artist had graciously kept refilling, so she wouldn't go without. Gazing at the artist, she watched the muscles in her shoulders and arms clench and relax as she painted. Thoughts of Evienne's relationship with the woman invaded her mind; she imagined kissing those shoulders, imagined touching the soft white skin of her upper arms. Madalane felt her nipples grow hard as she imagined the artist moving on top of her. In a sensual haze, she wondered if Evienne had glanced at her bosom. She arched slightly to see if there was any hesitation in Evienne's movements. Nothing. Evienne was implacable; she never seemed to respond the way the people did in books.

She knew she was more drunk than sober, but took another sip of wine as she allowed her mind to explore the secrets she wouldn't admit to anyone much less herself. A small drop of wine fell from the rim of the goblet and landed on her chest. It remained in place until Madalane took a breath and it began to slowly fall like a rivulet of dark red paint, along the inner curve of her left breast and down to the small round of flesh above her belly button, finally disappearing into the crevice. Madalane had been fascinated by the fate of the lost wine and had forgotten that Evienne was still painting her. She looked up quickly to see if Evienne had noticed. The artist was standing still, her breathing shallow and deep and her eyes seemed glazed with an intense stare.

Evienne watched the arch of Madalane's back and curiously studied what the woman in front of her was doing. It was a drop of wine slowly slipping down her white flesh that was her undoing. The red wine had a life of its own and Evienne wanted to pull the wine and Madalane into her mouth. She was hypnotized watching Madalane watch the wine. Both women consumed by the universe of one drop of wine.

"I spilled some wine." Madalane heard the words come out of her own mouth, but she felt strangely disembodied from her own voice.

Evienne found herself asking, "What were you thinking as you watched the drop of wine roll down your body?"

Blood flooded into the Madalane's face. "I don't know what I was thinking...I was distracted by the way the wine rolled." She broke her pose and covered her face with her hand that had been resting over her head. "I think I've had too much to drink Evienne. I am feeling a little light-headed." She felt embarrassed and exposed. What was she doing? Posing partially nude for her friend, having these thoughts about her friend. She leaned over, put the wine goblet down, and retrieved the modesty cover from around her waist. She covered her chest and looked up at Evienne with shamed eyes.

"I was thinking how lucky that single drop of wine was." Evienne was not sure why she had said something so provocative, but the words were true. "Do you want a bit of water? Or some baguette?" Evienne was stumbling, trying to quell her desire.

Madalane broke eye contact with her friend. Did she just say that the wine was lucky? What did that mean? She must have misheard. She felt more heat invading her body; the sheet seemed to be strangling her chest. She wanted to fling it away and rush to Evienne to hide her face in her friend's strong body. She shook her head and tried to clear the images that kept creeping into her consciousness. "I think I am done Evienne. I'm sorry. I can't sit still any longer."

Madalane hoped her friend would not ask any questions and just acquiesce to her request. Evienne swiftly went to Madalane's side to help her get up off the lounge, but Madalane waived away the help.

"It's alright. You don't have to apologize. It's been a long day.

We did a lot of work. You're a wonderful model. Let me help you—" Evienne wanted to help her friend who seemed to be having a hard time regaining her equilibrium. She was reaching for her, not sure whether to touch her or not. "You really did a great job, thank you Dove for today."

Madalane stood up and shook off Evienne's attempt to assist her. "No, I'm fine. I just need to get dressed and we'll go to the cafe, yes?" She looked at the artist who nodded.

She stepped behind the screen and dropped the sheet. Her body was enflamed and the rough texture of her clothes only made her blood boil even more. As she buttoned her dress, her fingers felt the slide of silk and then the tight bud of her nipple. Her index finger circled her nipple once, twice, and again. She imagined Evienne's lips circling her nipple. She heard a low moan and realized it was coming from her own mouth.

The sound coming from behind the screen was not unfamiliar to Evienne. She felt her heart skip; she picked up the wine Madalane had left behind and drank it. She closed her eyes and felt the heat of the wine moving through her. She wanted to push Madalane up against the wall. She wanted her splayed out on the chaise. She wanted to own her mouth and feel her hair wrapped around them both. Evienne licked the lip of the glass and rolled the curved edge back and forth over her bottom lip. Her heart was pounding; she thought she could hear it echoing in the silence of the studio. Unconsciously she murmured, "Madalane."

The sound of her friend whispering her name brought Madalane back to her present circumstances. She felt a jolt of excitement as she heard the soft voice. She gritted her teeth and finished buttoning her dress. Her body was incredibly sensitive; part of her wanted to drop her clothes and approach her friend. She wanted to let Evienne touch her the way she touched the artist's woman. She wanted Evienne to take control and demand that she step away from the screen. She waited a moment, and then another, praying that Evienne would release her from her indecision.

But no, Evienne made no move to rescue her from her thoughts. Madalane pulled on her stockings and slipped into her shoes. Her heart had slowed but the burn inside of her was still there. She stepped away from the screen and saw Evienne standing near the chaise with her abandoned goblet in hand. "Can I see the painting?" Madalane's voice sounded foreign and tight to her own ears.

Evienne walked to the painting without saying a word to Madalane. When she glanced at it, it stopped her. She had forgotten how intensely beautiful the woman staring back at her was.

Curious, Madalane walked around the easel and saw the canvas for the first time. It was her face, yet not her face. The face staring back at her was older, wiser, and prettier. It was a face she was not entirely familiar with, but more shocking than her friend's interpretation of her face was the fact that it was just her face and shoulders that her friend had painted. She had sat half nude all day, but Evienne had only painted her from the shoulders up. She was confused but relieved in a strange way. She glanced back at the face staring at her from the canvas and then looked at her friend. "This is how you see me?"

"You allow me to see your soul. You let me see inside you and this is how my heart paints you." Evienne stopped speaking and looked directly into Madalane's eyes. "Thank you for allowing me to see you."

Madalane felt the love and appreciation emanating off her friend. She wanted to embrace her and show her how much she loved her, but her body was so electrified that she feared any physical touch. Instead, she looked up at the artist and nodded. "Thank you for painting me. You are a remarkable artist."

My Dearest Madalane,

With my mind working my hands, I hope never to be confused with any other artist, no matter how great. My most enduring observation includes your arm demurely acting as your décolleté. The coverage of flesh leaves an ethereal conception to my eyes. The sunlight streaked across your face, slim neck and bosom softly illuminates your skin seducing me to believe you have been fed blue-topaz milk. The incandescent glow radiates from beneath your bones allows your beauty to flood to the surface demanding I attempt a recreation of the radiance in front of me.

You ask me if I see you this way, the way I have painted you, and I do. I pray to God to apprentice my brush, reviving every detail of your essence to my canvas. The hours we spent together seemed like minutes, lost in a dream-like haze. I was unable to gaze at you for too long because the moment was too private, too lovely, your touch soft, your recline sublime, too much for my mortal eyes to endure. I paint you because you are beyond words; you are a battle of love for my art. I stare at your painting blatantly because I can and wonder if my heart has created you. If I did not have your portrait in front of me, I would question whether you are real.

You live in my heart forever,

Evienne

Chapter 42

Paris, April 1929

It had been a miserably cold day. Even though it was almost springtime in Paris, the rain had been relentless. Evienne had stood outside all day at her stall. While the other artists had packed up early and headed to the cafes, Evienne would not submit to the temptation of warmth and comfort. She was low on funds, and she had promised herself that she would return to their warm cozy room if she sold one painting. Instead, she watched the rain drive the locals and tourists away. The few hardy souls who ventured out were not in a buying mood and as the day wore on, Evienne's mood became foul and dark. Why couldn't one of these bastards just buy one small sketch or painting?

The day grew dark and she knew the deal she had made with herself had been fruitless. She was angry with herself for putting a condition on the day. She locked up her stall and headed back to the small room she shared with Madalane. A few of the girls at the boarding house knew that Evienne was living there, but their shared hatred of the Madame encouraged them to keep their mouths shut if and when they saw the artist. She slipped in the unlocked window and stripped down to her under clothes.

She was shivering and felt nauseated from the coldness inside of her. She lit the fire that she had lain in the fireplace that morning, but it would take a while for the heat to permeate the room. Normally she slept in an old undershirt, but she slipped on Madalane's nightgown instead. She was cold and Madalane left her nightgown on the small heat exchange in the room. It was warm and smelled like Madalane. She loved the way the fabric breathed with her friend's scent and it gave her a small thrill to think of Madalane's flesh touching the same fabric she was now wearing. Madalane had a late class and wouldn't be back for another hour. Evienne sat trembling on the bed, wishing for Madalane's body heat. Exhausted she crawled into the narrow bed and burrowed beneath the quilt. She would just rest her eyes a few minutes and then get up to make tea for Madalane. She would be just as cold from her walk home from the university.

The heaviness of the quilt combined with the warmth of the nightgown with Madalane's scent clinging to it relaxed the artist and soon her body had fallen into a deep, contented slumber. Lying completely still, listening to the rain splash again the window, she felt the press of a body sitting on the bed. She felt so incredibly comfortable; she didn't want to move. With great effort, she raised her hand and let it slide along the silky skin of her friend. She knew it was Madalane. The weight of her body on the bed was familiar and comforting. Her friend's flesh was cold, but Evienne felt an incredible lassitude but she couldn't muster the energy to get up to help her friend.

She reached for Madalane, expecting some resistance, but instead her friend seemed to fold herself into Evienne's body. The artist pulled Madalane even closer until Madalane was on top of her body. Evienne's conscious mind rebelled at the closeness; it was too much of a temptation. But it felt too good, and she shushed her conscious mind. Madalane's scent was so powerful and the pressure of her body on Evienne's was almost too much to bear. She wrapped her arms around Madalane and pulled her closer.

Through Evienne's foggy mind, she realized that Madalane was brushing her chin and cheeks with small kisses. She felt a spasm in her belly shoot through her and she pulled Madalane even closer. Madalane's lips moved down to the artist's neck as Evienne shifted to accommodate the pressure of her friend's body. Evienne's heart was pounding as she heard a small moan escape her mouth as Madalane's teeth sank into her flesh. Evienne was afraid to move or to make any sound in case her friend would stop. She held herself completely still as she felt Madalane begin to move on top of her. Their bodies began to undulate rhythmically and Evienne's hands moved down Madalane's back to grasp her friend's hips. They locked into a cadence and Evienne focused her entire existence on this moment, on this sensation, on the heat that was spreading through her body.

Evienne craved Madalane's mouth. The pressure of her friend's lips and teeth on her neck was insanely pleasurable, but she wanted to connect more intimately. She needed to gain control of what was happening or she would lose any command of her senses that she currently held. Evienne pushed her head away and felt her friend pull back. The artist's hands traveled up her friend's back and threaded through her thick hair. The kiss she had been dying for was about to happen. She slowed her breathing, slowed her actions, slowed the moment. Madalane's scent was so seductive—it was alive in her brain. She wanted this to be perfect, to live in her memory forever.

As Evienne stroked her friend's neck, she heard the distant click of the door. Evienne's eyes popped open as her heart pounded in shock. She was alone in the bed, and Madalane was standing in the doorway looking like a drowned rat. Evienne winced as she realized that she had been dreaming, and she rubbed her eyes frantically trying to wipe the fantasy out of her mind.

Looking at her friend, Madalane shrugged out of her coat and rushed to the bed. "Are you okay? You look flushed." Evienne flinched as Madalane's hand pressed against her forehead.

"You are very warm."

Pulling away from her friend, Evienne shook her head and got up to stoke the fire. "I'm fine...just slept longer than I had planned."

Confused, Madalane watched her friend's stiff movements, absently wondering why Evienne was wearing her nightgown. Sometimes Evienne's behavior was more baffling than usual to her.

Chapter 43

Paris, April 1929

Evienne watched a little spark catch a piece of paper and the fire erupted, purple and blue flames licking the corners of the orange heat.

Evienne had been eager to get back to Madalane's room because earlier that day she had hidden Madalane's birthday present under the foot of the bed. As Evienne laid the fire, she could feel her secret building inside of her. She could feel Madalane's eyes on her back. She could feel the air of Paris, the Louvre, and their picnic lingering over her own body. She could still feel the coarse fibers of Madalane's sweater on her fingertips as she held her hand gently along the curve of her back and stared at art, knowing all was right with their world.

Madalane stretched her body and pushed off her shoes as she sat on the bed. Watching Evienne lay the fire was always so comforting. Her large hands, usually wielding a paintbrush, seemed equally at home placing logs into the cavity of the fireplace. She did it neatly, systematically, without one wasted motion. Madalane watched Evienne's back and shoulders flex carelessly as she moved the heavy logs around. Watching the flames lick at the kindling, she knew this fire would last for hours and their slumber would be warm and cozy.

Feeling uncomfortably like a voyeur, Madalane lay back upon the bed and stared at the small candelabra hanging from the ceiling. Madalane recalled seeing Evienne's face as she came out of her morning class earlier in the day. Walking with two of her classmates, she had spied her friend lounging on a bench across from the building's doorway. Evienne was smoking a cigarette, watching the flow of people cross in front of her. Evienne's face lit up as she saw Madalane and she had tossed her cigarette into the street, grabbed a large knapsack, and hurriedly crossed the street to greet her. Madalane nodded to her classmates to keep going. School was forgotten now that Evienne was here.

Today was Madalane's birthday. Evienne had woken earlier than her custom and had run out for croissants for her friend's breakfast. When Madalane stirred, she opened her eyes to a morning feast. It had been such a sweet thing to do and Madalane was thrilled that her friend had remembered the date. After breakfast, Madalane had to hurry to get to her first class on time. Smiling at her memories, she had had no idea that Evienne had anything else planned for her day.

As Evienne sat vigil at the fireplace's edge, the flames burning the flesh of her face, bringing the warmth of red to her white skin. The colors danced in her mind: the purples, the oranges, and the blues. She thought about turning around to look at the reclining woman on the bed, to think of the day of happiness they had shared, but the burn of the flames on her cheeks showed more of her heart than she was willing to expose with her eyes. She watched the burning embers practice ballet in front of her, small red and black snowflakes spinning into the air and effortlessly falling white at the end of a long, meaningful life. A tree offering air falling to the earth, turning to kindling and burning to give heat, returning to the dirt that once nourished its life.

Evienne wanted to dive deliciously into her love for Madalane, but the scorch of her heart created caution preventing her from touching the flames, keeping her distance, moving with vigilance although she felt the layers of her fears burning away. She pulled off her cable sweater and moved to the corner of the room where she stashed her bag. Last night she went to the cafe to fill an extra bottle of wine, saving it for this moment. Madalane watched Evienne move back to the fireplace to resettle a log. She turned and said "Happy birthday Madalane."

She opened her bag, took out the wine, and presented it to Madalane like it was a prized statue. "We should drink a toast to you in front of the fire and celebrate the gift God has given me by bringing you to me." She stopped and looked into Madalane's eyes and smiled, feeling the burn sear right into her heart.

Overcome by her friend's exuberance, Madalane felt her heart flutter. Evienne spent so much time keeping herself hidden, but sometimes, like today, she revealed the woman underneath the quietude. Impulsively, Madalane stood up, pulled the wine out of her friend's hands, and pulled a large swallow right from the bottle. She saw Evienne's amusement and she held the bottle out to her friend, waiting for her to take her own sip.

Evienne continued smiling, but she stood up and put her hands behind her back. She wordlessly beckoned her friend to hold the bottle to her mouth, briefly licking the top of her lip with the tip of her tongue. Nervously and very unsure, Madalane held the bottle to her friend's lips and as Evienne's head tilted back, she poured the wine into her friend's mouth. A splash of purple landed on Evienne's shirt, but neither woman noticed as their eyes met and focused only on each other. Madalane watched Evienne's lips wrap around the bottle and when she was sure her friend had a good amount, she reluctantly lowered the wine.

Evienne wiped the residue of wine from her mouth with the back of her hand. Her Bordeaux-red lips pursed as she pushed her knuckle into her mouth, her lips opened, her hand and then index finger slowly dragged inside the slight wet of her own lips.

Evienne wanted to feel flesh, taste passion; she wanted to touch Madalane's lips, touch Madalane's lips with her own fingers, matching the burn in her throat. Her own hand would have to do. Evienne stared into her friend's eyes, lips still slightly parted, her face expressionless as words whispered seductively from her mouth, "You should take a turn, hands behind your back." Evienne never left the connection of their stare. She nodded her head to motion her drinking partner's hands to move behind her back as she reached to take the bottle from her.

Madalane felt panic well up inside her chest. This little game seemed to be taking on a more provocative edge. Automatically she handed the bottle to Evienne, absently noticing that her hand was trembling. Evienne's face had taken on an almost feral appearance. Her eyes had darkened, her lips pursed in a tight regard, and her face was flushed with the heat of the room. Madalane gasped as her friend reminded her to put her hands behind her back. The words were said in a slow, husky tone that twisted inside her belly and made her feel slightly queasy. Apprehensively, she put her hands behind her on the bedpost, wrapping them around the tapered wood to keep her grounded. She had an overwhelming urge to get up and break their eye contact, to open a window and let a gust of cold air in, to shake off this inertia she seemed to be captured by. But she held still, waiting.

Evienne moved closer to Madalane; the artist could feel the heat coming off her friend's body. Madalane felt cornered and her anxiety continued to grow. She looked deeply into Evienne's eyes, trying to read the expression on her friend's face—why was this moment so different than the usual physical closeness they shared living together in this small room? Why was she so nervous?

Madalane squeezed the bedpost tighter behind her back as Evienne held the green bottle to her mouth. Slowly, the way she wanted to own Madalane's mouth, she tilted the bottle until the wine was freely pouring between her lips. The passion was building inside her; the feeling was riveting and compulsive. She was losing control and reached to hold the back of Madalane's head, to continue gently feeding her the red wine. Evienne towered over the Madalane. The orange and red glow of the fire filled the room. The fire was hissing and popping, calling her name—leading her on, igniting the drive inside her, tantalizing her rational mind. Evienne caught sight of her face in the mirror hanging across the room. She saw the animal in her, the survivor of her spirit. She realized at that moment that she was frightening her friend. She was dominating Madalane, so she would not have to deal with her own emotions. Fear of being seen, leading her to a need to consume Madalane so she could burn the demons of her loneliness, blinding herself so as not to see her own fragile heart.

Madalane felt the warm mouth of the bottle tilted against her lips. She forced herself to maintain eye contact with her friend. The Evienne standing before her was not the quiet tortured woman she was used to; this woman was intimidating her but there was also this spark of excitement she couldn't remember feeling before. She felt a tiny bit of trepidation as she felt the wine splash against her tongue. As she tried to figure out if she should swallow immediately or hold it in her mouth and then swallow, she noticed her friend's eyes flickered to something behind her. Confused as to what had taken Evienne's attention, she realized too late that she couldn't swallow all the wine that had filled her mouth and breathe at the same time. She felt a choking sensation and frantically she breathed in air through her nose, which promptly pushed the wine in her mouth up, through her nose. Coughing and snorting, she belatedly realized that she had showered Evienne with sunbursts of red wine all over her white shirt.

She clenched her eyes, horrified at her faux pas. Praying that she could disappear on the spot, she barely heard the chuckle that turned into a chortle that erupted into full-force hysterical laughter. Opening her eyes, she saw her friend doubled over in amusement. Her embarrassment turned into affection and she began to laugh too.

Unable to hold herself up any longer, Evienne rolled onto the bed and laughed for what seemed like hours; her roommate joined in until exhaustion set in for them both. Nonetheless, each time they looked at one another, they would convulse into giggles again. Finally, they both lay stretched out on the small bed, their bodies casually lying against each other, breathing hard as they got themselves under control.

At that moment, Evienne thought about giving Madalane her birthday gift. She stretched her lean body over the edge of the bed, retrieved the hidden gift, and laid it on Madalane's heaving chest.

Seeing the small wrapped package, Madalane felt a delighted spark echo through her body. She sat up, reverently holding the gift in her hands. She looked to her friend who was lying on her side, smiling at her. Madalane winced when she saw Evienne's ruined shirt, but the weight in her hands was distracting her. "You bought me a gift?" Her voice sounded overly girlish in her head and she blushed at how ridiculous she sounded.

Evienne nodded, but didn't say anything.

Madalane examined the red ribbon wound tightly around the rectangular package. Pulling gently at the satin, it came undone like a bow tie with one small tug. She moved the ribbon off to the side—she would keep it to remember this day forever. Unwrapping the brown paper, she saw that her friend had given her a book of poetry, A Few Figs From Thistles by Edna St. Vincent Millay. Madalane felt tears erupting from her heart. Keeping her head down, she traced the silver letters on the black binding. It was all so much—breakfast, the picnic, the museum and now this beautiful book of poetry. She felt the tears escape and run down her cheeks. No one had ever cared this much about her. So much joy was unfamiliar.

"No tears, my Dove." Evienne reached out to Madalane's cheek and caught a tear on her index finger. Evienne examined the tear glistening on her fingertip. She thought of the journey the tear had taken, traveling from her friend's eye to her cheek to her own finger. Evienne rubbed the tear between her fingers, absorbing the essence of Madalane. Evienne looked up at her friend and asked, "May I read you a poem?"

Madalane held the book out to her friend as the image of the wine bottle a few moments before flashed through her mind. Every move, every word held some sort of electric thrill tonight. She was falling into a chasm of contentment that was far beyond anything she had ever experienced before. "I would love for you to read to me." Madalane's voice struggled to be heard. She was deliriously happy, yet she felt a crushing sadness that this day would end soon. She pushed that thought away and waited for her friend to find the poem she was flipping pages looking for.

Evienne thought of how Adrienne, the proprietor of the bookshop, helped her find this book for Madalane and how she read every poem at her art stand for the following few day after purchasing it. "Here it is! We should honor the American poet by reading it in English, would you agree?" Evienne cleared her throat and in a deep contralto voice, her words flowed over Madalane.

> *My candle burns at both ends;*
> *It will not last the night;*
> *But ah, my foes, and oh, my friends—*
> *It gives a lovely light!*

Madalane had closed her eyes while her friend read, and as the last syllable echoed in the quiet room, the flow of words, the beauty of the image, the tone were all overshadowed by the realization that this was the first time she had heard Evienne speak her native English. Opening her eyes, she resisted the urge to comment on her friend's unaccented English. Instead, she focused on the words of the poem that had struck her so strongly, "That poem is about you Evienne. It captures your essence. I love that you read it to me."

"Reading it is my gift to you Dove, but I think it is about all of us who choose to live our lives and not the life others have chosen for us. Do you agree?" Evienne handed the book, open to the poem, back to Madalane.

Madalane considered her friend's words as she scanned the poem. Realizing her own rebellions against her mother had led her to this moment, she nodded. "You are so profound Evienne. How did you learn so much? You are only a few years older than I." Not expecting an answer, she stared at the words on the page. Silence descended heavily in the room. Madalane sat up, laying the book gently next to her. "Every day I wake up so excited to begin my day. I feel like everything I have done in my life has led me to Paris and my life with you. I spend my days in class, learning as much as I can and then I come home to you and my education really starts. I am finally living the life I dreamed about since I was twelve."

Evienne stood and pulled the lap blanket from the foot of the bed and draped it over her friend's shoulders and then turned her back to attend the fire. "We, as women, have lived hundreds of lives. It is like the statue we saw today at the Louvre, Madalane. The Statue of Victory—she has been on her journey for centuries and she reveals the mysteries of her existence without a face. We can learn from her journey. We can learn how our physical bodies take us on travels and experiences. We can learn from what we have and from what we have lost. We can learn from what others have and what others still do not have. We can learn from the beauty of their presence. The presence of beauty can melt even the most stoic of us, leaving us exposed and vulnerable to yet another experience."

Madalane grasped the blanket tighter around her body and thought about what she would say. Memories of standing at the foot of the staircase, looking up at the ancient statue filtered through Madalane's mind. Her friend's ability to explain the importance of her symbolic faceless beauty staggered her. Feeling horribly inadequate, she decided to pursue the subject that

Evienne loved the most: her art. "Is that why you paint faces so exquisitely? To show an individual's journey?"

"I look at you and I see beyond your creamy skin tones and unmarked flesh, and I know I can paint your innocence. But as an artist, I paint to unearth the unexplained—the mystery—to immortalize our purpose; perhaps it is the same reason you read. Is that true?" Evienne moved back to the fireplace, stoking the fire and turned to look over her shoulder to see her friend.

Madalane's mind churned as she tried to digest her friend's words. No one made her think quite so hard about life and existence. "I suppose you are right. I hadn't thought about it like that before. I read to give me an escape, to escape from my mother, to escape from bullies, to escape from unhappiness. Why I read was never a mystery to me. It was my salvation. Perhaps if I was a writer, I could interpret the world and unlock my purpose. I think people who create, like you, have a special insight into the world."

"Artists and those who appreciate the art just see it from different sides. Both are needed to appreciate the true meaning of a creation—even if they disagree on what the piece means." Evienne whispered as she rejoined her friend on the bed. "Your turn my Dove. Now, you must read a poem to me." Madalane's voice haltingly read the unfamiliar English words as the artist closed her eyes and listened to the language she didn't realize she missed so much.

Chapter 44

Paris, April 1929

Madalane stared at her father's precise handwriting. He had summarily agreed to her suggestion. Part of her was relieved and happy, but another part of her was devastated. The last tie between them was now severed and it broke her heart much more than she had anticipated. She stared with unseeing eyes out the window, hoping that Evienne would be home soon. This was what she had wanted; moreover, it was what she had asked for. Why did it feel like she was being abandoned again?

The panic had set in about a fortnight prior. She had completed her mid-semester exams, and on her way home, the feeling of relief was replaced by the gnawing anxiety that she would have to go home to her parent's house for the summer. Where would Evienne live? How could she survive the entire summer at home with her family, wondering what Evienne was doing? The realization had caught her unaware. She didn't know why she hadn't thought about this earlier, but the feeling was like a hammer blow to her chest. When she had gotten back to her rooms, she had sat staring at the painting Evienne had given her when she had first met the artist. Her eyes traced the lines of the old woman's face as her mind searched for solutions. Initially, she thought she could have Evienne come home with her for a few months. Paris was sticky and hot in the summer and Evienne would have a whole new crop of faces to draw in her village.

As quickly as that idea came to her, she understood that it would not happen. Where would Evienne sleep? In the storeroom with Madalane? It seemed farcical and yet Evienne had slept in far worse places. Nonetheless, her mother would be adamant. In her mind, artists were no better than prostitutes, opium fiends or Bolsheviks. No, her mother would certainly never allow Madalane to bring home an artist, and Evienne would not be able to hide who she was for any amount of time. Nor would it be fair to expect Evienne to hide herself from her mother just so Madalane could keep her close. Plus, the truth was that she wasn't sure that Evienne would ever consider leaving her beloved Paris.

Instead, she had decided to be honest with her father, or at least as honest as a young woman could be with the man who brought her into the world. She had written him a letter outlining the reasons why she should stay in Paris. Aside from the practical aspects of taking summer classes and working at a shop, she underscored the tension between herself and her mother. If she could stay in Paris, the family home would maintain its peace. And if her mother were peaceful, her father's life would be peaceful. Madalane knew that her mother's anxiety increased when she came home; she didn't know why—she tried to make herself as small as possible in her family's house, but her mother would be on inevitably edge for the entire tenure of the visit.

The letter had been sent and Madalane waited patiently each day for the post. She had not mentioned any of this to Evienne because she didn't want the older girl to talk her out of it. Finally, the return response came and with shaking hands, Madalane had ripped open the envelope and quickly scanned the letter. Her father agreed; he would allow her to stay in Paris and would send her a small housing allowance and continue to pay tuition, but she would have to cover any other expenses; it was all written in a perfunctory manner, like a contract with a vendor. As she read the words, she envisioned her summer with Evienne: picnics, walks and lazy summer afternoons, listening to the bands playing in the park. She felt so incredibly free; she couldn't wait to share the news with her friend. Yet, she couldn't shake the strange sense of abandonment, feeling like a foundling left on the church steps.

The sun was setting and Evienne would be home soon. Madalane's fog thickened as she reread the carefully formed letters of her father's handwriting. He offered no resistance to the idea, offered no alternatives. Perhaps this was what everyone had wanted all along, to get rid of her—to get rid of the problem. The old feelings of being unwanted shrouded her mind as the streets darkened. Where was Evienne? Madalane felt a chasm of pain opening in her chest and she needed her friend to remind her that she was worthy.

Standing at the window, Madalane saw the familiar silhouette of her friend's tall form strolling down the small street emerge from the darkness. Evienne appeared like a spiritual savior from the blackest part of the street. She felt a rush of relief and threw open the window to welcome her friend home for the night.

Evienne looked to the opened dining room window of Madalane's room and was surprised to see Madalane's face there. Evienne sensed a problem in her friend's expression. She knew Madalane's expressions like she knew the streets of Paris.

Madalane stepped back to give Evienne room to enter through the window. The artist handed off the baguette that she had been eating as well as the liter of wine she had purchased on her way home. Madalane put their dinner on the small table near the fireplace and turned to see her friend removing her coat. She wanted to blurt out the contents of the letter, but she knew she would have to broach the subject carefully. Evienne was skittish at the best of times and this conversation would have to be subtle.

Biding her time, she poured herself and Evienne a glass of wine.

Evienne was surprised that Madalane went right for the wine. She normally related the events of her day but on this evening, she appeared preoccupied by the garnet shade of the wine. Curious, she asked, "Madalane, are you feeling all right?"

"Yes Evienne. I'm fine. I just had a hard day." Madalane observed the measure of wine in the glass and drank it down in one swallow. She refilled her glass and turned to face her friend who was staring at her with a quizzical look. Madalane's hand trembled imperceptibly as she raised the glass to her mouth again. She felt the burn of the alcohol spread through her chest as the wine insulated her exhausted brain. It was better now. She felt her body start to relax and as she gazed at Evienne, an incipient bravery spread over her limbs. She could handle this.

"Dove, you don't seem very well. Did something happen in class today? Tell me what is wrong." Evienne's voice sounded urgent.

Considering her options, Madalane tried to sound playful, "I will trade you wine for a cigarette."

Evienne knew what the cigarette meant for Madalane— clearly, she was upset. She reached into her pocket, never taking her eyes off her friend, and pulled her fresh pack out. She put two to her lips and lit them both, handing one to her friend. "You seem uneasy. You only smoke when the air is too heavy for you to breathe; talk to me—you are acting jittery, like a fish out of water."

Madalane greedily sucked the smoke into her lungs. She had watched Evienne smoke for months; she had seen the calming sensation overtake her friend as she inhaled. She had recently tried it, and found like a drug, it seemed to have an immediate calming effect on her too. She got a little dizzy and felt the need to put the cigarette down for a minute. She knew Evienne was watching her and she knew she had to pull herself together. Madalane leaned back against the chair and held the cigarette in front of her between her index and middle finger, tapping the end with her thumb.

Madalane tried to focus on being practical; Evienne could be eminently practical so that seemed like a good place to start. "Evienne, have you thought about what we are going to do when the semester ends?"

Evienne feigned a casual countenance and leaned against the table to give Madalane her full attention. "Are you tired of keeping the window open for the cat to come in?" Evienne tried to lighten the mood. She knew her stay at the dorm room was too good to be true. Everything was bound to end in her life; her life had been filled with abrupt endings.

"Don't be silly! The cat is my best friend. I would never get tired of my cat." Madalane grinned at her friend, hoping she felt the same. "We need to plan for school ending. We can't stay here—Madame closes up the house for the summer; we have to find somewhere to live for the summer—clearly somewhere that allows cats." Still smiling, Madalane hoped that Evienne would understand that she was including herself in plans. Maybe the conversation would be easier than she thought.

Evienne grinned, purring her words, "Meow! I'll start asking around and see if we can't find a room nearby for the summer." Evienne took a drag from her cigarette and hazarded a question, "Don't your parents expect you home for the summer?" Evienne flicked a gray ash into the small ashtray and looked into Madalane's eyes.

"You know how it is...my family is counting the days until school is over...they are planning my homecoming banquet even as we speak." Madalane hoped her tone was sardonic but not overly bitter. Evienne didn't say anything, but she nodded, understanding her friend's point.

"I don't want to go home this summer. I don't ever want to go home ever again." Madalane took another drag from her cigarette, "I wrote to my father and..." Before Madalane could finish her sentence, the artist interrupted.

"You should go and enjoy your summer with them. This cat will find a safe place to curl up, don't you worry." Evienne was visiting the ticket counter at the train station in her mind. One ticket. One way. Her heart slowed and hissed like the steam exiting the engine pulling out of the station.

Madalane's faced flushed with a wellspring of irritation as she tried to control her temper. "Whether I should go home or not is irrelevant. The bottom line is that neither he nor my mother wants me to come home. My mother is relieved."

Evienne was shocked to hear those brutal words come from Madalane's mouth. She knew that Madalane did not get along with her mother, but she had not seen how deep the pain went. Evienne reached for her friend's hand but Madalane pulled away from her; Evienne leaned back in her chair and felt her heart stutter. What could she say? "Then stay in Paris." She drew from the cigarette and felt the heat warm her chest. "I suppose I should ask if you want to stay in Paris with me."

Irritation turned into anger. Madalane could not believe that her friend could be so cavalier about this conversation. She had virtually severed ties with her family to stay in Paris and now Evienne supposed that she should ask her to live with her. Suppose? Anger turned into fury and Madalane felt an unguarded moment of hatred towards her friend. A moment of hatred towards the world. She breathed deeply, hoping to sound normal when she spoke.

"You don't have to suppose anything Evienne. I'm staying in Paris and if you want to live with me, I would like that. However, if you get a better offer, then I suppose you should take it."

Quickly realizing that she had misjudged her response, Evienne countered, "No need to get upset. There is plenty of room for all of us in Paris." Evienne stood up and moved in front of Madalane. Madalane looked up to her, trying to camouflage the anger. Ignoring her plight, Evienne pulled the girl's head to her stomach and smoothed the brown flyaway hairs that had escaped her chignon. Madalane resisted at first but Evienne knew intuitively the fears Madalane was having. "I only want to stay with

you Madalane. We will do this together and we will be happy. I
will show you the pleasures of Paris in the summer."

The artist's soft words brought tears to Madalane's eyes. She
turned to bury her face in her friend's stomach and inhaled the
familiar scent of sandalwood. The anger and rage still throbbed
in her head, but her heart had given up. She gripped her friend
tightly around her waist and felt the hot tears fall from her eyes.
Images of working with her father in the small shop flooded her
mind and she felt completely alone as his words echoed in her
mind. "Madalane, you are right. Your mother and I both agree
that you should stay in Paris. There is no need for you to come
home again." Handwriting that was so familiar; words that were so
final. Had he really meant to say again or until Christmas break?

Evienne felt the intensity pouring from Madalane's body. Tell
me why you are so upset. Tell me." Evienne wiped the wetness
from the one side of her cheek and pulled her tighter.

Madalane didn't want to answer, but she knew her friend
would be relentless. "I am happy; I really am. I am thrilled that
my father wants me to stay in Paris." Madalane felt the anxiety
of his words roll around her heart. "I am just having a hard time
understanding why my parents don't want me around. It seems
they have been trying to get rid of me since I can remember. My
father started taking me to the shop when I was four or five to
keep me out of my mother's hair. Then when I was old enough
to go to boarding school, I got shipped off. I just wish I knew
what I did that made them hate me so much."

Evienne released her grasp of Madalane and took her face
softly in her hands. "They are your parents Madalane. They
couldn't possibly hate you. And the more I think about it, your
parents are doing me a favor by giving you the opportunity to
stay in Paris with me because, quite frankly, being a stray cat
doesn't suit me anymore." Evienne gave her friend a huge smile.

Madalane laughed as she wiped the tears from her face. "Do
you think Evienne? Do you think they want me to stay in Paris

because it is good for me and not because they don't love me or want me at home?"

"I think your father wants you to learn about life, your mother may be jealous and your father knows it. My father would always say follow your dreams. Will you follow your dream by staying here?"

Madalane shrugged her shoulders and shook her head not really knowing what to say to Evienne or herself.

Evienne had a realization strike her, and she thought of the ink jar in hidden in her art box. She went to her art box and carried it over to where her friend was sitting. Madalane's eyes followed her. "Let me tell you a story about my family." The artist sat down, facing Madalane, "When I was little, my mother used to let me play with this while I sat in her lap." Evienne lifted the art box to the table and opened a small cubbyhole, and took out the black inkbottle. She unscrewed the lid and pulled out a tiny wrapped object. "My mum would tell me even though you feel unnoticed to the world, you need to start someplace." Evienne carefully unwrapped the cloth and there sitting in the middle of her palm was an iridescent pearl. It was larger than any pearl Madalane had ever seen.

"She would say to me, 'Evienne this pearl started out as a grain of sand, a small piece of nothing and because the sand and the oyster worked together, they created this pearl. The pearl holds the answers to the universe.' Then she would take my hand with the pearl in it and put it on my heart. Rocking both of us, she told me my answers are inside me and I have to work for them to grow and then to shine. Some things start out curiously and then as they grow, their shape evolves and so does their purpose."

Evienne pushed the pearl into Madalane's hand, wrapping her long fingers around Madalane's hand forcing it to close into a fist. "I want you to take this so you remember you have a reason and while you are doing that, I will be your oyster. We will be each other's family, you and me together."

The young woman opened her hand and the smooth perfectly round pearl sat in the middle of Madalane's palm. She wanted to thrust it back at Evienne, proclaiming herself unworthy of such a gift. The roar of denial crowded her brain and yet, the pearl stayed in the middle of her palm. Impulsively, she grasped the pearl into her fist and felt the small presence as she gripped tighter and tighter. Part of her wondered if she held it tight enough, would it crumble back to sand? Still, it remained clutched in her hand. The presence as certain and steady as the artist watching her.

Pulling her fist to her forehead, she closed her eyes as her friend's words washed over her. How was it possible that such a generous and kind soul found her in the midst of Paris? She wanted to grasp Evienne as tightly to her as she held the pearl and never let either go. She opened her fist and the pearl caught the light, appearing for a moment like the moon watching over her.

"I don't know what to say Evienne. You make me feel good even when I am feeling at my worst; you take my troubles away. I will keep the pearl and I promise you, I will never let it go. It will be my most prized possession...along with the painting you gave me when we met of course." Through teary eyes, Madalane looked up at her friend through the fringe of her hair and smiled. "Thank you for being my savior."

Evienne pushed the black ink jar towards Madalane. "I have always kept the pearl in this old jar, so no one would find it. You know my life has not been the safest in Paris and I would just die if I had lost it. No one wants a little dried up ink jar do they?" Evienne winked at Madalane. "The most beautiful things are hidden in the strangest places. Imagine something so exquisite hidden in a slimy shell. My dad never found another pearl as beautiful as this." Evienne looked at the pearl rolling in Madalane's palm. "You look tired Mad; why don't you lie down?"

Madalane felt an overwhelming sense of relief. She had expected Evienne to fight her over living together for the summer, yet Evienne had been strangely accepting of the idea. The rage towards her parents had dissipated and now she wanted to lie close to her friend and enjoy the image of what the future could bring. She nestled the pearl back into its wrapping and set it inside the jar again. She smiled as she thought about the pearl being snug in its little home, like herself and Evienne in their little room.

"Will you lie down with me?" She hoped that Evienne would be agreeable. Her warm body was always such a comfort.

"I will lie down with you if you promise to always tell me if there is something wrong." Evienne picked up her wine and waited for Madalane's answer. "Do you promise Madalane? It worries me when you are that upset; everything is easier when you talk about with a friend. And I promise you, we will find a room to live in. It will be a magical castle, just you wait."

Madalane felt the weight of her friend settle in behind her and she knew she would be asleep in minutes. "I promise Evienne. I have to tell you anyway because you always already know when I'm upset." She reached behind her, grabbed her friend's arm, and pulled it around her like a blanket. Heat suffused her body as she dreamily whispered, "And just think, the cat will be able to use the front door of the castle every day."

Madalane felt her body immediately relax and as she fell into a deep slumber, she realized that they had a lot to do in the next six weeks, but the anxiety of separation was no longer present. She finally felt like her life had truly begun.

Chapter 45

My Dearest Madalane,

The pearl I gave you is genuine and true and I know it every minute of the day. Madalane, it is how I feel about you. The pearl has been a part of my life since I was a child and a witness to my memories. The pearl has allowed me to believe kindness and love did once exist in my life. As I have had to face my misfortunes, the pearl has taken me full circle to your love and kindness.

My father used to tell me the story of how the oyster formed the pearl. How it was a gift for the queen mermaid of the sea. He would tell me how the grittiest piece of sand lodged into the mouth of the mollusk over time would work magic to transform dirt into beauty. It was always with the dedication and faith of the heart. It taught me that we all possess the power to take nothing and turn it into something great.

My father, on the full moon, would remind my mother of the miracles they had witnessed, the love they shared, the many blessing the sea had given them and he reminded her of her beauty—she was his queen on this earth. The pearl was meant to adorn her although the pearl fell shy to her beauty he would often say. He repetitively promised he would set the pearl in a ring or necklace to be reminded how honored he was to have her love. Money to do such a thing always fell short. She would often offer it to him to sell to fix something on his fishing boat. He laughed and said there are always other ways. He would turn sand into coins. It was the promise passing between their hearts. It was the glue between them. The truth of their commitment; the living gem that told the story of their love.

The pearl is so small and yet when you look inside, deep inside, you see the magic of the sea and the moon, the iridescent glow of the sunrise, the mysteries of the world. When we dig deep into the earth, into ourselves, we uncover our truth, our strength, our faith, our experiences of pain and love and through all this life; we emerge as something elementally beautiful. Our bones like the grain of sand hold our truth, emit our splendors. You are this pearl to me, Madalane, you are my family.

Forever,

Evienne

As Stella's clear voice dropped to silence at the last few words of the letter, Eve surprisingly sprang up from the couch. The older woman moved quickly into the dining room and Stella heard the china cabinet being opened and faint rustling noises being made.

Eve moved the piles of old greeting cards and china from the front of the hutch. Tossing the cards onto the dining room table, she moved a stack of plates to the dining room chair. The object she was seeking was all the way to the right back corner of the cabinet, and the knick-knacks that were in the way were confounding her. Finally, Eve could reach back and she retrieved the small black item. Breathlessly, she returned to Stella and held out her hand revealing a small ink bottle. "Stella, look, I have it. The pearl...my mom gave it to me before she died."

"Eve, you have the pearl that Evienne gave Madalane? This is unbelievable..." Stella watched anxiously as Eve cradled the small ink jar in her palms. "What did you mother tell you about it?"

Eve's excitement was palpable as she tried to unscrew the top of the inkbottle. "My God, I haven't opened this bottle in years. My arthritis is getting the best of me; I can't loosen the top. Stella, can you try to crack the seal? I can't believe that Evienne gave my mom this pearl and I even knew where it was!" Eve thrust out the small ink bottle to the younger woman with exasperated excitement.

Stella took the bottle and attempted to break the seal. "Why do you think your mom separated this from the art box?" A peeling brown label was still evident on the bottle. She felt the slip of the lid loosening and she finished unscrewing the top. She gave the bottle back to Eve, so she could retrieve the pearl.

"My mother gave me the pearl after she got sick. I don't know why she separated it from the art box. I guess she must have figured that the pearl was the easiest thing to pass along to me without having to do too much explaining." Eve pulled a small black piece of felt out of the bottle as she continued her story, "She said it was a family heirloom, and that I had to keep it in the ink bottle. She said that the ink bottle was to remind me that being an educated woman was an honor and that the pearl represented that out of grit and determination, anything is possible. For some reason, I thought her grandmother gave it to her—Madalane's father's mother. She helped raise Madalane for the first few years of her life; my mom loved her very much."

Stella watched Eve unwrap the old dark fabric from the jar, slowly unraveling the fabric searching for the pearl. Eve opened the last fold of fabric and there sat a perfect milk-white pearl the size of summer pea.

Reverently, the two women stared at the iridescent splendor of a gift from sea to land. Stella, lost in the past, murmured, "Evienne was right, you know. In an ordinary grain of sand there lives something incredibly beautiful. The love they had for each other had no boundaries. Their relationship is documented and has passed beyond time and oceans. She really loved your mother." Stella looked to Eve for confirmation.

"Yes, it does appear that Evienne and my mother were truly in love. It just makes me sad to think of my mom being alone for so long and having to mislead me about her relationship." Eve sighed heavily. "My mother gave this to me after she found out about the cancer. She had been sick for a while, but she hadn't said anything to anyone, or at least she hadn't said anything to me. Like I told you, after college, I went to Europe and did the backpacking thing. It was the sixties and my mom wanted me to enjoy life and have an adventure. I met my husband in a hostel in Switzerland—we fell in love during a blizzard. He was like me—just an American kicking around Europe, soaking up as much as he could. We traveled around for a while longer, and when he asked me to marry him, I brought him home to meet mom. As independent as I was, I wanted mom's blessing. She would tell me if I was making a mistake. She told me to marry him before he changed his mind. Ha. She was funny in a very dry way. Anyway, my husband and I went back to Europe; we ended up teaching English as part of an exchange program. Then I got the letter from mom. She was sick. She didn't order me home or anything draconian; she just wanted to see me again."

Absently, Eve sat down on the couch, memories flashing before her eyes. "We came home and moved in with mom. She was already so sick. She had waited until the end of my school term; she was so proud that I had become a teacher like her. A few months after we were home and we had settled into the routine, mom called me in to her bedroom and gave me the pearl. In those days, there weren't a lot of drugs or treatments for lung cancer—much less than today, and she knew she was going to die soon. And she did...just a few weeks later."

"She gave you her pearl on her death bed?" Stella reflected on the timing.

Eve frowned at the term, "Not exactly on her death bed, but I suppose it was close enough. I sat with my mom almost all the time in the last couple months of her life. She was usually too weak to talk, but we watched television together and I read to her. I didn't really think about the pearl other than as an object to pass along to my child one day. And we know how that turned out." Eve gave a stiff little smile.

Stella nodded.

Eve leaned back against the back of the couch and dropped the pearl back into its fabric resting place.

Chapter 46

Paris, April 1929

So here she was, facing the window, feeling very exposed and foolish in the morning light as Evienne's eyes studied her. Madalane looked around at the small dormer they shared; it was getting tinier by the minute. The clock on the mantelpiece seemed to be ticking louder than she had ever heard it before. The morning sun made it stifling hot in the room; she felt sweat trickling down her neck and back. Evienne's eyes were searing into her. Her fingers fussed with the fabric of her skirt; she gathered the fabric into small rows and then smoothed them out. She performed this action over and over again trying to calm the panic she felt rising in the pit of her stomach. She wished they had wine but they had finished the liter the previous night and it was too early to buy more.

Evienne's eyes briefly glanced at the tension in Madalane's hands, but it was her face that captivated her. The lines of her jaw, the roundness of her cheeks, and the slight curve of her lips surprised her every time she woke and saw her face. For a reason she did not want to admit, she needed to have Madalane's face memorized inside her heart.

Madalane sat completely still, staring at the window, properly positioned by her mother's silent instructions.

There was purity in their uncomfortable silence. Evienne
absorbed every detail: the innocence of her expression, the lifting and falling of her chest, the whiteness of her skin captured
under the thin sheer fabric of her cotton nightdress, the fidgeting of her fingers, the light shining in on the auburn strands of
her hair, the golden rainbow arching around her head created by
the glistening of the morning light. Evienne's intense scrutiny
was interrupted by the realization that something, someone, a
face, a body, a soul, was changing who she was. They both craved
freedom, and yet Madalane sat for her at her command and Evienne was equally captive to anything Madalane would ask of her.

Madalane's childish impulse to fidget was strong, yet she
resisted the urge to move. She closed her eyes and forced her heart
to slow down. Watching the artist, Madalane was reminded that
this was her chance to watch her friend unguarded.

Evienne's hand hovered over her sketchpad, watching
Madalane's expression with hooded eyes. Each time she put a
mark on the paper, she felt as if she was reclaiming a piece of her
bruised soul. The artist did not realize it, but her own breath was
getting short. She was lost staring into Madalane's eyes intently;
Madalane glanced down feeling exposed.

"Do not avert your eyes. Look at me—allow me see who you
are—let me capture you." Evienne's voice was rougher and fiercer
than she intended. Realizing that her voice had sounded angry,
she softened her tone, "Please, I want to capture the warmth in
your eyes. I want to capture the beauty of you."

Evienne's words shot through Madalane; she momentarily
wanted to bolt from the room; however, the gentler tone Evienne used calmed her.

The ferocity of her own voice had surprised Evienne. She was
beginning to understand the depth of her need. It was more than
just a portrait. Her hand started to shake and she lost her con-

centration. Frustrated at herself, she set her sketchpad down and stared at the drawing then at her friend and back to the sketch.

Madalane saw her friend's hand shake a bit as she put the pad down. "Have I done something wrong?" she asked.

Evienne stared wordlessly at the sketch. Finally, after seconds stretched into minutes, she replied, "No, you've done nothing wrong Dove." Evienne gazed at Madalane sitting exactly where her mind had envisioned her. The sketch matched perfectly to her face.

Suddenly Evienne was standing in front of Madalane. Evienne's body had moved across the small room like a ghost, and she gently grasped Madalane's face in her hand. She thought to herself how perfectly her friend's chin fit into her palm. How the bond of her flesh was searing into her soul, becoming part of her. She could not even blink or breathe. She had stared into other women's faces, but Madalane stole her will and created a burn inside the core of her.

Evienne's movements were so swift that Madalane barely registered the movement. One minute she was on the stool next to the window and now she stood in front of her. Madalane's heart pounded hard in her ears. For a minute, she thought Evienne was studying her up close. Evienne's breath—so sweet and warm—stirred the skin on her cheeks. Her fingers were tender and firm, holding Madalane's face with a reverential touch. Madalane felt the heat from artist's fingers, desperately wanting her never to let go. She stared deeply into her friend's eyes—silently giving her permission to take anything she wanted. Madalane was close to weeping at the beauty of the moment. "Please, please, please," Madalane's mind formed the mantra as Evienne's eyes gazed into hers. Evienne's scent, an intoxicating blend of paint and sandalwood, made her feel drunk. She wanted to fall into the warmth of the caress, but she was afraid to move, afraid to breathe, not wanting this to end.

Without thought, Evienne's mouth was on Madalane's lips.

Evienne moved so slowly and naturally that it was as if she had kissed Madalane a thousand times and yet this was the first. She felt her body spiral into center of the universe's helix, and felt a surge of passion flood through her body. She was lost in a thirty-second kiss, a thousand mile journey, a lifetime of need captured in the moment of union. Under her mouth, the softness of silky skin fit perfectly along her lips. Bliss encapsulated them and as she pulled away, and took the sweetness of Madalane's breath into her lungs. Evienne felt dizzy, almost falling to her knees, gasping for any air left in the room, trying to compose herself.

Instinctually, Madalane had just let her lips move with Evienne's and had felt that flicker of heat grow. She felt like she was in dream, lost in the spice of Evienne's mouth. She was unaware of the time as Evienne continued slowly to caress her mouth with her lips. Madalane's heart was pounding and her body was enflamed, building into a fire she had never known before. In every storybook, in every movie, in every fantasy, Madalane had never witnessed the perfection of the kiss that she now felt. When Evienne's lips pressed against hers, the world slipped away and her universe became this small oasis of passion. She had never kissed a woman and the few kisses she had shared with boys were nothing compared to this. Madalane was unsure what she should do, so she held still wanting to memorize the feeling. She wanted to wrap her arms around Evienne's back and pull her closer, but she was not sure of the etiquette for when a woman was being kissed by another woman. She felt Evienne pull away and for a moment, she was confused as to where she was. Looking at Evienne with bewilderment, she wanted to pull her back. She wanted Evienne's mouth on hers. She wanted to drink from her lips for eternity.

Evienne's mind exploded. Oh my God! What have I done? What have I done? Madalane's eyes seared into the artist as if she had stolen something from her. The blood was running from the artist's body and left her standing there in a puddle of doubt and mortification.

"I am sorry Madalane. I am so sorry." Evienne suddenly felt helpless. She wanted to beg and plead, but the words were stuck in her throat. She wanted to speak of love and promise and how she cherished her, but no sound came out. At that moment, in the silence of the stare from the girl she had just kissed, she realized her chest was wide open and tears were rolling down her face.

Startled by the change in demeanor, Madalane had never seen Evienne so upset. Madalane just wanted her to wrap her arms around her and kiss her again. Couldn't she see that? She stared at Evienne as the words echoed around the room. The only words she heard with clarity were, "I'm sorry." Madalane brought her fingers up to her lips and felt the residual heat of Evienne.

It struck her that the artist was regretting her impulsive action. She must have done something wrong. Madalane stared down at her hands and felt hot tears escape from her eyes. How could she tell her that she wants her to hold and kiss her again and again; she could learn—she was an excellent student. She looked back up at Evienne and saw the look of horror on the artist's face. Her regret was intractable.

Evienne knew whatever had just happened was over. She desperately wanted to smoke and lose herself in the intricacies of sketching a face. Evienne vowed to herself never to put her lips on Madalane ever again. She would paint her face until she saw nothing else, despite the desire to pull her to her body and hold her there forever.

With her head bowed, Madalane heard Evienne pick up the sketchpad and light a cigarette. The air turned acrid from the smoke. Madalane looked up and saw Evienne sitting on the small stool with her sketchpad in her hand and pencil in the other. The cigarette was in the crook of her mouth and Evienne squinted to keep the smoke from burning her eyes. She started to sketch again.

Madalane's eyes traveled from Evienne's hands, up her arms, along her chin and mouth and finally she met Evienne's gaze.

The artist's eyes were flat and empty and dark. Madalane knew that her own eyes mirrored the artist's expression. As their eyes met and held, it was as if the kiss had never happened.

Chapter 47

The letters had been temporarily put aside. After delving so deeply into the lives of these two young women, Stella had asked for a break and returned to the photographs that were found with the packet of letters.

One shot in particular made Stella pause and stare. It was Madalane and Evienne sitting at a cafe table. Madalane was wearing a patterned dress with a light-colored jacket over the dress. She looked like the very model of a young schoolteacher in Paris in the 1930's. Her hair was crimped in the style of the day and she smiled broadly at the photographer. Stella, however, was captivated by Evienne's appearance who was sitting casually at the table, barely even noticing the photographer. She was gazing at Madalane with a look that defined adoration veiled with a nonchalant posture. She wore long pants, a light shirt, a vest and a wool jacket. Evienne had one leg crossed over the other and a cigarette held confidently in her hand. It reminded Stella of pictures of Oscar Wilde although Evienne was far more casual in her appearance. Her hair was in its usual long braid that was barely visible in the photograph. Stella closed her eyes, imagining the conversation that the young women were having when someone took their picture.

"Evienne, stop looking at me and look at the camera!"

"No...you are far more appealing than Berenice. I'd much rather have a picture of just you."

"You are the only one who sees me as something special."

"No, my Dove...the world knows you are beautiful, but only I know the depths of your passionate nature."

"Sh...you will embarrass Berenice. At least stop scowling...for me?"

Stella's eyes darted open and she looked to the older woman for answers. "Look at this picture—you can tell that Evienne is a woman, yet she sits at that cafe table with a man's confidence. They appear to be together, but are they more than friends? The 1930s in Paris is so intriguing to me; there was a level of permissiveness that seems so completely normal to them. I feel like a person could try on a hat and see if it fit, and if not find another until they found one that was comfortable for them. Is this way of life lost in a photo of another time?"

Knowing that Stella was watching her with rapt attention, Eve pulled her eyes away from the photograph and asked, "How much do you know about this time period? It's a rather interesting era of the 20th century."

"I am ashamed to say that I don't know that much. I know about Mann Ray's photography from a project that Sarah had to do, and I liked the movie about Josephine Baker—you know the one with Halle Berry. I am pretty sure she was performing in Paris during this time period." Stella looked at Eve hoping that she didn't sound horribly uninformed.

"You probably know more than the average American. People tend to focus on the history of their own country—you know what I mean, like the Civil War re-enactors who show up at Gettysburg every weekend. We like our own history. Luckily for us, my mother lived in Paris during this time period. I don't know if you knew that." Eve smiled with a sly smirk.

"Really?" Stella played along, happy for the respite of an exhausting day.

With a mock dramatic flair, Eve continued the fiction, "Yes,

my mother was a denizen of Paris in its Golden Age. Such a
sophisticate—doncha know?!" Eve laughed at her own joke before
reverting to a more serious, instructional tone. "I'll give you the
Reader's Digest version—Paris at that time was the place where
art, literature and music found its home. The greats—and I mean
truly great—all passed through Paris in 20s and 30s—people like
F. Scott Fitzgerald, Hemingway, Sinclair, Dreiser, James Joyce,
Picasso, Braque, Duchamp, Stravinsky and of course Josephine
Baker. Gertrude Stein called them the Lost Generation because
they all came from the generation of the Great War—what is
now called World War I. After dealing with so much violence
and death, art focused more on life and sex and creativity. There
was a large homosexual community in Paris at the time as well
as in Berlin. Berlin was more politically radicalized whereas
Paris was all about the creativity. I suppose it was quite normal,
relatively speaking, to see two women together, especially when
one was dressed as a man. Gertrude Stein and her partner Alice
B. Toklas seemed to have invented, in some ways, the dichotomy
of dress as a way of maintaining societal acceptance."

"The freedom to be yourself. It seems to me that this is something the present could learn from the past, don't you think?"

"Well said my friend." Eve was delighted by Stella's perspective. Eve thought for a moment then added, "Hemingway has a
wonderful book about being in Paris at this time called *A Move-
able Feast*. Have you read it?"

Stella shook her head, seeing the romance novel she was
reading on her nightstand, wishing she had a deeper appreciation for literature.

Eve continued, "His account of a road trip with F. Scott
Fitzgerald is hilarious. That particular story is worth the price of
the book alone. It is a bit earlier than Evienne and mom's time,
but Paris is its own character in his book."

Stella's romantic nature started to bloom and a thought
crossed her mind, "It's a lovely sentiment to think of Paris as a

lover or even as her own character. It is so interesting to think
about. I have heard people refer to Paris as if you could fall right
into her arms. The smells, the city of lights, the love, the wine,
and of course the French women." Smiling, Stella thought of how
Evienne fell in love with a French woman. "I feel as if Evienne
was in love with Paris first, and then let her go for Madalane
and then the two woman shared Paris and immersed themselves
into her heart—sort of a love triangle in a way."

Smiling inwardly, Eve nodded her agreement. Aside from it
being her mother, the love story between Evienne and Madalane
was very sweet. Two awkward post-adolescents trying to navigate
a burgeoning love affair amidst their own myriad of problems
and self-esteem issues. Eve knew she was considering it within
the parameters of modern day psychobabble and her own experiences with young adults, but nonetheless, it seemed a miracle
that her mother and Evienne were able to cross the threshold
into a real relationship. Stella's romantic notions were endear-
ing and it made Eve see the beauty of two young women trying
to work it out, especially in a time period decades before the era
of Ellen and Portia.

"They just lucked out to live in a progressive city during a time
of great artistic transition. Can you imagine if they were alive
today? They would just naturally presume they could be a couple.
Evienne would be stomping around Paris in her Doc Martens
and Madalane would be listening to the Indigo Girls on her iPod
during her walk to work!" Eve laughed out loud imagining her
mother in Birkenstocks.

"I prefer to see them lunching with wine and cheese under
the Eiffel Tower. You are wrecking my image of them for me."
Stella laughed with her.

"Oh come on...if they were alive today, their lives would be
so different. After their lunch at the Eiffel Tower, they could
go to the alternative bookstore so Madalane could browse the
Sapphic poetry and prose. Then later, they could have dinner at
the vegan restaurant."

"Do not modernize them—your mother would be appalled." Stella was laughing, but underneath her words, there was a serious inflection.

Eve laughed, glad she had ruffled the otherwise unflappable woman next to her. "Okay, you're right. Evienne and Madalane don't belong in the present. We'll let them stay in the past where they clearly were figuring things out. Shall we get back to the letters?"

Chapter 48

Paris May 1929

Evienne was consumed by the kiss she had given Madalane since it happened a few days before. In her darkest hour, after she and Madalane had slipped into bed for the night, she had lain awake and compared herself to the men who had tried to rape her at Christmas. Her hunger had been overwhelming and she had felt a fierce lust course through her body as she put her lips on Madalane.

On this beautiful clear morning, the world felt different as she walked to her art stand at the Seine. She allowed herself to think of the softness of Madalane's lips and the eagerness of her friend's mouth. How she had stared at her, no into her, with intense excitement. As her boot heels clicked rhythmically along the sidewalk, it hit her. She felt bathed in a wave of elation like when she knew with certainty that a customer wanted to buy one of her paintings.

The scene, which she had played and replayed a thousand times in her head, suddenly came into startling clarity. She wanted me to kiss her—she rolled the image back and forth in her mind. Evienne was sure of this. Madalane had stopped because she didn't know what to do next.

Enlightened, Evienne felt the craving to kiss Madalane return, even stronger than before. Arriving at her art stand, she opened up for the morning then turned to stare at the Seine. Although still early in the day, the mild temperatures brought both the Parisians and the tourists to browse along the boulevard of art stands. Evienne felt the heaviness that had resided in her heart slowly dissolve as she realized what she should do. She heard what her heart was saying and she went to her art box, found a pencil and ripped a piece of her brown wrapping paper to write Madalane a note.

2 May 1929

My Dearest Madalane—
  Your sweet lips and downy skin,
  perfection between my mouth and hands.
  Will you ever allow me to kiss
  your beauty with my eager mouth,
  again?
Always,
E—

Evienne re-read the note over and over as the day went on. She sketched rose buds around the border of the ripped paper— some soft and opening, and others tight and new, ready to burst. She filled the plain brown paper with what she knew best, her art. She drew a miniature portrait of Madalane with her eye closed, the way she remembered her face the moment before she kissed her. She allowed the previously repressed memories of the softness of her hair lying under her fingertips, her jaw trusting Evienne's hand. Evienne was lost for hours thinking of nothing but their kiss, thinking of nothing but Madalane.

On her return to their room, she slipped the note inside of Madalane's coat pocket while hanging her own on the hook at the door. Madalane's attention had been and was still distracted as it had been since the kiss. The two continued to go about their lives as if nothing had happened. They shared the stories of the day and settled into their evening work of sketching and studies and dinner.

When Evienne climbed into the small twin bed with Madalane that evening, she felt the warmth of her friend's back on her chest. She understood that her thoughts of never touching Madalane's mouth again were said in haste. She had spent many years learning how to protect her own heart from the disappointment of love and caring too much. Today, as she stood staring at the Seine, allowing the truth to take shape, she understood that she would sleep next to Madalane for the rest of her life.

For the first time in days, Evienne felt herself falling into a deep slumber, the lulling rhythm of her friend's breathing and the softness of the body next to hers melting into her; she unconsciously matched her own breathing to Madalane's. She forgot the war in her mind and slipped away into the dreams of the night.

* * *

Madalane woke up with the same melancholy feeling she had felt since Evienne had kissed her. Lying in the narrow bed, she felt her friend's steady breathing behind her. She ached inside. She loved living with Evienne, but this sadness that had invaded her soul was too much to bear. She had felt so foolish after their kiss; it was clear to her that even a bohemian artist found her inadequate. The voice in her head kept reminding her that she had failed. Failure loomed large, a leviathan of inadequacy filled her with horror. She wished she could stay in bed and hide under the covers, weeping at her own desperation. Miserable, she felt tears form and drop onto her pillow. She wanted to howl her pain, but instead she rolled onto her stomach and let the cotton pillowcase staunch her sadness.

Dragging herself out of bed, she stood at the window. It was a gray day. Yesterday had been beautiful and warm; it had given her a modicum of hope as Evienne arrived home seemingly in a better mood than she had seen her since they kissed. Whatever regret Evienne had carried with her had been replaced by good humor. Evienne's change of mood had made last night painful in its ordinariness. Her tales of tourists looking for Marie Antoinette's guillotine always entertained her and last night had been no different, except for the heaviness in her chest. Evienne had moved on; she was over the awkwardness of the situation. This felt even worse. While she was still moping in the depths of her misery, Evienne had put their kiss in perspective and was ready to resume their normal life.

Madalane turned from the window and gazed at her friend. Evienne had stretched out in the bed; her long limbs extending outside their normal boundaries. Asleep, she was even more beautiful; the ascetic purity of her raw-boned features gave her an almost religious guise. She was Joan of Arc, Mary Magdalene, Saint Teresa all bathed in the countenance of self-denial and total confidence in her faith.

Breathing deeply, her emotions ragged with anxiety, Madalane quickly dressed in the semi-darkness of their room. Most mornings, Evienne would be up, joining her for breakfast; however today, Evienne continued to sleep. Madalane felt tears well up again as she donned her dress.

Hearing Madalane stirring in the small room, Evienne came out of her dream. Without moving a muscle, she absorbed the breaking morning, opened her eyes, and watched Madalane pull her stockings up her thighs, slipping her hands under her skirt to fasten the garters.

This was not something Evienne would normally have the pleasure of watching, and she thoroughly enjoyed the scene unfolding in front of her, watching with half-mast blue eyes. Madalane felt the change in the energy of the room, looked up, and froze, finding Evienne staring at her.

"Good morning Dove."

The sleepy sultry voice of her friend stirred something deep inside of Madalane. She gazed at her, wondering how she can be so nonchalant while she felt such despair. "Good morning. Did I wake you?" Madalane's voice sounded foreign and stilted to her own ears.

No, I have been lying here considering my day. You should come back to bed. Oh! I know! We should play hooky today. What do you think? Come back to bed and I will rub your back." Smiling, Evienne stretched languorously across the bed and winked at her friend.

A shot of anger coursed through Madalane. How dare Evienne act like nothing was wrong between them. She felt a white-hot rage fill her body as she tried to keep her voice steady, "I can't. I have an exam next week and I'll miss the lecture if I don't go to class." She stared helplessly at her friend, tousled and relaxed, stretched out in their bed. Part of her wanted to dive back into the bed and cuddle, but the anger that had been simmering was stronger than the desire to shut out the world. "I have to go."

"Please, Dove. What about some breakfast; would you like something to eat? I can put water on for tea." Evienne rolled over on her stomach, contemplating getting up. She never lounged in bed. She would have smoked a cigarette by now and organized her day, but something made her linger.

Something about the way Evienne called her the familiar Dove stopped Madalane's anger from escalating any further. That and the way the sheet wrapped around the artist's body and the way her hair, the dark strands free from its usual tie, framed her face. Madalane smiled, "Really, I wish I could, but I'm already late. I'll get something to eat after my first class. I'll see you when I get back. You should stay in bed Evienne. You haven't been sleeping well and it's too cold to stand outside all day."

Madalane moved to the door, almost forgetting her coat because of the heat coursing through her. Even first thing in the morning, her friend's beauty took her breath away.

"I'll consider it. Don't be jealous that I'm having breakfast in bed!" Evienne shot her a winning smile. "I'll be here when you get back. I will miss you." Evienne thought of the note she slipped into her friend's pocket as she blew her a kiss.

Madalane closed door, her brow furrowed. What had gotten into her friend? Evienne was not the type of person to blow kisses. Focusing on getting through the day, Madalane quickly dismissed thoughts of Evienne from her mind.

* * *

And she was gone. Evienne imagined what might happen if she heard the key in the lock and Madalane came back to her, dropping her coat and laying her body on top of hers. Thanking her for the note, kissing her mouth deeply, wantonly.

Evienne could smell Madalane on the sheet. Her scent. Her delicious scent captivated her. Impulsively, she pushed her nose into the bed sheets and inhaled deeply. She could almost feel her in the bed with her by her smell alone. The musky warmth was powerful. It was pure perfection. The smell convinced Evienne to press her breasts harder into the firmness of the mattress, slowly grinding her hips as her breath caught in her chest. She could feel the electricity of her thoughts surge through her core.

With her face turned to the side, Evienne traced her own jaw line with her fingertips and tried to pinpoint the difference between hers and Madalane's. She followed the muscles of her neck, lightly touching the silky hairs under her curtain of thick hair. She imagined Madalane touching her as she rolled languidly onto her back. The brushing of the sheets over her nipples sent chills through her; the feeling dominated her attention. Evienne closed her eyes and fantasized her hands were Madalane's as she slipped into her own pleasure.

* * *

The rage and frustration had dissipated and was replaced by the more familiar feeling of misery, chilling Madalane's bones. She had arrived at the lecture hall just as the professor had started his rambling dissection of romantic poetry. She was freezing; the walk had been punctuated by a blowing breeze with occasional drops of cold rain. As she walked through the chilly Parisian streets, she thought about Evienne lying in their warm bed, which only enhanced her wretchedness.

Arriving as late as she did, she took the first seat in the lecture hall near the entranceway. Cracks in the doorway created a vacuum of cold air and she pulled her coat around her tighter. Musing at the circumstances of her morning, she considered her day: late, cold and now sitting in a breezeway. Could her day get any better? She took off her heavy wool gloves and slipped them into her bag as she searched for her pen. Had she spoken too soon? Was her day about to get worse? No pen? What was the point of being in class if she couldn't take notes on the lecture? She looked longingly towards her usual seat; her friends would have graciously loaned her a pen, but they were across the room. This professor pounced on unruly students with the precision and vigor of a Napoleonic soldier. Sighing she settled into her seat and decided to listen intently and hope she could copy someone's notes during the first break.

The professor was rhapsodically describing the similarities of Shelley and Keats. Meter, tone, theme...so many notes and Madalane felt herself growing more despondent at her situation. She reached down again and let her fingers slide along the pockets of her bag; she always kept her pen in there and often more than one. She tried to remember what happened at the end of class yesterday. Then it flashed in her mind; someone had borrowed it to write down a quick thought as they were walking out of class. She had stashed it in her coat when they exited the building, excited by the warmth of the sun and the brilliance of the early spring day.

Feeling somewhat relieved, Madalane reached into her coat pocket and felt the solid presence of her pen, but she also felt a folded piece of paper. Confused because she was scrupulous about not leaving things in her pockets; the nuns had called it a sin to collect things in one's pockets because it caused the pockets to wear out. Surreptitiously, she withdrew the pen and paper lest the professor sees and his ire falls upon her. The paper was brown and waxy, like the paper that came in big rolls that her father used to wrap packages. Keeping her eyes on her professor, Madalane eased open the paper and saw Evienne's handwriting and a series of small sketches framing the note.

Her heart leapt as she read the words.

My Dearest Madalane—
   Your sweet lips and downy skin,
   perfection between my mouth and hands.

Was Evienne reaching out to her? The words filled her with an emotion surging from the depths of her soul. It burned through her like a fire; her emotions were like a dam being released.

*Will you ever allow me to kiss
your beauty with my eager mouth,
again.*
Always,
Evienne

Was Evienne asking to kiss her again? All was not lost. Her
soul exploded into a million tiny reflective stars as she felt a surge
of joy rocket through her body.

Her fingertips traced the rose trellis as she imagined her
friend's mouth on hers. Would it be as sweet the next time?
Would it be sweeter? Would she survive another kiss if it were
sweeter? Heat suffused her body as she reread the words over
and over. Cautious of curious observers, Madalane folded the
note and cupped it in the palm of her hand, stamping down the
emotional storm fighting to be let loose. A honeycomb of pleasure swept through her, leaving her no longer cold

She wanted to jump up and run out of the room, but the
sonorous tones of her professor gave her pause. Uncapping her
pen, she opened her notebook to a fresh sheet of paper. If she
couldn't race home, then she would capture her feelings with
words. Evienne had seen a few of her poems, but Madalane had
been too shy and embarrassed to write anything for her friend.
Today, that would change. She would pour everything she felt and
wanted into a poem for Evienne. And just to teach her friend a
lesson, she would slip it into her art box while they slept tonight.
Two could play hide and seek. She just wished she could see Evienne's face when she read her poem.

Putting pen to paper, Madalane pursued her task with a
diligence rarely seen in a classroom.

Evienne,

    Your lips are made for mine.
    With eyes closed, slowly drawn,
    so slow and sweet I could not even
    think to take a breath,
    to know Paris, to know life,
    to know the inner most essence of your taste.
    I felt you upon me; I felt the strength
    of your earth, I believe nothing but your heart.

    My heart and I want to tell you this…
    you have my breath and my lips
    and everything that makes
    my lips plead for your breath
    and the sweetness of your lips
    on mine.

Chapter 49

Paris, May 10, 1929

The night was cool, yet Madalane was sweating. She had been nervous and excited when Evienne had told her about the invitation to the salon. Evienne had explained that these guests were from the highest echelon of literature and art; these people lived the lives others could only read about. They were the ones who were defining the latest and newest artistic and literary trends.

Madalane was eager to attend with her friend, but she wasn't sure what to expect. She asked a professor at school about the salons, and the instructor, wide eyed, was shocked that a student had been invited. That's when Madalane realized that these salons were something very special.

Evienne tucked her arm under Madalane's and led them both to the Rue de l'Odeon. Evienne was so excited that she could barely contain herself. She had heard from the others that recognizable painters and writers socialized at these private salons. If she had the chance to ask questions and learn from superior artists, this night would be stellar. On arrival, she remembered the instruction to knock on the door to the right of the store. Evienne looked into Madalane's eyes and said, "Are you ready?"

She pulled on the hanging knocker and let it fall, repeating this action twice more, and there without delay was Adrienne opening the door and inviting them in.

"Bonjour Evienne! Introduce me to your friend! Come in, come in—it's too cold to stand on the doorstep!"

Evienne made a quick introduction as their hostess ushered them into the warmth of the foyer.

Madalane felt Evienne's hand guide her through the doorway. She felt oddly comforted by the pressure of Evienne's hand on her back. Adrienne took both of their coats and hung them on the hooks inside the door. Madalane quickly counted fifteen coats already hanging.

Adrienne led them up a narrow staircase and through a small hallway. Evienne's eyes scanned the entryway. Voices made their way out to the corridor and Madalane felt her heartbeat increase. These were the elite intelligentsia of the city and she was just a student. She had resolved to keep her mouth shut and let Evienne do the talking for the both of them. She would be horrified if she embarrassed Evienne and they were not invited back.

The salon was a long thin room, four times the size of Madalane's room. The room was bracketed with windows on either end and the length of the far wall was covered with framed paintings and drawings. Evienne recognized the style of some of the paintings while others were unknown to her. The guests were socializing with each other, sharing conversation, drinking wine and smoking. Evienne felt she had walked into paradise. Two older women, sitting towards the front of the room, had an air of superiority about them. She had seen the heavier woman's picture before, but could not remember her name. Several women crowded around them, listening with rapt attention; the heavier woman's bird-like friend made eye contact with Evienne and smiled. Some of the women were sitting on settees and others were standing and talking to the few men in the room. The room had an energy of warmth mixed with the scent of smoke and red wine and champagne.

Madalane knew her whole body was fidgeting—she had not been this nervous since she had been sent away to live at the lycee. Evienne felt the tension and pulled her closer to her side, knowing the maturity of the situation would put Madalane at a disadvantage. Adrienne approached with two glasses of red wine, "Tell me about your friend, Evienne; how did you meet this delightful young woman?" A small smile played around the corner of her lips as the two younger women gratefully received the wine glasses.

Evienne introduced Madalane properly to her host. "Madalane is a student at Sorbonne, studying literature and humanities. She is going to be a teacher. We met when she demonstrated excellent taste by admiring one of my paintings." Evienne positively beamed as she spoke of Madalane.

Adrienne laughed and welcomed the women to her home, "You will find my guests most intriguing Madalane. Please, I hope you feel at home." Madalane returned the smile and thanked her for the invitation.

Adrienne, in a long gray skirt and white shirt, guided them to a small group of women and introduced them. Standing quietly and listening to the women, Evienne leaned down and whispered into her friend's ear, "Madalane, take a deep breath and look at where you are. We have the opportunity to see the internal mechanism of Paris' greatest artistic minds. These people here speak their minds and they are proud of who they are. They have taken long journeys and know what their truths are. Here in this salon, we can learn who and what we are and what we will become tomorrow."

Madalane looked at Evienne. Her eyes were glowing as if Evienne was having a religious conversion. Her words resonated inside of Madalane and she began to feel something, a realization that the she was proud of the strength of her soul. She felt her own transformation, the stirring of her maturity. Madalane listened intently to the conversation as Evienne easily joined in discussing whether cubism has already been replaced. Madalane felt like a twelve year old at an adult party, but she smiled and listened, soaking up everything.

During a pause in the conversation, Adrienne turned her attention to Evienne, "How are your paintings selling? I hope you will grace our humble walls with one of your portraits." Madalane glanced at the framed drawing closest to her; it was a small pencil drawing of a woman reclining and she recognized the scrawl of Picasso's name. She inwardly wondered if Evienne realized the compliment that was being paid to her by their hostess.

Evienne shifted her weight and smiled at her hostess. "I am proud to say that I have some regulars buying my paintings. In fact, they are Americans who travel quite often to Paris. I think they might have an apartment near the Renommee du Cafe. They buy three or four paintings with each visit. The wife is very interested in collecting and studies the paint and ink technique, and—"she whispered conspiratorially, "—they never barter for a better price."

Adrienne's eyebrows rose as she replied, "Americans? They are the only ones with any money these days and even they are not as well off as they used to be. Perhaps you have found your own Gertrude. Pablo was scraping by when Miss Stein started buying his art and now look at him." Adrienne furtively glanced towards the front before continuing, "Of course, she is here tonight, so we shall drop the subject in case she should overhear and take offense. Evienne dear, your fortunes are definitely looking up."

"I can only continue with what is given to me, Adrienne. I will be sure to bring you one of my finer portraits; in fact I know which one." Evienne looked in the direction of Madalane and took a sip of her wine. Evienne knew sure in her heart she would never give the portrait of Madalane away—any portrait but that one. "I do see Monsieur Picasso on the street occasionally. He is always rushing to get to his studio to paint. He is a very talented man, would you agree?" Evienne was desperate to know what Adrienne knew of Picasso and then it hit her—what if one day she was as recognized as Picasso was. It was her dream.

As Adrienne answered Evienne's question, a small thin woman disengaged from the group and came to stand next to Madalane. She was smoking a cigarette and her eyes were a bright blue despite the cloud of smoke that seemed to drift perpetually across her face.

"Hello, I am Sylvia—"She extended her hand, "I own the book shop across from Adrienne's. You are Evienne's friend?"

"Yes Madame." Madalane's nerves were getting the best of her; she felt like a student in front of the Mother Superior.

"Please call me Sylvia. You are so young; are you a student?"

"Yes."

Sylvia took a long contemplative drag on her cigarette, "I envy you. Your entire job is to learn as much as you can."

Madalane blushed. She was unsure what to say.

Sylvia smiled and said, "Learn today, and apply what you have learned when you come back next week." She noticed that Madalane's glass was already almost empty. She quickly filled it with a bottle of Cliquot that was sitting near the group. With an appreciative look into Madalane's eyes, she said, "I think you are a very lovely girl."

Evienne's hand found its way to the small of Madalane's back again. Madalane felt her body relaxing. As Evienne continued to chat with the other women, she felt immensely proud of her friend—she was so confident and informed. Evienne glanced at Madalane and wanted her to feel part of the group. She knew the wine would begin to ease Madalane nervousness; her cheeks had become softer and her expression calmer.

During a lull in the conversation, Evienne broke in, "Madalane has been studying the role of women in society. We were discussing on our way over how the freedom to create art is not a gift, but rather the manifestation of boundaries we have triumphed over."

Madalane realized that all eyes were on her, including Evienne's. She spoke hesitantly at first, but with intention as she warmed to her subject, "I have been reading the writings of Voltairine de Cleyre. Her point is that society has been created by men to maintain a man's dominance in the world. She thinks that the only way to undermine this system is to destroy it."

Adrienne's shrewd eyes appraised the young woman. "Wasn't de Cleyre a Communist?"

Madalane quickly responded, "Technically no. She called herself an anarchist although I will concede she was not a big fan of a money-based economy."

"We have had the pleasure of hosting Emma Goldman at one of our salons and she confirmed that de Cleyre was a Communist," Adrienne asserted.

Sylvia's peevishly called out, "Leave the girl alone Adrienne."

Madalane had witnessed the smile and spark in Adrienne's eyes and understood that she was being challenged in a gentle way, "No Sylvia, it's okay. Of course you and Adrienne are far more worldly and have met many great writers, and I should defer to your first-hand knowledge; however, I am quite sure that de Cleyre resisted the Communist label for her entire life, including in a letter to your friend Ms. Goldman, herself a Communist." Madalane paused, waiting for a denial from her hostess. Instead, the smile that had hovered around Adrienne's eyes burst out as a hearty laugh.

Turning to Evienne, Adrienne spoke with great appreciation, "Evienne, thank you for bringing this wonderful young woman. She is not only smart, but brave." Turning to Madalane, she squeezed Madalane's arm and said admiringly, "You will go far my new friend. You are fearless."

Nodding, Evienne thought it would be an opportune time to ask around for an apartment for her and Madalane to move. "Madalane and I have been looking for a new place to live; maybe you have a suggestion for us."

Sylvia exhaled a stream of smoke and replied, "Adrienne is the one who knows the best places in the city. She found the first location for my bookstore as well as the current location. She has a nose for sniffing out the best spots."

All eyes turned to Adrienne who was already contemplating the request. Finger lifted to her lips, she tapped out a secret message to herself as she considered the options. "I am assuming that you need someplace reasonably priced?"

Madalane nodded, "Yes and preferably within walking distance of the university and a good cafe."

Adrienne laughed, "My sweet child, you can't swing a cat in Paris without hitting a good cafe."

Evienne winked at Madalane at the mention of cats as Adrienne considered the request. "Now let me think; I have a friend who rents out rooms near the Luxembourg Gardens. It will involve stairs—the higher up you go, the cheaper it will be, so it is good you are both young and vigorous. In the summer, it will be glorious to sit in the gardens and enjoy the air."

An apartment near the gardens gave Madalane a burst of pleasure. She imagined the two of them picnicking on a summer afternoon, sipping wine and feeding each other grapes as the sun lingered overhead. Stairs were nothing to her if she and Evienne could live the life they wanted. "Yes, Adrienne, it sounds ideal. Evienne, what do you think?"

"Sounds perfect, you will have to give us the address. Madalane will be done classes in a few weeks and summer will be here, so we will have to settle on an arrangement soon." Evienne directed her proposal to Adrienne though her thoughts drifted to the top floor of a Paris apartment. Her body stretched over Madalane's. A kiss. The kiss. The taste of Madalane's sweat from her upper lip. Evienne licked the top of her own lip as she took a drag of her cigarette.

"Come to the shop this week and we will set you off into the right direction," Sylvia continued, "See I told you, my Adrienne knows all the right people in Paris. She fixed that problem perfectly and now we can continue with our party!"

Evienne moved her body even closer to Madalane's as their hostesses moved away indicating that their speaker was ready. Evienne's hand surreptitiously grasped Madalane's fingers, squeezing them in appreciation.

A small pinging of silverware to glass sounded. Their hosts, Adrienne and Sylvia, were standing at the front of the room with a small, dark woman. Everyone stopped their conversation, and gave them their attention. "Ladies and gentlemen, we are very happy to have with us tonight a very special guest—our good friend D'Juana Barnes. As many of you can attest, she is writer of great renown and a woman of incredible vision as well as a biting wit. She published not one, but two books last year—both of which I am sure you are aware of and I hope many of you have read and enjoyed greatly. She has recently begun writing a new novel and she has agreed to share with us a chapter she is working on."

Around the room, guests refilled their glasses and waited expectantly for the author to begin her reading. Evienne noticed an armchair near the back corner and she guided Madalane in that direction. Madalane insisted that Evienne take the chair and she sat at her feet with her back against Evienne's legs. Madalane gazed at the small woman at the front of the room. She was dark and wore a dramatic black cloak and a hat pulled low almost covering her eyes. A slash of ruby red lipstick bisected her face and when she began to speak, her tobacco-roughened voice startled Madalane.

The author's voice started low with a slight hitch in her breathing, "I know some of you found the Almanack a little too honest about our wonderful literary world, so instead I shall offer you some of the jottings I have made about a family whom none of you know. Truth is a memory someone else has forged in this case."

Madalane felt the energy in the room shift at the reference

to the Almanack. Several of the women appeared to be defiantly disinterested in the words while others smiled encouragingly at the author. The writer started to read disjointed lines that seemed only to make sense after she had finished a page. Madalane enjoyed the modernist take on writing, but this chapter was so unformed, she had a hard time following the thought process.

Evienne could feel the weight of Madalane's back on her shins. It was a comfort to have someone to share this evening with. Evienne gazed down at her friend, noticing the shimmering reflection in her hair from the nearby fire. Madalane's hair was always so carefully maintained in a tight chignon. Evienne leaned forward and pushed her hands below the neckline of Madalane's wool dress, massaging her friend's shoulders as they listened to the poet. Feeling the warmth under her fingers, Evienne continued to push her fingers into Madalane's tight muscles. She felt comfortable and peaceful, feeling the acceptance of being in this room with these amazing artists, knowing they were there same reason—to know freedom of speech, to know the feeling of community, to know the freedom of their art.

Madalane watched the writer and tried to listen to her words, allowing the phrases to flow and ebb through her mind like a river tide. But the temptation to observe the other guests in this moment was too great. She glanced around the room and realized that almost everyone in the room, now about twenty guests, were women except for three or four men. Yet, even the men didn't seem traditionally masculine. Many of the women were leaning against each other, like she was leaning against Evienne. Sylvia and Adrienne were on a wine-colored settee along the left wall, and they were holding hands. At the sight of the two women's hands intertwined, her eyes stopped and she watched them. Feeling a chill of the unexpected, she searched the faces of both women. It was not unusual to see two women holding hands, but their clasped hands seemed to communicate something so much more significant than friendship. She stared at the women trying to detect any other sign indicating the nature of their relationship.

Feeling like she was voyeuristically staring at her hosts' private affection, Madalane's eyes roamed the room as her thoughts flitted from one explanation to another. She settled further back against Evienne; Evienne's hands were rubbing the muscles of her shoulders. It felt so good. She tilted her face up and smiled at her friend. Evienne was smiling down at her. She sighed deeply, contentedly and turned to face the author.

As much as she tried to keep her eyes on the speaker, her gaze kept coming back to the clasped hands of Sylvia and Adrienne. Sylvia's thumb appeared to be stroking the soft skin on the back of Adrienne's hand, but Adrienne barely seemed to notice. Madalane mused at how so much affection seemed to be packed into the slight movement of a finger.

The feel of Evienne's hands and the knowledge that all of the women in the room were sharing affectionate touches intoxicated Madalane. She was succumbing to her yearning desire for Evienne to touch her body. She was beginning to understand something she had never comprehended before.

Evienne recognized in her own body the feeling of desire, a slow and steady feeling of want. The muscles of Madalane's neck became pliable, falling into a natural rhythm under Evienne's touch.

Evienne and Madalane were immersed in the heat of the room, the low murmurs of the story and the affections of women. It was subtle like water flowing over their skin, at times raging inside their soul like fire, owning every inch of the air in the room; freedom to touch and be touched, liberating, a unique sense of belonging.

Madalane's skin was flushed pink, and Evienne momentarily imagined turning Madalane's face towards her and kissing her lips. Evienne imagined the shape of her lips, having memorized each line, the fullness, the pink that sometimes appeared red. She thought how she would kiss the younger woman—the pressure of her lips, the taste of the honey living inside of her, the fire that would rage out of control as she owned her friend's mouth.

When Evienne had finished the massage, she leaned forward and wrapped her arm, clasping Madalane close to her. Her fingers still hungry, she gently moved her index finger along the back of Madalane's arm, thinking of the softness. She felt a surge of electricity as Madalane sighed and dropped her head to Evienne's knee.

Feeling drunk with warmth and wine, Madalane was overcome by a lassitude in her limbs. It had been delightful to be pampered in such a warm intimate way. Watching this amazing collection of people was fascinating, but the strong warm hands skimming her arm with the lightest of touches was entirely too pleasurable to not focus on. She shifted her head, so that it looked like she was watching the speaker, but as her head rested against her companion's knee, she could only feel the soft slide of fingers gently stroking her skin.

Chapter 50

Paris, May 10, 1929

Sylvia and Adrienne stood on the doorstep as they two young women prepared to leave.

"I will be by the book store on Tuesday or Wednesday to get the information regarding your friend renting us a room. We truly appreciate your help."

"Of course Evienne. I look forward to seeing you. I think I have a few new picture books that you might like to flip through."

Sylvia embraced Madalane warmly, whispering, "I hope you have a lovely walk home. It is a beautiful night and the full moon shall light your way; let the night take you where you want to be."

Madalane blushed, wondering if the older woman was psychic. She had thought of nothing but Evienne's lips on hers since the reading had ended. She knew Evienne had found the poem; she had surreptitiously checked the art box before they left. Was Evienne being cautious? Why had she not kissed her again? She had hoped that Evienne would gather her in her arms when she left the bathroom after getting ready; instead, she had merely gazed at her longingly, as if she was a piece of art.

After insisting that Evienne and Madalane return for the

next salon, kisses and hugs were exchanged and the two young women set off for their apartment on Rue Galande.

Madalane linked arms with her friend as they walked off into the dark, cool evening.

Evienne's voice broke the silence of the night, "Wasn't it fantastic?"

Madalane smiled up at her friend. "It was like no other I have ever experienced. Adrienne and Sylvia are very nice. They have quite an interesting group of friends."

Evienne laughed. "Is that a euphemism?" She glanced at Madalane to watch her reaction.

"No... I just mean that they are very unusual. I couldn't pay attention to the writer because I was so interested in the guests. I have never seen so many smart people in one place. I felt rather stupid. Most of them looked quite ordinary—like you would see them at the bakery or butcher shop, but their conversations were incredible...so esoteric and philosophical." Madalane was quiet for a moment, expecting Evienne to respond. Evienne said nothing, but continued to walk at a leisurely pace down the boulevard towards their room. Madalane let her mind wander to the scenes that played out in front of her during the party. Finally, she whispered, "Did you notice that all of the women were very affectionate with each other?"

Evienne seemed lost in thought. She was thinking how she had been thrilled to be in the same room with Madalane, sharing in the excitement of finding like-minded people. She wanted everybody to know that they were together. The thought excited her and she could only think of one way to respond to Madalane—I wanted to kiss you when you looked at me—but knowing that was not the answer to the question, Evienne slowly spoke—drawing out each word, "You learned something about what one woman can do for another. Did it create questions in your mind?"

Madalane's anxiety surged as she realized that her interest had been too obvious. Had she betrayed her secret? Recognizing that she was not ready for this conversation, she quickly replied, "No, not really. It's just unusual to see." Feeling frantic, she changed the subject, asking, "Did you see the way that the writer had her hair done? It's the newest style—it is considered very chic. If I'm ever brave enough, I might try it."

Evienne gave her a horrified look as Madalane started to laugh. Evienne pulled Madalane to her, feeling the warmth of her friend. She started laughing too. They continued their walk and something Madalane had been wondering popped into her head. "Why are people so against the Communists? What makes their system so abhorrent?"

Evienne sighed and shrugged. "I don't know why Adrienne is, but I think, in general, that most people see the violence that occurred during the Bolshevik Revolution and it scares them. The idea of using violence to control a population is spreading and it always impacts the middle-class first. I have nothing to lose if the Bolshies come calling. But Adrienne and Sylvia have businesses and savings—they would lose it all. On the other side of the coin are the fascists, but they use violence to achieve their ends as well. To me—no one wins when there is violence. I don't believe that violence can ever be an alternative to dialogue. Unfortunately, as de Cleyre points out, as long as there are armies, there will be wars."

Madalane's serious countenance broke into a large smile. "You do listen when I prattle on about what I learned in class!" She was positively delighted that her friend had paid attention. She had secretly dreaded that Evienne merely nodded, pretending to listen.

"Of course my friend. I am attending class through you. I learn from you. You are an outstanding teacher."

Madalane blushed at the compliment and grasped her friend's arm tighter. Her mind wandered back to her friend. Each day they woke up next to one another; each night they fell asleep next to each other. Her days were counted out by sunrises in her friend's arms. She wanted to lie in her friend's arms tonight and know that she would be kissed. She wanted to feel the pressure of Evienne's mouth on hers. Yet, as she walked along the wide Saint Germain Boulevard, Evienne looked like she always did: self-contained and self-assured. Would they slip out of their clothes and lie down to sleep as they did every night? Or would Evienne take her in her arms and take her breath away?

A small whisper swirled around Madalane's thoughts. She should take the first step. Why should she wait all night to see if Evienne would kiss her? She wanted to feel the confident suppleness of Evienne's lips. She knew that Evienne wanted to kiss her and she wanted to kiss Evienne. Surely, there was no rule about who should kiss whom, or maybe there was and she didn't know the rule. She was momentarily caught off guard by the idea that there were rules for kissing another girl. Were they in a book? How could she find out? Then as quickly as that thought had come into her mind, she recognized that Evienne was not the kind of girl who followed rules. They had turned the corner from the boulevard and were heading down the smaller Rue Dante. Madalane, determined to achieve her goal, stopped. Evienne looked down at her friend, curious why she had paused. "Is something wrong?"

Madalane stared up at her friend's concerned eyes. Her heart was pounding, her mouth was dry and she felt like she was about to jump off a cliff into a bottomless sea. She reached up, pulled her friend's face down to hers, and whispered, "Kiss me Evienne." Pushing her mouth against her friend's lips, she let her mind go blank as she felt softness engulf her. Madalane felt the gentle, feather-light kisses that barely brushed against lips. As desire commanded them both to fit their mouths perfectly together, they breathed the same air; kissing each other over and over again, stopping time. A vortex of energy swirled around them, consuming them, rendering them lost to the moment.

Evienne was lost in surprised pleasure as Madalane's lips covered hers. Instantly, Madalane mouth's was in command of her mouth, of her desire and of her intention. Evienne felt numbness in her knees. It swayed along her thoughts, back and forth between her heart and the honey of the kiss coating every exposed nerve of her body. She pulled only centimeters away to see the woman who had just kissed her, but her lips immediately begged her to return to Madalane. She tilted her head and blended herself into the perfection of the magic, the divine dance of her partner, matching the kiss she has been imagining. Madalane's mouth was a universe unto itself, a portal into heaven.

Evienne's long fingers delicately cupped the face below hers and balanced the entirety of Madalane's soul in the moonlight, both lost in the swoon of passion. Evienne pulled back again and stared into Madalane's eyes, kissing her slowly between words, "Madalane," followed with a wet silky kiss. "I will always kiss you." She slipped her hand down her friend's neck and then back up, slowly losing her hand in the warmth of the nape of her brown hair. Pushing her own mouth hard against soft lips, opening her mouth as commanded and drawing Madalane's lips back into softness.

Madalane's mind had become dizzy, an induced intoxication from the sweetness of Evienne's kiss. Her balance was pivoting on Evienne's mouth, consumed intention exchanged between two women, a kiss defining love, a kiss transforming nature, a kiss leading them both over a waterfall, falling into velvet ocean of comfort.

"Madalane." Evienne tried again to explain the tumble of thoughts cascading through her mind. "I am..."

Madalane touched her lips with her fingers and quieted her. "Kiss me Evienne, kiss me forever."

Accepting her powerlessness, Evienne kissed her again, a kiss that spun them both into oblivion, traveling through histories, revealing the mysteries of the universe. Forgetting the hours before, one kiss materializing on a dim street in Paris that lasted until dawn; a kiss that was born from love.

Chapter 51

Eve stood up and stretched her body, vexed by the sound of the popping noises coming from her spine. She looked down at Stella who appeared unfazed by their day of sitting. She rolled her eyes remembering how it felt to be 40 as opposed to being almost 70 now. As she gazed down, she realized that Stella is the age her daughter would have been now had she been able to have a child.

"Do you feel you know your mother? And your father? Do you think any child truly knows their parents?"

The image of her own mother shot through Stella's mind. "My real father was a drinker and a gambler, and he met some woman on a trip to Vegas and then he was gone. My mother essentially called my dad a drunken waste as a man and not a proper husband to her." Stella's tone grew quiet, "I really have to question now, as I examine the past, who was really telling the truth. I can remember phone calls where my mother was screaming that he didn't deserve to see me, so I guess he did want to see me now that I think about it. Maybe my father truly was a scoundrel or maybe Margo created stories so she could look like the better parent. Either way, I barely saw him. The more I think about it, I think my dad's abandonment of me might have been one of her stories too."

Stella held her hand gingerly in the other and studied her

wedding set. "It's the choices that we make from our memories and experiences that create our futures. Maybe my dad was not such a bad guy after all, but he's gone now, lost to alcohol. I have to accept what my mom did—I don't have to like it, but I do have to move on. I feel like I am figuring out my present as we look at the past." She squinted her eyes in confusion, "That can't be bad can it?"

"I think that is the hardest part of life. We have to accept the lies our parents told us, and still love them. Otherwise, we would be better off being raised by a pack of wolves." Eve was quiet for a moment, allowing the moment to breathe. "I think there are reasons why people do what they do except they are not always good reasons. It's a good reason for them at that moment, but eventually choices are examined and in retrospect, nothing is so clear cut."

Stella looked up to her friend, curious about Eve's parentage. "Your father seems to be a distant memory too; what happened to him, did you know him?"

Eve winced as the lurking suspicions that had been gathering traction were going to come to light as she answered Stella's question. "I never met my father. According to my mother's legend, he died heroically in a battle in France. My mother told me that she and my father knew each other a few months before she got pregnant. They married and right after they had me, he was drafted. She said he died in combat when I was eighteen months. She..." Eve stopped for a moment unsure how to continue the tale.

Silence permeated the living room as Eve felt the walls close in around her. "My mother saved only one letter from my father—it's a letter he wrote to me on my first birthday. I still have it. It's short and sweet and I've kept it at the bottom of my jewelry box since I was a child." Eve was silent again. Bitterly, she added, "After today, I don't think my father wrote the letter. I think it is a fiction, much like the picture of him I kept in my room. After learning about Evienne, I think my mom had a moment of weakness, slept with some anonymous man, got pregnant and created a fairy tale that would sustain my paternal yearnings." Eve's breathing was ragged and harsh and she bowed her head as her words colored the air.

"Do you really think your mother had a one-night stand?" Stella was shocked by the thoughts in her own head.

Eve rolled her eyes at Stella's naive tone. Sometimes Stella seemed to have been raised in a Masterpiece Theater mini-series. "My mother was a lot of things, but most of all, she was practical." Eve saw Stella cringe and she tried to soften her tone. "Listen—Mom did what she had to do—if she was lonely, I can see her having sex with someone although I may not have thought this a few days ago. I had always considered her sexless, which, I suppose, most people see their mothers as. Of course, I never actually saw my mom date anyone, so I think I had a valid perspective. She was, however, very sensible. Whether she was lonely, bored, or depressed, I can see her going out to find some companionship. I doubt if there were lesbian bars in Boston in the 1940s, so finding a man, maybe even a soldier who was shipping out, would have been the next best thing."

Dumbfounded by Eve's openness, Stella sat there staring at her.

Eve wondered if she had offended the younger woman. "Did I shock you? About what I said about my mom?"

"No, no—of course not." Stella reached for her wine sounding hesitant as the words came out slowly.

Leaning back into the softness of the couch, Eve sighed heavily. "It's just a feeling I got as we discussed it. I'm wondering about the fairy tales my mom used to tell me about her whirlwind love affair with my so-called father. I think some of the stories she told me were actually about Evienne, probably most of the stories now that I think about it. The letter about them bonding in church reminded me of a story she used to tell me about knowing that she loved my father when he took her to church to look at the architectural details. When we vacationed in England, we rented a car and drove around the perimeter. When we got to the northwest part, we drove along the sea where all these old fishing villages were. For some reason she wouldn't explain, we stopped at one and walked out on this rocky beach. I was bored. I wanted to do something other than stare at water. I think I whined and mom, who never lost her temper at me, called me a selfish child for wanting to leave. It was the first and only time she purposely denigrated me. I was hopping mad, but in retrospect, I was a bit of a horror."

Eve turned to face Stella. "It seems logical that fishing village was where Evienne grew up?"

Stella nodded slowly, understanding that there were few other reasons to visit a rocky beach in the north of England.

Eve felt the anger of being misled ring inside of her and she abruptly stopped talking. Everyone was long dead, yet she felt terribly betrayed.

"Eve, the fishing village in England, the pearl, and the museum trips—this all makes so much sense." Stella declared emphatically.

Scowling, Eve turned to Stella who looked like a puppy about to get a treat. "You know...I understand that this is interesting and fun for you, but this is my life—my life which in the last couple of weeks has unraveled. Everything that I believed has now been undermined and tossed away. Instead of my childhood memories being happy, I am now second-guessing everything my mother told me. I don't give a rat's ass about my father or Evienne, but my mother was the one person I trusted in my life, and now it's apparent that she lied to me more than any other person I have known."

" You have to believe she loved you and she wanted to tell you the truth, but in the 40's, or the 50's or even the 60's, the truth needed to be filtered in America—you know that—you lived through those decades. I know this is a lot to handle right now, but don't you think Madalane just wanted to do the right thing for you. If the right time had come, don't you think she would have put those pieces together for you?" Stella felt a passion for these two women

"Quite frankly Stella, I am not so sure. I feel like my mother made up a bunch of lies so she wouldn't have to deal with the ramifications of getting pregnant from some anonymous guy in the 1940s. Being a single mother now is no big deal, but we both know that it was completely unacceptable in those days. She came up with a plausible story, got herself out of Boston and came to Philadelphia with a fake wedding ring and a fairy-tale romance. Who wouldn't help a war widow in those days? I always saw my mother as a straight shooter, a no-bullshit kind of woman. It's what I loved most about her, but really…she's just like everyone else. She lied to protect herself and avoid any uncomfortable questions from me or her friends. I'm sick of this whole thing. I'm sick of these letters. I'm sick of Evienne and mostly, I'm sick to death that my memories are forever clouded by these revelations."

"Clouded? She was your mother. She loved you and did what was best for you and at the same time tried to tell you of the love she knew in her own life. And I really think it was the only love she knew in her life. From what you said, her own mother sent her away; she could have done that to you, but she didn't! I believe your mother did what she thought best for you. It's just like what you said about me with Sarah. You gave me the best advice and guidance I have gotten in a long time! And where do you think you learned that from—a life of lies?" Stella had both elbows on her knees, leaning into her words as she argued fervently for Madalane, Evienne and ultimately herself.

The validity of Stella's words washed over Eve's fevered brain. She was still angry, but she understood what it must have been like to want your child to have a good, happy life. Everything Stella said was true. Madalane had been an excellent mother and the fairy tale of her father had allowed her to be normal, not shunned for illegitimacy. She let out a long breath, as if she had been holding her rage in her lungs.

"Okay—you're right. You are. I loved my mother and nothing will ever change that. The fact that she used her relationship with Evienne as a model for my father is..." Eve awkwardly searched for a word, "...sweet in a weird way."

Irritated at being contradicted and proven wrong, Eve reached for another letter in the quickly dwindling pile. "Alright...let's get on with our reading. I need to know what happened to Evienne and how my mom ended up in Boston!"

Stella moved into the vacant seat between them on the couch and wrapped her arms around Eve, forcing the embrace until Eve relaxed into the hug. Stella murmured against her shoulder, "It is sweet Eve, it is really sweet. Your mother loved you. She did everything she could and left a few puzzle pieces for you really to understand her." She pulled Eve closer to her and felt the faint melting of the older woman's fears and doubts.

After a few minutes, Eve pulled back, tracks of dried tears evident on her translucent skin. She inhaled deeply, trying to gather her thoughts. A funny thought occurred to her as she glanced at the coffee table where the letters sat waiting for them to finish. "So...I know what you really want."

Stella's forehead knitted in confusion.

"Want to see my dad's letter to me?"

Stella laughed, realizing that she was an open book to this woman. She nodded vigorously and smiled widely. "Absolutely!"

October 25, 1943

My dearest Madalane and my beloved Eve,
My Madalane, so beautiful is the love growing beside you, sleep in peace and may my love protect you in my absence. My arms and legs are fighting in your honor.
My baby, I sat at your mother's side as she dreamed and

I rested my hand on her stomach and ached in a strange unfamiliar way. Your unborn body filled me with love; your life fragile and precious to us both. My heart wept when you were born and I wept again when my departure was imminent. I swoon at the passage of time and how it has given me the greatest love and now as time is lost; it steals me from you both.

As our child, you should never know the perils of war. It is my honor to stand for our country, it is my struggle that war takes me from your first step, war takes me from the love I have for you and your mother. War takes me from hearing your first word, and from the honor of watching you learning to run. I have faith in knowing our blood is filling the tiny veins of your heart, building strength, creating a purpose. It is in this honor that I know to be your father. Your father— I have been humbled by the duty of the word. My purpose is to teach you of family, of hard work. I am torn by my new family and my duty, by the stripping of choice. To be the man I need to be, I must live the words I profess.

In my absence, I will think of your hand, the hand we created, being held by your mother's. Believe me, under the oath of God, our rules need to be adjusted in time of crisis; I, as a soldier, have been called and I must go. Under the grace of God, I will return for you and your mother. I will fight with the honor of both your hearts. I will fight for the pride of peace and return to our family and your perfect face.

My dear child, follow your heart for it is your own. May God love and protect us all.

Your loving father,

Private First Class Steven Vale

Chapter 52

Paris, May 1929

Madalane watched the heavy rump of the old woman moving slowly up the stairs in front of her. She was breathing hard and Madalane was momentarily nervous that she would collapse before they would arrive at their destination. The last couple of weeks had been a blur. Evienne had picked up the information about the apartment from Adrienne, and between her school schedule and their potential landlady's recent illness, they had been unable to see the apartment until today. Walking with Evienne, they had both felt the excitement of starting a life in their own apartment. Although Evienne never complained about ducking in and out of windows, Madalane knew that it wore on her at times. Evienne needed space to call her own. This apartment that would be both of theirs was on the sixth floor of a beautiful beaux-arts building across from the Luxembourg Gardens.

The landlady's laborious progress up the stairs reminded Madalane of the walk home carrying the painting that Evienne had given her the day they became friends. The steps seemed to Madalane to be a reminder of how far she and Evienne had come, how far they had advanced into each other's lives. She wanted to weep at the memory of seeing her friend at the train station when she returned from Christmas break. Each step brought another memory from her heart into her mind. How they sat together at the church admiring the stained glass, blending the colors of their lives into the city. Last night she lay, as she had for two weeks now, in Evienne's arms and kissed her friend with a passion she never knew existed. Each night was filled with kisses, hand holding and small caresses. She felt loved for the first time in her life.

Each raspy breath their future landlady took convinced Madalane that this apartment would be perfect. She would never bother them because the steps would make it impossible for her to patrol the building like the Madame at the rooming house did. She fervently prayed that the apartment would be habitable. She had heard nightmarish stories from the girls at school about rotting floorboards and rain soaked ceilings.

Without realizing it, the landlady had stopped, and Madalane almost ran into her, losing her balance. As usual, Evienne was there to catch her. The older woman rummaged through a large key chain before identifying the correct key. As she slipped the key into the lock, Madalane turned her head to smile at Evienne who winked back at her.

The shared eye contact almost made Madalane laugh out loud. The love the two were sharing made everything seem perfect. The door flung open from the command of the landlady's weight, exposing the attic's wooden peak, sloping down to a window on either side. The attic apartment was massive compared to their little dormer and the knotty hardwood floors gave the room a clean, linear expanse of geometric space. Besides the stairs, it was clear that the apartment would not bring in the usual rents charged in this area because of the lack of headspace due to the slanting ceilings. "You know girls," the landlady gasped, "this is a mighty fine apartment—if you can manage the stairs." Standing in the center of the attic where the ceiling soared several feet above her head, Evienne gazed around the attic—it was twice the floor space than Madalane's dorm and she wondered if Adrienne had anything to do with the affordability.

The apartment had two windows on the end of each room: one facing the Seine in the distance and the other looked over the shimmering rooftops of Paris. Madalane immediately imagined how the feel of the breeze coming through the opposing windows would keep their apartment quite enjoyable in the spring and summer. "The bathing annex is on the 5th floor. There is a small toilette to the left." The landlady remarked as she vaguely pointed to an area beyond the open door. She made no move to join them, so Evienne and Madalane figured they had to offer themselves the tour of the apartment.

Evienne gave the eye to Madalane and reached for her elbow to lead her to the window on the left side room. On that end of the attic was a small closed off room with a toilette and on the other side, a kitchen counter with a small heating ring and a sink. The windows filled the room with light. Madalane stood on her toes to look for the view of the Seine. It would be perfect. She felt it in her bones. The two looked at each other and thought the dream they were experiencing was too good to be true.

"Girls, girls. What do you think? I have to get back to my work downstairs. If you want to discuss the place, I will meet you at my office. Come when you are finished and don't forget to check the bath on the fifth and lock the door. I will not do the steps twice on this day."

Evienne smiled, assuring the woman she would honor her requests as she shut the door behind her. The two stood quietly listening to the uneven thumps of her descending the stairs and Evienne took Madalane's face in her hand and asked her, between kisses, if she would live there with her. Melting into Evienne's seduction, Madalane knew she would do anything to live at 93 Boulevard Saint -Michel.

As the kiss ended, Madalane looked around the room again. Could this really be happening? Instead of a bare room, she saw the bed and desk in their place and most importantly, the space for Evienne's easel near the wide windows.

"Evienne, did you see the river? You can see the river from up here." When no response came, she turned to see her friend smiling at her. "Do you think I am silly for being so excited?"

Evienne had already memorized the layout of their rooftop apartment, noting the smell of hot tar from the rooftops, and the various places to paint. She was pleased to see Madalane so happy and answered her, "No Dove. I love that you are happy. I am happy. I am happy for us. This will be the best place I have ever lived in Paris. We should take it. What do you think?"

Feeling uncharacteristically bold, Madalane approached her friend with a wicked smile. "I don't know Evienne. Do you think you will be safe living here with me? Will you be able to protect yourself from my wanton ways? How will you manage when I need to feel your lips on mine? How will you Evienne? How will you manage?"

Evienne's face shifted from smiling to serious as she stepped towards Madalane. She rubbed the back of her own neck as she if the question flexed her mind to new possibilities. Madalane backed away from her pursuer as Evienne stepped towards her, her eyes locked into her thoughts, "I don't know Ms. Durand; how do you feel about me having a key. Being able to walk in through the front door at any time, day or night?" As the slow charismatic words came from Evienne's mouth, she slowly pursued Madalane's lips, moving forward then backing away from her, taunting her.

Madalane was smiling, but her words were husky and deliberate as she stepped towards Evienne. "It is not me who needs to worry. You are such a shy delicate thing. A girl like you wouldn't know the hunger another could have for your lips." The last word was said with a delicious emphatic tone, Evienne almost faltered in her step.

Madalane continued, her breathing coming in hard gasps, as she followed Evienne to the wall next to the window. "Would you succumb to the needs of another? Would you push me away and run from the apartment." Her voice was low as she pushed her friend against the wall, pressing herself against her length. Their eyes were speaking volumes as Madalane extended her body up to reach her friend's mouth. Her lips brushed the soft skin below her lips and then brushed again the flesh next to her mouth. Each pass was another tantalizing moment to relish the scent of sandalwood and Evienne.

"Would a girl like you resist my kiss in this apartment? Or would a girl like you pull me to her and kiss me?" As if to turn away, Madalane stepped back and whispered, "What would a girl like you do in this apartment?"

In a tone filled with mock seriousness, Evienne replied, "I would write a thank-you note to Adrienne." Dropping her voice to a murmur, she continued, "I would thank her for putting me on top of the world in a castle with a woman like you, with a woman with lips like yours, with a woman's words that speak to my heart, with a woman's scent that makes me want to pin her against the wall and devour every inch of her loveliness. Then I would thank her again after we both have had our fill and we fall sound asleep." Evienne leaned into Madalane and pressed her lips against Madalane's mouth. Lost in the moment, the two barely heard the knock on the apartment door.

"Madame wants to know if you are taking the apartment and don't forget to lock the door on your way out." A boy's voice echoed through the door. "She said you should come downstairs now and settle the arrangements." The voice disappeared down the stairs leaving barely a trace of his arrival.

The two broke into laughter and embraced in a hug. Evienne's voice rumbled in Madalane's ear, "I rather like a pushy woman."

Chapter 53

Paris, June 1929

The sounds of squishing water filled the narrow hall as the two girls made their way up the staircase. Walking home, they had been caught in an early summer rainstorm and now they were soaked to the skin. Although relatively warm today, the rain had cooled the temperature dramatically. The last few blocks had been torture—pounding rain and a breeze whipping around the boulevard. They were shivering as they trudged up the seven flights of steps to their attic apartment on Boulevard Saint-Michel, small puddles of water left at their footsteps. Arriving at their door, Evienne's hand shook so badly that she was barely able to get the key in the lock.

Madalane and Evienne rushed into their apartment as soon as the door opened. Immediately, Evienne went to their small brazier, loaded some coals, and stoked the banked coals until the new coals started to smoke. Turning around, she saw Madalane standing, wrapped in the blanket from their bed. She smiled because her friend looked like the painting of Venus rising from the surf. Madalane's hair had fallen loose from its usual tight chignon, and it fell in careless ringlets around her shoulders, still dripping with rainwater, a few drops of water rolling down her face. The bottom of her dress was soaked and it clung to her legs like a second skin; a replica of a marble statue.

As she felt the heat permeate the room, she moved to hang her wet coat and approached her friend who opened the blanket as an invitation to join her. Evienne moved into the little cocoon and felt the welcoming warmth of Madalane and the blanket.

Madalane knew that they should get out of their wet clothes, but it felt so nice to have Evienne's arms wrapped around her. She never wanted to move again. She murmured in contentment against her friend's chest, losing herself in the softness of her skin.

There was something about the mix of the fresh rain and the smell of Madalane's hair that forced Evienne's mouth onto Madalane's neck. She licked and sucked the damp flesh trying to taste each muscle of her neck. Drinking the rain and salt from her skin, trying to quench her thirst, each raindrop tasted better than the finest wine.

Small moans of pleasure escaped Madalane's mouth as Evienne ran her lips and teeth up and down her neck. Evienne needed Madalane. She needed her mouth, she felt her lips calling for her. She wrapped her fingers into the loose curls that hung around her neck and guided Madalane's lips to her mouth.

At the touch of her lips, Madalane was lost in Evienne as she consumed her mouth. Her universe began and ended with her mouth, forgetting everything in between. Her body swayed as Evienne deeply kissed her and lightly bit her lips, pulling her body into hers. Evienne thought how receptive Madalane was under her touch. How she received her passion and never stopped her desires, no matter how intense the moment would become. Their bodies naturally blended into each other, dancing together to music only they could hear.

Evienne's mouth covered Madalane's more passionately, sucking the breath from her lungs, demanding the moans of Madalane's pleasure, pushing her tongue lasciviously into her mouth. Pulling Madalane closer to her, Evienne's hand pushed deep into her curves of her body, slowly feeling the vertebrae and ribs passing under each finger. She was burning with need as her palms cupped Madalane's hips. Feeling almost insane with desire, she hiked the smaller body onto hers, practically lifting Madalane off the floor and kissed her mouth deeper. Evienne wanted to bring her pleasure and hear her moan as she had so many evenings when they would lay in bed and kiss for hours. She wanted more, she always wanted more, but this time the fever that raged in her was taking control of her senses.

Sternly Evienne told herself to slow down, as Madalane's arms remained tightly wrapped around her neck with the blanket locking them together. The passion of Madalane's kiss was creating a whirl of emotions in Evienne's mind. She could tell that Madalane was ready for her; she was ready to take her to bed. There was no room left for questions. Her only thought was to remove Madalane's clothes so she could feel her skin, remove all barriers so she could taste every part of her. She broke her mouth away from Madalane's.

"Dove, we need to get our wet clothes off—let me help you." Madalane released the blanket and it fell to the floor, her arms reaching to the sky. Evienne barely heard herself mutter the words and did not even wait for a response as she began pulling the wet dress up over her friend's body. Her skin was warm and soft under Evienne's confident hands, the smoothness overwhelming Evienne. She could only look at Madalane's face as her wet clothes lay at their feet in a puddle. Evienne turned Madalane around to unhook her bra, Madalane coyly looked over her shoulder and smiled; Evienne's chest burned with expectation. Before she turned back, Madalane unconsciously cupped her breasts in modesty and then turned to face Evienne. Evienne began undressing herself, unhooking her belt and unwrapping it from around her waist, letting it drop to the floor followed by her trousers.

Madalane stood there in front of her in just her white underwear. Evienne's eyes moved from her face and drank in the totality of her loveliness. She put her palms on the young woman's perfect shoulders. Evienne moved close to her lips, to feel the quickness of Madalane's breath on her, to see the pink flush rushing to the surface of her translucent skin. Evienne's lips needed another taste as she wrapped her arms around her back and kissed her lightly as she guided her reverently to the small bed. Madalane's hands never left her breasts. Evienne sat her on the bed and laid her down, lifting her legs and running her hands up and down her solid muscles.

Every pass over her skin ignited sparks and Madalane felt the tight heat build under her skin. She had felt this heat before with Evienne, but each time Evienne would pull away and dash to the window to have a cigarette and gaze at the stars, giving them both time and distance to cool their heated flesh. Tonight the heat was almost unbearable, she wanted to know where this tight flame would lead and she knew that she needed to convince Evienne that she was ready. Filled with anxiety, but determined to move forward, Madalane released her breasts and exposed herself to Evienne. Arms outstretched, she reached for her; it was a choice she had no control over.

Evienne stared at her friend in wonderment and impulsively pulled her own under shirt off. Finding a second of clarity, she memorized the moment—the beautiful girl lying in front of her, her body so white and delicate, the fullness of her alabaster breasts contrasted with the pink of her nipples. "Madalane, you are gorgeous."

A powerful, magnetic current pulled the two women's bodies together. Evienne crawled over the top of her, never losing eye contact with her; a connection of heat boiling between them. She must go slow, slow, slow. The word took on its on presence as Evienne could barely breathe as the flesh of her breasts touched Madalane's. Madalane was sweeping her hand up and down Evienne's bare back pulling her body to her with every pass.

Evienne was intoxicated with want and lowered the weight of her body onto Madalane. The pressure took the breath from her lungs. Evienne's eyes closed as she drank the sound of Madalane's perfect moan as the younger woman received the excruciating want of Evienne's desire. Evienne's strength held her to the mattress as Madalane's hips rolled with their own mind, needing the connection to the woman she loved.

Evienne kissed her slow and deep as if it was the only thing that would keep them both alive, pushing her own hips into her. Liquid heat coalesced over the two bodies, blending them into one. Madalane became Evienne's universe. Nothing else existed but their desire for one another, the ragged sound of their breath, and the softness of flesh.

Evienne's mind exploded in tremors, she felt her heart in her ears, she needed to take all of her, to bathe her in pleasure, to feel the pleasure in her own body from the sheer gift of just touching her, feeling Madalane's pleasure to find her own. The mantra of slow, slow, slow whispered in her ear and she found a reservoir of control and pulled herself away.

Madalane felt shock from the absence of Evienne's lips and rhythm of their bodies. The abrupt stop pulled her from her wave of bliss. Her mind mutinied as she realized that Evienne had stopped; they couldn't possibly stop this time. Madalane's mind demanded they fulfill their destiny, they had passed the point of no return; whispering in the growing darkness of the room, she pleaded, "Evienne please...don't stop yourself. Don't stop me. I love you. I want you to make love to me, show me how." Desperation underscored her words as she continued, not caring how she sounded, 'Promise me you won't stop. Please don't stop." Gasping for breath, trying to quell the tears that threatened to fall, she made one last plea, "Please, make me your lover Evienne."

The words cascaded around Evienne and she was simply unable to resist as Madalane pulled her lover to her mouth with a searing fire, a commitment to the pledge that neither woman would ever regret.

Chapter 54

Paris, June 1929

Hours later, Madalane was nestled tightly in the crook of Evienne's arm, resting against the solid firmness of her friend's body,
her own body creating a quilt over her new lover. The drops of
rain hitting the windowpane seemed to echo her heartbeat under
her head and the darkness permeated the room was like a blanket of solitude. She knew the burden of intimate expectation
had been lifted from both of their shoulders and replaced with
the most indescribable joy she had ever felt. Evienne's touch had
been gentle and sweet, yet memories of their frenzied lovemaking burned within her like a lava flow. She wanted more, but the
pleasure of lying in Evienne's arms was too delicious to move just
yet. Every time she closed her eyes, she saw Evienne's body over
hers, a slow curling smile that signaled her need to kiss, nip at
her flesh, and touch her intimately—each moment a reminder
of exquisite delight. Without realizing it, she sighed contentedly
and felt Evienne stir under her.

"Have I told you how much I love it when you purr?"

Only half-aware of what the noise she had made, Madalane's
head lifted and she gave her lover a questioning look.

Resettling her head on her chest, Evienne softly whispered the words into Madalane's ear. "The sound of pleasure my Dove, the sound of contentment, the sound of happiness. You speak a thousand words to me, you plant a thousand seeds of happiness in me every time I hear it slip from your mouth."

Madalane smiled but said nothing.

"You are quiet on this perfect evening in our castle in the sky." Evienne pushed her breasts into her lover's as she reached for her pack of Gauloise on the side table.

Smiling at the feel of Evienne's body, she shifted to face her lover, and she watched the flame from the match illuminate Evienne's face as she inhaled the first drag of nicotine. Slowly exhaling, Evienne glanced down at Madalane and offered the cigarette to her.

Madalane took a drag, replying, "Tonight's been perfect; I can't imagine a more perfect night. I don't even know what to say. There are no words." Reaching over to the night table for the bottle of wine, she took a small swig. Passing it to Evienne, she watched with amusement as her friend tried to juggle both the bottle and the cigarette with the one hand because she refused to move the other, which was still firmly wrapped around Madalane's body.

Settling back to her preferred spot, listening to Evienne's heartbeat, she tried to sound casual as she asked, "Ev, I don't want to sound naive, but is it always this good? How do people ever leave their houses if it feels this good all the time?"

"It is this good when love lives in the hearts of the ones making love. It is good because you feel love in its purest form." Evienne took a sip of wine and followed it with a drag of her cigarette. It was the perfect burn she craved. After exhaling, she kissed the woman staring at her lips. Murmuring the rest of her answer between kisses, the words were almost lost in the intensity of the moment. "We are paint and canvas. We were made for each other. Paint and canvas, Madalane, we are paint and canvas."

Tasting the tang of wine stoked the flames between them

again, and Madalane slipped her tongue into Evienne's mouth, seeking out the small remaining drops of wine that hid in the deepest recesses her mouth. She was proud of herself for being so blatant in her desire; she knew in her heart that Evienne did not want a shy lover, so she threw away the conventions the nuns had taught her. Passive submission would not be welcome in Evienne's bed and it invigorated her knowing that Evienne had been delighted when Madalane had rolled her over and had made love to her earlier in the evening. Always a quick study, she had paid attention to Evienne's lovemaking and she had done her best to give her as much pleasure as she had received. Memories flooded her mind as Evienne took control of their kiss.

The heat of the alcohol and the warmth of Evienne's mouth brought out Madalane's passion. Madalane pulled the bottle out of Evienne's hand and took another sip that she shared with her lover. Before their kisses made her lose her mind, she had a request and she was determined to ask for it. Lips sought hers as she turned her head and Evienne's confused gaze met her eyes. "I have something I want, Evienne."

Breathlessly, her lover replied, "Anything my Dove. My kingdom for your kiss."

Madalane blushed with pleasure at the chivalry her lover displayed, "Not quite a kingdom, my love. I want a letter. I want your words about tonight on paper. Will you do that for me?"

Without thought or hesitation, Evienne nodded. She was so pleased that Madalane valued her letters and that she wanted another that she would read to remember this night. Madalane could have asked for anything and Evienne would have agreed. "Anything my Dove, anything for you. It will be done."

They kissed, sealing the pact, sharing the rest of the wine back and forth between their mouths, trying not to swallow so quickly; small drops fell to their flesh until they were streaked in red wine. When the bottle was empty, Madalane set it down on the table and looked down at their bodies laughing, "We need a bath or someone will think we have the pox!"

Evienne slipped her body on top of Madalane's body and kissed her wine-soaked mouth. "We should be quarantined for days—maybe weeks, so we don't infect the city, yes?" Madalane giggled her affirmation as their kisses turned from sweet to passionate.

* * *

Later, deep into the night, the two young women quietly made their way to the bathing chamber. Evienne turned the water on and as they waited for the claw-foot tub to fill; she kissed Madalane's neck and shoulders, slowly drawing the robe she wore down her body. The small room filled with steaming heat and soon the tub was ready. Evienne got in first and she lay against the curved backrest. Standing above her, feeling bold and empowered, Madalane's eyes followed the line of Evienne's throat to her chest. She was so thin and pale, but effortlessly lovely. Her eyes traveled around Evienne's shoulders and chest, reveling in the privilege of examining her exquisite beauty with unguarded appreciation. The scar of a cigarette burn was the only imperfection in the sheer ivory expanse of the artist's skin.

Madalane remembered being shocked by it when she saw it after they had moved in together. Evienne had laughed it off claiming it was a moment of youthful exuberance and experimentation. There was something about its raw ragged intensity that made her wonder if there was something more. But tonight she only gave it a moment's notice as Evienne's arms reclined on the edge of the tub. Although at rest, Madalane could see the outline of how the muscles would tighten when she painted or made love. A lustful sensation in the base of her belly echoed her thoughts. She was so perfectly still—Madalane felt the desire to touch her skin to see if the alabaster sheen was real.

Glancing back up, Madalane saw patient amusement in her friend's eyes; she didn't care if she appeared foolish; she never gave herself such permission before to gaze upon Evienne's body, now her lover's body. Her eyes traveled back down to her chest, lower this time. The swell of her breasts pulled her eyes until she was blatantly staring. Evienne's soft round skin was puckered from the cool air above the water and her nipples were dark and erect. The feeling in Madalane's belly tightened even more and she looked away.

Evienne's husky voice broke the silence in the room, "Don't look away. I am yours. Look at me as much as you want. Touch me as much as you want. I want you to know my body better than you know your own."

The heat from the water made the air close and hot. Evienne's words seared a permanent need in Madalane as she stared with unconcealed lust. Evienne's eyes were slitted open and she was watched Madalane stare at her. They were locked in a passionate stillness.

Evienne's voice sounded thick as she spoke, "Come here, and let me wash your hair." Partly relieved and partly disappointed that the moment had ended, Madalane slid into the tub, cradled between Evienne's long legs, breasts pressed into her back and the strong arms she had been thinking about, cushioned them against the cool porcelain of the tub. Strong fingers caressed her head and it felt insanely wonderful. Madalane knew from that day forward, she would never want to wash her own hair ever again. When Evienne ran soapy hands along her shoulders and neck, Madalane unconsciously leaned forward to give her better access. Her hands were soft and strong, always knowing where the ache in a student's neck lay hidden. Evienne's hands moved up and rinsed her hair, slowly cupping water to wash the soap away.

Madalane felt an intense softness on her back, between her shoulder blades. It almost felt like a kiss, but it happened so fast.

Then it happened again, slightly higher. Evienne pulled her back against her breasts. Madalane felt rock-hard nipples against her back and she tried to steady her breathing. Grasping the bar of soap in her hands, Evienne started to lather her lover's arms; she worked slowly and thoroughly, working her way up to her chest. Madalane kept her head back against Evienne's shoulder with her eyes closed as slightly calloused fingers softly slid over her soapy skin. Over and over, the soap passed along Madalane's chest as she watched through half-closed eyes as her lover's hands came closer and closer to her breasts. The heat building inside her forced her adjust her position slightly and her nipples floated out of the water completely exposed, furiously tightening as the cool air and the tension in the room united.

Madalane's mind was screaming that Evienne should touch her again. Was there a limit to how much she should want? They had already made love for hours, yet she was burning with need again. She arched her back, encouraging Evienne's attentions, but Evienne was motionless. Ready to cry with frustration, Madalane suddenly felt the soap glide over her skin again. The soap skimmed the roundness of her breast over and over. Each time she came close to her nipple, Evienne would switch to the other hand. After an eternity of torment, the soap dropped from Evienne's hand and then it was only her flesh on Madalane's flesh. The warmth of her palm moved around, above, and below her breasts, avoiding the pink buds begging for attention.

Staring at Evienne's hands in rapt fascination as they skimmed the surface of her desire, Madalane watched fingers slide down her rib cage and as they came back up, her palm seemed to stop briefly on her nipple. Madalane felt her lungs contract and she must have gasped because Evienne stopped again. Minutes passed and after an agonizing wait, her hand began to move against her friend again. Each time her palm grazed her nipple, it seemed to swell. The light sensation of her fingertips gave way to harder pressure as Evienne's fingers pinched her nipples. The merest feeling of pressure, but it was sheer pleasure coursing through Madalane. Evienne became bolder. Her fingers circled Madalane's nipples and then pinched and tugged, a surge of pleasurable pain coursed through her. Madalane's body was thrumming like a humming-bird and her entire being seemed attached to Evienne's hands.

Unable to take another minute, she fell forward, desperately trying to catch her breath. Wild-eyed with unknown desire, she turned to face her lover, uttering a strangled cry, "I need…I want….I…" Unable to finish her thought, Evienne took mercy on her young lover, captured her flailing mouth with hers, and pulled her down into an embrace.

21 June 1929

My Dearest Madalane,

You became my lover tonight. The rain squalls, hiding in the shadows of our rooftop apartment, and the wind whispers of love. The rain vivifies the love I want to plant at your feet and tender sprouts mimic my trembling as desire grows through my spirit. I feel the pulse of your heart on every inch of your skin as my fingers gently sweep over your bare body. The flowers and sea mix around us and I watch you bloom into a fully realized woman under my touch. I feel the truth and the strength of your heart. You flower for me, as we lie naked, allowing our passions to envelope us. I come home to my own heart as you allow me to come into the depth of your soul. I want to live inside you—push myself deeper inside of you, so deep I could be lost inside of you for eternity.

As I slowly laid your body onto the bed and gazed at your loveliness, I was struck by the intensity of the truth I felt in my heart; you are the perfect fit to my pulse, we are a perfect fit together. You are my blanket on a cold night, the North Star guiding a lost traveler at sea, nourishment to a starving body. I wish to mirror your divinity in perfection. I wish to know every inch of you by heart. I will memorize the buds of your lips, the journey of your body, and the portrait of your face, the blood that fills your veins and the art I find in your soul. I want to take paint and blend every essence of you, to paint the flowering of your heart, blossoming in the garden of me.

You gave me the gift of sharing your body with me as the full white moon shares her light with the silvery surf, dancing with the arrival of every wave. Your body is all that the universe can give—images of God, the softness of new life, rose petals lightly falling from the stem, warm bread, cool red wine burning down an eager throat, and mermaids basking in the moon light. You give yourself to me, yet your arms carry the strength of a thunderstorm. I dream of your nakedness held to me through the night, your breath mingled with mine, and you are dependable as the morning light. Your scent is the only air I want to breathe. When you pursed your lips and whispered to me, 'make me your lover,' I felt I had lived a thousand lives and took a thousand breaths to hear these words from your lips.

'Make me your lover.' I waited for each molecule of your body to spin with mine—to live in this perfect moment. I knew, without question, this was our perfection. I would love you in way that would bring you pleasure. And you asked— you asked me—I needed you to ask me, to honor the communion of our love, the intimacy of our touch. As I slid my hand across the flat of your stomach, into the valley of your hip to the darkness of your purest pleasure, I melted into every inch of your world. You became the only thing that existed. I was made for you and every moment in between.

Making love with you completed that one thing in me that had always been missing. Your moans of pleasure and joy feed my only need, filling me with fierce love. You are my lover, you will always be my lover, and I will only know one lover. That is you. We have shared the same breath and know each other as we know ourselves. I need you to fill me. I need you even in the bright of day, in the quiet of night, in every moment.

I want you Madalane; I want you to be my lover forever.

Forever,

Evienne

Chapter 55

Paris, August 1937

The sun was shining in through the large window in the bedroom. It was a warm day in Paris—the kind meant for walking along the river to feel the breeze or sitting at a café watching the people walk by. Instead, Madalane Durand sat on the bed she has shared with her lover for eight years. Evienne had to run errands this morning and Madalane had found herself alone with nothing to do. A rare occasion to be sure and Madalane was delighting in the joy of doing nothing of consequence.

As a schoolteacher, she was always carrying papers to grade and lessons to plan. However, since it was summer and even her summer students were off in August, she was enjoying a temporary respite from the demands of her students. Initially, she had decided to stay in bed and enjoy a lazy morning, but her mind was too busy and excited. This afternoon, when Evienne returned home, they would go to the World's Expo. Paris was buzzing with tourists and visitors. Although the conservatives found the openness of the fair to be highly suspicious, the average person was excited to see the international exposition.

After a fruitless attempt to do nothing, Madalane sat up and contemplated her morning. She had several books sitting next to the bed, but none that held her attention. The apartment was tidy, and she didn't feel like tackling the clutter that seemed to congregate in the dining room. She lay back on the bed and enjoyed the sun on her skin. Staring at the ceiling, she smiled to herself. How many nights had her lover taken her with a passion that had left her breathless? Opening her eyes, she would find herself surprised to still be in the bed—the bedroom ceiling always grounding her, reminding her that she was in fact in their bedroom and not spinning around the city.

Grinning with the memories of sensual pleasures, she reached under the bed to a small box. Barely the size of a small hatbox, it contained the treasures of her life with Evienne. Gently lifting the lid off the box, she saw the letters first. They were always first. Over the past few years, the letters had come less often, but when they did, she secreted them away in her box of memories. Each letter brought a smile and sometimes tears. The memories of the first few years together gave her such happiness.

After they had moved to the attic garret of St. Michel Boulevard, they barely left the apartment the first year. Evienne's passion was unquenchable and she had discovered a hidden cache inside herself. Blushing slightly at the memories of Evienne covering her in watercolor paints, she felt the soft tip of the paintbrush on her nipples still. Each day with Evienne brought new sensations and new pleasures.

Despite being distracted by her lover, she had managed to finish University and after securing a teaching job, they were in a position to afford a larger apartment. They knew that an apartment had become available on the fourth floor and their landlady had been quite agreeable with the rent increase.

If truth were told, they could have afforded an even better apartment because Evienne's paintings had been selling well. A gallery owner had contacted her a few years prior after seeing her work exhibited at the annual amateur's exhibition; he had offered himself as an agent, which she had begrudgingly accepted. Madalane had rightly pointed out that even Picasso had sales agents who handled his business affairs. Evienne's reputation had grown in stature and she was being recognized for the depth and mastery of her portraits. She wasn't rich, but her paintings were selling well and after the gallery owner took his cut, she was taking in a tidy sum.

Madalane flipped through various pictures of their life together—each year represented by her own attempts to stay current with the latest hairstyle. Evienne's hair was the same as the day they met—long, luxurious locks kept tightly braided in a single rope down her lean back or along her arm. The only difference now was the thin white strands that could only been seen when Madalane sifted the soft silky hair through her fingers.

Tracing the lines of an old photograph from their first year together, Madalane felt a wellspring of love overflow for her partner. She wondered if they would stand together as they stood in this shot when they were old and very gray. Evienne, so much taller than she, posed next to her; a smile barely visible on her face whereas she, was beaming with impossible glee. They had been on a picnic that day when their friend Berenice had snapped the shot after posing them in front of the Seine. Would Evienne still put a protective arm around her and stare uncomfortably at a camera? Would she still feel the joy of being in the company of this remarkable woman? In her heart, she knew the answer—yes she would always thank God that she been given this wonderful gift. They would grow old together and in her last breath, Evienne would be the name on her lips.

Madalane's thoughts were interrupted when she heard the key in the door. Even after all of these years, the thought of Evienne coming home to her gave her a thrill. Quickly, she put her treasures back in the box and slid it under the bed in its usual resting place. Evienne walked in the door as she walked out to the front room.

"You are back sooner than I thought. Is everything okay with Adrienne?"

"Let's sit for a minute Madalane." Evienne lowered herself into a straight-backed chair as her partner looked at her quizzically.

"I was just with Adrienne and it seems Sylvia is moving out."

Madalane gasped in shock and on unsteady knees, held herself up by sheer willpower.

Evienne continued speaking, her voice devoid of emotion, "She stated it as if it were a change in the bookstore hours. It was matter of fact. She asked me to tend to the book store for a couple of weekends while she visits her parent's country home." Evienne took a cigarette out of it pack and examined the translucent paper. She could see the outlines of chopped tobacco, focusing on the cigarette instead of the breakup of Adrienne and Sylvia.

Staggered by the implications of their friends separating, Madalane's body began to tremble. "They are breaking up? Just like that? After all these years?" She felt sourness in her mouth and she felt an overwhelming sadness permeate her body.

"Sit with me my Dove; sit down and hold my hand. It will be okay once the shock wears off. I don't even remember the walk home, but as soon as I saw you, I knew that it would be okay." The two women were quiet for a minute and Evienne felt the need to fill the silence, "We should still go to the Exposition. You know Picasso, my old acquaintance, will be exhibiting at the Spanish pavilion" Trying to match the levity she was faking, Evienne reached for Madalane's hand and winked. The breakup of their long-time friends and mentors ripped a piece of her heart. It opened a box of abandonment she would rather not visit.

"Yes, of course Evienne. We are still going. I am just shocked, completely shocked." As the words left her mouth, she felt a crushing anxiety strike her body. She collapsed onto the settee across from Evienne's chair and grasped her partner's hand. Tears fell from her eyes unbidden. "Are they still friends? How did Adrienne seem? Who wanted this? Sylvia? How could she do this to Adrienne?"

Understanding the implication of her partner's words, Evienne whispered, "Dove, they are not us. We are different...you know that; I don't know who wanted the separation. They are private women and times are changing for everyone. I tried not to ask too many questions. I just told Adrienne that I would do whatever it was she needed me to do."

Madalane continued to cry softly and Evienne felt an ache in her soul. She continued speaking, "Think about it—you know how much you love being in the bookstores—we will see them both, just not together for a while. It will be okay, I promise. They are not us; nothing will separate our hearts."

As if to seal the promise, Evienne caught Madalane's tears on her fingertip and brought it to her lips. "You will forever be a part of me."

Pulling Evienne off the chair and onto the settee, Madalane settled her body next to her. "You always know what I am feeling. I don't know what I would do without you. I can't even think about it, it scares me so much." Evienne continued to hold Madalane as she wept. Being held so tightly, being loved so thoroughly gave Madalane peace in her heart and she felt her tears subside. She lifted her head and kissed Evienne's lips lightly, then more passionately, allowing her love to wash over them both.

Finally feeling normal, Madalane abruptly stopped kissing Evienne and stood up, smiling at the power she still held over her long-time lover. Evienne's startled lust-filled eyes opened wide as Madalane started to fix her hair in the mirror next to the door. Seeing Evienne's reflection in the mirror, Madalane could see the feral animal that lived inside of her friend, trying to take over. How could she feel so aroused now when just moments before, she felt the world shifting on its axis? She turned to face Evienne who was breathing heavily as she warred with herself over what path she should take.

"Come on lazy bones! Let's go, we can finish this later. You can have your way with me after we have seen the exhibit." Leaning down, she whispered a sensual promise, and slipped away before Evienne could pull her back to the sofa. Madalane rushed to the door, holding it open as the taller woman shook her head and made a great show of begrudgingly getting off the couch.

Madalane and Evienne left their apartment near the Jardin du Luxembourg and went northwest for their walk to the International Exposition dedicated to the Art and Technology in the Modern World. The rest of the world liked to refer to it as the World's Fair but the French in their indefatigable quest to be unique called it the Exposition or Expo. Evienne had heard that the best entrance was at the Trocodero, so they decided to skirt around the edge of the Expo and come in from above the Seine. She sold the idea to Madalane by reminding her that the walk home would be much quicker after a long day on their feet.

Thousands of tourists and visitors streamed into Paris anxious to see the marvels of their modern age. A worldwide economic depression had finally begun to subside and countries shook off their torpor to highlight their entry back into the world's stage. Mammoth architectural displays from Germany and the developing world power, the Soviet Union, flanked the Eiffel Tower, the landmark image of Paris. For the more politically astute, they might have felt the chill of military might staring each other down as the city of light and culture stood naked in between like a beautiful woman captured between two belligerent men.

Designed by Hitler's architect, Albert Speer, the German edifice was a massive rectangular building, the height of the building rising 500 feet in the air, topped with an eagle and a swastika. Columns along the front imposed the idea of ancient glory and historical greatness. The Soviet pavilion celebrated the 20th anniversary of the October Revolution that saw the assassination of the Russian royal family and the rise of the communist party. On top of the pavilion were two massive figures holding a hammer and sickle, representing the common worker and a peasant woman, posed striding confidently forward symbolizing the emergence of the Soviet Union's worldwide influence.

Despite Madalane's interest in seeing all of the pavilions, Evienne was focused on one and only one pavilion—the Spanish pavilion where Picasso's new painting was featured.

As the two women neared the 7th Arrondissement, they joined the unusually large throng of visitors streaming towards the expo pavilions. A cacophony of voices filled the air around them as they slowed to match the pace of the people around them. They had hoped that going in the middle of the day in the summer would minimize the crowds. Instead, it seemed like the entire continent of Europe had joined them on this particular day.

Madalane felt her hand being grasped and she recognized the familiar feel of calluses and strength. She looked up at Evienne who had a tight, tense look on her face. Evienne hated crowds, but she wanted to see Picasso's new painting. She had ignored the Exposition when it opened in May. Initially the Spaniards were still finalizing their pavilion when the Expo opened; once it was ready for the public in July, the world appeared at its entrance. Evienne had patiently waited until she could stand it no more. She had to see this magnificent painting that had Paris and the whole world buzzing.

The crowd had grown impossibly thick as they neared the ticket booth. Standing in line, Madalane stood on tippy toes to see over the multitudes surrounding her. Even at her maximum reach, she couldn't see much beyond a few feet. Frustrated, she dropped back to the ground. She noticed Evienne grinning at her; vaguely annoyed at her partner's height, she turned to look at the advertising poster near the entrance. To get her lover's mind off of the crowd surging around them as they passed through the ticket booth where they paid their six francs each, Madalane asked, "Why is this painting getting so much attention?"

"My Dove, the art that is housed behind those walls is painted by a man who understands the nature of what art is. He took a tragedy, an act of human horror, a thunder of displacement of routine and transported it with God's grace onto a canvas. He understood that horror hides the fragility of life, the ending to one's breath. The fear of not knowing what was to come next if there was ever a next. He was compelled by a muse, driven to make us never forget—to give permanence. Taking art to the final destiny...timelessness and without boundaries. He is a master of his art and you and I are going to witness his brilliance in the stages of it drying; we still might smell the turpentine and raw paint, I know how much you love that."

Evienne winked at Madalane knowing the scent of paint made Madalane want her with a passionate fury.

Intently listening to Evienne's explanation, Madalane blushed at the memories of how her lover could so easily seduce her after a day of painting. The smell of oil paint combined with Evienne's natural scent made Madalane helpless to resist. Staring at her feet, she tried desperately to recapture the seriousness of Evienne's words, but all she could see was her lover wrapped in streaks of magenta and blue. She closed her eyes and focused on their conversation. She finally recaptured the thread and looked up at Evienne as they inched their way to the entrance of the Spanish pavilion. "Do you think art can make that much of a difference? In terms of the politics? Will this stop Franco from slaughtering people in Spain?"

Evienne looked to the familiar clouding sky, "Will it stop Franco from supporting something I don't understand or will it be an inspiration to those fighting Franco? No one knows Madalane. This painting should drive others to fill their hearts with an honesty of violence. It will state the truth of war and brutality." Evienne stared at the spiraling statue guarding and honoring the Spanish pavilion, the sculpture stated the belief of the Spaniards. "See this Madalane; it is written here: 'the Spanish people have a path, it leads to a star'." Evienne pointed towards the base of the sculpture, and then shifted upwards, moving her hand as to replicate the waves and curves of the pillar. "We have our dreams, we have our inspirations, we follow what we believe is our destiny. You and I are going to be changed, changed by Picasso's interpretation, and challenged by the vision of our thought."

Madalane stopped and gazed at the statue by Alberto Sanchez Perez. She had never heard of the artist, but she tended to focus on paintings since her passion was one painter in particular. The soaring lines capped by the flame reminded her of the flame on the Statue of Liberty—a gift from France to the United States and an emblem of freedom now. Wondering if Perez had been inspired by France's love of liberty, she realized that Evienne had already moved to the entrance of the pavilion. She had her hands in her pocket and she was reading a statement inscribed at the doorway. Madalane glanced once more at the sculpture and hurried to join her partner.

Evienne's heart pounded knowing how hard she has lived to be the woman she, knew she would never be walked over, never be taken to a place she was not willing to go. Picasso was her hero and she wanted to honor him by allowing his interpretation to live inside of her. It was a somber moment as the visitors adjusted to the reason for their visit to this pavilion.

Keeping her head down and allowing the crowd to move her forward, Evienne cleared her mind so as to not to distract herself from the first impression of Picasso's Guernica.

As they moved through the entrance of the main building, Madalane glanced at the quote above the door: "More than half a million Spaniards are standing ready with their bayonets in the trenches; they will not be walked over." —President Azana. The young woman felt a chill go down her body as she felt the vigorous defiance in those words. Quietly, she followed Evienne through the open space. She felt nervous anticipation; not so much for herself but for her partner who idolized Picasso. Her style was so different than his, but she lived and breathed paint

just like he did. Meandering about the area, she felt a hush fall
over the crowd as they neared the Mercury Fountain.

Evienne felt the sure presence of her lover behind her. She
knew she would not interrupt her as she stared at the floor. The
two shared an unspoken understanding for the things that made
life real with another person. Evienne stayed true to her word and
held her head down, following the feet of the observers until it
was her turn to view the painting. She thought of the burgeoning
war machines that Hitler used to practice on the small Basque
village. She knew it could have easily been her own small town,
easily been her people screaming in the streets cut down by the
crumbling buildings. Her own sisters stolen from their Monday morning market. She thought about the newspaper photos,
the devastation, and the somber reminder of war. She reached
behind her for the comforting warmth of Madalane's hand. She
was the closest to home she would ever come again. She raised
her eyes to see the black and white and gray of every horror she
had known and not known in her heart. She stopped breathing
and squeezed her lover's hand in disbelief.

Evienne gasped for words, "Madalane." She said her lover's
name, avoiding the impulse to run and hide, to shelter herself
from the pain and anguish filling the canvas in front of her.
She had seen death in the nucleus of her family. The screams
of her mother finding her brother dead, the suffocating truth of
her father's last breath. She was overwhelmed by the images of
screaming pain falling from the mouths of women and children.
The horse struggling in chaos as it is gored by a bull underneath;
an animal killing an animal. Briefly, she wondered if this is what
Picasso intended? To teach man that we are no better than a
brutal animal killing its own kind? How could life be taken so
carelessly? How could breath be stolen by anonymous warplanes
so efficiently? She saw the newspaper photos flash in her mind,
the conversations in cafes with other painters at how Picasso was
inspired by the black and white truth.

Agony. Agony was the one word she wanted to force into the mind of the others standing around her. Did they see what she was seeing? Did they see the pain? She felt the loss, the hate, the fear, and the recognition that was intended by the painting in front of her. The fight would determine one's destiny, not the war. A tear rolled down Evienne's cheek; she did not need to see anymore. She did not need to feel anymore. She wanted to fight. Her body stiffened and turned; Madalane's hand slipped from hers.

A splash of sun striated Evienne's skin as she walked away from the Spanish Pavilion. She needed the Seine to relieve her heart of its ache, to inspire her art, to revive her soul. She needed to keep moving, to shake the unshakable. She looked to the sinking sun for answers and saw a clouding gray.

Following her partner, Madalane knew all too well that the set of Evienne's shoulders; her stiff walk and her isolated stance were signs that Evienne had been changed by Guernica. If Evienne had been disappointed, her scorn would have been on full display as soon as they walked away, but instead, her slow tremulous gait signified a powerful reaction. She knew their afternoon had come to an abrupt end. They would return another day and enjoy the exhibits set up around the expo, but today the sorrow that had infiltrated Evienne would require comfort and kindness. They made their way past the Soviet and German pavilions, facing each other with defiant brutality.

Madalane's initial desire to tour these pavilions was now replaced by disgust...disgust for war and death and the politicians who used humans like chess pieces in their quest for domination.

She caught up to Evienne and slipped her hand inside her lover's. Instead of the warmth she usually felt, a cold clammy sensation rocked her foundation. Evienne's reaction was more visceral than she had realized. An overwhelming desire to take care of her partner hit her hard in the solar plexus. She would take her home, bring her soup and wine and make love to her as if the world was ending tomorrow.

The sun dipped lower on the horizon as the two women made their way silently back to their apartment. A chilling wind seemed to blow through the city although only a few seemed to notice.

Chapter 56

21 August 1937

My Dearest Madalane—

As you and I stood between the Soviet and German pavilions, the grandiose hands of communist and Nazi power dictating the world's extremism, proudly there stood our Eiffel Tower between them. I fear the potential of power displayed here at the World's Expo. Does not anyone notice? Does not anyone see the potential for dictatorship and loss? Picasso did because I felt his cry within his paint.

My pain and my confusion rush to my hands and I pray it will flood my canvas as Picasso's did. Picasso's art, Picassos' strength and directness, and his ability to paint dark brutality will live in the minds and souls of the world long after the fascist names of Franco, Mussolini, and Hitler and his damn Gestapo thugs have faded. They will be vilified as Picasso will be memorialized. Every day that I paint after today, I promise to make a statement of my truth; my paint will reflect the emotions and validity of our lives. I feel I understand my true artistic purpose now and how one can grow from the art a person experiences. As with Guernica, art and even words can unfold life, and through the expres-

sion of art—their meaning reveals their purpose.

Your words of poetry confirmed the tragic pain I felt while witnessing Guernica. My sense of loss was a contradiction to the warmth of your hand as it slipped into mine and comforted me as we walked home, and now it is your poetry that consumes me here in the night. Your poetry impacts my senses the same way Picasso's paint captures a nation's pain. Your words and my pain allow me to feel complete. I found my home in your hand today. I love you…
Forever,
E—

As Stella finished reading the letter, Eve's mind wandered to the dates. Was it possible that her mother and Evienne had been together for so long? Most of the letters had been written in the first couple of years of their relationship. This letter was nine years after the relationship had started. Eve felt flummoxed by the realization that their relationship had gone on for so long—why didn't her mother ever mention someone that she had spent a decade with?

Stella murmured, "Seems she is quite mad at the Germans and moved by the Spanish. Do you know what she is talking about here when…wait, let me read it." Stella held the letter and slowly re-read the section that captivated her: *"Your words of poetry confirmed the tragic pain I felt while witnessing Guernica. My sense of loss was a contradiction to the warmth of your hand as it slipped into mine and comforted me as we walked home, and now it is your poetry that consumes me here in the night. Your poetry impacts my senses the same way Picasso's paint captures a nation's pain. Your words and my pain allow me to feel complete. I found my home in your hand today. I love you…"*

Stella was still reading when Eve interrupted.

"My mother wrote poetry." Eve's tone sounded on the verge of hysteria.

Stella nodded, but thought it best to say nothing.

"Just when I didn't expect any other surprises, here is another one. Jesus Stella—I don't think I knew my mother at all. In all our years together, she barely wrote anything unless it was with a red pen."

Stella felt the waves of frustration pouring off the older woman. She tried to distract Eve from the latest revelation. "I don't mean to be ignorant, but I am not sure I even know what Guernica was."

Eve replied as if she was answering a student's question, "Guernica was Picasso's political masterpiece. It is a mural about the German bombers that attacked a small Spanish town in the late 30s before World War 2 started. It was a practice bombing by the Nazis."

"Did your mom leave you anything that could contain her writing?" She looked in the direction of the piles of stuff around the living room. "Maybe she left a box with her poetry or possible more letters. Madalane being a poet just about made the love affair perfect, don't you think? A poet and a painter—a bounty of art."

Eve rolled her eyes at Stella's romantic enthusiasm. Her mind rebelled at the idea of going through the boxes of her mother's belongings she had kept in the spare room after she had died. It was too much, too painful and too hard to even consider it. Yet the idea that her mother had been moved to create poetry was a lure that she might not be able to resist. She ran both of her hands through her gray hair, compressing her skull, hoping to relieve some of the pressure. Maybe it was time finally to clear the clutter from her world. Go through everything she had packed up and stored, go through all the papers that had stacked up throughout the house, and finally get away from the encumbrances of stuff that she couldn't dig herself out from under.

She briefly glanced at Stella who had the excited expression that Eve dreaded. She was ready for a treasure hunt.

Eve took a deep breath, "I know you want to find my mother's poetry, but *before* we look for anything....you need to understand that I haven't gone through my mother's belongings ever. I always planned to, but couldn't face it."

Stella Simone's eyebrow rose at the idea of history and poetry and art and art boxes and her newfound passion for romantic detective work. She knew she needed to control herself. Holding back her enthusiasm, she said calmly, "Listen Eve, as I see it, your mother kept a tight hold on the things that she loved, including her love for Evienne, for you, and for her work. If you could visualize anything else, the way you remembered the art box next to your mother's bed, what would it be?"

Feeling panic rise up inside of her, Eve searched her mind for her mother's cherished belongings. The painting and the pearl were the only items that Madalane ever specifically referenced. "I don't know. My mother didn't hold on to much. She came to the states with a suitcase and the painting. She literally ran for her life. We barely had anything when I was little. Mom spent every dime she made on rent and food. She was a teacher; the only things that she ever spent money on or held onto were books." Lightning struck as she realized the implication. "Of course....my mother treasured her books—not all of them—just a few. She said they were her only friends when she came to this country. They reminded her of home and happier times. She kept them in a bookcase in her bedroom. That seems right, don't you think?"

Hope restored, Stella nodded her agreement as she watched Eve run to the cluttered dining room. Stella wondered if she kept everything of importance in that room.

A small burst of excitement shot through Eve as she ran past Evienne's painting. She lifted a stack of mail off the buffet, uncovering a small porcelain bowl filled with keys. She dumped the keys onto the pile of mail, separating them quickly from each other as she looked for the one she was seeking. Finally finding it, she tentatively turned to Stella, "Please don't judge what you are going to see." Her voice was tense and coiled. Not waiting for an answer, Eve hurried back through the living room and down a hallway leading to what Stella assumed were the bedrooms.

Placing the key in the lock of a bedroom door, Eve took a deep breath. She had installed the lock years ago when Hank had first started visiting because she was embarrassed and did not want him to know what lay beyond this door. Stella will be appalled—she already knew that, but hopefully she could find the boxes from her mother's bedroom bookcase and get back to the relative order of her living room. She wished she had asked Stella to stay in the living room, but the younger woman was behind her, virtually vibrating with excited anticipation.

The door did not swing open; rather, it required Eve's full weight to push it wide enough to see in the room. Eve winced at the disarray of the small room, stacked floor to ceiling with boxes, clothes, bags, toys and assorted detritus she didn't know what to do with. Her heart pounding, she quickly turned to Stella and sharply stated, "Stay here."

Wading through the piles of partially filled plastic bags, she felt humiliation fill her. She prayed she could find the boxes quickly, so she could lock up her secret again and hope that Stella didn't think too badly of her. The room was overwhelming—it always had been. It was the reason she had stopped even coming in here. Her breath was rapid and shallow and she felt the flush of anxiety rise through her. The boxes of books were near the closet. She remembered moving the boxes a few years prior when she needed to get something out of the closet. Of course, now, she couldn't remember what she would have needed from the closet. She pushed through a pile of coats thrown next to the bed. The two boxes were there, stacked neatly under bags of old Christmas cards and decorations.

Quickly moving the bags to the pile of coats, she picked up the first box, feeling the heft, confident that it had to be the books if it was this heavy. She moved carefully back to the door and handed the box wordlessly to Stella who placed the box on the floor behind her in the hallway. Eve returned to the second box, repeating the process. Handing the second box to Stella, she squeezed through the doorway and quickly relocked the door, pocketing the key, promising herself to start clearing out this mess. She picked up the first box that Stella had left in the hallway and turned to go into the living room.

Holding the second box, Stella had already moved into the living, fighting the overwhelming desire to organize and sort and categorize, but hushed those instincts for another day. As the older woman made her way to the couch, Stella saw the flush of Eve's cheeks and realized that Eve would definitely need a moment to get past this. Balancing the weight of her box, she said to Eve, "Maybe we should have some wine with our poetry?"

Grateful that Stella did not focus on her shameful secret, she heartily agreed. Eve put her box next to the couch and went through to the kitchen to get another bottle of wine. Returning, she saw that Stella had placed her box on the floor between her feet, having carefully moved the coffee table out to make space. Filling both of their glasses, she put the bottle on the coffee table and moved her box to the space between her legs, mirroring Stella's posture.

Stella reached for the glasses and confidently declared, "Let's toast to Madalane and Evienne."

Eve gave a faint smile of relief and the two toasted their wine glasses and drank. "Shall we just dive in? Or try to be systematic in our search?" Eve hoped that Stella would give her some direction

Stella slipped for a second back to her life with her husband. His clutter was a consistent job for her that she sort of missed now. The irony of missing his mess made her smile.

"Let's each take a box." Placing her wine glass carefully on the coffee table, she opened the Gallo wine box as if it was Evienne's art box. Stacked inside were old hardback books—maybe twenty in total. "I think we should look inside each book and see if your mom wrote in them or left papers or letters tucked in them." Stella looked at Eve for approval before she proceeded. Eve nodded, placing her own wine glass next to Stella's, and took the top off from the box at her feet.

Eve flipped through the first book in the box, realizing that it was a collection of essays from the ancient writers of Greece and Rome. Something seemed to click into place as Eve flipped the pages. She put the book down on the coffee table with an emphatic thud. "We need to find her poetry books. My mother loved symmetry. She always kept things in a particular order. She would put poems in a poetry book, not in a history book. Let's pull out all of the books, and check the spines. It will go quicker this way!"

Excitedly, Eve reached into her own box, pulled out a half dozen books, and scanned the spines: Sartre, de Beauvoir, and Colette...all novels or essays. She prayed that she was right—recently it felt like she had barely even known her mother. She needed to be right about this.

As she lifted the lid off her box, Stella felt certain that the book would be in her box; it felt like the day she had spied the art box on the top closet shelf of the spare room in Maggie's grandmother's house. She flipped through the first book of poetry by T.S. Eliot then one from Rimbaud. She skipped *The Great Gatsby*, absently wondering why it was packed with the poetry books. She picked up another book and the writing was French, but she found nothing. Stella felt Eve's shoulder pressing into hers. She too suspected that if anything were to be found, it would be in the box Stella had.

Flipping through the pages of a book of poetry by Edith Sitwell, Stella sighed as she found nothing. What were they doing? What were they looking for? She picked up a thin book, the cover brown from age, *A Few Figs from Thistles*, poems by Edna St. Vincent Millay. Stella flipped open the book, respecting the delicate paper, and there on the first page was a folded paper covering the poem, "The First Fig."

"Did you find it?" Eve gasped in excitement. "Is there more than one? Are there a lot?"

Stella quickly flipped though the antique book, and both women could see that between almost every page, there was a sheet of onionskin paper carefully folded.

Eve felt lightheaded, but she desperately needed to hear her mother's words. It had been so long since she had heard her voice. "Will you read one aloud? Any of them? I don't care which. Just find one and read it to me please."

Stella took a moment to consider how to proceed, and flipped to further back in the book of poetry. She slipped a poem from its resting spot, and opened the paper carefully.

Eve stared hard at her own hands, hoping to maintain a grip on her emotions as Stella began to read:

Her Mother Screams

> *We are fighting for the essential unity of Spain.*
> *We are fighting for the integrity of Spanish soil.*
> *We are fighting for the independence of our country and for*
> *the right of the Spanish people to determine their own*
> *destiny. (Paul Eluard)*
> *A rumble in the sky on*
> *a mother's walk in*
> *the sunny streets*
> *to Monday's market,*
> *clean children in tow;*
> *they shield their eyes to see.*
>
> *Their Basque village,*
> *their market*
> *filled with green apples*
> *brown potatoes, white eggs,*
> *baked bread, laughter, and bells.*
> *The hamlet turns their heads*
> *to the rumbling sound;*
> *curious children pause.*
> *The sun shaded by warplanes;*
> *the ground shadowed gray.*

Hitler has his sight on the
calculation of control.
He practices his massacre—
his bombs, his air raids.
A thousand deaths
in three hours;
Nazis experiment on life.
A thousand unpredictable lives
flee incendiary bombs for
three daylight hours.

Everything built is destroyed.
The gluttony of brutal reality,
living the responsibility.

Mothers cry for their children.
Vegetables are dropped and
trampled upon, tormented
outstretched arms;
there is nowhere to run
the ground is shaking, the
buildings are on fire,
the horses are screaming, the
town is turning red in agony.
Humans
shot down running.
All left for dead; burning
flames matching screams of chaos.
God's church crumbles back to
gray stone, steeple fallen.
Defeat of people
at the hand
of tormentors.

Chapter 57

Paris, April 1940

Madalane wrapped her coat tighter around herself as she turned the corner to Rue St. Michel. It had been a long day. The students were more distracted than usual and she had spent most of each class trying to maintain control. The sun was hiding today and the general atmosphere in Paris was cold and gloomy. She was looking forward to spending the night, locked away in the apartment she shared with Evienne, with a good book, a roaring brazier, and a glass or two of wine.

Two men, both dressed in Nazi uniforms were walking towards her. Their eyes cut sharply towards her like a chill wind as they approached, and she felt a small panic rise up in her throat. She was not Jewish; she had even taken to wearing her confirmation cross to ensure that there was no question. Rumors had filtered through the city over the past year about whole families disappearing from the Jewish sections of the city. No one would publicly discuss what was happening, but everyone knew. Hitler's men were in town to purge the city of Semitic influence. Even Gertrude Stein and Alice B. Toklas had fled their beloved city and were hiding out in the countryside.

The closer the soldiers got, the more Madalane avoided their eyes. She had done nothing wrong; she was not the wrong religion although rumors abounded that Hitler was not a fan of the papists either. However, she had also heard rumors that the Pope arranged for the Catholics to be left alone. As the men passed, they nodded almost imperceptibly and murmured, "Bon Soir Madame."

Words that normally came so easily to Madalane seemed to get stuck in her throat; finally, she managed to croak out, "Bon soir." It was a mere whisper but the men carried on, enjoying the fact that they intimidated a French woman. She stopped for a moment, turned and watched them continue down the street. They walked slowly with an almost extravagant presence, taking up the expansive sidewalk with their swinging arms and wide stance. She saw a few people cross the street to avoid them while others hurried past with their heads down. As she was about to turn back to continue her journey, she saw the two soldiers stop and engage a young boy in conversation. He appeared to be no older than fourteen, but he was tall and very thin. The soldiers backed him up against the red brick of the building and she could see them demanding his identity papers. She felt a sick apprehension come over her. She wanted to go back and pull the boy away from these men, but she was afraid. Stories of Nazi cruelty were all over Paris and she had been warned by Evienne as well as by the teachers at school that they should keep to themselves. These violent men would leave their city soon when they saw that there was no fight to be had here.

Without looking back to see the fate of the young boy, she started walking again. Some of the shop windows carried swastika flags, welcoming the Nazi soldiers. She felt scorn for these shopkeepers; they were welcoming violence into their world. It's one thing to wait on a Nazi, but something entirely different to invite them. She knew her own father had no control over who came into his shop, but he never willingly invited trouble.

She slipped through the entrance of their building and walked heavily up the four flights to their apartment. She and Evienne had discussed moving down another floor or two when they were closer to forty, but for now, it was still an easy walk up the stairs. Outside the door of the apartment, Madalane stopped to take a moment to ease the anxiety the soldiers had caused. She wondered what would happen to the boy, but she forced the image out of her mind. She couldn't worry about anyone but herself and Evienne.

Evienne sat looking out the window in her studio. The mix of Parisians and fear traveling down the boulevard seemed a trite game to her mind now; not long ago she searched the world for shades, angles, and inspiration to uncover the mysteries of art and the interpretation of meaning. Today she knew what loomed in her future—the potent image of the last of the Paris she knew with her lover. Evienne knew her choice was born from the threat to her art and the threat to Madalane. She slowly rolled her white Gauloise cigarette back and forth between her thumb and her index finger contemplating the words she was about to say to Madalane.

Evienne searched her worktable for an unused match. Fingering through the horsehair paintbrushes, the half-used tubes of oil paint and finally the art box where she found a stray match. Instead of using the match, she closed the box, and she placed her hand on top of it as if it was a Bible and she was swearing to God to tell the truth.

Evienne had already put each of her most valuable treasures into the box. She put the few black and white pictures of her and Madalane's early days as lovers along with the most beautiful drawings she could find of her Dove. Carefully, Evienne placed her final love letter to her companion of ten years between the pictures. She felt as if she had slipped her heart into the art box, packing her heart away with her art. Hot tears rolled down her cheeks as she removed the vesta case from around her neck; an object that had become part of her body. It had been her communion gift from Madalane while the two sat in church and watched the sun set through the stained glass. Evienne slipped the case into the box and closed it again. She touched the small latches of her sealed art box and she stared at her hands as she bound the leather strap.

The art box was consistent. It was the one thing intimately connected to her; what she had counted on before she discovered she could count on Madalane. She closed her eyes, rubbed her smoky, turpentine-stained fingers under her nose, and tried to clear the well of tears splashing on her lap. Her heart cursed her for her choice. She had sworn to herself that she would never paint again until she knew Madalane was safe from the brutality of the Nazis. She feared for the safety of Madalane in their beautiful city—a city where the blooming flowers were threatened because of the nature of their prosperity. She would take the thorns of inhumanity and fight the construction of lies to reconstruct the vitality of their city.

Evienne's heart felt the harsh reality of fear from the necessity of change. She prayed the contents of the art box would comfort Madalane's heart. She prayed every word she wrote in the letter reflected the truth in her heart and Madalane would forgive her for the lie she was about to tell. The cigarette remained unlit as she heard the key slip into the door of their apartment on 93 Rue Saint Michel.

* * *

Shaking off the images that had filled her mind, Madalane took a deep cleansing breath and opened the door to their apartment. Walking in, she felt an odd chill in the room. The front parlor was empty but that was not unusual. Evienne always stayed in her studio until Madalane came home. She looked around briefly, trying to put her finger on the differences in the room. It was tidy, as always, but it seemed like something was missing. Did Evienne clean today? Madalane's nerves started to jangle. Now even more concerned, Madalane moved through the parlor to the hall that led to Evienne's studio, which was the second bedroom. Out of the corner of her eye, she glanced into the bedroom they shared. Her suitcase was sitting at the foot of the bed. Shaking her head, she frantically wondered what was happening. Madalane's mind raced as she took in the room; the framed picture she kept next to her side of her bed of she and Evienne was gone. Anxiety welled up in her as she ran into Evienne's studio. Evienne was sitting still at the worktable. She was facing the doorway, expecting Madalane's arrival. "Evienne! Are you okay? Why is my suitcase out?"

Nothing came to Evienne's lips. Everything she rehearsed in her mind evaporated as she stared at Madalane standing frozen in the doorway, her bag clutched in her arms, her coat still on.

"Madalane." Evienne stood up from her small stool. Her cigarette, still unlit, fell to the floor. "We have to go. It is Hitler. It's not safe anymore."

"What are you talking about? It's just another day Evienne! What makes today the day we have to go?" Madalane's tone was hysterical. As more and more Nazis had entered Paris, the two women had discussed various possibilities. When their friends started to leave the city, they had discussed contingencies. Yet, neither of them had felt it necessary to leave over the past year.

"I need to be sure of your safety Madalane." Evienne firmly placed her palms on both of Madalane's shoulders, partly to steady the sound of her own words. "I made our travel arrangements. My sisters in Boston. They will sponsor us."

Evienne's eyes burned. "I could only get one ticket for the ship to Boston. I will be following in three days. I have to settle out with the gallery, so we have money to start our life in America together. We need to go Madalane. You know the conversations on the streets and in the cafes! The Nazi's will take over Paris. You know people are fleeing Madalane. I need you to do as I ask. It is time." A haze of panic filled the room as both women stared at one another; Madalane could hear by her partner's tone that Evienne was sternly committed to this course of action.

"For God's sake! How many times have we heard these rumors? I can't leave in the middle of a term; I will get fired. Let's just wait until the summer break and then we'll decide. And if we decide that we should leave, then we'll go together." Madalane's defiance was palpable in the small room.

"The tickets have been bought and the train will be leaving shortly. There is no other way." Evienne turned to her art table and felt the hollowness in her stomach as she reached for her art box. "I want you to take my art box with you."

Madalane's mind had been racing, but at this request, she was literally stopped in her tracks. "You want me to take your art box? Why?"

"Madalane stop asking so many questions." Evienne quickly turned to face Madalane once again, extending the art box towards her. "I want you to have it. I want you to take it. Keep it safe for me. Please Madalane—just take it and hold it for me until I join you in America." The words blundered from her mouth.

Staring furiously at her partner, Madalane's mind tried to register what was happening. She shrugged her coat off and ran her fingers down the front of her dress, trying to smooth away all the wrinkles in her world. Evienne was adamant about them leaving. Maybe giving her the box was meant to ensure her compliance. Evienne would never abandon her art box—it was an extension of her soul. Tears sprang to Madalane's eyes as she connected the dots. The only person in the world Evienne would trust with her heart or her art box was she. Feeling the fight leave her, Madalane felt she needed to make one last effort to hold off and wait for her lover, so they could travel together.

She grasped Evienne's hand and pleaded, "Evienne, please... cash in my ticket today and let me travel with you in three days. Nothing will happen to me if we wait three days. I don't want to travel alone. If we are going to start a new life in America, I want us to do it together, at the same time. Please, love? Please?"

"Dove—everyone is fleeing. There was only one berth on the ship to Boston to secure, and I secured the only one available for me in three days." Evienne pushed herself away from her partner to retrieve Madalane's suitcase. "Is there anything else you want to take with you?" Evienne left Madalane standing in the doorway and headed to the door of their home. Pausing, she looked around the apartment. "Is there?"

Heartsick and despondent, Madalane looked around the apartment they had shared for the past five years. The furniture, the knick-knacks, and the clutter on the sideboard all reminded her of their life together, and now they were just walking away from it all. She knew, deep in her heart, that they would have to leave Paris eventually. Most of their friends from the salon had left, even Janet who made a living writing about Paris, had fled the city.

She glanced around the room once more and her eyes rested on the painting that Evienne had given her when they met. She would not leave Paris without it; she did not care if Evienne had to wait—this was far more important than clothes or jewelry to her. She gingerly lifted it off the wall and carried it into Evienne's studio to wrap it. She knew Evienne was watching, but her silence said volumes. Before returning to the parlor with the painting wrapped in brown paper, Madalane slipped into their bedroom. Kneeling down next to her side of the bed, she reached for her treasure box.

Evienne's voice sounded from the parlor, "I already put it in the suitcase." Madalane stood up and stared hard at the room they had shared, memorizing everything until she heard Evienne grow restless in the next room. She stepped out to the parlor and nodded at her lover and they proceeded out the door.

The setting sun skipped off the glass windows of the building, framing the boulevard as the two walked in silence. Evienne had her arm clasped tightly at Madalane's elbow, their shoulders pushed firmly together. Evienne carried Madalane's suitcase, Madalane carried Evienne's art box, and the painting as the two women walked to the train station.

Evienne started to recite the plan: "You will take the train to Calais and then the ferry to Dover in England. You will then catch the train in Southampton and then board the ship to Boston.

The words seemed to robotically fall from her mouth. She did not even want to hear her own voice, she wanted to bury herself into Madalane's neck and swear what she was promising to be true. They turned left heading towards the Seine and the distance between Madalane's train and the rest of their lives was quickening.

The clipped sounds of Evienne's boots hitting the sidewalk created a metronome in Madalane's head. She had a horrible sense of unease. There was something wrong with Evienne's attitude and yet the art box under her arm comforted her. Evienne would never go anywhere without it; by giving it to her to carry, it felt like a contract that they were both signing. However, even the sturdy weight of the art box did little to diminish the feeling that something wasn't right. She looked up at her partner of so many years—they had just celebrated their anniversary a few months before. She wished she could see into her mind and know what she was thinking. There was something going on, but she couldn't put her finger on it.

There was an unusually large crowd gathered around the front of the train station. Any nagging worries were lost as they struggled to get through the crowd and get to the platforms. Madalane stopped for a minute to hear the worried cries of the people surrounding the newspaper vendor—the Nazis had invaded Denmark. Her heart sank as she heard the news. Evienne was right. Hitler had no intention of leaving France alone.

"Here are your tickets."

Madalane's attention was focused on the crowds' voices, straining to hear what the news of Hitler was.

"Madalane, listen to me." Evienne stopped her near the hissing train, putting Madalane's case down. She turned Madalane's face to hers and looked deeply into her eyes. She was scared to release a word, knowing tears would never stop if she started to tell her what her heart was screaming. "My sisters will be waiting for you in Boston. I will send word when I arrive." With both palms cradling her lover's face, Evienne stared into the eyes of the loveliest person in the world to her. The stare between the two women melted their surroundings into silence.

Ignoring the voice that was whispering doubts about Evienne's plan, Madalane focused on her lover's face. "I don't want to go without you." The words escaped Madalane's mouth without her even realizing she said them.

Slowly Evienne turned her head slightly almost quizzically and lowered her mouth to the lips of the only woman she would ever love. She need to hush her own doubts and needed to fill Madalane with the one last thing she could give her, her eternal love. She deserved to know it and feel it. She closed her eyes to pray and took a deep jittery breath. Evienne could feel hot tears rolling over her fingers. She could smell the sweet breath of Madalane; opening her eyes and looking to her lover's, she drew her mouth towards hers.

Madalane's eyes closed again as Evienne pulled her lover's lips into her mouth, kissing them over and over, trying desperately to keep this part of her lover with her forever, internalizing and consuming the greatest love she had ever known. Evienne knew she was second guessing herself. The moment was at a crisis, and she could not let her go. She would never let her Dove leave without her. She would bring her home and make love to her for the rest of their lives; Hitler be damned!

Her soul whispered to her that she would put Madalane in terrible danger and she ached deep inside. Powerful words demanded their release—"I love you," she said between kisses. "I love you Madalane," and she kissed her mouth over and over. "It is you I will only love." The salt of the tears, the sweetness of Madalane's mouth trembled through Evienne's body.

The conductor's voice rang over the din of the crowd, "All aboard, Paris to Calais departing in five minutes! All aboard!"

Tears ran down Madalane's face as she kissed her lover back. "I love you Evienne. You know that, right? I loved you from the first moment I saw you selling your paintings. I loved you before I even knew your name." Madalane's memories came rushing back into her mind. "I will see you in a few weeks, yes?" Her voice sounded tremulous and she needed Evienne's reassurance.

Evienne nodded as she held her tight. Madalane's anxiety struck hard and she pulled away, "Promise me. You promise me now. You will see me in a few weeks, right? I need you to say it. Please Evienne. I'm not getting on this train until you promise me."

The stone of her decision hardened her voice. "Yes, my Dove, yes. I promise, I will be there." The all-aboard whistle blew.

Madalane's eyes narrowed at Evienne's words. She had to believe her. She grasped her lover to her once more and buried her face into the thick plait of her hair. She inhaled deeply, smelling the familiar sandalwood, tobacco and paint that defined Evienne. She held the scent in her lungs for as long as she could; she wanted to memorize it until she could inhale it again.

"Final boarding call to Calais! All aboard!"

The conductor's voice ripped Madalane's heart in half as she pulled away, Evienne's plait of hair rippling through her hand. She stopped and stared into Evienne's eyes, taking the braid to her face, she rubbed the softness to her lips and kissed the hair and let it drop to Evienne's chest. The platform was mostly deserted; only a few last minute goodbyes echoed above the roar of the train's engine. Madalane stepped up to the entrance and Evienne handed her the suitcase, which the porter took into the depths of the train. Madalane stood in the open doorway, clutching the art box and the painting to her chest as the train started to pull away. Her eyes locked on Evienne's as she shouted one last farewell, "Goodbye Evienne. I will love you forever."

Evienne's mouthed a silent, "I love you."

The two women stood staring at each other until they could see each other no more. Finally, as Evienne's form blended into the shadows of the train platform, Madalane reluctantly turned to find her compartment.

10 April, 1940

My Dearest Madalane,
I only understand one thing in my life and that is you.
I am drinking my last cup of tea in our apartment and I
dream of the last time I drew your face, our last kiss this
afternoon, the taste of your lips, and the feeling of being in
your arms. I can still smell your hair, your neck. I know your
love although I sit here empty memorizing the life we shared
together. Have I done the right thing? I feel your fingers in my
hair. I feel your presence behind me, I turn and you are not
there, I am desperate. I need you to know, I will never love
another. You have my art box filled with everything that is
of significance to me, I put a letter in the box with our picture.
You will find me there.
After leaving you at the train today, I am desperate to
write. My chest pains at the thought of lies. Forgive me for
what I am about to tell you. Please, my Dove, forgive me. I
have been living a lie in our life. I have been working with
a secret group, helping disrupt German communications and
blocking supplies within Paris. I am fearful even to write
this to you, disgusted about what has happened to our Paris.
I cannot sit solitary in another country knowing the life Paris
gave to me is being destroyed. She has been my companion
through the worst and the best days of my life and this leaves
me with one option, I need to defend her. I cannot read in a
paper how our city has become an icon of a conquered nation.
And this is why I needed you to be safe and to understand, our
rules needed to be adjusted in times of crisis. I cannot allow
Hitler to win.
I know you are angry. I feel the tears slipping from your

eyes. Do not lose your trust in me. I can feel your anger stream from your golden eyes, but you will forgive and understand me in time, when our Paris is free. I will protect her for you, and I will bring you home.

I will come for you, I promise, I will come for you.

I love you Madalane, my Dove.

Forever,

Evienne

Chapter 58

Paris, April 1940

The tears kept burning her face as her wool coat sleeve raked over her cheeks. As soon as she passed through the entrance of the train station, she felt compelled to run deep into the streets of Paris. She wanted to be eaten up by the city, so she could forget what she had just done. She wanted to rip every swastika from every shop window and claw at the ones painted on walls. She wanted the Germans to feel the pain that was throbbing in every cell of her body. She wanted to scream at every injustice scarred into her heart.

The choice she made that day with Charles changed her life; she knew it. She stared at the Seine as she did almost a year ago, and felt his words flood back into her mind.

"Can you believe that we are still slogging away with our paints and brushes after all these years? I love painting, but don't you ever feel like there is more we could do?"

Was it on impulse or boredom that she said yes to him? It was not boredom, and she knows now in retrospect that it was on impulse. "Charles you need to find a new technique for your brush or a new woman." she said pushing the hair behind her ear.

"I am serious. I want to tell you about a scheme I'm working on, but you have to promise to not say a word to anyone, especially Madalane." Charles voice was serious and quiet; Charles was never serious or quiet, so Evienne looked at him with concern.

"Do you promise Ev?"

"Yes, yes of course. What is it?" She saw a nervous bead of sweat slip from his hairline, her own heartbeat faster. "I promise, tell me. What is it?"

Charles stopped and looked out at the river. "You read the paper... this madman in Germany has his sights set on Europe and none of the politicians are doing a damn thing to stop him."

Evienne opened her mouth to say something, but Charles held up a finger indicating that she should let him finish.

"I have become involved with a group who believe that some- thing has to be done to stop the Nazis and they are doing it quietly in every corner of France. We have realized that if someone doesn't, we will be goose-stepping down the Champs d'Elysee with swastikas on our jackets. I don't want that to happen to Paris. It is my home and I know you feel the same. You can join us and take a stand. It's easy work my friend—just painting canvases, like we do anyway. There is virtually no risk involved."

Was it a thrill that she felt in her bones that day on the Seine? A day eerily like today. It was her truth to be living for what she believed in—she had lived and worked for Paris, and now she had to go underground or it would be her death. She said yes to Charles before she understood exactly what it meant. She was now living another life painting coded messages into paintings they sold next to the Seine. Had she known this secret would separate her from Madalane, had she known the secret would take her from her lover, she would have said no.

When she found out that their identities had been uncovered, she had wanted to tell Madalane. She had wanted to bring her with them as they left their old lives behind, but Charles told her stories of men, women, and even children being tortured and burned. Evienne's mind flashed to the horrible rumors of the Nazi camps where prisoners were either killed upon arrival or were worked to death, or starved until they couldn't work anymore. She had heard terrible tales of attractive women being turned into sex slaves for the Nazis and her heart rebelled at the idea of her Dove being raped by some Nazi brute. Her father would have never let anything happen to her mother or her sisters. How could she ever let harm come to the only family she had? It was the right thing to do putting her on the train, getting her away from the madness in Europe. It had to stop. Hitler had to be stopped. She had committed herself to this destiny.

The pending night was haunting her; she needed to find her focus and execute her plans. There was no time to weep, there was no time to feel loss, and there was no time to think of her past, not even of her lover. After months of planning, Evienne rationalized and almost believed the lies she had told Madalane. When it became clear that the Nazis had identified her and Charles as part of the resistance group, this became their only move. They had to go underground. She had to devote herself to the faith of saving Paris. She had to. She had to undermine the Germans and drive them out of her city. She believed in the mission—and it was the only way she could reunite safely with Madalane.

Automatically, her feet moved her through the streets, people, children, cafes all still living; she saw nothing but a gray blur, her body moist with a thin layer of sweat. Just over an hour ago, Madalane was next to her. Now she ran over the Pont Neuf Bridge alone and terrified that Madalane would hate her for what she had done. Something made Evienne stop, gasping for breath and her fingers gripping the stone, she looked down at the river. She had often contemplated life while gazing at the water, always feeling her father's spirit filling her when she stared at the placid surface. Nothing was different on this early solitary evening as Evienne prayed and the sun dipped beyond the horizon and the air cooled around her: Father, I had to stand for something that I believed was true. You would have sent mother away too, for safety. Will Madalane forgive me? Will I forgive myself?

Impulsively, Evienne pulled her father's cap from her head, buried her face in it, smelling what may have remained of her father's life mixed into hers, kissed it and asked for his blessing. With a sharp controlled flip of her wrist, the worn cap went whirling through the air and into the Seine.

Turning back to her path, Evienne felt the urgency again. She had to get home, retrieve her things, and get to the meeting place that she and Charles had settled upon. The two friends had given up their lives and were now going completely underground to work on covert communications. The two worked on coding messages with invisible inks and watercolors, transferring messages on canvas by day at the art stand. Charles had pulled her into this world; she owed him her life as she owed her loyalty to Paris.

Making her way to 93 Rue Saint Michel, then up the four flights of stairs, barely out of breath, time did not seem to matter to her anymore. Life had been so contrived until today and now it seemed driven. Her key slipped effortlessly into the lock and into the safety of their apartment. She hooked her key on the hook Madalane put there for her and shut the door with her foot. Madalane should have been here. She would have been here; Madalane would have never left her. As she thought of her life with Madalane, tears swelled from the core of her chest and burst through her heart, dropping her to her knees, a blank feeling surrounding her. The pressure of Madalane's absence was almost too much to bear. Evienne sobbed in a long forgotten way—the way death and loss had stolen her life so many times before Madalane's arrival in her life.

Evienne's hands clasped her head. The heat of her heaving breath and tears awakened her to her reality. She stood, wiped her face, and mechanically walked to her studio as she has done so many times before. She found the long metal shears on a shelf with her paints. With her right hand gripping the scissors, she opened and closed them to assure their working condition, and pulled her long braid taut and lopped it off. The braid, just kissed by her lover, fell limp in her hand. It was her other life. She kissed the plait as Madalane did and dropped it on the table in front of her. She continued clipping away at her head until she was barely recognizable as a woman. It was time to go underground, time to disappear.

Evienne went to their armoire, hidden in the back was her knapsack; it held her tools and black beret signifying her role. She pulled opened the flap and searched for the hat, feeling the black felt, she pulled it from the bag and put it on her head. It was time to go; it was completely dark now. The apartment had no comforting light glowing; it seemed to be mourning the loss of its lovers. Evienne looked around feeling slightly lost in a place she loved as her home, threw her sack over her shoulder and went to retrieve her art box. Her aching chest stopped her from entering her art room. It was like a brick wall barricading her—it was gone and so was Madalane.

Straightening her back, she turned and walked down the hall to the wood door, kissing the key hanging on their hook. She let the metal key go and as it hit the plaster wall, it shattered a life that was once living inside their home.

If God were with her, he would give her a chance. The door clicked shut behind her and she disappeared into the night leaving the only life she loved behind.

Chapter 59

If I do not make it back to your side to see your smile, to look into your eyes, to feel your heart, know I am a better person because of you. You are my one and only heart and I love only you. Forever,
Evienne

Stella's voice struggled to finish the last line of the last letter that Evienne wrote to Madalane. The room had taken on a funereal silence as the two women sat contemplating the words Evienne had offered up as a sort of benediction.

Finally, Eve broke the quiet, "I half expected that Evienne had run out on my mom, but I had no idea that it would be for a noble purpose." She lapsed back into silence, both lost in their own thoughts.

Stella fell deeper into the sofa and contemplated the gravity of the letter she just read. Evienne lied for love and lied for honor; a chain of horror must have followed, knowing she could be leading herself into death. Worse yet, she knew the consequences of abandoning the one person who she trusted and who had trusted her—Madalane.

Choking on the words, Stella replied, "Evienne walked to her death thinking she could outsmart it. She failed even as she wore her armor of faith. It just breaks my heart."

"Love of country is the only thing more powerful than romantic love." Eve glanced at Stella who seemed to be half listening and half lost in her own reverie. "How many men have marched off to war, leaving behind wives, children, and parents to wonder what will become of them? I have always seen it as a very foolish thing to do—probably because I came of age during Vietnam when war was proved to be a futile endeavor. However, Hitler was a bad, bad man and I can't help but admire Evienne's dedication to Paris. To be honest, I can see why my mom never found someone to equal Evienne. How can you compete with a woman who placed honor above life and love?"

"What do you think happened to her?" Stella glanced back down at the letter she still held in her hand, "I can't imagine living in a time of an invading war. I can't believe this is the last letter Eve. I want more." Clutching the letter to her chest, she slumped even further into the sofa.

"I will absolutely try to find out what happened to Evienne. How hard could it be to find one female artist in a sea of 12 million victims of a war?" Eve gave a wry smile to Stella who nodded, not quite sure if the older woman was kidding.

Realizing Stella's uncertainty, Eve assured her, "I will do my best, but World War 2 was a massive war over multiple continents and millions of people were displaced or died. The Nazis kept good records but even with that, I may not find much."

Stella had a crestfallen look on her face, which made Eve reach over to cover her hand, "Don't worry. I am really good at this type of thing—I have been doing research for fifty years. If there is anything to find, I will find it. I will do everything I can to find out what happened to Evienne. I owe it to you and I owe it to my mother."

Eve felt emotion washing over her. "Can you imagine living your whole adult life hoping for someone to come back to you?"

Stella looked away as she replied, "I understand. Victor held a part of me that I thought was real, and now after all this, I see what is real. Real love is honesty and integrity between two people. Love is not the fantasy of Cinderella; it is the truth that a person is willing to share their heart with you no matter the pain or the happiness. I feel that way about David; it is funny how his love weaved its way into me through the years. When we love someone so much, the soul of the other person lives inside us, takes up residence in us and we grow together in our existence. Evienne's soul was the blood in your mother's veins. They were everything to each other, and even in death, they still are."

Chapter 60

Eve's fingers twitched as she stared at the Google search screen. She normally preferred using the resources at the college, but she was home and the online databases the college subscribed to were accessible only from the college network. She started with the most obvious search—Evienne Lavelle. The few responses that came up didn't reveal anyone with that exact name. Eve drummed her fingers on the keyboard. This is a woman who had died almost sixty years before, a woman who had died before she could make a significant impression on the art world. She stared at the cursor inside the search box. What next?

The last letter to Madalane indicated that she was joining an underground group, fighting the Nazis. Eve typed in French Resistance and hit enter. She got six and a half million hits and as usual, the Wikipedia website was first on the results page. Sighing because she felt slightly hypocritical about using a site she had warned her students about. Nonetheless, when the page loaded, she quickly scanned the information. The section about women in the French Resistance was relatively short and did not provide much for her quest. She clicked on the few women's names that were in hypertext. There was nothing of significance other than most of them had been sent to a prison camp at some point during the war.

She clicked back to Google's main search page. Inside the search box where she had typed French Resistance, she added the word 'women', hoping that another term would focus her search. She hit enter and watched as over a million results registered. Wikipedia was first, then another commercial site, but the third site was a university—San Francisco State University. Eve was encouraged and she eagerly clicked on the link. It was an article written by a woman—it didn't indicate if she was a student or a professor. Eve scanned the article, snorting when she read about the 3K's in Hitler's manifesto—women should be pregnant, in the kitchen and in the church.

She continued to read—it was a standard academic article— plenty of footnotes and assiduous research. A woman's name jumped out at her—Marie-Claude Vaillant-Couturier, a reporter and photographer born in Paris in 1912. Eve did the math in her head; this woman would have been close in age to Evienne. The article indicated that Couturier had been arrested and put in Auschwitz and then eventually she was transferred to Ravensbruck Concentration Camp. This camp held mostly women and was more of a work camp than a death camp. Eve's eyebrows rose as she read that Ravensbruck seemed to be populated by political prisoners, significantly resistance fighters from all over Europe as well as the expected Jews, Gypsies and other undesirables.

She sat back and stared at the screen. Could Evienne have ended up in Ravensbruck? She wasn't Jewish and she was tall and strong with no children. She would have been a good candidate for a work camp. A few more clicks and Eve was staring at photos of the women held at Ravensbruck. Tall, short, fair, dark—all of them emaciated—women who stared at the camera with defiance and hope. The few photos she had seen of Evienne were no help in trying to locate the artist amidst the blurry faces of desperation.

She continued to surf and look at images that made the bile in her gut rise up and burn her throat. She found a link that informed her that she could contact the Red Cross for information about concentration camp victims. Ravensbruck had been on the eastern side of the Berlin Wall. After the Soviet Union fell, the incredibly detailed records of the Nazis finally became available about Ravensbruck to the west. Eve pulled up the Red Cross site and saw that she had to mail a form to their Victim Tracing Center to track Evienne down. She wondered if her academic credentials would allow her to see any of the primary documents.

As she returned to reading about Ravensbruck, each page brought worse and worse atrocities to Eve's screen. Her heart felt heavy and she wanted to take a break to call Stella to let her know what she found. Yet, she felt compelled to keep scrolling through each web site, hoping for Evienne's name to affirm her suspicions. She clicked on a group shot of twenty or so women standing behind barbed wire, which led to a site that documented medical experiments on Polish women and children. Sickened, she continued to read and a jarring fact jumped out at her. The article was based on a book written by a Polish countess who had also been an art history professor. She had been housed at Ravensbruck for two years starting in 1943. Curious about the book, she brought up Amazon and typed in the information: A Wartime Memoir by Karolina Lanckorońska. She hit search fearing the book was out of print or lost to the world.

Amazon's search engine had so such worries as it gave Eve what she desperately wanted—not the book she was looking for, but another book entitled Michelangelo in Ravensbruck by the same author. Not only was it available, but it could be purchased in Kindle form, no less. Eve laughed as she got up to retrieve the Kindle she had been given by Hank and barely ever used. Remembering she had left it on her bedroom bookcase (at the time she had considered it a personal ironic statement), she quickly pulled it off the shelf, wiped the dust from it and uploaded the book.

Eve scanned the pages until she got to the details on Ravensbruck. She briefly thought about calling Stella again, but she realized that Stella would be happier if Eve had more solid information. The atrocities of the medical experiments and the structure of the camp seemed to march through each chapter as an unflinching indictment of Nazi terror.

During the two years the author spent in the camp, she had taught art history classes in the camp barracks to some of the women who showed an interest. Eve wondered if Evienne had been her student. As she flipped through some of the gorier accounts of medical experiments, she read a paragraph that made her blood go cold in her veins. Lanckorońska related a story about an artist in the camp who used to draw portraits of the other prisoners in the hard-packed dirt of the camp. She had been desperate to escape. She tried over and over again to jump the barbed wire, even resorting to bribing the Nazi guards with portraits and drawings if they would turn away when she made her escape. Each time she was captured and beaten severely. The beatings never deterred the artist. She was relentless in her attempt to escape. Finally, the commandant of the camp decided to punish her with death by the Walzkommando. Eve put the Kindle down for a minute and Googled the term. She gazed at an old black and white photo. It was a large concrete cylinder attached to a metal harness. Inmates who were particularly problematic were punished by being harnessed to the heavy cylinder and then forced to pull it until they died.

Eve shuddered at the image and then went back to the Kindle. Lanckorońska's story about the artist ended without her ever revealing the inmate's name. Eve scanned the rest of the section about camp life and the photos in the book. There was nothing else except the pain and horror inflicted on these poor women. Lanckorońska had died in 2002, so there was no way of finding out any more details from her. Perhaps the Red Cross would have more information. She printed out the form to fill out and mail. Eve finally stood up from her desk, feeling cramped and miserable.

Rubbing the ache from her shoulders as she moved away from

her office, she thought of calling Stella, but she felt despondent over what she had discovered. She knew from the couple's passionate love letters that Evienne would have found Madalane had she survived the war. The inevitability of her death was certain, and yet Eve had hoped that Evienne had somehow outwitted the Nazis.

She thought about what she really wanted at that moment, and she realized more than anything, she wanted her mother. She wanted Madalane to cradle her against her chest and stroke her hair. Eve wanted her mother to affirm that her daughter's presence in her life had taken away some of her pain and filled her life with love.

Eve sighed, briefly considering something to eat, but the ache in her stomach was not hunger. Bones creaking, she felt every one of her almost seventy years as she moved through the kitchen and into the dining room. She stood in front of Evienne's painting and traced the paint with her fingertips. Suddenly she felt exhausted. Running her fingers once more over the painting's signature, she turned and moved unsteadily to her bedroom where Tiberius was already splayed out at the foot of the bed. Joining him, she stared up at the ceiling allowing the reality of the moment to infiltrate her consciousness. Had her mother's heart not been broken, she would never have been born. She was a child of misery and solitude, yet she had never suspected any of this. Her carefully controlled, cluttered life had suddenly become much more complex than she had ever thought possible.

Eve rolled onto her stomach and stared at the photo of her and Hank she kept next to her bed. She had put it there because it made Hank happy. Realizing that she wanted him next to her, she reached for her cell phone and pushed his number. She knew he would come to her, hold her tight in his arms, and not ask any questions until she was ready to talk.

Chapter 61

Stella pulled the cork out of a Meritage, giving it time to breathe before Eve arrived. She paused to look out the window, winter was still in force but a few hearty birds were hanging around the yard—months had passed since David left. Opening a kitchen cabinet, she reached for two wine glasses. How time had changed her. She felt a new sense of independence, a womanly character emerging from inside of her. Maybe this is what it felt like to grow into herself, she had allowed herself to mature and breathe like the wine.

As she put the glasses down next to the wine bottle, she questioned why it took so long to feel like this. Just a few months ago, her life seemed empty and unfulfilled. She realized that she no longer felt guilty about not loving David enough. Who defined love? Who defined a marriage? The only two people who had a say in her marriage were she and David. She longed to share with him the passion and confidence that was growing inside of her. She had written to David expressing her desire to commit to him. His response was tentative and neutral and she had cried for days that she had lost him. A few days after his first response, he had sent another email that gave her hope.

```
Dear Stella—
I'm sorry if I seemed aloof in my last email.
I have spent the last couple of months try-
ing to imagine my life without you, and I had
finally reconciled myself to knowing that I
would grow old without you. Your email was a
shock. I almost wondered if I had dreamed it
but the email is still here.
I want so much for us to be happy. I love you
with every ounce of my being. My homecoming is
still months away, and I hope you still feel
the same after I return.
Love, David
```

She knew she could have the passionate love that Madalane and Evienne shared. Their love was a commitment to each other that lasted beyond a lifetime, and still was touching souls who never even knew them. She was committed to David and she believed that despite her emotional rollercoaster, he was still committed to her. She may have never known a real love, a true love if it had not been for the unfolding of this love story hidden in an art box, a story boxed away in time.

Granger's ears perked drawing Stella's attention, "Is Eve here, baby?" Stella had become comfortable with the long conversations she had with her dog. The pineapple doorknocker hit the door and Granger went running with Stella following behind.

* * *

Pulling into the driveway, Eve gave a low whistle. She had suspected all along that Stella had some money; now that she was seeing her house, it was very clear that she and her husband were very comfortable. Stella's house was a beautiful classic Georgian bricked house with five windows along the second floor and two large windows at the ground level, one on either side of the door, all accented with white shutters. Two additional dormer windows in the attic area gleamed in the mid-day sun. The long line of the roof was intersected by two opposing chimneys. Eve slipped out of her Camry, reached into the back seat for the art box and followed the flagstones to the steps leading to the front door. A simple white portico shielded the front door. Eve lifted the doorknocker and marveled at the elegant simplicity of the house. She was gazing at the rather sparse garden in the front, imagining it filled with a rhododendrons and a variety of rose bushes when Stella opened the door.

"Hey, come in." Stella reached for her friend and embraced her, Granger earnestly trying to get his allotment of attention from the visitor.

Stella took a deep breath of the cold air before shutting the white door. "Come in, come in. I am anxious to hear what you learned about Evienne." Stella reached for Eve's jacket and hung it on an oak coat tree in the foyer.

Eve followed Stella into the kitchen, looking around at the black and white photos expertly placed along the hall. "These shots are amazing. Are they Sarah's photographs?" She asked as she gazed at a photo of a woman's head and shoulders taken from behind, the musculature emphasized by the plait of hair that shadowed the spine.

"Yes, this is my daughter's work. David says it our personal shrine to her brilliance." Smiling, Stella stopped and turned to look at the photos with Eve. "The series of women through the iron gates is what got her the internship slot in Europe. It blows my mind how much talent this kid has. She sees life through the lens of her camera." Stella paused, embarrassed that she was being so stereotypical. "Can you tell I am not too proud of my baby?"

Eve laughed at Stella's rueful comment. "You have every right to be the proud mama."

Stella looked back to the photographs, pondering the intensity of the woman's face staring right at the observer through the iron gate. That particular photo always gave Stella feelings of pain, loss, of being locked into societal ways. "Sarah wants her photos to evoke the struggles women go through and how they are caged into certain roles. I would love for you to meet her. I think the two of you would find your individual perspectives of life fascinating." She smiled warmly at her friend.

"She is very talented. I can see why she got the internship. Has she decided if she is going? Still trying to choose between a fabulous adventure or staying home and playing house with the girlfriend?"

Stella rolled her eyes and nodded, clearly not wanting to talk about it.

The two women moved into a large modern kitchen. All of the appliances were stainless steel and the counter was gleaming black marble. Eve ruefully thought of her own small cluttered kitchen and wondered if Stella could make it look half as good as this. There were two wine glasses and an open bottle of red wine on the large island in the center of the kitchen. "Your house is gorgeous Stella. I love the old houses, but a good modern kitchen is priceless!" Eve slipped into a high-backed iron bar chair and reflected on the luxuriousness of the kitchen. Calphalon pots gleamed in the sunlight against the far wall, and a wine fridge was snugged up against the large Sub-Zero refrigerator. Eve thought she could easily get used to a clean, fully stocked kitchen.

Stella put the art box on the island, off to the side of the wine glasses, and reached for the bottle of Meritage. "You are going to love this wine." Stella picked up the glass and swirled the liquid, closing her green eyes and inhaling the wine's bouquet, seemingly lost to the moment. She opened her eyes to see Eve's tense face staring at the wine glass.

"Eve what is it? Why do you seem so sad?"

Looking at Stella, Eve felt her chest tighten. She had been dreading talking to Stella about her research, but she knew she had to tell her what she had discovered. Yet, she had put it off multiple times already. She had even talked to Hank about it. Always practical, he had pointed out that this meant that Evienne did not abandon Madalane. She went to her death loyal to her mother.

Stella's eyes seemed to bore into her as Eve searched for what to do. "It's not sadness as much as some information I found out."

"What is it Eve? Tell me." Stella concern overrode the thoughts of Paris.

Eve took a deep breath, and recounted her research to Stella. Stella was quiet but alert through the explanation of what she had found. Eve finished her report with the story that she had found in the book about the artist at the camp who tried to escape repeatedly only to be caught and tortured to death. She had sent the tracing form to the Red Cross, but hadn't heard back yet. She saw Stella's steady gaze falter for a moment as pain seemed to wash across her features. Both women were silent after Eve ended her explanation.

Eve put an arm around the rigid woman sitting next to her, "Are you okay Stella? I know this is so heartbreaking. I spent the day in bed after I found out."

"It's terrible, but it's tragic in a beautiful way; Evienne's first thought was to save Madalane. I believe that Evienne loved your mother so much that she died for her in the most terrible of ways?"

Acceptance washed over Eve like a warm shower. She knew in her heart that her mother and Evienne had truly loved one another. Her mother had not been alone all those years because of a broken heart; she had made the choice to be alone because she could not bear loving anyone else. Instead of words, tears came as Eve tried to speak, "Yes, I understand now. I understand so much more than I did...about so many different things." Unable to say anymore, Eve's head dropped into hands and she wept for her mother, for Evienne, for her husband, and for herself. She gave in to the extravagance of crying. She reveled in her own sadness for the first time in decades. Finally she had a friend who she believed understood her pain.

Hot tears rolled down Stella's face as her arm enveloped the sobbing woman. She knew in her heart that Eve understood that Madalane and Evienne loved each other. "We are going to Paris." Stella whispered the words into Eve's cranberry cardigan. "We are going to go to Paris and memorialize your mother and her lover and give them both a proper burial. It is the one thing we can do for them, bring them back together." The feelings flooded through Stella's chest, leaving her sobbing on her friend's shoulder.

Pulling back from Stella's embrace, Eve immediately thought of the reasons why she couldn't go. She hated long plane rides, she had to finish the semester, she was working on several committees, she had agreed to teach at least one summer class, and Paris was ungodly crowded with tourists in the spring....every reason seemed an insurmountable hurdle, and yet, she heard herself say, "Yes, we should. We need to go to Paris." As the words left her mouth, she felt tears prick her eyes again. Eve hastily wiped her eyes and ran her fingers through her hair. "I must look like a fright," she murmured as she tried to pull herself together.

Stella raised her wine glass and proposed a toast, "Paris in the spring for Evienne and your mother."

Eve raised her glass. "My mother was cremated and I've had her ashes in an urn for 40 years. I am not getting any younger. It just seems right that we scatter her ashes in Paris as we memorialize Evienne. I think my mother would be happy to finally go home."

Chapter 62

Paris in April

On a small side street in the 6th arrondisement, two women exited their hotel. One carried a canvas satchel while the other firmly gripped the leather handle of an old wooden art box. They both breathed deeply of the fresh Parisian morning, filling their lungs with the scent of crisp spring air and the lingering smells from the boulangeries.

Stella and Eve looked at each, smiling eagerly for their day to begin. They had been in Paris for four days, wandering around the city, looking for the buildings and landmarks that filled the letters that Evienne had written to Madalane. They had been to the church and the Sorbonne. They had frequented the art stalls along the Seine and had even walked the steps of the apartment building where Evienne and Madalane had lived in before the war. They had knocked on the door of the attic apartment as well as the apartment that Evienne and Madalane had eventually moved into on a lower floor, but no one had been at home. Feeling the spirit of her mother, Eve had not been disappointed by their inability to step into the rooms that her mother had once lived.

Stella had never been to Paris, so they indulged in the requisite sightseeing. They had picnicked at the Eiffel Tower and wandered the grand halls of the Louvre and the Musee d'Orsay. Each day had been a revelation to Stella, and Eve had enjoyed sharing the city with the younger woman. Although Eve had been to Paris before, she had never felt the connection to the city that she did this time. When she had visited before, Paris was just a city where her mother lived before the war, but now it was the city where her mother fell in love and lived happily for many years. She was always reminding her students to look for context, and now, she ruefully admitted, she finally had the context to love this city.

The women turned right and headed towards the Seine. They walked in the narrow road as the grey stone sidewalks were barely wide enough for one person much less two. The occasional car would come down the small street and they stepped up on the sidewalk to allow it to pass. The sunlight glinted off the black wrought iron decorative gates that punctuated the second floor windows. As they walked, Eve gripped each of the small black balustrades that were spaced a few feet apart, preventing any overly enthusiastic car owners from parking their car on the narrow sidewalks. Her hip was sending sharp pain signals, but she was determined to complete their task this morning. They were flying out this afternoon; their suitcases already packed and left with the concierge at the hotel.

Pensively, they made their way to the end of the street, turning left onto the wide sunny avenue of Quai des Grands Augustins. Stella felt the warmth of the day and the hum of the electricity surging through the city as they joined the flock of humanity strolling along the Seine on this gorgeous April morning.

"Eve, wouldn't it be lovely to live here? Can you imagine stepping out to this view every day?" Stella adjusted her cream-colored chiffon scarf so the breeze would catch it over her shoulder, the action making her feel quite Parisian.

Glancing at the younger woman, Eve smiled at Stella. Stella

really seemed to be in her element in Paris, much more so than at home in the suburbs of Philadelphia. "I would weigh 400 pounds if I lived in Paris, but the view along the bridge might be worth it." As they approached Rue Seguier, Eve saw a crosswalk, "Let's cross here!" Without waiting for Stella, Eve bounded across the wide boulevard, so they could stroll next to the river. Stella laughed and ran to catch up with the older woman.

Sighing with the pain that caught up with her, Eve reflected, "I have been to Paris many times, but it's always been another city to me. I love being here with you Stella. For the first time, I really feel my mother here. I can see her on the streets, see her walking through museums. It gives me so much happiness. I feel a connection to this city and especially to the Seine—it's like my heritage lives in this river." Eve stopped for a moment, gazing at the sun glinting off the glittery surface of the Seine.

"I see Madalane and Evienne in every café, on every corner."

Eve continued to stare at the water; Stella could feel the trepidation in Eve. She put her hand on the older woman's back and waited.

Eventually the women continued walking, passing the entrance to the Pont Neuf. "I have such a different picture of my mother these days. She gave so much of herself to me, to her students, to her friends. I suppose I thought that my mother was a closed book. I just assumed that it was a mother's job to dedicate herself to her child." Eve saw Stella smile. "I know that is selfish, but how else could I rationalize in my own mind why my mother never had a boyfriend or husband. I thought I was all she needed. I know why my mother didn't say anything about Evienne, yet it is so sad to think of the loneliness that must have lived inside of her for my entire life."

They were passing the small stands filled with art, books, and touristy items that were easy to bring home. Stella was in love with these stands—she could barely stand to pass a table of old books or even the trinkets literally set up on the sidewalk. Every time she saw one of those tiny Eiffel Towers, she promised herself that she was going to buy one even if it was the most clichéd thing to do. Pausing at a stand, she glanced at the book titles.

To the left of the stand, Stella saw something that caught her eye, and she abruptly exclaimed, "Oh look Eve—I love that painting of the Paris side street. Do you see it?" Stella pointed to a painter who had spread his paintings out on the sidewalk to sell.

Eve focused on the tall thin boy rearranging his few canvases. They were approaching the Pont des Arts, their final destination, and she was thankful for a brief respite from their walk. "That is a remarkable painting," she observed.

The artist turned and smiled at the women and then called out to them in halting French, "Bonjour, are you looking for a painting?"

Surprised, Stella and Eve looked at each other. The boy's voice was that of a girl. Stella realized that Eve's face was pale despite the warmth of the day. She gazed at the young woman who was smiling nervously at her, wondering why the older woman was staring at her. In Eve's mind, the tall young woman had morphed into the Evienne of the sketches. Thin, almost ascetic with hollow cheeks and an intense expression.

Stella too was staring, but she realized that they were making the girl uncomfortable. Stella nudged Eve gently. Eve came back to reality with a start, and realized that she was expected to answer. "Perhaps," she heard herself say in French. She felt faint and queasy but held herself together, "My friend is interested. Do you speak English?"

The artist smiled, revealing a youthful face of a girl who was still a child in many ways. "Yes. I am English." She pointed to the art box that Eve carried, "Do you paint? Are you a painter?"

Eve had momentarily forgotten about the art box she carried, glancing down, she realized why the young woman had asked her that. "No, I am a teacher."

"It is a wonderful art box. Anyone would be lucky to have

it." The young woman turned her attention to Stella, her potential customer. "Would you like to look at the paintings I haven't displayed yet?"

Still shaking off the time warp, Stella nodded and leaned down, flipping through a small stack of paintings leaning against the side of the stone Seine wall. In the back, she found one of an older woman. In a modern way, it reminded her of the way Evienne had painted. She wanted it to be the way Evienne painted but the colors were strong and primary and the lines faded. It was nice but not up to Evienne's quality; nonetheless, she wanted the painting anyway. "Eve, what do you think of this one?" Stella stood and showed her friend, who was still gazing at the young woman. "I know it is not a true Paris scene but look at her face and there is a faint sky line in the back."

Noticing the vague parallel with the painting in her dining room, Eve nodded. "I like it. We can ship it home on the way back to the hotel. I'm sure the artist would hold the painting for us while we finish our task." Eve glanced at the young woman who nodded vigorously at the women. Satisfied with their plan, Stella decided to take another look at the paintings.

While Stella browsed, Eve noticed a sketchbook and a shoebox sitting on the sea wall. Eve pointed to the small pile of supplies, "Is that what you carry your paints in?"

The girl blushed furiously. "Yes madam. I had an art kit, but it was damaged in a fire in my apartment building. It was unusable. I am saving up to buy a new one, but paints and canvases are always needed first."

Stella had turned to listen to the exchange and her eyes met Eve's. Eve shook her head, but Stella continued to gaze steadily into her eyes. Finally, Eve opened the art box and took out the cache of letters and pictures tied with the red ribbon, and handed them wordlessly to Stella who stowed them in her canvas satchel. With a deep steadying breath, Eve handed the empty art box to the young painter.

"You are a wonderful artist. My friend and I want you to have this. A real artist deserves a real art box for her....tools." Eve felt a tremendous weight press against her chest, but it was not unpleasant. It was more like the feeling one got when a person knew they were making the right choice albeit the hard choice.

"Madame, oui, oui, merci bien. Are you sure? This is a very old art box—a family heirloom." The girl pointed to the metal medallion attached to the front of the box written in English as she cradled the wooden treasure in her arms.

Eve smiled kindly at the young woman. She didn't know how to explain the overwhelming sense of generosity that surged through her. She looked to Stella who had walked over to the pair.

Stella slipped her arm into the crook of Eve's elbow to support her, "Eve's mother had a friend who painted like you do—maybe even at this very place. Her name was Evienne Lavelle and she was born in England; her father brought her this box when she left home to come to Paris. You remind us of her."

"Madams, this is so precious. This art box is a beautiful gift." The young woman held the box in her arms, holding it against her heart. Looking back and forth between the women, she seemed stunned by her good fortune. Holding the box with one hand, she took her black beret off letting the sun catch the shimmering black of her pixie hair. "S'il vous plait take any painting you want as a gift from me." She looked at Stella and pointed to the painting in her hand. "You may have that one if you choose and your friend—please choose something. It is the only way I can thank you."

Stella looked to Eve who smiled at her and nodded. "Yes, I will have this painting. Thank you."

Slipping her hat back on her head, she took the painting from Stella's hand. "Eve what do you think? I saw the most beautiful painting of the Pont des Arts. It will be a wonderful companion to Evienne's painting in your dining room."

"Madam, I will get it for you." The girl put the box down

next to her shoebox and placed Stella's painting on her vacant easel. As she turned to the wall, Stella turned to Eve and whispered, "You did the right thing Eve; you changed her life. It is an auspicious day."

"Is it this one Madam?" She asked, handing it to Eve.

Feeling overwhelmed by the gratitude, Eve felt herself slide into the passive acceptance of the painting. She didn't really care about the painting. She wanted to get on with their plan. Divesting herself of the art box seemed like the kind thing to do, but the grateful exuberance of the artist made her uncomfortable.

Stella explained to the young woman that they would be back shortly for their paintings. Eve began to walk away, not able to stand still any longer. She moved to the entrance of the Pont des Arts, waiting patiently as Stella spoke to the young woman in low tones. Eve felt hot and cold, tired and energized, ready to let go and desperately wanting to hold on.

When Stella joined Eve, the two women walked in companionable silence until they reached the mid-point of the bridge. Stella followed Eve's lead and as she stopped, so did she. They were finally at their destination point on the bridge. Stella's heart began to beat a bit faster. Eve settled on the right side and Stella thought it appropriate that they were facing the Notre Dame Cathedral even though it was a bit up the Seine. Stella put her bag down between them. Eve stood staring at the water.

"Eve, the artist was so thankful for the art box. She is going deliver the paintings to the hotel herself."

Eve thought for a moment before replying. "It was weird, wasn't it? I thought she was a boy and then I saw Evienne emerge. I'm not sure if it was wish fulfillment or a trick of the eyes, but I felt Evienne as strongly as I know you are standing next to me." She turned to face the other direction and she stretched her back against the bridge wall. They were standing near the famous wall of padlocks which lovers left together to honor their devotion.

Turning back to Stella, Eve glanced at the couples and singles walking along the bridge. It was a pedestrian bridge and the lack of traffic made it easy to linger. "Sometimes I wonder, Stella."

"Wonder what, Eve?"

"I wonder if my isolation is self-imposed or inherited. Maybe I come from a family where you only get one chance at real love. I mean, I love Hank, but not like I loved my husband. He was my passion. When he died, I shut down for many years. I couldn't even contemplate loving someone else. When I met Hank, he was living in his own purgatory. His ex-wife had put him through the wringer, so he was happy to have his own space. We were each other's companions and escorts to social events with a little sex thrown in once in a while. I think we were together a year before we actually spent the night together. We've been together for decades now, and I'm beginning to wonder if I haven't cheated him out of real love. Maybe I should have let him go, so he could find a woman who wanted to be with him on a full-time basis."

Stella felt as if she had been having this conversation with herself for a long time. A few months ago, she would told Eve to let him go, but she felt differently now. She had a new under-standing about the choices people make, and it helped her see the truth that lay below the surface. "There are many kinds of love, and the love that you and Hank have is perfect for you right now, and if Hank wanted something different, he would have told you."

Eve nodded in acknowledgement, and then changed the subject, "Shall we begin?"

Stella bent down and pulled a lock from her bag. "I have a surprise." Holding a padlock in her palm, she showed Eve that she had written Madalane and Evienne inside a heart with April 19th on the other side. "I couldn't resist. I had to bring one when we decided to come here. Do you think it's silly?"

"No, I think it is wonderful." Eve watched Stella move down and place the padlock on an open piece of the crowded fence. She thought about Hank and how undemanding he was. Occasionally, in a fit of pique, he would demand that she speak to him about her feelings, but usually he was content to let her be. Maybe that was the best either of them could hope for. She smiled as she watched Stella rub her fingers along the padlock. This journey with Stella had been life changing, and maybe it was time to sit down with Hank and discuss their relationship. She was ready to retire and it would be cheaper to live in one house than two. As she watched Stella run her hand along the myriad of locks, hearing the clink of metal hitting metal, she realized that maybe, just maybe, she really did want to live with Hank, and not just because of the financial savings. It would be nice to know someone other than the dog was waiting for her at the end of a day. When she got home, she would broach the subject, but first she would start cleaning out the spare room. Her clutter would never disappear, but the stuff she had stored away needed to be cleared out before she could move forward.

Stella resumed her spot next to Eve; she was smiling broadly, looking younger and happier than Eve had ever seen her. "The day is going so fast. We need to leave for the airport soon. Are you excited to see David?"

"Yes, I just hope he is excited to see me. I feel like the past few months have changed me, my heart, and my life. I am so ready to see David. I'm also excited about traveling to China, but I'm really looking forward to seeing him." Pausing to rearrange her perfectly arranged scarf, Stella's voice deepened with emotion, "It is as if I have fallen in love with him all over again over the last six months. I owe so much of that change to your mother and to you. My life is different because Madalane and Evienne taught me what love really is. Love is not just a promise or a desire; it's a devotion to something or someone, like Evienne's devotion to painting and her devotion to your mother. I spent so many years wondering if I made the right choice that I forgot to pay attention to the little moments of devotion that David shared with me every day. Then I understood that I was just as devoted to him although in a very different way. I never wanted to hurt him. That helped me realize that I love him as passionately as he loves me; I feel like Madalane and Evienne gave me this gift." She looked at her friend and then back to the river. "It is a perfect day, and with every end, there is a beginning."

Eve smiled, hoping that Stella's trip to China would bring them time to talk. David would be home for good next month, but Stella needed to be with him.

"It's time." Eve looked to the east to see the sun moving across the sky, reminding them of their deadline. "Now that we are here and ready to do this, I'm nervous. Tell me that we are doing the right thing."

On hearing those words from Eve, the final end of the journey crashed into Stella's heart making her chest hurt a bit. "Yes we are." Stella sounded more confident than she felt as bent down to open her bag. She took out the urn that held Eve's mother's ashes; Eve had added the engraved vesta case that Madalane had given Evienne so many years ago. She stood up, holding the urn like a bouquet of flowers, and smiled at Eve.

Blinking away her own tears, Eve reached into the pocket of her jacket. She pulled out an envelope and retrieved a sheet of paper. Her voice rough with emotion, she held it out to Stella. "I read through all of mom's poems and this was the last one in the book, and I think it must have been the last one she wrote. I think we should use her words to say goodbye to them." Eve took a deep breath...she felt lightheaded and was grateful for the solid feel of the bridge wall. "I would like you to read it before we drop the ashes. Would that be okay?"

Tears were beginning to escape Stella's eyes. In a soft voice, she responded, "Reading Evienne's love letters has brought me more joy and love than anything else I have ever read. I would be honored to read your mother's poetry."

The two began their exchange. Stella took the white envelope from Eve and secured the urn in Eve's hands. She took a deep breath as the two turned to face the river. Eve pulled the urn to her heart as Stella took the poem.

Solemnly, Stella began with the date:

10 April 1958

The Last Time I Saw Your Face

> *Where ever you are,*
> *you live inside me.*
> *Your mind captured me,*
> *you are my one and only heart.*
> *Your soul soothed me,*
> *each layer of your complexity is*
> *lost inside our last glass of wine.*
> *Your body enflamed me,*
> *alone you will find me, and*
> *you must bring me home again.*
> *Your nobility astounds me still.*
> *You are my one and only heart*
> *and I love only you.*

Eve felt her tears falling; the story of her mother's relationship with Evienne had been told in Stella's warm contralto voice, and it felt so right that she would narrate the last part of their journey again. She pressed her forehead against the urn, feeling the spirit of her mother rise up in gratitude for this moment. She cleared her throat and looked at Stella who was still gazing at the poem.

"Stella...would you do me one more favor?"

Stella looked up at Eve and nodded, "Of course, anything."

"I want you to have the letters. You brought me the gift of my mother's life. I don't need to hold on to them, but I need to know that they will be loved and respected."

Stella was shocked that Eve was giving such a huge part of her mother to her. "Yes, yes, a thousand times yes. I love these letters. I will cherish them forever." Stella looked to the sun, felt the warmth of Paris, and heard the passing voices behind her—they were like a symphony of happiness. Impulsively, she declared, "Let's put your mother's poem in the urn with the last letter Evienne wrote to her. Both of their writings filled with love and commitment. A time capsule devoted to their love."

Eve nodded, knowing with a certainty that Stella's suggestion was exactly the right thing to do. "Of course, it's an absolute necessity." Eve opened the lid of the urn and glanced inside, looking for the silver vesta case, but it already been embraced by the ashes.

Stella bent down and retrieved the letters from her bag. The final letter had been saved to read on arrival in Paris. It was on the bottom of the pile where Madalane had left it. As Stella stood, she stuck the poem Eve had given her under her arm and pulled at the red ribbon that had held the letters together for almost a hundred years. Two lifetimes she thought. Two people intertwined, changing other lives, weaving into so many destinies.

Stella read the letter aloud, tears falling from her eyes as Eve gazed at the water. The sound of bells echoed in the distanced as the last words Evienne wrote to Madalane resonated in the space between them. At the end of the letter, it seemed as if everyone on the bridge acknowledged a moment of silence as the two women let the words wash over them.

Stella broke the silence as the sun seemed to dip lower in the sky. "I want to tie this ribbon around the two letters before I put them in the urn. Is that okay?"

Eve nodded in agreement.

Stella put the rest of the letters back securely in her bag leaving the ribbon out with the letter. Retrieving the poem from under her arm, she opened the letter and placed them together. She was compelled to reread the last line of Evienne's last letter: *you are my one and only heart and I love only you.* She realized they were the same words used in Madalane's poem. It was meant to be—truly meant to be. Chills covered her sun-warmed body. Carefully, she folded them together, like lovers falling asleep wrapped around one another, and tied them together with the tattered red ribbon, and handed them to Eve.

Eve accepted the papers and kissed the small bundle before gently placing them inside the urn. She pressed down a bit to ensure that they were securely anchored in her mother's ashes. She exhaled hard, realizing she had been holding her breath while Stella had secured the papers together. She twisted the cap back on the urn, and returned it to Stella.

"Ready?"

Stella nodded and placed her hand on the urn along with Eve's. The two women took a moment to reflect on their journey before holding the urn out over the perimeter of the bridge wall. They glanced at each other, smiling shyly, with one trembling pause, and ten fingers let go. The accumulation of energy splashed into the water, dipping into the dark depths, sinking and settling into a resting place of their union.

Eve's tear-filled eyes nearly miss the distorted mass as the urn splashed into the water. She viscerally felt the silver ripples of lifetimes as the small waves traveled and knocked into the edges of the square stone barriers, each wake a memory and each circle too soon forgotten as it blended into the current. Madalane and Evienne were gone. Evienne and Madalane, who had sought peace in each other's arms, were slowly embraced by the resolve of history.

Two worlds created by a river, the left and the right bank, both impacting innumerable lives. The river survived over a hundred decades like the heart of a woman, solid as stone, but always filling the empty spaces. Indefinable and as tangible as the way a woman slips in and out of life's tragedies with patient strength. Within this river, the truth exists for every woman, alive and dead.

Eve closed her eyes feeling as if her mother was beckoning her as the river whispered by. "Yes." Eve said out loud to Stella. "Yes, it is the home my mother once had, and it is the home she will have again with her Evienne. Yes, there is love, and yes, there are two quiet hearts finding their devotion to one another once more on the river's bed." She looked at her friend standing next to her, tears slipping into the Seine River, one after the other, and she smiled, "Shall we have a glass of wine?"

My Dearest Madalane,
　　As sure as the daylight has come, I sit here lost in uncertainty, and yet the day has come with certainty. The day has come where the crushing feeling of love lives inside me, but is laced with the lies I have told you. My Madalane, my dearest, my Dove— you have taken my thoughts with you, my heart, my soul, my everything. Please leave me with your forgiveness.

　　Time keeps me from you—I know you are miles from me, but I feel your presence behind me, the merest shadow, a slight noise, the twist of your key in our lock. The bare whisper of your voice makes my heart jump. Wistful of me, I pray to be able to turn life backwards, back to the day we met and start again. My heart beats faster with mere thoughts of you; you always have had that reaction on me, as simple as your sweet lips talking gave me a gentle hum inside my heart, tickling me with your soft words of love. My God, what have I done?

　　The first time your eyes looked upon me, I fell in love with you. Actually, you and my heart demanded that I fall in love with you, over and over again. From that moment at my art stand, I fell into your eyes and found your heart as well as my own. You leave me delirious. A thousand times, I fall in love with you, equal to a thousand strokes of paint to immortalize your lovely face. There was a time, as you know, that I wanted a solitary room for my shriveled heart—my nightmares teased me until the morning light came and then thankfully I could lose myself again in paint. Lose myself in the faces of my past. And then I met you...and you filled every crack inside me.

　　I love you as no other. I tried to memorize each strand of your hair as I have brushed it so many times in the moonlight after our baths. I would bring your hair to my face and smell your truth, you essence, and I would silently pray that I would never have to leave that exact moment. You, your hair spread over me like the moon filled me like the Seine filled my soul. You own me today like Paris once did.

Tonight there will be no chance of kissing you all through the dark. No, no kissing until daybreak like the days in your cozy dorm room. On that day, I knew the inside of your mouth, the taste of your very being; I memorized the shape of your lips and I felt your breath warm my throat and insides. I kissed you until you made me whole; I kissed you until I was lost inside of you. On this day, I would give anything for that moment once more.

It is time for me to say goodbye; it will be only minutes before you walk in the door and our lives will be changed forever. You taught me to believe in something and if I should die, then we will be together in the afterlife. If I do not make it back to your side to see your smile, to look into your eyes, to feel your heart, know I am a better person because of you. You are my one and only heart and I love only you.

Forever,

Evienne

Epilogue

Four Months Later

Sarah Simone slipped in through the staff entrance at the museum in Amsterdam. She quickly passed the small break room and made her way through the labyrinth of halls, which would lead her to the temporary exhibition space reserved for special events and displays. She had no business being up in this area, but the student who was interning in the portraiture and painting program at the museum would be guiding a tour around this time, and she made Sarah's heart beat a little faster. The girl's name was Aniky and she was from a little town in Hungary. She was, in Sarah's opinion, the loveliest girl she had ever met: long dark hair, short but with an athletic build and the most beautiful hazel eyes.

Sarah saw a large group of people standing in a semi-circle. She knew intuitively that Aniky would be in the midst of the group, explaining the intricacies of a painting. Sarah slipped into the adjoining room, hoping for a moment to say hello to Aniky. The museum was presenting a special exhibition of artwork recovered after various wars. Most of the paintings had been damaged and extensive work had been done in the restoration room. The restoration department was next to where Sarah had spent the last few weeks working on the photography exhibit that was going to be mounted the following month. It was in these workrooms where Sarah had initially spied Aniky, eventually approaching her as a fellow intern. Their status as students allowed them to become friends, but their attraction to one another created a whole new bond that neither had anticipated.

The paintings did not interest Sarah; the object of her fascination was currently surrounded by a group of American tourists who seemed captivated by a particular painting. Sarah scanned the paintings in the room; they were all lovely, but none of them captured the vivacity and depth of a photograph. She leaned around the corner and caught a glance of Aniky who saw Sarah out of the corner of her eye. She smiled and winked at Sarah as she directed the group to the next painting of note.

Sighing, Sarah stood indecisively between the two rooms, wondering if she should go to the photo room and get on with her work or if she should wait a few more minutes in case Aniky could give her a moment. The internship in Amsterdam would be ending soon and she would be off to Florence. Aniky was staying on until the current exhibition ended, and then she was headed to Rome. A two-hour train ride and they could spend their days off together. Aniky was the most amazing woman Sarah had ever met and it made her crazy that they would be in different countries for a few weeks.

Finally, Aniky's group began to disperse on a short break. They fanned out around the room, examining some of the less discussed work in more detail. Sarah saw Aniky speaking to an older couple who gestured repeatedly to the painting behind her. Aniky nodded and adjusted her glasses, a nervous gesture that Sarah now recognized with affection. Everything Aniky did was adorable. Finally, the older couple walked away and Aniky turned to see if Sarah was still there. Sarah was already walking towards her.

When they were close enough to share the same breath,

Sarah whispered, "Those tourists are so lucky to have you all to themselves. I miss you when you are on the floor."

Aniky smiled a shy, disarming smile that completely unnerved Sarah. "What were those people asking you, the ones who monopolized your time when I only get mere minutes with you throughout the day?"

Aniky's beautifully accented English brushed against Sarah's nervous system like warm caramel. "The American couple? They think they know some information about that painting." She pointed behind her to a portrait of an old woman, thick layers of paint and inks creating the history of her life.

Sarah glanced at the painting, and then looked again at it. It was striking, something that even she, an avowed photographer, found extraordinary. "Who is the artist?"

"We don't know. It was found along with thousands of other paintings in a warehouse filled with the art that the Nazis looted from museums and galleries. No one has ever been able to identify the painter of this piece. It was seriously damaged around the edges from being cut out of frame. The artist's name was cut off when the painting was appropriated by the Nazis."

Sarah loved the way Aniky discussed art. She was so rhapsodic in her tone and inflection that it often made Sarah swoon. She forgot the painting and gazed at Aniky, wishing there were more places in the museum to find a moment of privacy.

Staring at the painting, Aniky continued, "Many of the second and third tier artists and their work were destroyed during World War II. The painter was probably one of the poor souls lost to the war, but his or her painting will live forever."

Aniky looked back at Sarah, "The Americans think they have other paintings by the same painter, a woman from Paris. The man's parents were avid art collectors in Europe in the 1920's and 30's. I am going to introduce them to the curator at the end of the tour. Maybe one of our mysteries will finally be solved." She smiled at Sarah who was still gazing at her in stupefied adoration.

Laughing at her companion's lustful expression, Aniky pulled Sarah into the next room that was still empty. She kissed her deeply, then softly and then returned to her tour group.

Sarah's lips tingled from Aniky's soft kiss. Today would be a good day. Sarah smoothed her hair back and returned to the main gallery room, walking by the portrait of the old woman once again. She glanced at it, and swore for a brief moment, the old woman in the portrait smiled at her. The visceral reaction made her pause for a moment to really study the painting.

Shaking her head, Sarah started to head back to where she was working on the proper lighting for the photo exhibition that she would not see when she heard Aniky call for her, "Ms. Simone."

Sarah snapped around to the direction of the familiar intonation of her name to find the confident tour director approaching her. Her clipboard in hand with a multitude of tourists' eyes still upon her, she efficiently folded the top piece of paper on the clipboard and stated, "Would you be so kind as to make this appointment for me. It is very important I do not forget this time sensitive appointment." Aniky looked over the top of her black Italian frames and winked at Sarah. "I must get back to my group, thank you." She spun around, her brown hair like the mane on a galloping horse and rejoined her group.

Sarah nodded as her heart continued to leap in her chest. She could tell this day was turning out more promising than the walk along the canal she was planning for later.

Holding the note tightly in her hand and heading back to the photography area via a discreet passageway, she stopped and leaned against the cool white wall to unfold the note that was just placed in her hand. Images of Aniky's lips made her hands tremble; she had it bad she realized as she shook her head a little giddy and a little embarrassed for herself. America seemed a lifetime away—her life was filled with the muse of photography, filled with the passion of desire, every frame filled with Aniky. Slowly, she opened the last fold of the white paper to find the words written by her lover's hand.

Sarah,

I still taste your lips as I return
to my group of strangers. They look at me.
I blush at the thought of your kiss.
I want more of you. I need you.

Meet me at 4:15 in storage room c.
You will not make me wait.
My need will lead you to me.
My lips will cover you.

Aniky

A gleeful smile rounded her cheeks as she folded the note and brought it to her lips. Sarah kissed the paper and slipped it into her shirt pocket closest to her heart.

The End

Acknowledgements

Beginning in 2009, two lifelong friends set out to write a novel about the journey of women. They wrote in coffee shops, in bars, and at kitchen tables for years and produced a book to represent all women. Women have devoted their lives to so many causes—from saving others to saving themselves, or fighting injustices. Most of the time, these women went unnoticed and unacknowledged for their heroic deeds.

From season to season, we wrote, battled, laughed, created, wrote more, and rewrote a story that mirrors contemporary life as well as history. We want to take this opportunity to thank the people and places that gave us the inspiration to continue and finish a project that holds more than a story to us.

Thank you to our families, who supported us while we wrote very early on weekend mornings. We wrote the entirety of the book via email, which demanded extensive computer time at our kitchen tables—so thank you for bringing coffee and breakfast, for being patient and understanding, and for keeping quiet. Your support made our story richer and our lives deeper. We want to thank the coffee shops that stimulated progress and the wine bars that inspired creativity and settled disagreements.

We want to thank the small community of writers, intellects, artists, and readers (and you, gentle reader—we cannot live without you) who we serendipitously attracted, and who helped us launch this story to a wider audience. Starting with our first draft readers—Cheryl Baals, Janice Barlow, Rae Bettinger, Tory Kane, Michelle Kane, Jessye Kuhn, Patricia Kuhn Zuckschwerdt, Terry Larsen, Linda Macht, Andrea Space, and Renee Wayne—we needed each one of you to reassure us that we took a dream and turned it into a novel.

We want to thank Roseann Lentin for her invaluable publishing advice and support, and Steve Morrone for his captivating artwork on our cover and his wife Jennifer who reminded us to laugh in good times and in bad.

Thank you to Todd Kraft for a very fun (bordering on silly) photo shoot.

We owe Jack Dixon a debt of gratitude that is beyond compare. You have guided us through the publishing business, demonstrated what true generosity is, and listened with an open heart and circumspect mind.

Lastly, we would like to thank our friends and family who gave us the time to devote to being authors. This is a lifelong dream for two women who turned an idea into a story.

From our hands to yours—Rachelle and Tracy

About the Authors

Two young women in their early 20's figured they would have the rest of their lives to write a book. We met at the Woodbine caterers and spent most of our time either in the office or behind the bar, talking about art, poetry, literature, and of course, our dreams, hopes, and aspirations. We went out, had a drink (or two) and talked about a plan. We made a promise to write a novel together. Our words were caught in the web of intention—the universe listened, and our promise was fulfilled, but many years later.

Time passed and our lives separated us—families and college classes replaced the fun of our single lives. Rachelle became a Professor of English and Humanities at the Pennsylvania Institute of Technology. Tracy raised three children, became a healer, an accomplished poet, and Jill of many trades.

After almost 20 years of planning to write together, Tracy sent a letter to Rachelle, reminding her of their promise. We met at an Irish restaurant in Philadelphia in 2008 to catch up, and to finally talk writing. By 2009, we discovered that we did have a novel brewing between us. Email after email, our idea of long ago became a writer's reality. We thoroughly embraced the— "I am right!" "No, you are not! We can figure it out."—policy, leaving us with a bond that grew stronger through each chapter of our novel. We diligently woke up before sunrise and wrote through our weekend mornings. The banter of our friendship molded our journey and encouraged us to continue the creation of Her Mother's Lover.

As the joy of writing turned into the publishing process, we found that writing a book is more than just writing words, it is creating a need in our readers. We are honored by all the people who have supported and encouraged us.

We love the fact that this is OUR book and we can be contacted directly via our email or web site to answer your questions or simply to say hi. We want your suggestions; we want your opinion! We LOVE a well-thought out opinion. So shoot us an email and let us know what you think.

From our kitchen table to yours,

Thank you,

Rachelle and Tracy

www.hermotherslover.com

hermotherslover@gmail.com

ISBN: 978-0-989-15411-6 (pbk)
ISBN 978-0-989-15410-9 (ebk)